BURNT ENDS

A Mystery

BURNT ENDS

Laura Wetsel

CamCat
Books

CamCat Publishing, LLC
Fort Collins, Colorado 80524
camcatpublishing.com

Hardcover ISBN 9780744311211
Paperback ISBN 9780744311228
Large-Print Paperback ISBN 9780744311242
eBook ISBN 9780744311235
Audiobook ISBN 9780744311259

Library of Congress Control Number: 2024931445

Book and cover design by Maryann Appel
Interior artwork by Demianvs, Denys, pop_jop

5   3   1   2   4

FOR KANSAS CITY.

Chapter One

HERE IT WAS—SMOKING MEAT, the sweet stench of my childhood. Hickory, molasses, tomato, brown sugar. Kansas City's love letter to everyone but me.

Darnell, my best friend from our early rehab days, drove us into the parking lot of Rocky's BBQ Smokehouse, and I gagged on the meat-thickened air. *Don't toss your waffles, Tori.* The giant statue of Rocky the Pig—"Rocky the Cannibal"—smiled down at me in his chef hat and apron, holding a platter of ribs like he was trying to turn my stomach.

Darnell parked his truck with a displeased grunt. "Seriously, Tor," he said, wiping the sweat from his bald head. "I said I'd help you move, not run a stakeout in a hundred degrees."

"Don't worry." I took a gulp of Topo Chico to help settle my queasy gut. "My target should be here soon. Then you can help me move into my aunt's place." I twisted the zoom lens onto my digital camera and aimed it at a family tottering out of the restaurant with sauce-splattered shirts.

"Fine, then I'm running in for some brisket," Darnell said. "At least, assuming they've got any with the meat drought they've been—"

"Hold up," I cut him off and nodded at a green sedan rolling into the lot. "That's her." I pointed my lens at the driver's door, getting ready to fire away. When a woman stepped out with crutches, I groaned.

"Guess she wasn't lying." Darnell shifted the car out of park. "The brisket will have to—"

"Wait."

Darnell hit the brakes, jerking us forward. "Now what?"

"I want to see if she uses them inside. It would be hard in a buffet line."

"You're kidding, right?" He raised his brows at me. "If you go in there with that huge camera, there's no way she's ditching her crutches."

"That wasn't what I was thinking. I only knew to come here because my target's sister posted this online." I pulled out my phone to show Darnell the selfie post of Sasha Wolf with the caption, *Waiting for @GinnyWolf. #RockysBBQ #SisterLove.*

"Okay," Darnell said. "Am I supposed to be seeing something here?"

I tapped on Sasha's photo, zooming in on her sunlit head. "See that sunlight shining on her ponytail?"

"Yeah, and?"

"She's under an atrium, which means I'd have a great shot from the roof."

"The roof? You're not seriously thinking of climbing Rocky's, are you?"

"Why not?" I said, tying my blonde curls into a fist of a ponytail. "You've seen me scale walls and trees before. I'm a nimble little freak."

"I meant about trespassing." Darnell pointed to his police badge like he might arrest me.

"You know us private eyes don't have to follow your rules." I gave him a reassuring smile. "Just have a smoke, and I'll be back before you've even put your butt out."

"One cig, Tor," Darnell warned, tapping a pack of Marlboro Lights on the face of his watch. "Otherwise, have fun moving by yourself."

For a recovering addict, Darnell was a horrible liar. I knew he'd never abandon me, not for anything. Hanging my camera around my neck, I hopped out of the truck into the afternoon sun, where I already felt like I was sucking meat-flavored steam through a cocktail straw. I'd just have to deal with the nausea. I hustled toward the black and orange pavilion, noting its unclimbable plastic siding and security cameras mounted at the entrance. Maybe I'd have better luck in the back.

I circled around and found luck in the form of a supply truck parked right beside the restaurant. No driver, no cameras, no people. This was my way to the roof.

I hoisted myself onto the hood and made my way up the windshield to the top of the truck. The gap between the truck and building was only two feet, so I made the easy jump. Soon as I hit the roof though, my phone started buzzing in my pocket. This wasn't an ideal time to take calls, so I let it ring out while I got on my hands and knees to crawl toward the atrium.

When I got to the glass, I peered down below at a buffet hall where six dozen carnivores were dressed for the upcoming Fourth of July weekend and savagely stuffing their smeared, sticky faces with brisket, thighs, and ribs. My stomach surged at this familiar scene. I'd been avoiding the barbecue world for nearly fifteen years, and now that I was looking down on it like some floating deity, I remembered why I'd stayed away. Barbecue didn't just upset my stomach. From my head to my chest to my teeth, it made me mad everywhere. But I didn't want to think about why. Not after what I'd done last night.

As I searched the crowd of meat-eaters, I found Ginny, my target, at a table with her sister, her crutches against the wall. I raised my camera to my eye and focused on Ginny's face. She was teasing Sasha, lifting her brows and puckering her lips, and as she stuck out her tongue, a memory flashed in my head—I was a fourteen-year-old again in an inflatable pool of barbecue sauce with my cousin Annie. My hands shook, releasing the camera, but I jolted my neck back before the camera hit the roof.

That memory was another reminder why I avoided meat, but it made sense why the past was on my mind when Annie was the reason I was on this stakeout. She'd filed her case to investigate Ms. Wolf with my agency yesterday afternoon.

I had no idea who this Ginny Wolf was to Annie as I placed the burning hot camera back on my face and snapped pictures of Ginny, her crutches, her gold pendant and butterfly tattoo, all material things identifying her. When she stood up for the buffet, leaving her crutches behind, I videoed the fraudster walking free and easy without them.

As I'd thought, another liar.

My evidence secured, I returned to the restaurant's edge and jumped onto the supply truck. I wasn't loud, but I must have made noise inside the truck because the driver's door opened. When I saw who stepped out, I knew an apology wasn't cutting it. This was the largest man I'd ever seen. Not only was he around seven feet tall with brisket-sized arms and an ugly blond bowl cut, his steely blue eyes were fixed on me like he wanted to rip out my throat.

"Hey," his tuba voice bellowed. "You taking pictures of me?"

"No," I said, but my answer didn't put him at ease, because he jumped onto the hood to come after me. I didn't think it wise trying to fight a guy triple my size, so I rolled to the back of the truck, caught its back edge, let myself dangle, and released my grip.

Soon as I hit the pavement, I sprinted.

I had a head start on the driver, but I'd only gone a few strides before I heard his monster feet slapping the ground behind me. Around my neck, my camera thumped against my chest. I tried calling out for Darnell, but the heat and the exertion started making me choke. Behind me, the slapping feet were only getting closer. *You're not gonna make it.*

Just then, my ponytail got yanked, and I was thrown to the pavement. I tried pushing myself up fast, but a boot crushed down on my spine.

"Get *off* me," I gasped.

I strained to push up again, but the heel only dug deeper between my shoulder blades, cutting off my breath.

"I'll teach you not to spy on people," the voice said, before my camera strap was snatched off my neck. "This is mine now. Better not see you here again."

The boot then lifted, and the thug ran off.

I turned over. "Darnell," I wheezed, choking to breathe.

Darnell heard me this time and opened his door. "Tori?" he called out. "Are you okay?" He ran over and helped me up.

"Yeah, thanks," I said, patting my chest.

Darnell's lip curled in distress at my arm. "Damn, what happened?"

I looked at where he was staring and saw my arm bleeding. Not the worst cut I'd had, maybe an inch long, but I could barely feel any pain. "That truck driver over there stole my camera." I pointed at the giant, now on the other side of the lot. "I'm getting it back."

As I took a step forward, Darnell grabbed me by the shoulders.

"I don't think so," he said, like he was my dad. "You see the size of that guy? You're lucky he didn't crush your skull."

I tried to shake loose, but I was weak in Darnell's grip. "Please," I begged him, "my camera's priceless."

"Tor, your life's priceless." Darnell opened my door. "Now get in. I got something for your arm." I obeyed and climbed inside where he wrapped my wound with paper towels. "That should help with the bleeding. Now you stay put while I charge that man with assault and theft."

I cleared my throat with protest. "You can't do that."

"Excuse me?" Darnell's eyebrow rose. "Why not?"

"I was trespassing. If you charge him, he'll report me."

"So what? He's dangerous." Darnell opened his door, and I grabbed his arm with my uninjured hand.

"Do it and I'll lose my license."

His eyes widened with fury as he sucked on his teeth. "The things I do for you."

In case I didn't know Darnell was mad, he slammed his door and peeled out of the parking lot so fast my backpack flew to the floor of the car, spilling open at my feet. I couldn't blame him for getting angry about this situation when I was even angrier.

As I bent over to gather my stuff, my seatbelt tight against my body, my teeth were grinding hard.

That asshole stole your camera.

Darnell lit his fifth cigarette of the hour, and my phone buzzed in my pocket again. This time I pulled it out to check. "Great," I said. "My boss."

"Good, you can tell him how your assignment almost got you killed by an ogre."

I answered the call. "Hey Kev."

"Hi Tori, got a minute?" Kevin said, sounding nervous or drunk. Or maybe drunk because he was nervous.

"Sure, what's wrong?"

"Nothing," Kevin lied. "We got a case request last night about an accidental death case. The widow's saying it wasn't an accident and specifically requested you, but I can give it to someone else if you'd still rather stick to fraud cases. Thought I'd ask you first."

"Why is she asking for me?" I said, my stomach hardening for a punch, though I knew the answer to my own question.

"I think it has to do with your last name," Kevin said. "Aren't you related to Kansas City's Favorite Uncle?" Hearing that nickname made me gag like I'd smelled bacon. "Tori?"

"Yeah, he's my uncle."

"Well, Luis Mendoza was a cook at the Uncle Charlie's location in Leawood. His widow claims she's getting death threats and that the police aren't looking into it . . ." Kevin's voice stirred beneath the buh-*dump* of my heartbeat. Turned out getting my camera stolen wasn't the worst part of my day. I just needed to stop hearing about this case before I smashed something.

"Don't want it," I said, before hanging up and shoving the phone in my pocket. Darnell stayed quiet while I took staccato breaths. *You're fine. You're fine. You're fine.*

It wasn't until we reached Victory House, the sober house I was leaving for my aunt's, that Darnell turned to me and broke the silence. "So what did your boss say to get you so worked up?"

I was still in disbelief at my hysterical reaction that the words came out like I wasn't the one saying them. "He asked if I wanted a case at Uncle Charlie's."

"Uncle Charlie's? Man, good call turning that down. Your family's your worst trigger, and you've only been sober two years." Darnell reached into the back seat for a fresh Topo Chico, which, though warm, was still a Topo Chico. He handed me the bottle.

"Thanks," I said. With the black bottle opener ring I wore on my thumb, I popped off the cap and started chugging down the prickly bubbles. It wasn't a drug, but the sparkling water did calm me down.

"Was it about Luis Mendoza?" Darnell asked.

I nodded, while swallowing.

"I remember that case," he said. "Memorial Day. Guy was on heroin, fell, hit his head, passed out in the cooker. Ruled an accident."

I sipped the bottle with more restraint. "Sounds like his widow doesn't agree with that story."

"Denial's the first stage of grief." Darnell smashed his cigarette into the ashtray he'd taped to the dashboard. "Guess she's stuck there."

"Yeah, you don't got to tell me about grief."

"You know," Darnell said, nodding at my bottle of water, "you shouldn't drink that so fast. You'll give yourself indigestion with all that carbonation."

"Don't worry, I've got my resources." From my bag, I pulled out an orange bottle and pointed to the label for naltrexone, my anti-narcotic prescription.

What Darnell didn't realize, though, was that the pills inside weren't naltrexone. In fact, I'd stopped taking those a few months ago because they were making me too groggy to work. The pills I had were OxyContin, my opioid of choice, my gateway to heaven and hell.

Darnell gave me an incredulous glance. "That stuff treats heartburn too?"

"What can I say?" I chased down two oxies with a gulp of water. "It's a miracle drug."

As I chugged the bottle down to its bottom, my mind returned to Kevin's call and what had happened last night. After I'd seen Annie's case request, I got so upset I stole all the oxies from the girl next door and hit them hard. Then my anger boiled over, and I looked up my treacherous family online, discovered Luis Mendoza's suspicious death at the drive-in only a month ago, and saw an opportunity to finally get my revenge. That was why I submitted a case request to myself as Luis's widow yesterday.

In that drug-induced euphoric state where I felt invincible, my big plan was to investigate Uncle Charlie and bring him down. Now that I was only mildly drugged-up, though, I saw the danger in my vision. Because even if my gut knew Luis didn't die by accident, it also knew I couldn't investigate the truth. Like Darnell always said, my family was my worst trigger. And seeing as I was already hiding my recent relapse from him and my aunt, I didn't need to make my situation any worse.

Chapter Two

OFFERED TO GIVE DARNELL A hand moving my stuff into his truck, but he wouldn't hear none of it. Not with my bloody arm. So I cooled off in the AC instead and rode the warm wave of those two oxies I'd taken while reassuring Rebus in his cat carrier. "Don't worry, Reebs," I told him in my mothering voice. "We're going back to Aunt Kat's. Remember? You grew up there as a kitten."

But he didn't care what I had to say. Instead, he scowled at me with his mismatched eyes—one yellow, one blue—and once we hit the road, his grumbling escalated to a growl that didn't let up until Darnell pulled into the driveway of the canary yellow house with the dark purple door.

"Man." Darnell blinked at the house. "Your aunt sure likes purple."

"That's an understatement," I said.

I looked at the porch with its lilacs, dream catchers, and wind chimes, and a lump formed in my throat. Though I visited Aunt Kat all the time, I hadn't lived here since she took me in as an orphaned teenager. Now I was back, broke and desperate after Victory House gave me the boot for relapsing, and I had to make sure she never found that out. Otherwise, she'd definitely send me back to rehab, and I really didn't need to go through that drama again. I was planning on resetting myself tonight, anyway, by throwing the rest of the pills down the toilet. I just wanted to escape myself a little while longer.

The purple door opened, and my purple-haired aunt hopped onto the porch in her paint-smattered smock. "Tori," she shouted, waving her hands. "You and your friend can set your things on the porch. Nobody inside but you."

I nodded, and she went back into the house.

"Sorry," I said to Darnell. "She smokes weed all day for her back pain and gets paranoid around cops."

"I get it, but you gonna be okay around her pot?"

"Yeah, never did like the smell."

After Darnell unloaded my stuff on the porch and left, I took a seat on a box of books while the fan overhead tickled my neck hairs. This occasion called for another Topo Chico, and I reached over to grab a new one, popping its cap off with my thumb ring. It was one of those days when I might drink the whole crate.

"He gone?" Aunt Kat called out from behind the screen door.

"Yeah, you're safe."

Aunt Kat came out onto the porch barefoot, arms open and ready to squeeze me until her bloodshot eyes bulged at my arm gash. "Holy cow, you're bleeding."

"Yeah, but I think it's stopped." I patted the blood-soaked wad of paper towels. "Took a spill moving stuff."

"You need to disinfect that immediately."

"Probably."

I downed the rest of my water and picked up Rebus in his carrier to follow my spindly aunt into the lavender living room stinking of citrus skunk. When I unlocked the cat cage, Rebus darted under the plum couch to cry. Aunt Kat dropped to the ground to comfort him.

"Poor kitty," she said, tapping the hardwood floor with her violet nails. "I've got some grass-fed raw beef, if that'll cheer him up."

"Nah, he'll be on a hunger strike until he feels like hunting."

"Well, he's not going outside while he's a guest in this house. I don't want him bringing any of those pests in here like he used to do."

"He can't go outside anyway right now since he'd only run back to Victory House."

"Right." Aunt Kat gave a nod. "Cats do have that homing instinct, don't they?"

I looked around the living room to see if anything had changed. There was the purple couch, the purple rug, the purple table with the purple pipe, vape, and bong. But the display case was empty, meaning my aunt's American Girl doll collection was missing. Guess I couldn't be too offended she'd hidden them when I'd appeared on her doorstep with only one day's notice—and I *had* actually relapsed. I'd told her Victory House wanted me out because they needed my room for someone else and thought I was ready to be on my own. Clearly, Aunt Kat suspected I could be lying.

"Is that supposed to be a Scottish cow?" I gestured to her new painting of a long-horned, shaggy cow in a kilt playing bagpipes, its strokes of violet, magenta, and cyan so thick the paint could be yarn.

"Yeah, I was commissioned to do a Highland Cow with bagpipes," Aunt Kat said. "It's fun, don't you think? Thought I'd hang it in here a few days before sending it to the buyer."

There was a knock at the door, and my aunt jumped to her feet. "Tori," Darnell shouted. "You left your mail in the truck."

"I did?" I rummaged through my backpack. Only two envelopes. "Mustn't have scooped everything off the floor."

"Feed it through the mail slot," Aunt Kat instructed. Three envelopes plopped into a basket beside the front door.

"Thanks for helping me pay my bills," I said.

"Anytime."

Aunt Kat grabbed the mail and held up a star-spangled, glittery envelope without a stamp. "Going to a party?" She handed it to me with an elfish twinkle in her eye.

"Yeah, must be a social thing for NA that someone threw in my mailbox."

But I already knew what was in the envelope before I ripped it open, and as I pulled out a card written in my attempt at florid handwriting, my face flushed to see it again. Aunt Kat leaned over my shoulder, and I shoved the invitation back into the envelope before she could read it and worry.

"What is it?" she asked.

"You're right. It's an invitation."

"From who?"

"A friend you don't know."

"No, I saw your reaction." She shook her head at me. "You're hiding something, I can tell."

"Fine," I said, since I knew she'd only pester me until she got her answer. "Go ahead and find out." I handed her the envelope. "But don't say I didn't warn you."

"I'm sure it's nothing—" Aunt Kat pulled out the card, and it leapt from her hands like it was cursed. "My gosh! Why on earth is Charlie inviting you to his Fourth of July Barbecue tomorrow?"

"Technically, you don't know it came from him. There's no return address or postage."

"Then who sent it?"

"How should I know?" I plopped down on the couch to consider how to best deal with my aunt's curiosity. If she knew I'd invited myself, she'd be suspicious and would probably consider that I was using again. "You know," I began, popping another bottle of Topo Chico with my thumb ring, "my boss just offered me an accidental death case at Uncle Charlie's. The widow requested I investigate what happened to her dead husband."

"What? Why would she want you?" Aunt Kat reached for the overstuffed ashtray. "And why are you getting this invitation at the same time? That can't be a coincidence."

"Exactly." I took a swig of water. "I don't have any online presence saying I'm a PI with my agency, so I don't know how the widow knew my name. As for the invitation, I have no idea how it got to Victory House either. Maybe someone in the family's been watching me."

"Watching you? Tori, don't you give me a panic attack with that kind of talk. Please tell me you turned that case down."

"I did. Thought it would be a bad idea getting involved with the family."

"Of course it's a bad idea." Aunt Kat flicked her lighter at a joint. "It's been years since Charlie screwed you over." She took a drag. "He's nothing but trouble."

"Yeah, maybe the widow's working with whoever invited me," I said. "If Luis didn't die by accident—"

"Like he was murdered?" Aunt Kat's forehead puckered up. "Then even better you turned it down. You know you're not supposed to be working murders anymore, especially ones involving Charlie."

"That's why I was good and turned it down," I reassured her. "But I wouldn't be surprised if Uncle Charlie did murder this guy. You know I've always suspected he had a hand in Dad's death to steal the drive-in."

"I know," Aunt Kat sighed. "And I want to be honest with you right now. I don't think you're wrong about that either."

I leaned forward. "What?"

"Well, I've always kept my thoughts on this subject to myself, but seeing that you're doing so well managing your addiction and anger issues, I think I owe it to you to tell you my theory."

"Your theory on what?" I exclaimed, my pulse shooting up. "That Uncle Charlie killed Dad?"

"I'm sorry, are you okay to hear this? I really don't want to set off your temper."

I took a deep breath. "Yes," I said, more composed, "go on."

"You were too young to remember, thank goodness," Aunt Kat continued, "but Charlie and I saw what happened to Billy when your mom left and how he turned to heroin. Probably would have killed himself if not for you, and he was clean for a long while, but Charlie understood Billy's addictive nature. What I think happened is Charlie got so jealous of Billy's success that he deliberately got Billy hooked on drugs again."

My face was fever-hot, hearing this. "What do you mean?" I pressed her. "How did Uncle Charlie get Dad addicted to heroin again?"

"This is making you upset, I can see it in your face—"

"Tell me."

Aunt Kat sighed again. "I don't think it was an accident what happened with that scalding sauce falling off the barbecue cooker onto Billy's hands. My hunch is Charlie planted it there on purpose because he wanted Billy addicted to painkillers."

"Oxies," I stated as if I wasn't on them now.

"Right, and you know better than anyone how addictive they are. Billy tore through his first bottle in a blink, and that's when Charlie began dropping off heroin baggies in Billy's mailbox. I wouldn't be surprised if Charlie cut that stuff with something deadly either, if only to be sure he'd got the job done."

I strangled the Topo Chico bottle as if it was my uncle's neck. "What do you mean he dropped off baggies in the mailbox?"

"I saw Charlie's car at the mailbox," she said, "and found a baggie of heroin inside after he'd gone. I told Billy about it, but by then he was hooked and didn't care. Then he overdosed soon after that. The way I see it, Billy poisoned himself to death, but Charlie gave him the poison."

"So he could steal the drive-in," I said under my breath.

I thought back to that Fourth of July weekend, half my life ago, when Swensons Barbecue became the most popular joint in KC, with cars lining up for hours to get a taste of that smoky, sweet brisket.

Weeks later, Dad was dead, and when his will turned up, revised days before his death, it blew all our minds because it said Uncle Charlie was the heir to the barbecue business. Aunt Kat argued in court it couldn't be right, claiming there was a different will that said I was supposed to inherit my dad's business when I came of age, but with my uncle's connections in high places, he got away with his scheme.

So Uncle Charlie cut me out of the business and got super rich off my inheritance. His role in my dad's relapse, though, was a new twist to the tale.

Now my chest was heaving, especially with those two oxies I'd taken. Though opioids were supposed to calm you down and make you feel all cozy warm inside, they could also, depending, incite explosive rage. This situation called for it. Everything in me was at a boiling point—my heart rate, my blood pressure, my breath. I needed a release.

A shrill scream tore out my lungs, and I smashed my bottle on the coffee table, spraying water and glass everywhere.

"Oh my God, Tori," Aunt Kat said. "Are you okay?"

I was still panting short breaths as I looked up from the mess to my aunt's terrified blue eyes. "Sorry," I muttered, "I'll clean this up later." I got up and made for the door.

"Where are you going?" She snatched my arm. "You're red as a chili pepper. I'm sorry I upset you. I only thought you should know the truth at some point."

"I'm fine." I shook myself free. "I just need a moment."

Chapter Three

S NAPPED OPEN MY FOURTH Topo Chico of the hour and paced on the porch. The rehab doctors said not to blame others for your problems, but this wasn't my case. My uncle was the reason my life got destroyed. I couldn't blame Aunt Kat for wanting to protect me from the truth all this time, so I wouldn't burn my uncle's hands off myself. But now that I knew my intuition had been right all along, I wasn't sure I'd be able to restrain myself.

The bottle jiggled in my hand as I thought of my uncle on billboards, smiling a usurper's grin while holding my dad's barbecue burger, the same burger that had got my dad murdered by his own brother—if Aunt Kat's story proved to be true. Now I really understood Hamlet.

You could still get revenge.

After all, my uncle deserved to suffer for what he'd done. It wouldn't even be hard when I knew in my gut—the place that never lied—that Luis didn't conveniently fall into a cooker and destroy evidence of his track marks. More likely, someone killed him and covered up their murderous tracks, and whether that was my uncle, a cousin, or some bitter curb server, I knew exposing a murder at the all-American drive-in would discredit, if not crush, my uncle's fraudulent barbecue dynasty. No more Kansas City's Favorite Uncle.

I also knew Aunt Kat and Darnell would lose their minds over what I was about to do, but I messaged Kevin anyway. *Okay, I'll take the case*, I texted him.

Already, I was feeling much better.

When I went back into the house, Aunt Kat was again on her hands and knees in front of the couch. "Here, kitty, kitty . . ."

"I took the case," I announced drily.

"You what?" Aunt Kat whipped around to face me. "Didn't you hear what I said? Charlie is dangerous."

I ignored her panic. "Can I please borrow your car?" I still didn't have one since my accident two years ago. Though I'd been borrowing a friend's car at Victory House, that wasn't an option anymore.

"No, you've come too far," Aunt Kat said. "I won't be enabling trouble."

"Don't worry, I'm armed." I dug into my backpack and pulled out my police-strength stun gun to show her. Though I hadn't used it since catching the Amity Woods Killer some years ago, I still carried it with me.

"Your safety's not my only concern." Aunt Kat rubbed her temples in distress. "What about another relapse?"

Her question was a dart of anxiety to my chest. I could see in her expression, though, that she didn't believe I was on drugs now. If she did, she'd be tearing up. Unlike me, she wasn't very good at hiding her feelings.

"I'll be careful," I said. "But I need to get to Leawood and talk to Luis's manager so I'm ready for the party tomorrow."

"You're not going to that party."

"You're not stopping me." I gave her a firm look. "But if it makes you feel better, I'll keep you in the loop. You could even give me some pointers seeing as you know your brother better than I do."

"I shouldn't have told you anything," Aunt Kat moaned as she picked up a glass pipe and lit the bowl in defeat.

My phone dinged. It was a message from Kevin with an email attachment from Luis's widow, Isabella Mendoza, the same email I'd written last night.

"Clue number one." I cleared my throat to read the message aloud. "Dear Bullseye Services, I am writing because I have received anonymous threats and am too afraid to go to the police. My husband, Luis Mendoza, died on Monday, May 30, at Uncle Charlie's Bar-B-Que Drive-In in Leawood, Kansas. The coroner stated that Luis had been abusing heroin when he fell, hit his head, and died of a traumatic brain injury.

"However, this cannot be true because Luis never used drugs. He was a good man. Please, I must find out what happened to clear his name. I have included a $3,000 cash advance and am requesting that Victoria Swenson investigate because I believe she is related to the drive-in's owner, and would have additional resources for solving the case. I do not wish to meet in person because I fear I am being watched. If you need to contact me, or require more money, you can write me at this email address. Thank you, Isabella Mendoza."

"Is that a joke?" Aunt Kat scrunched her eyes together. "Who the heck sends that much up front?"

I nodded and regretted my empty bank account. This was why I had no choice but to move in with my aunt today.

Since Kevin discussed a new case with the client before assessing payment, I had to pretty much drain my savings, and $3,000 was enough for Kevin to move forward with the investigation without meeting the client.

"Mrs. Mendoza did say she was scared," I said. "Desperate people will pay whatever it takes."

"Rhetorical question, dear." Aunt Kat released a puff of smoke that for a second masked her disappointment. "Seriously, why are you pursuing a case that's obviously a trap?"

"Because I'm an investigator and angry enough to punish my uncle for killing my dad and destroying my life. Sound reasonable enough to you?"

Aunt Kat swallowed, the guilt resurfacing in her rosy cheeks for having told me the truth. "I understand you're mad, but you got to know you can't bring Charlie down."

"We'll see about that." I took out my phone. "But if I can't use your car, I'll start wasting what little money I have ordering rides."

Aunt Kat didn't call my bluff. She set the pipe down, opened her purse, and dropped the car keys on the coffee table. "Here. You'll do what you want. Always have. Always will."

"Thanks." I slipped the keys into my pocket.

"You might want to bring a cooler with you though," she added. "The AC broke last week, and I haven't got around to fixing it yet."

"Hey, I don't mind sweating." I gave her a smile. "But seriously, thanks for the wheels."

I'd need them for the ride I was going on.

Chapter Four

KANSAS CITY COULDN'T MAKE UP its mind about what it was or where it belonged. With about a million people in the metro area and the highest—per capita—amount of highway lane miles in the nation, it wasn't an urban city, but it wasn't a town either. During the Civil War times, the area was split on Union and Confederate issues. Now it straddled the border of Missouri and Kansas, two different states with different laws and systems. Some claimed KC was the Midwest. Some called it the Heartland. Others said it belonged to the South. I didn't care about these debates. To me, it was just home. And I liked it enough.

As I started my journey to Kansas, the dead air conditioner wasn't the only joy of my aunt's eggplant sedan from the early '90s, the same car she'd had since before I was born. There was no audio jack, and the scent of stale weed made me cough. I manually cranked the windows down, letting the humid air spank my face with street grit while I sailed along Southwest Trafficway for the new Uncle Charlie's in ritzy Leawood, Kansas.

My phone sat in the cup holder, tempting me to call Darnell. It would be pointless, though. Instead of getting police knowledge on the Mendoza case, I'd get a sermon on how stupid I was for taking the case. I knocked my head against the headrest.

Maybe you are stupid.

Right when I was almost cured, if such a thing was possible, here I was, on relapse number four. I'd had good intentions of throwing the rest of my pills down the toilet tonight, but I couldn't do that anymore. Now I needed them more than ever to deal with my estranged family. So long as I didn't take too many and have a violent outburst, I'd be fine. I'd quit again after the investigation. *Just watch the dose.* I opened the orange bottle and swallowed another round pink pill. So far today, I was up to 100 mg.

Not bad, not yet.

Over the next ten minutes, the oxy worked its magic of lifting me out of my lousy reality onto a tingling cloud, and I pushed a jazz cassette into the car's tape deck. Though the stereo system wasn't great, the gentle sax came out of the speakers, making me float even higher. This was my favorite Kansas City Charlie, Charlie "Yardbird" Parker, who'd lived a full life until his wheels flew off at thirty-four from a heart attack. Like Dad, heroin was his undoing. As if teasing me, Yardbird was playing "Summertime." If only I could believe the living was easy when I was cooking alive in this car and on my way to Uncle Charlie's.

The sax soared as the road dipped into the Plaza, America's first car-friendly shopping center built after World War I to resemble Seville, Spain. With its restaurants, hotels, apartment buildings, and boutique storefronts done up in colorful mosaics, terra-cotta roofs, and enough fountains to give KC the nickname "City of Fountains," it was such a charming wonderland that you'd swear you were in a snow globe if there was any snow. But as I imagined myself living a sober life in one of these enchanted condos, a little black dog flew out of nowhere right in front of me. I slammed on the brakes. My heart beat heavy in my head.

Thank God you didn't pancake that thing. I stayed there for a moment, chugging water as I watched the owner snap her fingers at the furball prancing before me. This was a warning to be more careful behind the wheel, especially since I was on opioids.

At a slower speed, I resumed my journey by turning onto Ward Parkway, Missouri's wealthiest boulevard, with its gated mansions and gardens.

Of course, Uncle Charlie lived on this decadent street, and when I saw his orange palace in the golden afternoon, I did what I always did and spit out the window. This time, though, my mouth was dry. I swallowed the air, tasting dirt. Hard to believe that in less than twenty-four hours, I'd be with my uncle putting on the show of my life.

Over the border into Leawood, Kansas, I drove past more fancy homes —until the odor of burning flesh stung my nostrils. Up ahead, on the side of the highway, stood the metallic monster, which didn't look a thing like the original drive-in my dad had converted from a gas station. This new one was shiny with a glass front, so curb servers could immediately spot a customer's headlights flashing for service. I hung a right past a sign that read *Home of America's Best Barbecue Burger,* then rolled into a parking lot packed with teens on summer break.

Down went the rest of my Topo Chico. Going into that shiny place wasn't something I'd ever wanted to do, but there was no point sitting in the car agonizing over the inevitable. At least the oxies had mostly numbed my fears about going inside. I stepped out, gagging on the smoky air, and walked toward the drive-in.

When I was almost to the front door, however, my attention got pulled in another direction. Parked in the front row was a familiar black Toyota with its TOP GUM vanity plate. I knew that car, since I'd had sex in it a few times way back when. As I approached the vehicle to knock on the window, it rolled down to reveal Gabe's chiseled Italian face. He gave me a playful though faint smile.

"Victoria," he said, sweeping his fingers through his thickly gelled hair. "Funny seeing you here."

"You know I don't like being called that," I said stonily.

Gabe didn't take the hint. Instead, he picked up his chocolate milkshake and obscenely slurped on his straw, his mirrored sunglasses reflecting my flushed cheeks. "How about Vicky?"

"What are you doing here?" I asked.

"Excuse me, wasn't I here before you?"

I looked at his lap and his half-eaten barbecue burger. "Guess it's a co-incidence then that you're having dinner here when I show up."

Gabe smiled. "You should know there's no such thing as coincidences in our line of work."

"All right, then what are you doing here?"

"The case you're here for was mine before you had a change of heart," he said, frowning. "Though I suppose your heart's been fickle before."

He raised the meat mountain to his mouth, chomped, and let the sauce dribble down his chin like he was Dracula. Even though it had been two years, Gabe was still sore I'd put the kibosh on our spring fling. Maybe he would've understood better, knowing that the world shutting down for a virus had sent me into relapse number three. Over those few months, I spiraled to the point I nearly died in my big car accident, and that's when Aunt Kat and Darnell got me into Victory House. But I never shared this story with Gabe, and I wasn't planning on it either.

"Sorry I inconvenienced you," I said in an unapologetic tone. "I was waffling since this case involves family."

Gabe dabbed his chin with a paper towel. "Oh, that's right," he said. "You're related to Uncle Charlie. I remember your tragic story. No wonder you're so fired up to take this case." He lowered his sunglasses to reveal his gold-flecked hazel eyes, which bore into me with the same intensity as in the bedroom. Since I was on oxies, I couldn't feel much of anything for him except impatience.

Ignoring his seduction attempt, I replied, "Yeah, he's dead to me."

"And do you really think it's a good idea for you to investigate your family's business? You're not exactly objective, are you? Perhaps it would be better if I helped—"

"No thanks. This is my case."

"For now," Gabe said with a smirk. "But while you're here, you might as well try the new UltraCharBurger. Twice as many burnt ends as the Char-Burger, smoked provolone, two onion rings, special barbecue sauce, on an extra-large buttered Kaiser roll."

"Sounds like heart disease."

"But it's extra saucy, just how you like it. Let me know if you want to grab a bite sometime."

"Sorry, don't eat meat."

Before Gabe could try another come-on, I left him and continued walking toward the drive-in. No doubt that made him mad. Not only had I taken my big case back that he'd wanted for his resumé, but I'd scorned him again. If only he was better at reading body language than engaging in wishful thinking.

I reached the glass door, which opened in my face as a lanky curb server stepped out. "This is a drive-in," he shouted like he was law enforcement. "Customers get served in the parking lot. Only employees are allowed in the Hub."

"I'm Uncle Charlie's niece," I stated, and presented my driver's license. The boy squinted at the fine print. "See." I pointed at my name. "I'm a Swenson. Can I please speak to your manager?"

The teen reluctantly led me into "the Hub"—or the loud, steaming, meat sauna, with a ceiling of harsh fluorescent lights and a few surveillance cameras. Though it had been years since meat had actually made me lose my lunch, my stomach was rumbling in dangerous territory now. I took out a Topo Chico from my bag and opened it to guzzle away my nausea.

Meanwhile, cookers sizzled in back, and robust, young curb servers dressed like Scouts sprinted in and out of the drive-in, swapping food orders as if passing batons. Then a round man, shorter than me, marched out to greet me. He was wearing tinted glasses, a buttoned-up shirt splattered in sauce and armpit stains, with a wisp of gray hair and a forehead shimmering in sweat and grease. His name tag read *Walter Meadows*.

"Hey there," he said. "I'm Walt. I hear you're a relative of Charlie's?"

"You bet," I said, giving him a smile to calm his nerves. "I'm Tori. Uncle Charlie's my uncle."

"Wow, Uncle Charlie's a real uncle." Walt forced a chuckle. "What can I do for you?"

"Sorry to show up unannounced," I began, "but I'm a private investigator, and I'm here to investigate the death of Luis Mendoza who used to work here. Were you the one who found him?"

Walt's face reddened while his mouth contorted with obvious pain. "I ... Yes ..."

"I understand this is difficult for you, but we wanted to hear from you again to prevent any future accidents like this from happening. Sometimes distance provides a fresh perspective on events."

Walt wiped his shiny forehead on his sleeve. "It's certainly been hard," he said. "Especially since I got the flu right after it happened. That's why I'm still shaking if you hadn't noticed, but I'll try to help if I can."

"Thanks. Mind if I record you?"

He consented, and I turned on my phone's recorder while following him into the kitchen, where a dozen workers prepared orders for the early supper crowd, some spritzing meat at the barbecue cookers, others making side dishes in bright red pots and pans.

Walt stopped near a cooker in the Hub's corner and pointed at it with a trembling finger. "That's where I found him, his arms burnt up—" He choked on what seemed like genuine emotion.

"I'm sorry, that must have been horrific." I approached the black iron and steel cylinder that looked like any other, cooking a brisket where it once cooked Luis. "You know how he landed in the grill?"

"The cops said he hit his forehead by accident after shooting up heroin." Walt slapped his own forehead in case I'd forgotten where it was. "Then he passed out in the cooker."

I still didn't buy this story of Luis accidentally dying in a cooker, but I went on with my questions. "Did you see any heroin?" I said.

"There was a needle on the ground, but that's all I saw."

"Right, and did you know whether Luis was a legal U.S. citizen?"

Walt blinked at me. "Of course he was," he exclaimed. "All our employees are U.S. citizens."

"Just asking standard questions. How long was he a cook here?"

"He started back in March, so over two months. Had a baby on the way and was working overtime. A real friendly, honest, reliable guy. I'd have promoted him fast to assistant manager."

"Anyone else working the night he died?"

Walt bashfully dropped his head. "There should have been two closers and me since it was a holiday night," he said, a crack in his voice. "Memorial Day, you know. We always have two closers on weekends and holidays, but I got sick and left early, and the other guy never showed." He leaned toward me and lowered his volume. "Not unusual in the restaurant business, I'm afraid. On average, a third of the staff doesn't show."

I remembered my dad making similar complaints about the unreliability of restaurant workers. "Who was this other guy who was supposed to be working?"

"Don't remember his name. I'd have to review an old schedule. He was only here a few weeks until I fired him for not showing."

I pointed at the surveillance camera above us. "Did anyone check the video feed to see what happened to Luis?"

"The police checked, but the footage was deleted for part of that night."

I nodded. *Yet another coincidence in the accidental death of Luis Mendoza.* "Who has access to the surveillance footage?"

"Just the executives." Walt pressed his lips together like he shouldn't have said that.

"So my uncle and cousins?" I stated for clarification.

He nodded, his cheeks reddening. "Yeah, unless someone hacked the system. Lots of kids these days know how to do that kind of high-tech stuff."

I placed a hand over my mouth to conceal my smile. If the footage had been deleted by one of my relatives, or someone working for them, then there was no doubt in my mind that my family had to be connected with Luis's death. I cleared my throat to ask another question. "So you can't be certain Luis was alone if there was no surveillance footage, right?"

"I guess he could have let someone in." Walt squeezed his sticky fingers and looked down at the floor again.

"Something bothering you?" I said.

He swallowed, then whispered quickly, "I don't know if your uncle knows this, but the police found heroin baggies in Luis's locker."

"Really? Can you show me where?"

Walt took me to the only hallway in the drive-in, one lined with lockers and leading to employee bathrooms and an office at the far end. We stopped by a locker, where Walt's shaking hand struggled to twist the key into the lock. When the door popped open, the empty locker was scented in lemon cleaner.

"The cops had me open it," Walt said. "There were baggies stacked all the way up to here." He raised his hand a foot from the locker's bottom.

"That's a lot of dope." I leaned my head inside and sniffed the citrus-scented chemicals. The locker had been thoroughly scrubbed. "Do you think Luis was dealing drugs from Uncle Charlie's?"

Walt's wet forehead flushed rose gold. "Could have been. He was acting pretty strange the night before he died."

"What do you mean?"

"We were closing up. I was in the office doing money stuff, and he was cleaning. When I went back into the kitchen, I saw him carrying a box. I asked him what it was, and he said the meat supplier had dropped off a delivery, but they never dropped off only one box, and anyway, they weren't scheduled that night."

"Did you look inside this box?" I said.

"Oh no, I was too afraid to ask about it. Luis was in pretty good shape."

"Do you think it's possible this box was a shipment of heroin and that he put it in his locker the night before he died?"

"I . . . I guess?"

"Who had access to his locker besides you and him?"

Again, Walt swallowed before giving his answer. "The executives."

Another strike on my family. I thanked Walt for his time and the free chocolate milkshake and returned to Aunt Kat's hotbox to get out my phone and run a background search on Walter Meadows. There was certainly something shifty about the guy, so I wasn't shocked to find he had a record. Last year, he'd been charged with a sexual harassment claim that got dropped, but what interested me more was his drug history. Though he hadn't had a drug-related charge for nearly twenty years, he had several counts of drug possession as well as two hospitalizations for overdoses. Clean half his life, at least according to his record, but I knew addicts. Most didn't stay clean. They just got better at hiding it.

Chapter Five

THERE WERE POTHOLES IN WALT'S story, but I still had to test it out. If, for example, Luis had been dealing drugs from the drive-in, was that why he got killed? And if someone in my family had cut the camera feed, was my family possibly covering up a major drug scheme? Maybe Luis was working for them. Maybe my family had to silence him because he knew too much, or wasn't on board with their program.

Whatever happened, though, I couldn't just show up at a friendly family gathering after years of absence with questions about Luis's death. That was a subject I needed someone else to bring up for me.

I started the car, cranked the volume on Yardbird, and hit the road for the West Bottoms. This was an area of town I avoided because my dad's original drive-in, now a national treasure, was still there and being run by my uncle. Just being near the place raised my blood pressure, but I didn't have a choice now. I had to find someone in the vicinity to interrupt tomorrow's party.

Twenty minutes later, I was flying off the highway for the West Bottoms. This was a neighborhood that had seen its fair share of change. Way back in its heyday in the mid-nineteenth century, it used to be KC's former economic center, with its railroads serving as the nation's distribution hub for Midwestern cattle. But after some floods and fires, it went from

Cattletown to Deadsville. Nothing but empty warehouses for years, which was why Dad could buy the abandoned gas station for next to nothing. Now the neighborhood was up-and-coming, full of stoned hipsters covered in tattoos and body piercings, while the brick warehouses had been converted into giant antique stores, haunted houses, new apartment complexes, brew-pubs, and wine bars.

Still, this part of town wasn't somewhere you wanted to be alone at night. Hitting the locks on the car doors and manually rolling up my windows almost to the top, I laid my stun gun on my lap and headed toward the train tracks. A man was sleeping in the underpass. Exactly the kind of person who could help me out—an addict.

"Hey," I called out to the stranger.

The man stirred and lifted his head limply at me, eyes flickering through a tangled mess of greasy hair. "What?" he called out.

"Listen, I got a job for you if you want to make some extra cash."

He pushed himself up and hobbled toward me. "How much?" he mumbled.

I pushed a hundred-dollar bill through the top crack of my window. "How about I give you this for just hearing me out," I told him. "You do what I ask, you get another two hundred. How's that sound?"

"Sounds all right to me." The man snatched the bill out of my hand and stuffed it into his pants. "What do you want?"

I scribbled instructions into my notebook and tore out the page. "Here." I handed it to him. "Be at Uncle Charlie's tomorrow afternoon and mention what I've written. But don't point me out at the party because I'll be there too. I'll come back and pay you once everyone's gone. Believe me, I'm good for my word."

"Hey, you don't gotta worry about me remembering you," he said, laughing through a mouthful of missing teeth. "Most days, I hardly remember my own name."

"Just remember to be there," I said, hoping he wasn't too drugged now to forget our arrangement.

The sun was blood orange on the horizon when I got back to Aunt Kat's canary house with the purple door. Inside, I found her snoring on the couch, the TV news blasting something about the joys of summer insects. I turned the TV off, and she didn't stir. A hard sleeper, unlike me. She didn't even wake as I lugged my stuff up the stairs to my teenage bedroom, a place steeped in bad memories that my aunt had tried covering up by repainting the black walls fuchsia.

Otherwise, it was the same old room I'd left for college, with its queen bed, the oak desk marked in black nail polish, and the antique Victrola—the only thing I scored from Dad's. Seeing the room again, though, knotted my stomach. *You'll be out in a few months.* After all, solving this case could even expedite that process because if I caught a big-fish murderer like Uncle Charlie, I'd get such a nice bonus I'd be able to afford something decent, maybe even in the Plaza.

Assuming you survive whatever's coming. That was my sober inner voice, the voice of rational pessimism. It wasn't wrong either. Seeing my uncle tomorrow meant putting on a smile while resisting the urge to rip his face off. Seeing my cousin Annie, my old best friend, meant pretending like I was completely fine with how she'd ghosted me after Dad's death, while also pretending I didn't know that she'd hired my agency to chase Ginny Wolf for fraud.

As I opened my closet to move my boxes inside, my eyes shot straight to the floorboard where I used to stash my dope. The piece of loose wood was still there. I backed up away from it. I couldn't do this right now. I closed the closet door and left my room.

I didn't want to think about whether I was making a mistake going after my family when I knew I was, so I picked up my clarinet, named Bird after Charlie Parker, and headed outside for the treehouse that Aunt Kat had gotten me as a place of refuge for playing music and reading books. Music was the only healthy outlet I had that wasn't a drug, and I needed to play. Of course, I wouldn't be good with the oxies in me as they slowed down my rhythm, but I didn't care.

Outside the treehouse, I looked around at the surrounding homes and apartment complexes. These people were my audience, the people smoking and drinking on balconies, thankful to have survived another blistering summer's day, while the swarmageddon of cicadas sang their mating calls. My body was heavy with exhaustion as I forced myself up the ladder, rung by rung, into the treehouse.

I made it, though. Then I opened Bird's case, put him together, and sucked on a fresh reed. *That sweet arundo donax cane.* As I held Bird to my chest, my fingertips tingling on the cool keys, I breathed in the silence before the music, always louder than the first note. There was ecstasy leaving this world and anxiety going to the next. Closing my eyes, I surrendered to whatever was coming, took a deep breath, and flew to the moon.

Chapter Six

MY EYES OPENED TO THE sound of gunfire. Like they'd taught us in defense training, I saved my questions for later and took cover by rolling out of bed to the ground. The pops continued firing outside, like rounds from a bazooka. I crawled over to the window and lifted a blind. Across the street, the sun shone on the neighborhood kids, setting off firecrackers. I snapped the blind back. "Happy Independence Day, Reebs," I said, but my scared baby boy was already under the bed for the day.

On my desk, the invitation to Uncle Charlie's party glittered back at me, reminding me yesterday's events had been real. Though I wanted to crawl under the bed along with my cat, I had research to do before my family reunion.

I downed a morning Topo Chico with a pair of my pink friends and waited for the warmth of a loving hug to envelop me. Then I was ready to run background searches on my family.

First up was Uncle Charlie, and the results were as expected. No arrests, no parking tickets, impeccable credit, one divorce. Thirty-eight cases in his court files, but sued only twice, both by family. As my adopted legal guardian when my dad died, Aunt Kat was the first who'd sued him on my behalf. The other was my former Aunt Marie, who'd since fled to Florida. In both cases, Uncle Charlie had won. His remaining lawsuits with customers, employees, competitor restaurants, the EEOC, and the USDA had all been settled outside of court. As for my cousins, their records were clean too.

I had to run an image search next. This was something I hadn't done since college, when I'd found Annie's wedding photos online and gotten so worked up that I ended up swallowing all the oxies in my possession. If not for the freebie Narcan they'd passed out at the campus center, I'd probably have oxycuted then.

That was relapse number one.

My cursor blinked at me, slower than my pulse. Not a great sign I was still so anxious after taking two pills. Not to mention I wasn't even at the party yet. I popped another 20 mg. So long as I didn't exceed my self-diagnosed tolerance of 120 mg, I'd be fine. I'd done way more than that before without having a real problem anyway.

I entered *Swenson fundraisers* into the search engine, and a montage flashed at me that could have been from a magazine, with charity balls, baseball games, boat outings, ribbon-cutting ceremonies, and sparkly Uncle Charlie's Angel ads.

I pushed my tongue into my cheek, my eyes glazing over their smug faces. Uncle Charlie might have stolen my dad's drive-in, but my cousins were just as guilty for what my life had become. Not only did they benefit from my loss, but they never once reached out to see how I was doing. Of course, it was Annie's silent complicity that always stung the most.

"Tori?" Aunt Kat knocked at the door.

I jolted in my chair. "Hold on," I shouted back at her. I did a quick scan of my room to make sure she wasn't stumbling in on something she shouldn't, but she barged right in before I could close my laptop.

"Morning." Aunt Kat planted a glass of purple froth on my desk. "Thought you could start your day off right with an immune-boosting smoothie. It's got elderberries from my garden."

"Thanks," I said, though I was biting my tongue from lecturing her on privacy invasion. Being an addict meant losing your privacy privileges for life. That was why there were no locks on any doors in the house.

My aunt smacked her lips at my screen. "I've seen that before." She pointed to a family photo at the Royals game, where everyone was smiling so hard they were wearing down their bleached enamel. "There's also a video of Charlie giving a motivational speech on the pitcher's mound where he talks about busting your butt to achieve your dreams." I pretended to gag, and Aunt Kat laughed. "Why are you looking at these?"

"Doing research." I took a gulp of ice-cold smoothie. It was refreshing, but very filling, especially since the oxies robbed me of an appetite.

"Better to be prepared I guess," she sighed. "You know, I'm still not thrilled you're going to that party, but I'm not here to stop you. Actually, I have a favor to ask." She pulled out an envelope from her robe pocket. "Could you please give this to Charlie?"

I took it. "It's not a death threat, is it?"

She shook her head. "Just something from the good old days."

"I'll need to see what it is first."

"Go ahead."

I opened the envelope and pulled out a Polaroid that made my chest tighten. It was a picture of Dad, Aunt Kat, and Uncle Charlie, standing together in stonewashed jeans at Missouri's first official barbecue drive-in, the famous gas station with the neon sign for *Swensons Barbecue*. Dad was in an apron and floppy chef's hat, sober and radiating joy. Uncle Charlie was frowning at Dad.

"Uncle Charlie looks upset," I said, shoving the photo back into its envelope.

Aunt Kat gave a nod. "I'm sure he was. He was always jealous of Billy, even as a kid."

"Why?"

Aunt Kat plopped down on my bed. "Because Billy had a passion that Charlie lacked," she said. "When your grandpa taught us kids how to barbecue, Billy was the one obsessed with it. Even in the blazing hot summers, he served barbecue from a cart on the street. That's when I first noticed Charlie's jealousy. Not only was Billy passionate, but he was making money."

"I remember Dad talking about that food cart," I said, taking another sip of smoothie. "He called it the prison sweat box. Probably like your car now."

"It was hot all right," Aunt Kat said with a chuckle. "And I'm not sure the fan helped when it made you feel like you were getting blown by a hair dryer all day. Your dad certainly put up with a lot trying to master his barbecue skills, and it didn't get any easier when he bought that gas station and had to work all day, every day, including Sunday. Of course, Charlie criticized him endlessly, saying it was a big waste of time and money since there were already hundreds of barbecue joints in town. Truth was, he was jealous Billy was taking the risks he wasn't. And when those risks made Billy successful, I think Charlie lost his mind."

"Maybe Dad would still be alive if he hadn't been so successful."

"I've considered that," my aunt said. "What if *KC Pitmaster* hadn't put Billy on the cover of their magazine? That's when the cars started rolling in from Oklahoma or Illinois to get a taste of what was already being called 'Kansas City's best burnt end burger,' though it wasn't really a burger. With so much business coming in, me and Charlie had to step up and help Billy out in the kitchen. Then a few days later, your dad had his so-called accident and burned his hands."

I didn't want to think about my dad's hands again, with how angry it had made me yesterday. "What do you mean it's not really a burger?" I asked instead.

"No patty, no burger."

"So what is it then? A meat monster?"

"A sandwich." Aunt Kat laughed. "There was a dispute when Charlie had to sign a settlement with The Big BQ over the word, 'burger,' but right after that he bought them out of bankruptcy, liquidated them, and went back to calling it a burger. That's why I can't warn you enough to be careful with him. If he thinks you're a threat, he'll try to destroy you."

With these reassuring words, Aunt Kat headed downstairs to marinate her Fourth of July ribs. Meanwhile, I filed the Polaroid in my bag and pulled out a suitcase in search of something red, white, and blue. Not that I cared about holidays, but I knew I shouldn't draw any more attention to myself when I was already shocking everyone with my sudden appearance.

I put on a pair of jean shorts and a cherry red tank, tied my blonde ringlets into a ponytail with a white scrunchie, and completed the patriotic look by slapping my arm injury with a bandage of Mickey Mouse waving the flag. To better perform the role of Tori—the charming, long-lost cousin—I dug out my makeup, reserved only for costumes, and applied royal blue eye shadow, sparkly red eyeliner, and mascara that made my green eyes pop.

"The all-American girl, Reebs," I said to my invisible cat under the bed. "That's me."

Chapter Seven

SOON AS I PULLED OUT of the driveway, I swallowed another pill. Then another. Now I was up to 100 mg, which made my skin extra clammy in the burning hot car. At least the streets were emptier for the holiday as I was swerving here and there, my focus less on the road and more on my horrifying destination. Every time I went through another intersection, the same thought stabbed me in the chest: *Another block closer.* The fourteen-year time gap was closing. I was really about to see my family again. And I really didn't want to.

Somehow, I wove through downtown inner-city traffic without hurting myself or anyone else and hung a left on 12th Street for the West Bottoms. The gravel road crunched beneath the tires as I passed warehouses overtaken by spaghetti grass, their parking lots cleared out for the long weekend.

When I turned past a giant warehouse called Heavenly Antiques, I slammed on the brakes, my breath sucked out of me. My head was a thumping subwoofer. But there it was. The same unassuming white pavilion with the shamrock green roof, as featured in all the magazines, TV shows, and KC tour guidebooks, unchanged except for the false name of *Uncle Charlie's Bar-B-Que Drive-In* that glowed in blue neon letters across the roof.

I coughed at the barbecue smoke and turned into the drive-in's parking lot. My eyes went to the glass front door. I swallowed the lump in my throat remembering Dad standing there, yelling at me to come inside because it was too hot to play.

These memories and more were waiting for me. In fact, they were even coming to life because I could swear my dad was standing behind the door now unless I had developed visual hallucinations from the oxies. I stopped the car and closed my eyes.

Sure enough, when I opened them, the ghost was gone. Just a glass door.

I rolled toward the corner of the parking lot, passing luxury cars while a band played "Stars and Stripes Forever" from behind the drive-in. When I passed the neon red *Closed* sign Dad loved and the vintage gas pumps I'd almost destroyed in a fit of teenage rage, I parked the car. At least in the back, Aunt Kat's beater would be less conspicuous.

But my hands were shaking worse than Walt's. *You're fine. You're fine.* This self-talk did nothing for me when I was throwing back more pills. Darnell would tell me to get the hell out of here, and he wouldn't be wrong.

But I was in a pickle. Going to this party would certainly be torture, but if I didn't go, I'd be tortured—with guilt—that I'd never tried settling the score with my uncle when I had the chance.

As I sucked on my water bottle in deliberation, an older man in a black T-shirt and jeans threw back the glass door and stumbled outside like he'd escaped his kidnappers.

This had to be the guy I'd mistaken for Dad's specter, which was somewhat encouraging since it meant I hadn't been hallucinating. I'd have to make do without my camera, so I grabbed my binoculars instead. The man was coughing and clutching his chest. When he flung his head back to come up for air, I dropped the binoculars in my lap.

My uncle pointed right at me. "We're closed," he shouted, then coughed into his elbow and started shuffling his bare feet across the parking lot toward me.

My hand moved for the keys, still in the ignition. *Get out of here.*

"You can't be here," he said, more adamant this time. "You need to leave."

Hearing this command, heat flushed through my body. I yanked the keys from the ignition. My uncle wasn't driving me out of my drive-in this time. I tapped twice on the horn, which could either be interpreted as a sign of greeting or a sign that a fight was beginning. Then I grabbed my cooler of Topo Chicos and stepped out into a scorching afternoon thick with barbecue smoke.

"You can't be here," my uncle repeated when he saw me coming.

I said nothing as I walked toward him, squeezing the cooler against my chest like it protected me from whatever disease he was carrying. This man was hardly the evil uncle I remembered. He looked like he was about to die. Still, I wasn't letting my guard down, and when we finally came face to face at the gas pumps, we stopped to let the silence pass between us. More heat flashed through my body, and I pressed my lips together so I wouldn't say anything I'd regret. Up close, I examined the scaly blotches on his cheeks, while his glassy gray eyes, red and swollen, narrowed on me with suspicion.

"I know you," he said, his voice surprisingly mild-mannered for someone who'd had the worst coughing fit I'd seen.

"You could say that." I smiled so hard my teeth went numb. "I'm your niece."

Chapter Eight

"B ILLY'S DAUGHTER," UNCLE CHARLIE STATED matter-of-
factly, like he wasn't at all shocked to see me. "You're not
broke and looking for money, are you?"

"Nope," I said, holding onto my smile as I fished out the sparkly invitation from my bag. "Got this in the mail."

Uncle Charlie swiped it from me. "Bullshit." He spat on the ground.
"This isn't ours. Emma had ours designed with piglets."

He threw the card back at me, his eyes drilling into mine like he suspected I'd invited myself.

"That's strange." I stepped back. "I can go if you'd—"

"Don't be stupid. You're a Swenson. Why should an old family beef
prevent you from reacquainting with your cousins?"

My jaw clenched at his dismissal of the past.

I honestly wanted to strangle him, but I could also read in his hard-
ened gaze that he was testing my allegiance. *Don't squander your revenge on
a cheap outburst.*

I just widened my grin. "I'd love to see my cousins. They all here?"

"Yeah, and I'm sure they'd love to see you, though they're pissing me
off."

"Why, something happen?"

"You—" Uncle Charlie stopped talking to cough into his fist like gravel rattling in a tin can. Then he wheezed, "You might as well know what's going on since you spent some time at this drive-in."

"Sure," I said. "What's going on?"

"Ever hear of Yummy Foods?"

My eyebrows shot up. "The fast-food conglomerate?"

"Yeah, they've offered to buy Uncle Charlie's for a shit ton and spread the business nationwide. It would be the first fast-food barbecue chain in American history. In airports and gas stations. Everywhere."

To think of my uncle richer and more famous than he already was, his name associated with flights and road trips, his face a nationally celebrated brand—it made me almost gag. I hurried to reassure myself so I wouldn't explode and give myself away. *You'll stop him with this investigation.* After all, no conglomerate worth its barbecue salt would do business with my uncle if the drive-in had a murdered man's blood on its hands.

"That's great," I said. "But would it still be called a 'drive-in' if it's at an airport?"

"Of course it would," he grunted. "I'm not selling if they change the damn name."

"So when's the sale happening?" I asked, probing him as deep as he'd let me.

"That's the thing. I don't know what I'm doing yet. Annie and Teddy say yes. Chuck and Emma say no. Not that I give a shit what any of them think." Uncle Charlie glanced at the drive-in and clicked his tongue against the roof of his mouth. "I'm ready to sell and be done with it. I just don't know if I'm getting the best deal. I might be able to get more—" He again stopped to grab his guts and cough.

I leaned forward as if concerned. "Are you okay?"

He waved his hands at me. "Stay back."

"I'm sorry you're sick. What do you got?"

"I'm not sick." He held one nostril and blew out a snot jet. "I'm never sick."

This man was delusional, but I wasn't about to argue with him. Instead, I followed his tortoise pace through the meat-infused air, circling around the drive-in—my beloved childhood hangout—to a beer garden decorated with flags, balloons, and streamers. Some fifty people were in attendance, most of them holding beer or wine and a paper plate weighed down with meat, beans, and potato salad. The band, all decked out in patriotic costumes, was on a podium playing "You're a Grand Old Flag," and I was relieved not to recognize the players. Somewhere out there, too, was Annie. I could already feel her eyes on me.

Uncle Charlie coughed, this time on purpose to get everyone's attention. The chatting and music came to a halt, and the party turned to stare at me, which made my cheeks burn. Unless I was playing for an audience, I hated being the center of attention. I set my cooler down on the ground, and my uncle's trembling, bony hand clasped my shoulder.

"Everyone, this is my niece, Tori," he announced. "She mysteriously reappeared after years of silence. But in our world, the barbecue world, blood is blood. Please make her feel welcome."

"Hi Tori," the party chanted in a drunken chorus, like I'd just introduced myself at an NA meeting.

I gave my best happy-to-be-here smile before the band started up again, and everyone got back to their drinking and meat-chomping except for the picnic table nearest the drive-in. The two people sitting there looked up at me with puzzled expressions, and a flush of adrenaline tingled through my body when I recognized that the slender woman in the white shorts, leopard print tank, and chunky gold bracelets, peering at me over opaque sunglasses, was Annie.

Chapter Nine

"**T**ORI, WELCOME TO OUR LITTLE party," said a husky twang in my ear. I turned to find a busty, violet-eyed redhead in a low-cut American flag cocktail dress. The woman swallowed me up in her perfumed arms. "I'm Jean, Charlie's girl."

I reciprocated by giving Jean a quick squeeze back. "Nice to meet you," I said.

Uncle Charlie wrapped a shaking arm around Jean. "Jeanie here," he began in a proud, paternal tone, "was an Uncle Charlie's Angel a few years back."

"It's the only ad where he gets squirted with barbecue sauce," she said, giggling. "A naughty boy then, a naughty boy now."

"Thought you looked familiar," I lied. You couldn't go wrong flattering your suspects, which, considering she was my uncle's girlfriend, Jean now was.

"See, Charlie. I'm famous." Jean gave me a wink and pointed a glossy nail at the buffet tables covered in tin foil platters. "Now hon, you help yourself to whatever you'd like. There's more meat here than people. Dark, light, sweet, dry. We've even got barbecue-pulled jackfruit sandwiches with homemade slaw and veggie burgers. All gluten-free buns. Charlie and I are gonna grab us some food. Can I get you a drink?"

"No thanks." I picked up my cooler. "I brought my own."

I looked back at Annie, her sunglasses now disguising her glance. Even with all the oxies in me, my heart ached. I knew I'd taken too many pills with how foggy I was feeling, but there was nothing to do except ride out the storm. Slowly, I moved over to the picnic table with my cooler. When I set it on the grass, I let out a grumble, as if its heavy weight justified my sluggish speed. Then the moment I'd been imagining for years was finally here: it was time to face Annie.

"Hi," I said, trying to smile.

Annie grinned back at me and snatched off her sunglasses, revealing the same bright blue eyes from my memories, now framed with bold make-up. Maybe it was the drugs skewing my perception, but there seemed a wary glint to her smile, like she already suspected that, just by being here, I was up to something.

"OMG, Tori," her high-pitched voice rang out. "I am absolutely thrilled to see you." She shot up from her seat. Still a head taller than me, and still model thin. When she grabbed me for a firm hug, my chest tightened even more. "Seriously," she cooed in my ear, "I can't believe you're here."

I hurried to shield my constricted pupils with sunglasses and open an emergency Topo Chico with my thumb ring. "Pretty crazy, right?" I said, as I sat on the bench beside her.

"So what made you sneak up on us today?" Her tone was teasing, but serious.

"I got an invitation."

"That's interesting. I don't remember seeing you on the guest list."

"Yeah, I thought it was strange myself, but I figured why not go. Thought it would be nice to see you all."

"Oh, absolutely," Annie said. "It's been way too long."

"Fourteen years," I said, and drank more water, looking away from her analytical gaze to her lipstick-rimmed wine glass. When I'd finished drinking, I dropped the empty bottle on the grass and reached for another Topo Chico in the cooler.

"I don't remember you being so thirsty." Annie laughed as she picked up her wine glass. "Do you compete in drinking contests?"

"No, just super dehydrated in this heat. These summers kill me."

"Really? But you loved the summer when we were kids. Like when we put on those concerts in my backyard." She took a sip of wine. "And there was that one summer when we tricked those barbecue customers, remember that?" She squeezed my arm. I flinched, but didn't pull away. "You wrote letters and put them in the to-go bags, right?" She gave me a knowing smile.

Now my cheeks tingled with anger. I never did such a thing, but I knew what she was doing. She was alluding to the letters I'd sent her after Dad died. She never wrote me back. I'd always hoped Uncle Charlie had intercepted them and kept them from her, that she hadn't really blown me off because she didn't know about them in the first place, but here she was letting me know she'd got them, ignored them, and wanted me to know that she'd purposefully ignored me.

"I remember writing the customers those letters," I said, playing along. "We were Betty Beef and Sally Sow."

"Oh totes, one hundred percent." Annie made cow horns with her hands, our secret blood sister sign. "I was Betty Beef, wasn't I?"

"No, we alternated roles."

"No way, I was most definitely Betty," she snipped. "Of all things, I can't believe you forgot that, Tori."

A chill passed through me as I squeezed the Topo Chico bottle in my hands. *Don't you break it.* I turned away from Annie to face Chuck, gangly and pasty as floured pizza dough, his pale blue eyes observing me with fearful fascination. He was an awkward kid, and now he looked like an awkward adult.

When I smiled at him, he dropped his nervous gaze from me to his chocolate shake that had a pair of Oreo mouse ears peeping from its frothy top. The cocktail made sense when you considered his outfit. From his hat to his watch, to his shirt to his suspenders, all of it featured Mickey Mouse.

"Hi Chuck," I said. "Is today Mickey Mouse Day?"

Chuck kept his head down, while Annie tickled my ear with a whisper, "Every day's a Mickey Mouse Day for Chuck."

"Right," I said, though I had no idea what she meant. "I also love Mickey Mouse," I said to my shy cousin, tapping on my cartoon bandage.

He glanced up from his shake with a thin wet smile. "Hi Tori." His voice was nasal, like a poorly tuned French horn terrified to hear itself play.

Chuck opened his mouth to say more before his eyes widened at something behind me. In an instant, he clamped his mouth shut and dropped his head down to the ground again.

I turned around to see what had scared him. Uncle Charlie and Jean were coming back to our table with plates of food.

"So what kind of shenanigans are you up to these days?" Annie's question fired out at me like an accusation, which she hastily autocorrected with a smile. "I mean for work *and* life."

As Annie's curious tone seemed genuine, I felt more assured that she didn't know I was a PI at the agency where she'd filed her case two days ago.

"I'm in the KC Jazz Orchestra," I said. Like all great lies, it wasn't a total lie. Not only did I play at the Green Lady Lounge and other jazz venues around town, but I also filled in for sick clarinetists in the KC Jazz Orchestra.

"Really? You support yourself entirely on music?"

"Yes, I'm a professional. Do you still play?"

"Not much," she said, refilling her wine glass. "But you seriously can't imagine how busy I am with being the Chief Marketing Officer for Uncle Charlie's. I have no time for hobbies like music, but that's so great that you still play jazz."

"Jazz?" Jean exclaimed, as she and my uncle returned to the table with meat platters that prickled the back of my throat. I swallowed more water, hoping not to lose my stomach. I hadn't been this close to meat in years. "Charlie, we'll have to invite Tori to play at our little club parties." Jean picked up a chicken wing, puckered up her lips, and started licking off the sauce like she was afraid to take a bite because the meat was still too hot.

"Whatever you want, my sweet," Uncle Charlie said and reached for a slab of ribs blanketed in barbecue sauce. "Where are you living these days, Tori?"

"Actually—" I started, before clearing my throat at the meat steam going up my nostrils.

Jean dropped her sauceless chicken wing on her plate. "You okay, hon?" she asked.

"Yeah, must have swallowed a bug," I said.

"I hope it didn't have a stinger." Jean picked up a fresh chicken wing and began licking off the sauce on that one too.

I turned to Uncle Charlie to answer his question. "I'm staying with Aunt Kat for now. Had a horrible breakup. Long boring story."

"Is that right?" Uncle Charlie scrunched his wiry brows together. "And how is my dear older sister these days? Still painting lions and tigers and bears?"

"Yep," I said. "Still painting. Doing well."

"You mean, she's not angry you came here today?" Uncle Charlie chomped into a rib.

"Not at all."

I watched the Adam's apple bob in my uncle's throat as he struggled to swallow his bite.

When he'd finally gotten the meat down, his voice came out even gruffer. "Good, tell her I miss her pork butt. She always cooked it 'til the bone slid out." He stripped off another piece of flesh with his teeth and chucked the bone into the bone bucket.

I turned to Annie and lowered my voice. "Does he normally act like this?"

"Well," she began in a whisper, "he's always been an asshole, but he's an exceptional one today." She pointed above my right eye. "Why are you missing hair there?"

"Oh, that was from a car accident a few years back." I tugged on my brow ring. "Got this hardware to cover up the scar."

"How funny. I have something similar." She kicked her sandaled foot up on the bench, and the sterling loop on her middle toe sparkled in the sun. "It's the *om* sign, the mantra which cleanses our aura—"

"Annie's religion is yoga," Uncle Charlie cut in. "Her husband, who avoids our parties because he thinks they're satanic, converted her to his cult."

"Yoga isn't a cult, Dad." Annie swished her dyed blonde hair. "Rick's a certified yoga instructor and healer, and it's a legitimate exercise designed to open and align your chakras to heal your energies so you can live a more peaceful life. Maybe you should try it."

"Bullshit," Uncle Charlie coughed into his elbow. "You think that worked on you? Look at you, tough as sirloin steak. You might be able to bend backward and count to ten, but you're still an uptight, yuppie hypocrite. You won't even eat our barbecue, and you sell it."

"Not true." Annie stiffened. "I eat it for our promos and guests."

A plush woman with short black hair interrupted the father-daughter squabble, plunking down beside Chuck with plates of sandwiches, fries, and cookies. Chuck raised his head to peck a kiss on the woman's cheek. "Tori, this is Marigold," he said, sighing with affection as Marigold shoved a saucy sandwich into her mouth.

"Nice to meet you," I said. "What kind of cookies are those?"

"Vegan."

"Marigold made them herself," Chuck stated, his tone more confident now with his girlfriend at his side. "Chocolate chip and peanut butter with coconut."

"And oatmeal," Marigold added, spraying jackfruit sandwich on the table.

"Sounds delicious," I said.

Chuck continued singing Marigold's praises. "She's such a great cook. She makes these dairy-free Mickey Mouse cocktails we call mouse-tails." He presented his ice cream drink.

"I didn't make that one," Marigold snapped at Chuck.

"Yeah, I made it all by myself."

"Silly mouse." Marigold snatched the glass from Chuck and stood up with it. "You forgot the whipped cream. I'll go add some in the kitchen."

Chuck turned to me and smiled. "See, isn't she the best?"

I watched Marigold hurry across the beer garden and disappear through the kitchen door. She emerged a moment later, stirring Chuck's mouse-tail with the Mickey Mouse straw. When she sat back down and handed the drink back to Chuck, I noticed that the vanilla ice cream had taken on a bright yellow glow.

"Before I met her," Chuck went on, "I wouldn't have thought I could stop hunting or that I'd even like vegan food, but she proved me wrong with her insights and fabulous cooking. She even has some recipes published with HETA."

"HETA?" I asked.

"Humans for the Ethical Treatment of Animals," Marigold stated as she presented a golden pig bracelet on her wrist, which must have been the organization's logo. "I've offered to make recipes for the Uncle Charlie's menu, but no one listens to me." Marigold turned to my uncle, oblivious to his sour mood. "I mean, why can't you put a plant-based burger on the menu?" she said, while my uncle chewed fast and twisted a stained paper towel. "You already slaughter hundreds of animals every day, contribute to greenhouse gas emissions and global warming, and poison people with sugar, carbs, high sodium, and saturated fats that promote heart attacks and diabetes. There are meat shortages everywhere, especially after the pandemic, and people are dying. The world is suffering now more than ever, and you want more blood?"

With a groan, Uncle Charlie swallowed his meat. "Barbecue is America, sweetie—" he began, before his coughing fit returned to punctuate his speech. "People want— comfort and meat comforts them. We use only the best ingredients. All locally sourced. Real butter— on our buns. We rub our meats with spices and slow— cook them over a variety of woods with a thick tomato-based barbecue sauce we make onsite. But you'd prefer we serve genetically modified soy— organisms so full of estrogen they give men tits? Listen, I'm not gonna— stop people from eating shit, but if you're gonna eat shit— you might as well eat gourmet shit."

I nodded, though I couldn't relate. Of course, my uncle had a point for those who didn't eat or drink to excess, but that wasn't my case. If I was drinking a chocolate shake, I didn't care whether it was gourmet or from a vending machine. I'd take whatever I could get and down it in seconds.

Marigold dropped her half-eaten sandwich, got up, and hustled toward the drive-in. As Chuck jumped up after her, she waved her piggy bracelet to signal she wanted alone time. Chuck sunk back in his place, head down, sulking while sipping his dairy-free mouse-tail.

Uncle Charlie spun a paper plate at me. "Don't be shy," he said. "Load up."

My stomach backflipped at the empty plate. I hadn't had anything all day except Aunt Kat's fruit smoothie, and though I had no appetite, I knew I should eat something to blend in with the party. If only I was certain I could hold the meat down.

Ever since my uncle had made me an orphan, though, I'd been a strict vegetarian. This wasn't because of any morals or ethics. It was because meat made me viscerally upset. The sight of it alone reminded me of my dad's death and Uncle Charlie's theft of the drive-in. I used to throw up walking past picnickers grilling out.

Right now, though, as I stared at Uncle Charlie's sauced-up brisket, my stomach tightening, I felt like I needed to force myself to fit in. I already stood out enough, showing up with a weird party invitation, and I didn't want to be exposed for my true intentions.

Jean stopped licking her chicken wing to grab my plate. "Brisket, hon?"

"Thanks," I answered automatically.

I watched Jean prance over to a buffet table, grab a pair of tongs, and pluck the blessed meat strips fated for my intestines. This could be a terrible idea, especially if my stomach lacked the proper enzymes to process flesh. For all I knew, I could get sick all over the table after one bite.

"Hey, happy party people," called out a drunk voice that made everyone's heads spin. Swaying outside the beer garden was the greasy-haired addict I'd paid last night.

Annie whipped out her phone. "Beat it, or I'm calling the cops."

"No cops," Uncle Charlie said, picking up his knife. "No need for a scandal—"

The man raised his arms in surrender. "No need to start a fight," he mumbled. "I heard this is where the smack's at. Can I get me some of that China White Snow to celebrate my freedom?"

"Why is he bringing up China?" Chuck blinked.

Uncle Charlie coughed, "He's talking about heroin."

"Heroin?" Annie frowned.

Actually, China White Snow was fentanyl, the synthetic opioid much deadlier than the oxies I was on, but I figured it was best to stay quiet on my knowledge of drug slang.

Uncle Charlie raised himself, his knuckles white clutching a steak knife. "Beat it, you bum. We don't sell dope here—" He coughed so hard he stumbled back in his chair.

"Not what I was told," the man laughed, shaking a finger at our table. "Uncle Charlie's is where you go if you're looking to score, and since your Leawood man got taken out, this is where we're all coming now. Flocks and flocks of us."

"Bullshit." Annie shot up from the bench. "Now get the hell out of here before we call the cops."

"Whatever, bitch." The man spat and staggered off, his curses dragging behind his untied shoes.

The party broke into a loud chatter while I took a victorious swig of Topo Chico. That was the best three hundred bucks I'd spent. Now I could bring up Luis.

Chapter Ten

ANNIE WAS ON HER SECOND bottle of wine and denouncing drug addicts as irresponsible wasters of oxygen that deserved to suffer—but not in public where she had to bear witness—when Jean sashayed back to the table to save us all, but especially me. Before my eyes was a steaming plate of carcass.

"Bon appétit," Jean said.

Bone appetite.

The smell of the saucy heap wafted into my nose, and I gagged.

"You don't like the smell?" Uncle Charlie said.

"No, that's not it," I hurried to say. "I'm just feeling emotional being here is all." Then I cut off a piece and forked it into my mouth, tasting the sweet, smoky flavor of my childhood. Dad's recipe. I swallowed and warmth flooded my veins. The bovine was divine. I hurried to cut another bite before I could think about it.

"Glad you like it," Uncle Charlie said.

"I'm hooked." The words oddly came out sincere.

"Tell it to the cook," he said.

"Tell me what?" said a woman who had to be my youngest cousin, Emma. She set a platter of burnt ends on the table, sat down beside me, and gave me a quick side hug. Unlike Annie, Emma had grown into a makeup-free tomboy. Her unadorned barbecue-stained jeans and black T-shirt were certainly a different look from when I last saw her. As a kid, she was always trying to be a princess in pink dresses and tiaras.

I nodded at my plate. "You know, I was just at Rocky's yesterday, but this is by far the best barbecue I've had in years."

"Of course it's better than Rocky's," Emma snapped like I'd insulted her. Her voice was sultry like a smoker's, which made sense since she smoked dead animals for a living. "But anyway," she continued in a calmer tone, "it's great to see you again, Tori. I don't think you've grown an inch."

"Yeah, I pretty much stopped growing after middle school." *Probably because my dad killed himself because of your dad, consequently stunting my growth.*

"Teeny Tori," Emma giggled.

"Emma's one to talk about height when she steals my heels for our events," Annie said, swirling her wine without spilling a drop. "Then again, she is the runt."

Emma smirked back at her sister. "And Annie's the—"

"Go to hell."

Emma laughed again, plucked up a fork, and stabbed an especially crispy, blackened burnt end, oozing with grease. I stared at the dripping meat chunk with fear and longing. Of all my dad's dishes, his burnt ends were my favorite.

"Is the end the best part?" I said, playing dumb as if I'd forgotten I was raised in the kitchen behind me.

"Of course." Emma held up a burnt end as if to torture me. "KC loves burnt ends because that's our thing. But the truth is the end's the worst part. It's just tradition that whoever cooks the brisket, eats the end." With her knife, she slid the burnt end off her fork and onto my brisket mountain.

Everyone was watching, so I stuffed the morsel into my mouth and chewed. I couldn't believe it. Just like in the old days, it was a butter that tasted like meat. I hurried to swallow it down before I could spit it out.

"Like it?" Emma asked.

"Love it." I grabbed my Topo Chico to cleanse my palate. "Why is it tradition that the cook eats the end?"

Uncle Charlie swiped a burnt end off Emma's plate and answered for her. "Because in the end, you're only as strong as your weakest piece of meat." He jammed the juicy square between his lips. "Smokier than I'd like—" He coughed, and the burnt end shot out of his mouth and over the table like a meat bullet.

While Chuck drank his mouse-tail with more desperation, Jean whacked my uncle's back. "Honey, I think you should lie d—"

"No," Uncle Charlie coughed again. "I told you I'm not sick."

Emma's brow crinkled. "You don't like it, Dad?"

"You burnt the hell out of it. Let's hope you didn't ruin the rest of the brisket." As Uncle Charlie launched into another epic coughing fit, he pushed himself up from the table and stumbled toward the drive-in. Moments later, Jean, apparently his nurse as well as his girlfriend, ran after him. Chuck had now finished his ice cream drink and looked around.

"I thought he liked the ends charred," Emma murmured, her bottom lip trembling. "They're succulent, not dry."

"Oh, boo hoo," Annie said in a childish voice. "No need to pout, Em. He's been a coughing maniac all day and is too proud to acknowledge he needs a doctor."

"Yes, he's worse than usual," Chuck whispered. "Marigold even ran away after he attacked her. Poor thing."

Emma's cheeks brightened in anger. "Is that why she burst into my kitchen and threw a slab of ribs on the floor? I don't care if she's a vegan, she's a damn hypocrite. You don't disrespect the animal's life by wasting its good meat."

As I watched my cousins argue, a pair of hands seized my shoulders from behind. On instinct, I grabbed the fingers, crushing them as hard as I could. A man wailed in my ear. I turned to find a fit, stocky man in a white polo and khakis, his dark hair thick with mousse, neck thick with muscle, waving his hand around like it had been caught in a meat grinder. This was

Cousin Teddy, the all-American frat boy who apparently still loved pulling pranks.

"Man," he said, wincing. "You've got some good reflexes."

My cousins stared at me like I was someone else, a look I'd seen a thousand times. No one expected so much strength from you when you were the size of a ten-year-old. Of course, I didn't tell them I'd acquired my reflexes from defense training courses.

"Sorry," I said. "You surprised me."

"Guess that's the risk of sneaking up on people who are secret ninjas. Now give your cousin a hug, but don't squeeze me to death." I stood up, we embraced, and Teddy laughed in my ear, "We thought you were dead."

I laughed back, "So did I."

Behind Teddy was a stringy brunette whose face seemed cast in a permanent scowl. "This is Susanne." He pointed at her with his beer bottle. "The Queen of the Hallmark Empire and Camelot Castle."

She had to be Susanne Hall, of Hallmark Cards. She offered me her hand, and I clasped it lightly, afraid I'd crumble it. "Would you excuse me?" she said, in a reedy voice. "I need to check on the children." As Susanne drifted away, I had to admit I wasn't surprised Teddy had settled for her. He'd always valued money and social standing above everything else.

Teddy and I sat down at the table. Finally, with all my cousins again. The last time this happened we were at Loose Park, celebrating Dad's success. How much we'd changed since then, with my life getting awful and theirs getting rich. My presence had to make them uneasy, though, when they knew they were only wealthy because I wasn't. Did it bother them what their dad had done? But as I took another swig of Topo Chico, searching their faces for remorse, all I saw was a bunch of entitled brats and a sniveling Chuck.

Annie addressed the table, a playful gleam in her eye. "So who invited Tori to our party, anyway?"

My cousins all looked at me suspiciously, and I stopped drinking. "Oh—" I began before pretending to choke on my water. I patted my chest, choking louder. I coughed harder, straining my face, and letting myself fall backward over the bench. As I squeezed my eyes tight, I writhed on the ground.

"Jesus," I heard Teddy shout over me, "does someone know the Heimlich maneuver?"

I didn't want anyone touching me, so I turned my face into the grass, jammed my fingers down my throat, and threw up the burnt end I'd just eaten. Gasping, I then opened my eyes to my cousins standing over me with startled expressions.

"Gross," Emma said.

Teddy extended a hand to pull me up. "Damn," he said, "are you all right?"

"Yeah, sorry." I trembled in his arms since I'd actually exhausted myself from all the fake coughing and real vomiting. "I think I had a reaction to the burnt end."

"You didn't like it?" Emma asked, offended.

Annie let out a tipsy giggle and cocked her head at me. "Convenient timing."

"What timing?" Emma blinked.

Though drunk, Annie's eyes were clear and shrewd. She stared at me like she was waiting for me to admit I'd faked the episode. "Well," I began, "Uncle Charlie choked on a burnt end, too, right?"

"What's wrong with them?" Emma demanded.

"Too dry," Chuck said quietly. "That's what Father said."

Emma grunted and we returned to our seats where I got to chugging water, relieved I'd avoided the topic of my mysterious invitation. Before Annie could repeat herself, I turned to Teddy. "So you're a dad now?"

"Three boys," he said with a grin. "Lots of testosterone, but they've got a real castle to play in."

"Obnoxious little shits too," Uncle Charlie called out as he and Jean reappeared, back from the drive-in. "Hopefully, they'll grow out of it, unlike their father."

Teddy's mouth fell open. "How dare you insult my children."

"What are you going to do about it?" Uncle Charlie grumbled. "Between your cowardice and your wife's anemia, your kids are fucked."

"That's enough, Dad," Annie said. "You'll blow your blood pressure with one of your angry flare-ups."

"It's not an angry flare-up, it's a fast reaction to bullshit."

"Yeah, you should get some rest, Dad," Chuck chimed in with a quiet, shaky voice, his gaze on the ground.

"Says the son who's always been a sick parasite. Maybe you should shut the hell up before I throw you out of here."

Chuck gave a sharp sniff, then reached for his empty cup and pretended to sip. Clearly, he was more terrified of my uncle than anyone here. With his eyes now glazed over, he looked toward the kitchen door like he wanted to run away, but then he turned back to look down into the bottom of his glass, his knuckles whitening as his grip tightened.

"You know what I think is going on?" Uncle Charlie slammed the table with his fists, and everyone shifted in their seats. "I think one of you is up to something."

"Here comes more Dad paranoia," Annie sighed.

"No, did you know Tori was invited here anonymously?"

Now my face burned while everyone looked at me with even more suspicion. When Annie nudged a knuckle into my arm, I reached for my sparkling water again.

"Or did you invite yourself?" Uncle Charlie shouted at me. "It's no secret we have this party every year." He pounded his fists on the table again.

"No," I said.

"Dad, you're hysterical," Emma said. "Why would Tori invite herself?"

"She wants revenge," he wheezed.

I took a long pull of water while Teddy said, "Dad, Uncle Billy left you the drive-in fair and square. You're speaking nonsense."

"You're right. It's more likely one of my own children is conspiring against me and invited her."

"Especially with this horrible cough you've had all week," Jean said, her eyes watery. "I don't know where on earth it came from."

"Exactly," my uncle said. "Which is why I have something to announce."

Chuck ran a hand through his thinning, gray hair, and I thought he was about to say something but he stopped himself.

"I signed the Yummy Foods contract," my uncle continued.

"You did?" Annie exclaimed.

"Yes, I signed the sucker and got it notarized."

"You did?" Emma's brows slanted in horror.

Uncle Charlie coughed. "I wanted it to be legitimate in case—" He stopped talking to enter another terrible coughing fit. As he gripped the table, his face turning turnip white, he was at least making my choking incident seem forgettable. When he finally caught his breath, he slumped back in his chair and panted, too exhausted to speak or move.

No one said anything until Emma flicked a brown bug off the table. "Stink bug," she said.

Chuck let out a scream that sounded more like a squeak, it was so high. "Oh God!" He jumped up from the table and ran for the drive-in.

"Pathetic," Teddy snickered. "Look at him run from a bug."

"Is he all right?" I said.

"Is he ever all right?" Teddy scoffed. "He's squeamish about insects. I used to put spiders in his bed when we were kids to scare him. Funny how he never cried about that, just ran away screaming. I think it ruined him for life."

"That boy's squeamish about everything," Uncle Charlie managed to rasp through more intermittent coughing. "Always has been—the weakest link in this family, and now that he's a bloody vegan because of his girlfriend—he's never been more stupidly sensitive—a huge disappointment for a firstborn son."

"But you have to admit," Annie began, ignoring her dad's struggles to speak, "Chuck and Marigold do have a point pushing for vegan items on the menu. It would attract more customers, and you know the five-person rule. If you have four Mikey Meatlovers in a car with one Vicky Vegan, they won't come to Uncle Charlie's."

Emma swung around to face her sister, her eyes squinting. "But it's not real barbecue," she hissed. "Barbecue is meat."

"Who cares if it caters to more customers?" Annie said. "Our competitors are adding vegan items, why shouldn't we?"

"And our competitors serve factory-farmed shit." Uncle Charlie stabbed the table with his knife, so it was sticking straight up. "We're the best barbecue in Kansas City—which makes us the best in the world."

Emma stretched across the table toward her father. "Then why sell out to a conglomerate and destroy everything you've built?"

"And why do you little—shits think you deserve what I've worked for? You know what I think would happen? You'd ruin it. All second-generation businesses—fail, but remember, I don't need to justify myself to you when it's—my business. I'm calling the shots."

Uncle Charlie's claim to my dad's drive-in made me want to empty the bone bucket over his head, but I kept still to observe the family dynamic. While Jean licked another chicken wing and Annie guzzled down the rest of her wine, Emma pursed her lips in obvious irritation, skewering a burnt end with a knife and shoving it into her mouth. As my uncle gasped like he was breathing through a brick, I opened my mouth to ask my hot button question.

"What about that accidental death with that cook in Leawood?" I said innocently enough. Everyone's faces went blank with the horror of verbalizing a taboo. "Didn't that hurt business? I mean, isn't that what that junkie meant when he said he was looking for a dealer here?"

Uncle Charlie grabbed the knife sticking out of the table and used what little strength he had to push himself up, his face straining so much his forehead vein popped out. The blade shook in his hand as he staggered toward me, but I didn't budge.

Not that I wanted to advertise my defense skills again, but I could easily disarm a knife-wielder as frail as Uncle Charlie.

"No," his voice crackled, flailing his knife about like he was a drunk conductor. "That cook deserved to die—stealing from our register—a dope-head—just like your father." His words sputtered between sharp gasps. "Billy—Billy—Bill—"

"Dad, sit down," Teddy demanded, shooting up from the bench. "You'll give yourself a heart attack."

"You son of a—" The knife slipped out of my uncle's hand and he fell to the ground. The music and chatter stopped, and everyone at the party circled my uncle to watch him wallop for air like an angry fish on a cutting board.

At the commotion, Chuck and Marigold rushed out of the drive-in. Maybe Chuck didn't know how else to react given the insanity of the moment, but when he saw my uncle on the ground, he laughed in a strange cartoonish voice. "Did Father fall?" he said in the same high-pitched voice.

"Charlie?" Jean shrieked as she knelt beside him to shake his wrists.

"Is this a joke?" Teddy bit his lip. "I mean, he once faked a seizure on Christmas—"

"Oh dear Jesus, his lips are turning blue," Jean howled. "He can't breathe. He can't breathe. Someone *do* something."

Annie took out her phone. "Yeah, I need an ambulance at Uncle Charlie's in the West Bottoms ASAP," she said as if ordering takeout. "My father seems to be having a heart attack."

"What about CPR?" Emma called out. "Doesn't anyone here know CPR?"

I looked around, expecting one of these rich people to be a doctor, but no one was making a move. I pushed through the crowd to where my uncle was lying in the grass. I'd seen enough people down to know he wasn't getting back up, but I still dropped to my knees, locking his dry mouth with my own and breathing what little breath I had into him before pumping his chest.

Again, I breathed and pumped, breathed and pumped. I did it harder, with more urgency, trying to save a man who deserved to die, but at some point in the useless cycle of breathing and pumping, he'd already stopped moving beneath me. I didn't need to feel for a pulse. I slid back and buried my head in my hands to hide from the hundreds of eyes on me.

"Tori?" Jean took me by the shoulders. I lifted my head to meet her violet gaze, bright with panic.

"He's dead," I said. "Uncle Charlie's dead."

Chapter Eleven

IREWORKS ERUPTED OVER THE PLAZA, bursting tendrils of sparkling dust over the city. I wasn't celebrating, though, even if my wicked uncle of the West Bottoms was dead. Uncle Charlie had got off easy. My plan was for him to suffer deeply for years. I'd wanted him gutted by the press for Luis's murder, his reputation so tarnished that he'd have been forced to shut down the drive-ins, sell his mansion, move to Nowheresville, Missouri, and die poor and alone.

I gassed for the yellow light and a brick building flew out at me. I swerved. Something clipped the mirror. I stopped in the middle of the street. *You shouldn't be driving.* I'd lost count of how many pills I'd taken, but it had clearly been too many. Though I was only a few blocks from Aunt Kat's, I pulled over to the curb to stumble out of the car and walk my high ass home. In the morning, I'd have to get the car before Aunt Kat knew it was missing.

When I was back at the canary house with the purple door, the dread of telling my aunt the bad news made my stomach swell with so much anxiety that I got sick on the lawn. Even if she did hate Uncle Charlie, she wasn't going to be happy hearing he was dead. And as if enough wasn't going on, my phone dinged with a new message from Kevin.

"Tori, call me ASAP," he wrote. "It's about the Mendoza case."

Of course it was, but Kevin would have to wait until I'd told my aunt her other brother was dead. I trudged up the porch stairs, opened the purple door, and found Aunt Kat on the sofa, her face glowing with an eager, stoned smile I was about to destroy.

"How'd it go?" she said, perking up. "How'd Charlie look? What did he say about the photo?"

"I didn't—" I began, then swallowed my dry mouth.

Aunt Kat put her pipe on the coffee table. "You okay?" she said. "You're pale and sweating at every pore."

"Yeah, I know I look bad, but that's because of what I have to tell you."

"What?"

"Uncle Charlie's dead."

Aunt Kat's bloodshot eyes beamed, as if I'd said it was snowing in July. "What do you mean he's dead? I haven't seen an obituary."

"That's because he died at the party." This time my news registered, because she sunk back into the couch and dropped her chin into her chest. It couldn't be good she was getting this info high. She sat in a stupor while the fireworks kept blasting outside.

After some time had passed, I said, "Aunt Kat?"

She raised her fearful eyes at me. "Charlie's dead?"

"Yeah, I'm sorry."

"My little brother," she gasped, and the tears started flowing. "I know we hadn't spoken in years and that he was a horrible person, but he was still my baby brother."

Though I wasn't sad my uncle was dead, I didn't like seeing my aunt sob. I did the best I could, rubbing her arms and hugging her before she finally exhausted her tears and let me help her into bed. After that, I lumbered upstairs until I reached my room, where Rebus was still camping out under the bed.

"It was a wild day," I told him like he was my spouse.

I thought again about Uncle Charlie dying under me, feeling his last breath leave his body. Even though I didn't kill him, I had to admit it was strange timing for him to collapse right after I'd showed up. Would he still have died if I hadn't? Maybe seeing me was enough to send him over the edge.

I pulled out the photo Aunt Kat had wanted me to give him, and my gut ached seeing my uncle between my dad and aunt. He was standing right where he died. I didn't need this memento hanging around, making me want to pop pills. I opened my window and let the wind take it where it wanted. Not bothering to change out of my dirty clothes, I got under the covers. I needed sleep. But soon as I shut my eyes, my phone started ringing and I groaned. Kevin was calling, probably impatient I hadn't called him back.

"Hey Kev," I breathed into the phone. "What's going on?"

"Listen, Isabella Mendoza dropped the investigation," he said.

"Oh?" I said, though I wasn't surprised. After Uncle Charlie had died, I swallowed too many pills and wrote another email as Mrs. Mendoza again so that I could drop the case. I didn't see a point working it anymore when my uncle was dead.

Kevin divulged more info that I'd mostly forgotten, because of the oxies blurring my memory. "Mrs. Mendoza said she didn't want to do it anymore. Didn't say why, and her email came from a different address than the first. Both accounts were deleted when I tried writing her back, so I don't know what's going on."

"Sounds like something's going on, but whatever. Anyway, I need to go to sleep now and forget about this day for the rest of my life."

"You okay there, Tori?" Kevin asked. "You sound out of it."

"I'm fine. Just been an exhausting day."

"Well, get your sleep. I'll send you the next fraud claim on deck tomorrow morning."

"Can't wait."

We got off the phone, and I closed my eyes again. This time, I entered that transitional zone between consciousness and dreams, where you weren't quite yet asleep but could hear voices streaming in and out like a radio turner while seeing images flash. I saw rib comets, then a brisket waterfall, then chicken tenders twirling like fallen leaves from a glitter tree. A burnt end danced in a pan. A bacon-stuffed needle sparkled. Grease oozed from the tip. A barbecue cooker smoked. A bathtub of barbecue sauce bubbled. Dad's body floated to the surface. His honey-glazed eyes turned on me. His bloated white feet slipped over the rim.

I opened my eyes. My phone was ringing again. But this time it wasn't Kevin. An unknown number.

Still breathing hard from the vision of my dead father, I answered, "Hello?"

"Hi Tori."

My hands jolted at the high-pitched voice, sending my phone to the floor. I rolled out of bed to retrieve it and switched on the speaker function. "Annie?"

"Yep, it's me," her voice blasted from the phone. "I wanted to see how you were doing. You were so upset when you left, I was worried about you."

"How did you get my number?"

There was a pause. Maybe that came out too accusatory.

"What do you mean?" she said. "You gave it to me."

I blinked as I tried to remember tonight, but from Uncle Charlie's death until my near car crash, my memory was mostly slush. Yet another sign I'd taken too many pills. "Tori?"

"Yeah, sorry, I'm pretty foggy right now," I said. "There's been a lot to process."

"I can't imagine. This must be so awful for you, showing up to our family reunion and then Dad dies."

"It's nothing compared to losing a dad. I'm sorry for your loss."

"Yeah, I know. I can't even. I'm sure I'll feel it later, but right now there's too much work to waste time grieving. We're having a will reading tomorrow at Dad's, and we'll discuss funeral arrangements. I'll keep you in the loop if you're interested in attending the service."

"Of course, anything I can do."

"Great, and please let Aunt Kat know. It would be so nice to see her despite these tragic circumstances and—" She stopped herself.

"Yeah?" I said.

"I know this might sound strange given my dad dying, but I also wanted to say that I'm thrilled we got reacquainted today. I hope we can get together again real soon."

I swallowed at this suggestion, my eyes watering with a mixture of nostalgia and anger. She wasn't being sincere. She was deliberately working me, provoking me to lose my shit like Uncle Charlie had done when I'd first showed up at the party. "Sure," I said, forcing myself to pretend. "I'd like that."

"OMG," she exclaimed. "I have a fantastic idea. Do you remember what Betty Beef and Sally Sow did in the kiddy pool?"

I laughed out of discomfort. She was bringing up the same memory I'd had on Rocky's roof. "I remember," I said. "Instead of water, we filled the kiddy pool with gallons of barbecue sauce and rolled around from head to toe, snorting like dirty piglets."

"Oh God, yes," Annie laughed. "We had so much fun, I mean, until Uncle Billy got super mad at us for wasting the sauce. Honestly, I was beyond terrified of setting off his temper again after that. Guess that's why he turned to drugs, right? To cope with his anger issues?"

My face lit hot at this obvious dig at my dad. There was no way Annie had forgotten about that barbecue sauce falling on his hands and burning him, not when we were the ones who'd found his oxy prescription and tried them out for kicks.

With each syllable firing off like a gunshot, I said, "I think he wasn't too pleased we wasted so much sauce."

"Right," Annie said in quick defense. "Anyway, I was thinking it might be fun to dive back into the pool for a fundraiser photo-op once Yummy Foods takes over. Only thing is we'd have to do it before I move to New York."

"New York?"

"That's the plan. They're headquartered in Manhattan, so I'll finally have the glamorous big city life I deserve."

Soon as we were off the phone, I screamed so loud Rebus shot out from under the bed and into the closet. I hugged myself like my body was a straitjacket I needed to escape. I hated Annie. Not only for insulting my dead father, but for rubbing her fake success in my face. But here she was about to get her way. After all, Uncle Charlie had announced that he'd signed and notarized the Yummy Foods contract. It was a done deal. She was going to New York.

I yanked my brow ring, repeating her words to myself. *The glamorous big city life I deserve.* I grabbed a vinyl, breaking it against my desk into shards of unlistenable music. Then I reached for my bag. My pill bottle was there, my escape, but I wasn't watching my feet, and before I noticed my clarinet case, I tumbled and landed on the ground.

Fortunately, Aunt Kat slept hard, or she'd have thought I was dying up here, which might have happened if I hadn't fallen. Too many pills could be fatal, and Annie had almost got me to cross that line again. Though I'd regret it in the morning, I grabbed the oxies, charged for the bathroom, uncapped the bottle, and raised it over the toilet like I was toasting to my victory over her. *But you're not victorious.* She was still getting her way and moving to New York. At least, that was what would happen if the drive-in wasn't connected to Luis's murder.

I stepped back from the toilet to reconsider my situation. It didn't matter that Isabella Mendoza had allegedly dropped the case—I could still investigate Luis's death.

Because if I was right about Luis getting murdered at the hands of my family, Yummy Foods wouldn't want anything to do with Uncle Charlie's, and Annie would be forced to stay here and suffer the shame of being connected to a murderous scandal.

That was the life she deserved.

I twisted the cap back on the pill bottle. *You'll quit after the case.* Stopping now wasn't an option, not when the withdrawals would incapacitate me. But I'd have to really watch the dose and not get super wasted like I'd done tonight.

I desperately needed sleep, but I needed to keep working. I sat down at my laptop and ran a background search on the widow, Isabella Mendoza. A clean record. She didn't even have a speeding ticket and was a nurse at Saint Luke's Hospital. First thing in the morning, I'd call and find out her hours.

Chapter Twelve

I WOKE UP FEELING LIKE MY head had been in a slow cooker all night. I couldn't wait for relief. I tapped an oxy into my clammy palm, threw it into my mouth to suck on it so I could rub the pink coating off on my arm. Using an empty Topo Chico bottle, I crushed it on my desk, then rolled up a dollar bill and snorted the heavenly powder straight into my bloodstream.

Seconds later, my headache was magically gone. Back in warm waters. Then I swallowed another pill and buried the orange bottle at the bottom of my backpack.

The narcotics were disguised in my anti-narcotic bottle, but I was still worried I'd be found out. Not so much by Aunt Kat, since grief had overtaken her skills of perception. I was mostly concerned with Darnell. Beyond being a hard-nosed cop, he was an addict himself and aware of the signs. Of course, I could defend some odd behavior with the stress of the case, but that would only get me so far. I had to be extra careful I didn't give myself away, because if either of them realized I'd thrown my two-year sober coins into the trash a few days ago, they'd waste no time dragging me to an inpatient clinic to sober me up and stop me from working. That was one of the unfortunate problems with relapsing. The people closest to you became your secret enemies.

Seeing as I had to keep up sober appearances, I headed over to Unity Temple for my weekly Tuesday NA meeting, short for Narcotics Anonymous.

Darnell was perched on the steps, wiping his glistening forehead with a sweat rag while a cigarette dangled from his mouth. When he saw me coming up the stairs, he exhaled smoke through both nostrils.

"Almost late, Tor." He flashed his brows at me with judgment.

"Almost on time's more like it," I said.

"How's that purple zone treating you?"

"Can't say I've noticed since I took the Mendoza case."

"Oh, is that why you look like shit?" He flicked his ash with an angry wrist snap. "Thought you turned that case down."

I rehashed my interview with Walt, the anonymous invitation, Uncle Charlie's party, Uncle Charlie's death, that the Mendoza case was dropped following my uncle's demise, and that I'd gone rogue as I wasn't stopping the investigation.

Darnell rubbed the bridge of his nose. "What do you think you're doing? Looking to lose your job or your mind?"

"Maybe both, but I need your help."

"Hell no," he said. "This is the kind of shit that ruins everything you've worked for."

"And what's that exactly? A boring life taking pictures of petty liars?"

Darnell took a slow, steady drag of his cigarette. "Better bored than dead," he said, exhaling.

"What's the difference?"

"Please, you know your family's bad news. You've barely been sober two years, and your brain's never fully recovering from the damage you've done. You keep on this case, bad things are coming. Honestly, I can't believe you haven't relapsed already."

Honestly, I couldn't believe his words. While he had little faith in me, he had more than I'd thought. I pretended to act offended, since that was how I'd behave if I wasn't secretly using again.

"I'm still here, aren't I?" I gave a sharp nod at the temple doors. "Anyway, you're a cop. You know Luis didn't die by accident. Don't you think a murdered man deserves justice?"

"It doesn't matter what I think. That case is closed, and you've got no good reason risking your life trying to solve it. Learn to quit shit that's bad for you." Since he coughed as he said this, I took it as an opportunity to point at his cigarette, which he inhaled harder to spite me. He held in the smoke and let it out slow, so it circled up around his head.

"I'm keeping this case with or without your help," I told him. "But with your help answering a few standard questions, I might be able to figure it out faster."

Darnell's gaze narrowed on me. "Depends on the questions," he said. "I'm not telling you anything classified."

"Sure. Anything you can share is appreciated."

He'd never let me record him, so I got out my notebook and pen. As I flipped through the pages, I saw the draft of the email I'd sent to Kevin last night where I was pretending to be Isabella Mendoza dropping the case. I flipped to a new, clean page.

"You gonna ask me something?" Darnell said.

"Yeah." I uncapped my pen. "Do you remember the time of Luis's death?"

"Around midnight."

I made a note. "Cause of death?"

"Blunt force trauma to the head. That's why he fell into the cooker. They say he hit his head on the lid."

"What about the heroin?"

"What about it?" Darnell shrugged. "They found it in his body and a used needle on the ground. The coroner said that's why he hit his head."

"But his arms were burned up, so the coroner couldn't verify his track marks, right?"

"Yeah, I guess so."

"What about Isabella Mendoza, the widow? Anyone talk to her?"

"See, that's as confidential as the surveillance footage." Squashing his half-smoked cigarette into an ashtray of burnt ends, Darnell opened the temple door. "Let's go. We're almost late."

Like every other building in summer, Unity Temple was pumped full of so much air-conditioning that you got goosebumps just stepping through the front door—unless you were on opioids like me.

To hide my sweats and play my normal freezing-to-death self, I threw on my black hoodie. The fluorescent lights offered a defense for my constricted pupils. I had my bases covered, so long as I didn't say something stupid.

I followed Darnell into the usual white room with the pastel chairs that reminded me of a dentist's office and grabbed a baby blue chair in the circle. If I weren't so high on oxies, I might have felt guilty I was about to deceive the people there to support my recovery.

"Any new members today?" said Zak, our unappointed leader who had been a hippie priest before converting to recovering addict. A guy in a black shirt raised his hand and introduced himself as Bill.

NA wasn't a religious group, or wasn't supposed to be, but since the majority of addicts who showed up were religious, or had converted to some religion in sobriety to make peace with themselves, we started our meetings with a prayer. This made me an outsider, since I never believed I'd been saved by Jesus, and it didn't matter to me if there was a God or not, but since everyone else got excited squeezing their eyes and murmuring big words, I played along and held hands while Zak read a Bible passage aloud.

After that, whoever wanted to get something off their chest could confess, the idea being that vocalizing your trauma would help you face it so you could move on. This time around, though, I planned on keeping my mouth shut.

Darnell was anxious to purge and stood up first. As usual, his wife was stressing him out with house repairs, his kids were stressing him out with violent video games, and his job was stressing him out because KC's homicide rate skyrocketed in the heat. Darnell had consequently doubled his smoking and been triggered to drink. When he was done venting, we all clapped, and he sat back down.

Zak got up next to confess how he'd failed God, because a few days ago he'd left the candles going at his church and caused a fire. He was praying and biting his nails more than ever, but his eyes were too guilty to fool me. If I had to guess, Zak was in agony thinking God burned down his church as punishment for him using again.

Bill the new guy then stood up. New people were always raw and ready to reset. He told us he'd lost his wife, his kids, and his house to fentanyl, but it took Bill overdosing himself to near death to check himself into a clinic and stop for good. This was his first time quitting, and we applauded him for making it to twenty-seven days.

More members shared stories, and the meeting would have been over, with me in the clear, if Darnell hadn't given me a skeptical look, because I hadn't spoken like I usually did. *He's onto you.* I sighed and got to my feet, rubbing my arms as if I was cold, and opened my mouth to lie better than Zak.

"You'll have to forgive me if I sound incoherent today, but some crazy stuff happened last night," I began. "Most of you know my dad fatally overdosed a while ago, but what I didn't know until recently was that my uncle had given my dad the heroin that killed him so he could steal my dad's drive-in empire. You all know Uncle Charlie—"

"Wait, Uncle Charlie's your uncle?" Bill blurted out, impressed.

Zak interjected to remind him of our protocol. "So you know, we don't interrupt the speaker."

Bill blushed. "Sorry," he murmured.

"That's fine," I said. "To answer your question, yeah, he's my uncle, or he was. He died last night at his barbecue party." Everyone's eyes widened while Darnell shook his head. "So Uncle Charlie's dead, and though I can't say I'm grieving, I also can't say his death makes me feel any better either."

There was a splatter of applause, and I sat back down. In the clear again. The meeting was over.

"You should take a lesson from yourself," Darnell said as people filed out of the room.

"Meaning what?" I said.

"You told us your uncle dying didn't solve your problems. Do you really think this Mendoza case will either?"

"I don't know. But take a lesson from yourself and stop telling me what to do. You're wasting your time."

Darnell leaned so close to me I could smell the stale cigarette on his breath. "And what if it kills you?"

I gave a shrug. "Guess I'll be too dead to care."

Darnell bolted out of the room right after that. He'd be mad at me for some time, and while I felt sorry about this since he was only trying to be a good friend, I was also relieved I'd driven him away. Now I didn't have to worry that he'd discover my relapse and try to stop my investigation.

Chapter Thirteen

I DROVE TO SAINT LUKE'S HOSPITAL to catch Isabella Mendoza after her work shift. The deceased's spouse usually had important info if they were willing to talk, but I wasn't that optimistic, considering I was about to terrify her with the news that someone, who happened to be me—though I wouldn't share that detail—was impersonating her. I pulled into the parking area marked for employees, got out of the car, and knocked back another pill with a slug of Topo Chico.

When I saw a pregnant, face-masked nurse tottering toward me, I knew this was Isabella. I held up my badge and smiled since she was under no obligation to talk to me.

"Isabella Mendoza?" I said.

"Yes?" Her confused eyes darted from my face to my badge. "Am I in trouble?"

"No trouble. I'm Victoria Swenson, the private investigator you hired with Bullseye Services."

"What?" she snapped at me as if I was a solicitor selling a scam. "I never hired anyone."

"You didn't?" I pulled out my phone and opened the original email I'd written as her. "So you didn't write this?"

She snatched my phone and scrolled through the case request.

Now she looked like she'd heard me right, recognized I wasn't soliciting a scam, and was terrified because what I was saying was real.

"I didn't write that," she whispered, reaching for the crucifix around her neck. "What's going on?"

"It's okay," I said. "I believe you." I advanced toward Isabella as she panted beneath her mask. "So someone's impersonating you then?"

"I . . . I guess?"

I nodded. "Well, you can press charges if you know who it is. Got any ideas?" She shook her head and waddled off to her car. "Isabella," I called out, following her.

"Please." She fumbled with her key to unlock the car door. "I don't want to get involved in any investigation. I've already had a long day working with sick people. I need rest."

"But Mrs. Mendoza," I pleaded, while she buckled herself in, "this discovery is disturbing, don't you think? Don't you want to know what's going on? How about just five minutes of your time?"

"No, I need to get home."

"But—"

"No," she shouted, angrily this time. "My husband's dead, I've got no money, I'm alone and five months' pregnant, and I'm not risking my baby's life."

She reached for the handle and slammed her door in my face.

I'd had witnesses run from me before, afraid they'd get in trouble for talking. It was always disappointing, but if Isabella got away, it would be more than disappointing.

It could mean the difference of me losing critical info for solving my case. Even in my drug-induced numb state, I forced myself to push my nose up to her window.

"You could be in serious danger if you don't speak to me," I warned her. "Please tell me what you know so I can help keep you safe."

"Leave me alone," she shouted again, turning on the ignition to an exhaust pipe in need of a better muffler.

I raised my voice over the noise, "Don't you want justice for your husband and baby's father?" As she backed up, I shouted even louder, "Do you want your kid hating their daddy for being a junkie?"

There it was. The brake lights lit up, and Isabella's face scrunched up red and tearful like the face of her newborn baby coming out. She rolled down the window. "Five minutes," she said.

"Thank you." I switched on my phone's recorder. "Do you know who might have wanted to hurt Luis?"

Isabella shook her head. "I've thought about it over and over again, but he had no enemies. He worked hard and cared about his family. I don't know why or how this could have happened to such a good man."

"I'm sure he was a good husband. Can you think of anything unusual before his death? Any strangers visit you? Any packages? Any suspicious behavior from Luis?"

Isabella nodded. "Yes, something strange happened a few weeks before he died. I told the police, but they didn't seem to care."

"What was that?"

"He'd left his phone at work and went back to Uncle Charlie's to get it, but when he came home, I could tell something was weighing on him. I asked him what it was, but he said nothing. I don't think he wanted to stress me out because of the baby."

"Interesting," I said, considering this likely meant one of two things: either Luis discovered something at Uncle Charlie's that night, or he was lying about his phone missing, so he could do something without his wife knowing. "Have you ever found anything unusual in your home?"

"No, I've never found any drugs if that's what you mean."

"And you've checked your car?"

"No? Do you think that's necessary?"

"Why not? Better to be thorough."

Isabella groaned with irritation, but hopped out of the car and waited while I climbed into a faux velvet interior stinking of air freshener. I examined the glove box and console, the back seat and side door pockets, under the mats. As I slid the passenger seat back, a thick envelope fell to the ground. I opened it to a stack of clean, crisp hundred-dollar bills. *Nothing suspicious here.*

Maybe this was what Uncle Charlie meant when he'd claimed that Luis had stolen money from the register.

"You know what this is doing here?" I fanned out the cash wad. "Looks like ten grand."

Isabella slapped a hand over her gaping mouth. I could tell she was genuinely shocked. "Dios mío." She closed her eyes, crossing herself. "I swear I don't know where that came from, believe me."

"I believe you," I hurried to reassure her. "But what do you think it's doing here? Did someone owe Luis money, or did he owe someone money?"

Her chest heaved, and she spoke with so much panic she removed her mask to breathe. "I don't know," she said, her bottom lip twitching. "But I know it's not drug money. He'd never do that. I'm sure of it. I'm sure."

"I'm not saying he was involved in drugs, but if money was as tight as you say, and Luis was stressed about supporting his growing family, he might have been involved in some risky behavior and keeping it from you. Is it possible he wasn't working overtime at Uncle Charlie's, but instead running a side hustle he never told you about?"

"Oh Luis," Isabella moaned while gripping her crucifix necklace. "My poor Luis."

Isabella leaned against her car and cried while I continued my inspection. Getting on my hands and knees, I switched on my phone's flashlight and looked under the car. A quarter-sized disc reflected at me. Fortunately, being small came with its perks, like fitting in tight spaces.

"What are you doing?" Isabella shrieked, as I wormed beneath her car.

I took a picture of the wireless tracker, snapped it off, and pulled myself back out. "I'm guessing you didn't know about this either?" I held up the tracker.

"Oh God," Isabella shrieked. "I'm being impersonated and stalked." She turned her head frantically. "What if we're being watched right now?"

I didn't want to lie to her and say her fears weren't warranted. The envelope of money and wireless tracker suggested Luis had been up to something he'd kept from his wife, and her wheels were probably spinning as she considered what else she didn't know about her husband. As for me, I wasn't shocked by what I'd found. Usually, people got knocked off for some reason. But I kept this thought to myself as I helped Isabella get back into her car.

"I know this is hard," I said, "but is there somewhere you can hide for now?"

"Hide? No, I have to work."

"Someone's impersonating you, and your husband could have been involved with some bad people. I don't think it's safe for you to be in KC right now."

Isabella bit her trembling lip as more tears trickled. "I have a brother in St. Louis," she conceded, wiping her eyes.

"Good. Get there fast, and take this." I handed her the envelope of cash.

She didn't argue and put the money in her purse. "One more question," I said through her open window. "Do you know the name of the co-worker who was supposed to be working with Luis the night he died?"

"Yeah, there was a guy he drank with a few times after work. Victor? Victor Green? I think that's his name."

Soon as Isabella's tires squealed around the garage corner, I ran a background check on Mr. Green. A few charges for possession, but nothing major. I dialed his number. Straight to voicemail.

"Hi Victor, my name's Tori Swenson," I said. "I'm a private investigator looking into the death of your former co-worker, Luis Mendoza, and I'd appreciate hearing your account. All confidential, of course."

Still in my hand was the wireless tracker, tangible proof Luis's death likely wasn't an accident. I might have been able to trace it back to its owner if I'd had Gabe's high-tech surveillance equipment, but I wasn't about to involve him in my case. My grip tightened around the plastic shell until I heard—and felt—the satisfying crunch. Now it was time to offer my condolences to my grieving cousins.

Chapter Fourteen

I HIT THE BRAKES AND kissed the curb of Uncle Charlie's estate, otherwise known as the Mack B. Nelson House, built a century ago by KC's famous lumber baron. My entire body was hot, my throat like sandpaper. *But Uncle Charlie's dead now.*

Behind the spiked fence stood the double-decker, orange palace, with its balconies, columns, and terra-cotta roof that looked like a sleeping dragon. I never thought I'd be here to ring the bell, though, I wasn't exactly invited to ring it either. Now that I was doing it though, I wanted another pill, badly. *Don't you do it.* I couldn't afford another yesterday. If I was going to solve this case, I needed my mind and body to work. Resisting the craving, I instead took a hearty swig of water and reached out the window to twist my thumb into the buzzer.

"Hello?" Jean drawled sorrowfully from the intercom.

"Hi, it's Tori," I said. "I'm here for the will read—"

"You were invited?" she shouted as if I'd done something wrong. Unless it was her grief talking, I had no idea why she'd be angry with me.

"Annie told me about it," I said.

"It's already been read. Nothing for you."

"I wasn't expecting anything."

"Just go around to the garage. Everyone's in the back."

The fortress gate drew open, and I rolled down a rose-lined driveway, circling around the mansion until I was greeted by a golden fountain where water gurgled from animals' mouths into a marble trough. After passing a flower garden, a charming gazebo overlooking a man-made pond, and a tennis court, I slid into the garage. Stepping out of the car into the warm evening, I then cautiously made my way toward the backyard, where I could hear my cousins shouting at each other. What good timing I had. Maybe I'd overhear something incriminating.

I approached the iron fence and looked into a manicured courtyard of rose bushes, statues, water fountains, a pool, and a patio decorated in black streamers, tiki torches, and balloons. My cousins sat at a patio table, far enough away that I couldn't hear what they were saying. I squatted and crept through the open gate, hiding between the fence and rose bushes, and quietly moved closer to the patio. When I was near enough to hear Chuck mumble, "I think we should wait for the autopsy," I switched on my phone's recorder.

Teddy knocked his beer bottle on the table and shouted, "We're having his funeral on Saturday. He was our father. He's Uncle Charlie. He shouldn't be stinking up a funeral parlor."

"Will you stop making so much damn noise?" Annie cut in. "You're giving me a migraine."

"But—but maybe—" Chuck sniffled, "we should wait for the report in case—"

"What?" Teddy shouted louder. "In case they find out one of us killed him so that stupid Slayer Rule goes into effect? You know, we'd all be disinherited if that happens, right? Great idea, Chuck."

"Why are you even suggesting he was killed?" Annie said.

"Yeah," Emma agreed. "You seriously think one of us killed Dad?"

"I never said he was killed," Chuck moaned. "I only think understanding the cause of death might help us with the grieving process."

"Doesn't matter to me how the asshole died." Teddy took a swig of his beer.

"Anyway," Annie said, "none of this matters as I'm sure his death was natural."

"He probably just gave himself a heart attack from all that Yummy Food contract stress," Emma added.

"You know what?" Annie picked up her phone. "I'm supposed to call the coroner's office back anyway, so let's settle this right now." Everyone went quiet as she pressed her phone to her ear and inquired about the death of her father. After saying "I see" and "absolutely" several times, she hung up. "Anaphylaxis," she announced, like it was the winning word on a game show. "An allergic reaction."

"A natural death?" Chuck flung himself on the table into his folded arms and started to cry.

"Look everybody, Chuck's crying," Teddy laughed, clapping Chuck on the back. "Congratulations, old boy. Looks like Daddy finally helped you to find your tears again."

"I wonder what he was allergic to," Emma said.

"It's a food mystery," Teddy laughed. "Was it the barbecue, the baked beans, or the cherry pie?"

"It probably was the food actually," Annie said. "The coroner said there were no bug bites or stings on his body, and that he'd have to run a toxicology report to find out the details, which could take weeks."

At this news, I flinched behind the flowers, and Annie's head swiveled in my direction. Now my pulse was soaring.

I'd been spotted. With a smile, I stepped out onto the lawn. "Love these roses," I said, as if I'd only been back there because I was enamored with the garden's beauty.

"Tori?" Annie frowned. "What are you doing here?"

My stomach contracted at her tone, but I wasn't surprised after our tense phone conversation last night. "Sorry to interrupt," I said. "Just thought I'd drop by, see how you all were doing."

"Great to see you again, fuzzy cuzzy." Teddy raised his beer bottle at me. "Beer?"

"No thanks." I slid on my sunglasses to avoid eye contact with Annie. "Couldn't help overhearing you talk about the toxicologist. That's nuts Uncle Charlie died of an allergy."

"Maybe it was nuts," Emma snickered.

Annie smirked at her sister. "Or maybe it was your burnt ends. Remember how he choked on one?"

"You're such a fucking—"

"You know," I cut in, "if a toxicologist knows what to test for, they can run the specific test and get immediate results."

"That's great, but we don't know what to test for," Annie said. "Plus, we don't need to waste time and money when he's already dead."

As Annie glared at me, I glanced around. "Where's Jean?"

Emma pointed to a pair of glass French doors leading into the house. "She got mad she wasn't first in line in the will."

"And why should she be?" Teddy raised his beer. "It's not like she was his kid. She was just his titty toy."

Emma laughed, "She's probably what Dad was allergic to. He didn't get sick until she showed up."

On cue, the French doors opened, and Jean slunk out in a tight black dress, her face smeared with mascara and eyeliner. Looking straight at me, she pointed a bejeweled finger. "Murderer," she declared.

My eyebrows shot up at this accusation, but her flaring nostrils indicated that she really believed what she was saying. That explained why she'd been so short with me on the intercom.

"Excuse me?" I said.

"Come on, Jean." Teddy banged his beer bottle on the table again.

"No, think about it," she appealed to my cousins. "Charlie went from red, to white, to blue after she mysteriously showed up. Then she gave him CPR when she was probably suffocating him to death instead."

"Wrong." Annie shook her head. "The coroner said Dad died from an allergic reaction."

"An allergic reaction." Jean clapped a hand to her chest. "To what?"

"You know," I said, speaking up in my own defense, "I'd like to point out that when I'd arrived at the party, he was already coughing and having a hard time breathing. It sounded like he'd been sick for a while."

Jean raised the volume of her voice, "That must be because you poisoned him with an allergy before you got there."

"Poisoned him with an allergy?" Emma snorted a laugh. "That's absurd."

Annie gestured to the cameras on the patio. "Jean, you of all people know how paranoid my father was about his safety. How many cameras are in there anyway? Fifty?"

"Fifty-six," Jean corrected her.

"And guns?" Annie asked next.

"How would I know?" Jean said. "It's not like I counted them."

"Anyway," Annie continued, "my point stands that Dad was always accusing everyone of trying to kill him or steal from him, and Tori couldn't have possibly killed him with an allergy. I'll agree with my sister for once because that hypothesis is absurd."

"Unless Tori plotted it out." Jean waved her phone above her head. "I have it all on tape right here."

She presented her phone, and my throat went dry. It was the surveillance footage from Uncle Charlie's in Leawood. There was no sound, but when I entered the Hub and met Walt, Jean paused the video. I swallowed as my cousins turned their astonished faces on me.

"What were you doing at Uncle Charlie's the day before Charlie died?" Jean screamed at me.

My skin prickled. I didn't know what to do now. My cover was blown. *No use trying to dig yourself out of this hole.* I fished out my badge and tossed it on the table. "I hope you all don't take this the wrong way," I began in a friendly tone, "but I'm a PI investigating the death of Luis Mendoza at Uncle Charlie's."

While my cousins stared at my badge in disbelief, Jean rushed back into the house and slammed the doors behind her.

"You're a secret agent?" Teddy mused. "So that's why you crunched my fingers yesterday like that. What else can you do? Bungee jump off burning buildings?"

"My job's really not that sexy," I said.

Annie turned to me, nose crinkled. Her silver toe ring sparkled in the setting sun. "So your friendly visit was nothing but a lie to get the dirt on us?" Her tone was shrill. "Guess I'm not surprised when you showed up with that bogus invitation story."

My stomach tightened. I wanted to give her harsh words back, but I had to be careful now that they knew I was investigating them. Showing any anger could get me kicked off the property. I softened my voice instead. "I was only investigating you because it's my job. Believe me, I've wanted to see you all. I wrote you letters, Annie, if you remember—"

"Okay," she interrupted me with a mocking laugh. "That makes it all better then. How nice you got to mix business with pleasure by catching up with us while also trying to ruin us. Get anything juicy besides feeling my dad die under you?"

"I'm sorry I upset you," I said.

"Whatever. You just want to take us down because you're jealous we're rich and you're not."

Again, my stomach clenched, and I might have launched at Annie with my fists out if Teddy hadn't spoken first. "Who cares if Tori looks into Luis? It's not like she's going to find anything. He was just some dopehead thief who died by accident." He opened another beer and let the head fizzle onto the table.

"My client alleges it wasn't an accident," I said. "That's why I was at Uncle Charlie's on Sunday. I was interviewing the manager."

Emma twisted her hair into a ponytail. "And did you find anything suspicious that suggests it wasn't an accident?"

"I'm afraid I can't discuss my findings with you, but I'll tell you something odd. I was anonymously invited to the party on the same day I was put on this case. Then my client dropped the case right after the party."

"You know what else sounds odd?" Emma smacked a mosquito on her arm, splattering blood. "That you're still on a case you got dropped from."

"Yeah, maybe it's your client who's compromised," Annie said. "There are lots of people out there who want to take us down. You know, people jealous of everything we've worked for."

"As I said, I'm only doing my job." I swiped my badge from the table. "In fact, now that you all know the truth, maybe you could help me."

"Yeah, right," Annie snorted.

While Chuck continued crying in his arms, Teddy turned to me with wide eyes. "Wait a second. Do you actually think one of us could be a murderer?"

"I don't think anything without evidence," I said.

Annie rolled her eyes. "Seriously, this is a huge waste of time and bad PR."

Emma raised an eyebrow at me. "Help you how?"

"I'd love to interview you all. Maybe tomorrow? You might know something that could help shine a light on what happened to Luis."

For a few seconds, only the sound of the peaceful fountains could be heard splashing.

This was my trap: if they said no, they'd look guilty.

"Go right ahead," Teddy declared, taking the bait. "I haven't killed anybody that I know of."

"I guess it could be a fun diversion from burying our dead father," Emma chimed in. "I could even give you a special pitmaster tour if you'd like and show you all my juicy barbecue secrets." She winked at me.

"Wonderful," I said, biting my tongue. I knew the recipes well, and Emma knew better than anyone that her secret barbecue recipes came from my dad.

Teddy clapped a hand on Emma's shoulder. "The boss with the sauce."

"Ugh," Annie groaned, "no way am I giving you an interview."

"Why's that?" Emma turned to Annie. "Because you're the killer?"

"No, I just don't see the point of wasting my time voluntarily divulging info that she could twist around. She's already pretended to be someone she's not. Who knows what she'll do with her so-called evidence."

"Oh, is that why you don't want to talk?" Emma gave Annie a smirk. "Or is it because you're afraid Yummy Foods will rescind their new contract if they hear about this murderous development?"

"Shut up," Annie shrieked at her sister. "Shut up."

"What's going on with the contract?" I said, as if it was my business.

Annie glared at Emma. "No one here seems to know where my father put it."

Emma shot daggers back at Annie. "How do you even know he signed? He was talking nonsense and making threats because he was dying."

"Maybe," Annie said. "But even if that's true, Yummy Foods has been gracious enough to accommodate our tragedy by extending their deadline to us, the new owners of Uncle Charlie's." From her leather tote bag, she pulled out a folder with a fresh contract, flipping its pages to show that she'd already signed. "We have until Saturday to sell. That's in four days."

Emma's face shriveled with deeper disdain. "Yeah, and for that to happen, we'd need a majority vote."

"That's right." Annie shoved the contract in front of Teddy.

"What are you doing?" Teddy said.

"Getting your signature."

"You think you can boss me around like that?" Teddy pushed the papers away. "How about the only way I'm signing is if you agree to talk to Tori?"

"What?" Annie gasped. "Why?"

"Why should I get interviewed for a murder when you aren't?"

"I'm saying, why don't we all refuse to talk to her?" Annie ran a hand through her hair. "That's the smart thing to do, but apparently, I'm the only one at this table who isn't a dumbass."

Teddy gave her a country club smile. "Well, if someone here is a murderer, they'll lose their share of the inheritance. More money for me."

"That doesn't matter, you idiot," Annie said. "Even if you killed some stupid cook and went to jail, you'd still get Dad's money."

"Then maybe I'm tired of you acting like you own me. In case you forgot, I'm way richer than you'll ever be. And I have a castle."

Annie closed her eyes before covering a nostril and breathing in long and exhaling longer. When she opened her eyes, she gave me a resigned sigh. "Fine, I'll spare you a few minutes. I'll even send you our surveillance feeds, if you want to waste more time going through them."

"Thanks," I said. "I'd appreciate that."

Teddy grabbed the contract and scribbled. "All right, we're officially split. Me and Annie want to sell. The losers don't."

"Guess we're not selling then." Emma swatted the contract to the ground, sprung out of her chair, and hustled across the backyard for the garage.

"Cunt," Annie huffed under her breath as she stooped down to retrieve the contract.

I tried not to show it, but I couldn't deny Annie's irritation was bringing me pleasure. With my cousins split on the sale, she'd have to fight for New York by either finding Uncle Charlie's original contract or convincing Chuck to sign the new one.

I turned to Chuck, still moaning in his arms. While he did seem sad with grief—visible in his tears—the uncontrollable twitching of his head in his arms suggested he was more than bereaved. Even in death, my uncle seemed to have some torturous power over my cousin.

"What about you, Chuck?" I called out to him. "Can I interview you too?"

Not bothering to lift his shaking head, he muttered into the table, "I don't care. I'll show you whatever you want. I've got records of our financial transactions."

"Great, I'd love to see them."

Annie, Teddy, and Chuck had nothing more to say to me, or each other. They took off, leaving me alone on the patio to drink a victorious Topo Chico. Strangely, my exposure had turned into my gain. But there was something I still needed to find out while I was here. I knocked on the patio door.

"Jean?" I called out.

I kept knocking until Jean appeared behind the glass with a scowl on her face. "What do you want?" she yelled.

"I know you don't want to talk to me, but can you at least tell me how you knew I was at Uncle Charlie's on Sunday? Sounds like someone is trying to jeopardize my case."

When Jean disappeared back into the house, I didn't know whether to stay or go. I waited a few minutes until I took her absence as a sign she wasn't coming back, then headed to the car. It was only when I was rolling past the flowers toward the front gate that I saw her in my rearview mirror, rushing toward me. I hit the brakes, and she ran up to my window.

"Wait, I was getting this." She held up an envelope. "For the record, this doesn't mean I trust you."

Through my window, she handed me a Priority Mail Express envelope, addressed to Uncle Charlie in black magic marker. No return address. I opened it, pulling out a note card. The paper twitched in my hand. Beside a sticker of a smiling sausage, the handwritten message read, *CHECK LEAWOOD SURVEILLANCE SUNDAY JULY 3 @ 5PM.*

"You know what this is about?" Jean asked.

"Yeah," I said, my cheeks burning. "I've got a pretty good idea who sent this."

Chapter Fifteen

DIDN'T CARE IF I was pushing my quota. I threw back two pills and called Kevin. "Where's Gabe?" I asked him.

"Why do you want to know?" he said.

"Oh," I feigned a heartfelt sigh, "I feel guilty about initially refusing Uncle Charlie's case, only to take it back from him once I changed my mind. Thought I'd apologize in person."

"He's on a stakeout at Rocky's in Westport," Kevin said. "Just be careful you don't blow his cover."

"Of course. I'd never do something amateur like that."

Apparently, this holiday season's crime scene was barbecue. Not only had I been to both Uncle Charlie's locations the past two days, I was heading back to Rocky's. Maybe Gabe was working Annie's same fraudulent workers' comp claim for Ginny Wolf, since I'd messed it up after that troll stole my camera.

I parked a block from the diner and followed the scent of meat to Rocky's while trying to grasp an extra-large vanilla milkshake too big for my hand. I'd ordered chocolate for myself and already annihilated it, but I'd also gotten vanilla, a flavor I detested, so I wouldn't be tempted to slurp the ice cream meant for Gabe's face. When I reached the parking lot, I whiffed in the smoking meat. It still didn't smell appetizing, but there was a perverse part of me that was curious to test it again. Maybe I'd try one of their burnt ends after taking care of Gabe. I snuck up behind a grotesque ad for the Holiday Rib Sandwich Special, where the sauce was oozing out of the bun, and scanned the parking lot—no sign of my colleague. If he was here, he was behind the diner.

Like I'd done a few days ago, I circled to the back of Rocky's. However, as soon as I peered around the loading dock, I almost dropped my milk-shake on myself.

There he was. The monster truck driver who took my camera was pushing a dolly up a ramp into his truck. My eyes widened to see him again. I'd forgotten the size of him. He really was huge, like a bodyguard. Instinctively, I wound back my arm with the shake before Darnell's words came to me. *He could crush your skull.*

At this reminder, I lowered my arm. Darnell was right. This would be reckless. If I threw my shake at this guy, I wouldn't stand a chance in a real fight, especially since I was buzzed on oxies and had left my stun gun in the car. Before the driver could see me standing behind him, I retreated alongside the diner to wait until he was gone.

A moment later, the back door of Rocky's opened. "Squishy," a man said, presumably another employee. "Want to do another bump before you bounce?"

"Sure," said the tuba voice I couldn't forget. Funny he went by "Squishy" when he was anything but soft, unless he had a reputation for squishing in brains. "One for the road never hurt nobody." Two short snorts, and a wheeze. "Thanks, man."

"No, thank you for hooking me up. This shit's gold."

"Anytime."

That Squishy liked coke and sold it wasn't shocking. That could explain why he'd lost his temper with me, thinking I was taking pictures of him selling or snorting. Paranoia and anger were trademark side effects of coke. But maybe there was another reason for Squishy's paranoia, maybe something more legitimate, like he was selling drugs for the KC mob and using barbecue restaurants as a front. Maybe he was afraid of someone bigger than the law.

The other coked-up employee went back inside, and Squishy slid the truck door down with a click. Then the truck started up and rumbled off into the dark blue dusk, and I stepped out from my hiding place. Sure enough, parked in the back corner of the parking lot was the black Toyota with its TOP GUM vanity plate.

My grip tightened again around the wet waxy cup of melted milkshake as I watched Gabe, his face behind binoculars, follow Squishy's truck down the road. When he turned his binoculars toward me, I waved, smiled, and strolled up to his window.

"Tori," he said, smiling back at me and grazing a hand through his slicked-back mane. "You must like me a lot since you've stalked me twice in one week. Did you come here for the Holiday Rib Sandwich Special?" He presented a ball of red mush in his hands. "It's not too bad, but it's all they've got. Guess that could have something to do with those meat shortages that started in the pandemic."

"I might like some ribs," I lied in an agreeable tone. "But the reason I came over was to apologize for taking that Uncle Charlie's case from you. It wasn't nice of me to change my mind like that, and you know, my karma bit me back since the client ended up dropping the case."

"Really?" Gabe raised his eyebrows.

I nodded. "Anyway, I wanted to make things right between us." I stuck out my hand, which he examined with reluctance. "I'm saying sorry," I went on. "I brought you a peace offering." I showed him the milkshake.

Gabe wrapped his warm grip around my free hand. "I remember your tiny hands," he said as he squeezed hard, pulling me close. "That's so sweet of you to get me a milkshake on a hot summer's night, but it looks too big for one person. How about you join me in here, and we indulge in it together?"

"Okay, I'll come around to the passenger's side." He released his hold on me, and I popped off the plastic lid with a quick thumb maneuver before hurling the vanilla ice cream right between his eyes.

For a few seconds, Gabe sat in cold silence while the ice cream dripped down his face and off his chin. "What the hell, Tori?" he screamed. He scrambled out of his car after me, but I was already on the other side. "Are you psycho?" He wiped shake off his face with the bottom of his barbecue-stained shirt. "What's your problem?"

I looked at the ice cream in his hair, feeling neither guilt nor triumph. He simply got his just desserts. "That was for trying to thwart my case," I stated.

"Thwart your case?"

"Yeah, for sending that anonymous note to Uncle Charlie's house informing on me. That was you, right?"

Gabe seethed. "Don't you think you'd better be damn sure of that before you douse people in milkshake?"

"I'm sure," I said. "Beyond the fact that only you knew I was there, you gave yourself away with that sausage sticker."

"All right," Gabe snorted a laugh. "I was pissed you took the case. Sometimes I get impulsive when I'm mad. Like you." He pointed to his back seat, flicking his brows up and down. "So why don't we make things right between us? You know, maybe we could work out our aggression in a more productive manner? We weren't so bad together before you cut things off."

I couldn't believe he was still trying to get with me after I'd thrown ice cream at him.

Maybe I should have told him the truth about why I'd ended things, but I wasn't telling him anything about my drug history when I was presently on drugs.

"Sorry, got work to do," I said.

Gabe's smile folded into a frown. "What work?"

"That Uncle Charlie's case."

"But you said your client dropped it."

"Did I say that?" I pretended to zip my mouth shut and throw the key behind me.

"Fair enough. You keep your juicy bits to yourself, and I'll do the same. Just know there's more than one big barbecue case in this town. Why do you think I'm here?"

I pointed at where the truck had been. "To watch Squishy sell dope?"

"Who?"

"The truck delivery giant you're watching goes by Squishy and likes snorting coke." I smiled at Gabe, and his bedroom eyes tightened into angry pellets. "Sounds like I know more about your case than you do."

Leaving Gabe to clean up his mess, I made my way into Rocky's, immediately regretting it as I started choking on the smoky air. I pinched my nose, which helped me to breathe better, then took in my surroundings as I'd only seen this place from up on the roof. It wasn't a drive-in like Uncle Charlie's, but a regular diner with red cushioned booths and red-and-white checkered tablecloths. And while there wasn't anything particularly special about its interior, Rocky's had almost as high a reputation when it came to barbecue in KC for its epic buffet. When I got to the line, still holding my nose, I saw that Gabe had been right about their selection. Most of the steel containers were empty except for the ribs. I gestured to the one labeled *Burnt Ends*.

"Got any in the back?" I asked the girl behind the counter.

"We're out," she said.

"How's that?"

"They're real popular" was the next line in her script. "Can I grab you our Holiday Rib Sandwich? It's on special."

"Wait a second," I said, confused. "How does a barbecue joint as esteemed as Rocky's run out of everything besides ribs?"

"We've also got chicken." She pointed to a canister of chicken wings. "We just got real busy over the holiday weekend and ran out of lots of things. We should be restocked in a few days."

That sounded like another line in her script, but I went ahead and ordered the Holiday Rib Sandwich Special with a side of fries and baked beans. When it arrived a few minutes later, I released my nose to pick up the burger. With my fingers dripping in sauce, I stared at the monstrosity in my hands.

Just try it.

I swallowed, lurched forward for a bite, and dropped the burger to chew. The meat was succulent and sweet, and the sauce had a zippy tang that complemented the crunchy pickles, but I couldn't handle it. As I spit it out into my basket, a nearby customer gave me a horrified look. I got the hell out of there.

Back at Aunt Kat's, the house was dark, and her snores were coming in sharp squeals from her bedroom. At least the poor woman was getting some sleep. I pulled out my pill bottle, desperately wanting one to finish off the day so I could melt into my bed. I unscrewed the cap, but the inner voice went off like an alarm. *Don't compromise your case.* I wasn't a fan of self-control, especially since I'd only reactivated my cravings a few days ago, so I opened my pill bottle and threw back a couple oxies.

As I opened the fridge to guzzle them down with an ice-cold Topo Chico, I eyed Aunt Kat's Fourth of July ribs sitting on the shelf. She hadn't touched them on account of her grief, and though I wasn't hungry and had zero interest in trying meat again at this moment, I had an idea.

If it looked like I'd had a huge appetite and wolfed down all her ribs, she'd never suspect I was on drugs again. Maybe that was a wasteful idea, but I really had to be sure she didn't find me out. For my own protection and hers, I grabbed the meat platter and headed upstairs with my water supply and a roll of paper towels.

King Rebus was sprawled across the bed, licking his paws. "Hey Reebs, want some meat?" I dangled a cold rib under his nose. Squinting at me like I'd brought out the nail clippers, he leapt onto the windowsill to twitch his tail at some critter outside. "Guess that's a hard no," I said.

I set the ribs on my desk and got to work. One rib after the other, I ripped the plump, fatty flesh, feeling like a lion attacking its prey. When I had a mound of meat on the right and a mound of bones on the left, I wiped my sticky fingers on a paper towel, got out of my chair, and hurled the meat out the window to whatever hungry creatures waited down below. By morning, the meat would all be gone, and Aunt Kat would never have to know.

My phone dinged, and I pulled it out of my pocket with a tired exhale. A text from Kevin. *Tori,* he wrote, *I received a strange call asking whether you were working the Mendoza case with us. I said you were our employee, but that you were supposed to be off that case. The caller said you were working this case today, which means you've broken our policy. Therefore, consider your employment with us terminated. I hope you understand. Best of luck.*

Maybe it was the drugs in my system, but this made me laugh. Here I was, already broke and living with my aunt, and now I didn't have a job because I'd pretended to hire and fire myself. Though I couldn't get too sad about never having to work another boring workers' comp case again, I wondered who'd informed on me. Was it Gabe trying to get even for the ice cream? Or Isabella worried over our conversation in the parking garage? I didn't think it was either of them. Kevin wouldn't have said the call was "strange" if it came from someone familiar. My hunch was that one of my cousins, or Jean, was trying to stop me from working because they were afraid I'd nab them for murder. In this case, getting fired wasn't such bad news. If anything, it only confirmed I was on the right track.

Chapter Sixteen

"T HE NATIONWIDE OPIOID EPIDEMIC CONTINUES to soar this summer," the sunburnt anchorwoman on the TV stated without emotion. "Though overdoses almost doubled from 2010 to 2019, from over 38,000 deaths to over 70,000, the onset of the COVID pandemic only exacerbated the opioid crisis. Nearly 107,000 people overdosed last year, and this year is anticipated to have even more deaths. As a result, life expectancy is declining for the first time in the U.S."

A video played of an unconscious man with a blurred-out face receiving Narcan, the medicine used to prevent you from dying of an overdose. Showcasing someone's near-death at breakfast seemed in poor taste, but the news was in the business of scaring you.

The sight of Narcan was enough to send a chill through my veins. I switched off the TV.

"Hey, what did you do that for?" Aunt Kat hollered from the kitchen. "I was listening to that."

I approached my aunt, who was heavily salting a newborn-sized lump of marbled red meat. The sight of raw flesh made me nauseous.

"Sorry," I said, "but I can't think with the TV on so loud. You should get a smaller one in here." I emptied the bowl of rib bones into the trash can. "Making more meat?"

"Yep. Pork butt."

"Pork butt?"

"It's the upper shoulder cut, and one of the cheapest cuts there is, but it was Charlie's favorite. Thought I'd cook it in honor of him." She squirted a dollop of hot mustard onto the pork, massaging it into its muscle.

I didn't ask why she was honoring a murderous traitor, but I figured it had to do with her grief. "I'd be interested in trying it later," I lied.

"I bet you would after you wolfed down my ribs last night." She said this less as a judgment and more as an observation.

"Yeah, sorry. Hadn't eaten anything all day. Was super hungry when I got home."

"You know you shouldn't be waiting until night to binge. You're looking after yourself, right?" She turned to me with an intense glance that commanded only one answer.

"Sure am." I took out my orange bottle from my bag and rattled the pills. "This will help with that." I didn't like lying to her face like this, but it was the right thing to do, especially since she was upset enough over Uncle Charlie.

"Good," she exhaled with relief. "Since when did you start eating meat again anyway?"

"Since the party. Guess it activated my curiosity."

"Sounds like it activated more than your curiosity."

"Yeah, but it had been a while, and you know, I'd forgotten how good it tasted. I'm glad it doesn't make me sick anymore."

This part wasn't exactly a lie. I'd succeeded so far in keeping the meat down that I'd eaten.

"I'm happy to hear you can handle it again." Aunt Kat dumped paprika over the mustard-lathered meat. "Just try not to eat all my pork butt. Otherwise, you'll turn into a meatball."

"Maybe you should stop being such a great chef if you don't want me gobbling down your food." I gave her a smile and cracked open a fresh Topo Chico.

Then I chased down three pills while Aunt Kat obliviously patted the pork butt with more spices.

"Hear anything about the coroner's report?" she asked.

"Yeah, you're not going to believe this. Turns out Uncle Charlie died of an allergic reaction."

"An allergic reaction?" She spun around to face me. "To what?"

"Beats me. Got any ideas?"

"No, I don't remember him having any allergies when he was younger, but they certainly can develop as we age. I never used to be allergic to pine nuts until a few years ago, and now I can't eat pesto." She reached for a joint in the ashtray. "But something tells me there's something more going on with this so-called allergy."

"What's that supposed to mean?"

Aunt Kat lit the joint and took a hit. "How often do people die from allergic reactions?"

"I imagine it's rare." I got out my phone and asked the internet for the answer. "It says here in a medical journal that food-related anaphylaxis is common, but the risk of fatal anaphylaxis is less than half a percent. So it's rare, but it happens."

"Being born with teeth is rare too, but I'm not biting. Charlie dying of an allergic reaction sounds about as convenient as you simultaneously getting an invitation to his party and a case to investigate a murder at Uncle Charlie's."

I recalled Jean's bizarre accusation that I'd poisoned him with an allergy. "Do you think it's possible someone gave him something on purpose, knowing he was allergic to it?"

"I don't think that sounds outlandish if they knew what the allergy was," my aunt said. "I'm sure a lot of people wanted him dead."

"Well, however he died, I don't care. My only concern is finding Luis's killer."

"And how do you know the two deaths aren't related?"

"I guess that's a possibility," I said. "Maybe Uncle Charlie knew who killed Luis and why and that's how he ended up dead a month later."

"Maybe." My aunt took another drag of her joint and let out the smoke. "But no matter all that business, I'd personally like to know how my brother died for my own peace of mind."

"Then I'll do my best to find out. That also reminds me, you were invited to the funeral on Saturday."

"Hell no," Aunt Kat blurted out, blowing smoke in my face. "Sorry." She hurried to wave the air around me. "But I wouldn't trust his kids as far as I could throw them. I fear I'd do or say something inappropriate."

"Yeah, and they're not as clever as they think they are, when they agreed to let me interview them. About to head out now."

"What? They know you're investigating them?"

"Yeah, my jealous colleague blew my cover, but I think it worked out better this way. If I'd come around knocking on their doors uninvited, inquiring about their whereabouts the night Luis died, I'd have received nothing but suspicion. Sometimes the truth beats lying."

"No." Aunt Kat shook her head. "You know you just made yourself a target, right? What if one of them is a murderer and wants to kill you when you figure that out?"

"I'm not too worried." I tossed my empty Topo Chico bottle into the recycling bin, while the pills I'd taken started making me float.

"That's careless, Tori," my aunt went on. "You should be worried. How do you plan on defending yourself if you get attacked?"

"Listen, if it'll put your mind more at ease, I'll show you what I'm packing." I reached into my bag and pulled out my yellow plastic weapon. "This is a police-strength stun gun."

Aunt Kat was stunned seeing it again. "Okay," she said. "And is that supposed to make me feel any better?"

"Essentially, it sends a shock wave to the nervous system and overworks the muscles, causing temporary pain," I explained. "Has an instant incapacitation rate of eighty-six percent, a range of fifteen feet, and can be used multiple times."

"But what if someone uses that thing on you?"

"They won't," I said, putting the gun back in my bag. "Because they'd have to beat me in a fight to get it."

"Just please be careful," Aunt Kat sighed. "Charlie may be dead, but who knows? His kids could be even deadlier."

Chapter Seventeen

O F ALL MY COUSINS, TEDDY was the most attractive and the most insecure. When he was a kid and Uncle Charlie was middle class, Teddy was so ashamed about his social standing that he lied to his schoolmates about where he'd lived, or the vacations he'd taken. Though his record was clean, I knew it had been scrubbed.

He'd been caught shoplifting expensive clothes in high school. I also knew he'd bribed a limo driver with drugs he scored at football parties so he could show up to school in a limo. Anytime I saw him back then, it was money, money, money.

He bragged about having so much that he'd one day buy the Chiefs and the Royals, though he never said how he'd make this fortune. Lucky for Teddy, Uncle Charlie took care of that part for him.

I was still soaking up the day's first sunny high when I reached the moat of Camelot Castle, the Great Disneyland of the Midwestern Plains. *Luxury Living Magazine* claimed it had thirty-eight rooms, along with pools, pool houses, and playgrounds—everything you needed that started with "p" to live a decent life.

But before I could stick out my middle finger to ring the bell, the majestic gate swung open, and Teddy stumbled out of the medieval front doors looking like the court jester.

Would I ever see my cousin sober?

"Tori," he sang out, giving me the beer bottle salute. "Come on in. I'll give you the grand tour. Should only take a few hours." He let out a burp and laughed.

"Mind if we stay outside?" I said, sniffing the air as if I loved humidity. Because there was no way I was going in that castle. Should Teddy be the killer and accidentally expose his crime because he was drunk, he'd have a much easier time murdering me in there. He could even have one room designated for torture and another for body disposal. "It's so pleasant out," I added.

"Fine," Teddy groaned. "We can sit on Lake Weatherby, the cleanest lake in Missouri." He proceeded to ramble on about the idle joys of sailing as he led me through the castle's arcade and across the lawn toward a stone fire pit at the water's edge. Another great place to get killed, but at least from here I could sprint into the forest if he tried bashing me in the head with his beer bottle. Teddy dropped into a chair and stared at the half-empty bottle in his hands. "I should get more to drink."

If he drank any more, I feared he'd be incoherent. "This won't take long," I said, fishing out my notebook of questions and turning on my phone's recorder. "Again, thank you for agreeing to talk to me. You're doing a great service."

"I live to serve," he laughed. "You know, I've done some of those escape rooms where you have to solve clues to get out. I'm really good at it, so maybe I'll figure this thing out right now."

It didn't matter to me whether my cousin was playing dumb, ignorant of the situation's severity, or drunk off his ass. If thinking of his interview as a game got him to spill his guts, I was willing to play along.

"Sounds like you're a natural detective," I said. "Let's see if you're any good with whodunits."

Teddy eagerly patted his thighs. "Let me guess question number one. How amazing is it to live in a castle?" He paused, while trying not to laugh before he let out a snicker. "What can I say? It's a party every day."

"I'm sure it is, but I have a different question for you." I looked at the first question in my notebook. "Can you tell me what you were doing on Memorial Day, the night Luis Mendoza died?"

"So official."

"Yep, pretty crazy," I said. "So do you know where you were?"

My cousin nodded, his face assuming a forced seriousness. "First, I golfed with my friends at the country club, then I suffered through Dad's dreadful barbecue party, and finally I partied all night long in my castle."

"So your wife can verify you were here that night?"

Teddy's jovial face crumpled into worry, his eyes squinty, nostrils ballooning. "No, no." He shook his head. "Suzie was in New York with the boys that weekend. You can check her Instagram."

"Is there anyone who can verify you were here that night, or did you party alone?"

"How could it be a party if you're alone?" Teddy gulped more beer. Then he looked at my phone, and gulped the air. "I know you're recording." His voice was now shaky. "But this conversation is confidential, right?"

"Yes," I assured him, "though I'm obligated by law to report any felonies, like murder, to the police."

"Well, I'm no murderer or felon, so if I tell you something, it better stay between you and me."

"Of course."

Teddy sucked in a deep breath and confessed, "I was messing around that night."

How shocking. I picked up my pen. "Can I get a name to verify your alibi?"

"Penelope Hall, but please don't contact her."

"Hall? Is she related to—"

"Yes, she's Suzie's younger cousin. Only twenty-one." When he said her age, he beamed with the same pride of living in a castle. "She was here that night, partying with me in the Crown Room."

"Do you have any surveillance footage that proves you were here with her?"

"No, I turned all that stuff off so Suzie wouldn't find out I was cheating, but I can show you me and Penelope's private tape if that would help clear my name."

Though Teddy's sex tape wasn't something I wanted to store in my memory bank, I had no choice. "Any material evidence would help remove you as a direct suspect in Luis's death," I said.

Teddy took out his phone and played the video of himself and Penelope performing gynecologist and patient in a room wallpapered with Hallmark Cards. It was dated on the night of Memorial Day, and the duration exceeded two hours.

It proved that while Teddy was lying to his wife and enjoyed role play, he was telling the truth about where he was that night. He didn't kill Luis. Still, I couldn't discount the possibility that he'd hired someone else to do it for him.

"Thank you." I waved at him to put his phone away. "Does your wife know about this affair?"

He laughed. "Not this one. Believe me, she'd blow a fuse knowing I was banging her hot cousin, so this better stay between us."

"Don't worry." I returned to my notebook of questions. "Do you know who might have wanted Luis dead?"

Teddy's cheeks flushed. "No, how would I?" he uttered in quick defense. "I barely knew the guy. He was just some drugged-up cook."

"Listen, I'm not accusing you of anything. These are standard detective questions."

Teddy nodded, his drunk eyes drooping. "Yeah, I know."

"Okay, then let me ask you another standard question. Do you think Luis was dealing drugs from Uncle Charlie's?"

"Drugs? No way. Dad would have told me if he was up to a scheme like that."

I'd like to know what other schemes Uncle Charlie was up to that he *did* tell Teddy about, but that question would probably get me thrown off the estate. Instead, I asked, "So you were close with your dad?"

"Are you kidding?" Teddy scoffed. "You saw him at the party. He was a paranoid jerk who thought everyone was trying to kill him."

"Did he expect you to work for him one day?"

"Of course, I'm the good-looking, prodigal son. He wanted me to carry the name and brand, though he made it clear I'd never be him."

"How did it feel hearing that?"

"Whatever, he was right." Teddy gestured to the castle and broke into a chuckle. "I'm twice as rich."

Teddy was back to his cheerfully drunk self. I moved on to my next question. "This Yummy Foods contract is a contentious subject in your family. Why do you want to sell Uncle Charlie's to a conglomerate?"

He threw open his arms and crowed, "Freedom, baby. Even if we don't sell, I was thinking of quitting anyway. It's not like I need the money, and without work, life would be a party all the time. What's better than that?"

"I really don't know because I have to work," I said. "What about your siblings? Why do they want to sell or not sell?"

"You want me to shit-talk them? Easy." Teddy rubbed his hands together. "Annie's a nose-to-the-grindstone careerist who wants to expand the business and grow her own someday. Emma's obsessed with barbecue, and considers Uncle Charlie's her birthright. And Chuck's being bossed around by his vegan girl—" Teddy stopped talking, his red cheeks turning onion white. Glancing over my shoulder, I saw Susanne on the lawn moving toward us, a tumbleweed in a toga.

"What's going on, Ted?" she said when she reached us. "I didn't realize we were having guests over."

Teddy's posture stiffened. "Tori's paying an impromptu visit," he said meekly. "You know, it's been so long since we last saw each other. We wanted to catch up properly."

"Why haven't you offered her refreshments?" Susanne blinked at the empty table and turned to me like a robot maid. "Can I get you anything? Coffee, tea, cookies?"

"Thanks," I said, "but—"

"Tori's actually on her way out," Teddy volunteered.

"Oh, that's too bad," Susanne said. "You'll have to stop by again soon."

As Susanne drifted back to the castle, Teddy whispered, "We need to stop now. I don't want Suzie knowing you're questioning me about a murder, or she'll lose her shit."

I didn't understand why Teddy was so scared of his wife when she was already gone, but there was no point arguing with him. I returned to the car, uncapped a new Topo Chico, and pulled out my phone. To be sure Susanne wasn't my killer, I opened her Instagram.

True to Teddy's words, there, at the top of her page, were pictures taken from the week of Memorial Day of herself, her kids, and the decorated veterans of Central Park.

Chapter Eighteen

A S I PASSED A BILLBOARD of a smiley Uncle Charlie holding an UltraCharBurger, and left Missouri for Kansas, Gabe's words returned to me: *It has twice as many burnt ends as the CharBurger.*

I couldn't imagine eating that thing and still being able to zip up my shorts, but I wasn't hungry anyway. Not after my morning dose. What I really wanted was another oxy, just a little boost to lower my anxiety since I was on my way to see Annie next.

I was especially anxious because even after years of silence, she knew me better than anyone. Of course, Darnell knew me well as a struggling addict, but Annie had watched me transition from a happy kid to that addict. The month before Dad died was when Annie and I found his oxies, the prescribed pain medication for his burnt hands, and didn't know what they did. We were young and stupid, and thought it would be fun to try something new. That's why Dad ran out of his prescription so fast.

The first pill I had was like warm barbecue sauce entering my veins, and I had to have more. Annie saw me get hooked, and after Dad died and my uncle banned me from seeing her again, I wrote her letters about my continued addiction.

If anyone suspected I was on them now, she would. That was why I had to resist another dose. If she knew, she'd try to exploit the situation, especially since I was about to be alone with her. But that horrifying scenario, of me sitting there trapped alone with her in her house, was exactly why I needed another pill.

The shiny new Uncle Charlie's drive-in appeared, rising like a steel sun over the I-435 entrance ramp, and I hit the accelerator to fly onto the open four-lane highway while the wind whipped my face with hot, suburban, strip-mall air. The closer my destination, the tighter my chest. I was fighting it, but I needed a pill like a burn victim needed to scratch her healing scars. I tried controlled, deep breaths, like they'd taught us in rehab. *In deep, out slow.* Like that ever worked.

Finally, I gave in and grabbed the orange bottle to throw back an oxy, chasing it down with sparkling water.

After about ten minutes, my tension and anxiety had lowered enough that I was back on a safe warm cloud. The steering wheel was heavier, though, as I turned into the sprawling Johnson County suburbs—or "JoCo" as the locals called it—where every house was an oversized cream and taupe box. Annie lived here in Whispering Winds, an extra yuppie neighborhood. Her house was of the taupe stone variety, with three taupe turrets, a cream portico supported by columns, and a beige balcony with French doors leading nowhere.

I pulled up to the curb and parked beside a bright green lawn, where a sign proclaimed that pesticides had been sprayed. In the mirror, my tired face and tiny pupils reflected back at me. It would be better to hide behind sunglasses. I slid them on, stumbled out of the car, and walked up the driveway. When I pressed the doorbell, it glowed the deep red of a 60 mg pill of oxy.

Inside, I could hear heels stabbing a hardwood floor, each step louder than the last. Then there was silence. Annie was watching me through the peep hole, studying me. I cleared my throat, raised my fist to knock, and the taupe door flung back to Annie in a zebra tank, white yoga pants, and black heels. Meanwhile, I held my fist in the air and forgot what I was doing there.

"All right," she groaned, "let's get this over with."

"So you know," I began, my voice heavy and far away, "I need to keep my sunglasses on because of my light sensitivity."

"Whatever." She rolled her eyes and led me through a marble foyer into a sunlit dining room.

I took a seat at the large walnut table covered in cardstock, stickers, and glitter. "Do you scrapbook?" I said.

"Yeah, right. Does it look like I have time for that?" She shoved the work aside, putting space between us. "But if you must know for your investigation, this is a marketing promo for my husband's expanding business, Yoga A-Go-Go. It really took off during the pandemic, and now he's launching an online special. Seeing as I'm a good wife, I'm helping him with his ad campaign."

"How long has he had his business?" I asked.

Annie exhaled hard through her nose. "Listen, you don't have to act like we're besties anymore. Being a successful career woman myself, I understand playing games to get ahead, so let's be clear. This friendship is totally canceled."

My stomach muscles clenched at this, and I could feel the pills inside me trying to bubble off my rage. I shifted my gaze away from her to take in some deep breaths so that I wouldn't feel tempted to throw her scrapbooking in her face. *You're fine. You're fine.*

"So are you going to ask me anything?" Annie crossed her arms. "You know, I've got lots of work to do preparing to bury my dead father."

"Yes, I'll get right to it." I swiped at an angry tear from under my sunglasses.

"Are you crying?" Annie laughed. "How pathetic."

"No, I told you my eyes are extra sensitive, which means they can water up. Kind of like migraine symptoms."

"What a shame." She made a dramatic pout. "Maybe you should take more medicine for that."

My stomach squeezed again. She was alluding to oxies, which meant she knew I was on them. "Yes," I said with a tight smile, "maybe I should."

I switched on the phone's recorder and flipped to my interview questions. "Luis Mendoza died around midnight on Memorial Day," I began. "Do you know what you were doing at that time?"

Annie inhaled a sip of air and spoke with easy recall, as if she'd rehearsed her answer. "I was with a Yummy Foods executive, who was visiting our drive-ins to determine whether they'd be interested in purchasing Uncle Charlie's."

"How long were you together?"

"I showed him a good time like I do all our clients. You know, wining and dining, that sort of thing. We had dinner in the evening and were at a bar until early the next morning."

I picked up my pen. "What's the name of this executive?"

"A name?" Annie stiffened in her chair. "I'd prefer you not bother Yummy Foods when they've already been gracious enough to accommodate my father's death by extending the new contract deadline to us. If you contact them, they might suspect something is actually going on and renege on their offer."

"But something might actually be going on."

Annie lurched forward at me. "*Might* isn't strong enough to ruin this deal."

"Then let's hope it's not true for your sake." I gave her another closed-lip smile. "I just want to be sure that no one working at Uncle Charlie's was involved in an innocent man's death."

"How altruistic of you, but want to know what I think you're up to?" Annie squinted at me. "I think you're fabricating some bullshit story about this dead low-life cook to prevent us from selling, because you're envious of our wealth that you didn't get to cash in on. But I'm absolutely confident you won't find anything by Saturday, or by any other time, because Luis died from an overdose. Never even heard of the guy until he was already dead, and good riddance."

Annie closed her eyes, covered one nostril, and inhaled and exhaled through the open one before covering up the other nostril and repeating the process. She did this ten times before she opened her eyes and exhaled through her mouth. "Nodi Shadhanam," she chanted. "Alternate nostril breathing to recenter my chakras. You may continue."

"Very well. Why do you want to sell Uncle Charlie's to Yummy Foods?"

"Simple. Beyond the obvious capital gain, there's an opportunity for significant career growth and advancement. If Uncle Charlie's goes nationwide, Yummy Foods said I could keep my job for five years with unlimited funds, meaning I can market exactly how I'd like. It's also headquartered in Manhattan, so I'd get the hell out of this Midwestern shithole that you'll be stuck in for the rest of your life. However long that is."

I bit down on my tongue before I could use it. Like at Uncle Charlie's party and the will reading, she was provoking me to explode. After all, she knew how angry I was over what had happened to me, and she also knew that oxies could make me even angrier. I'd told her all about it in my unanswered letters.

To calm down, I grabbed a Topo Chico from my bag and snapped the cap off with my thumb ring. "What are the reasons for your siblings wanting to sell or not?" I said, before taking an especially bubbly first sip that burned my esophagus.

"Teddy wants to sell because he's a lazy drunk who hates work," Annie said. "My little sister refuses because she's the pitmaster of one of the most important barbecue restaurants in the world, and without it, she's nothing. As for Chuck, he's too much of a coward to sell because Marigold doesn't want that."

"Why doesn't Marigold want to sell?"

"Have you met that pig?" Annie laughed. "She's a militant vegan in HETA, trying to stop the evil spread of meat consumption."

I recalled what Teddy had said about Chuck and Marigold's relationship, that she was bossing Chuck around. "Do you think Marigold's using Chuck?" I asked.

"Oh God, one hundred percent. But Chuck's never had a girlfriend in his life until now, and worships the ground she stomps on. She's up to something, though, with the way she seems to be casting a spell on him. Believe me, the minute we sell is the minute she dumps his Mickey Mouse ass."

"Do you know why he's so into Mickey?"

"Oh Mickey, you're so fine, you're so fine, you blow my mind, hey Mickey," Annie sung. "No, I don't know and I don't care. Chuck's always been a weirdo. I'm sure you remember him talking to his stuffed animals as a kid. Probably because he didn't have real friends."

"Or maybe it was because his family's been mean to him his whole life," I suggested. Annie made no response to this as I looked down at my next question, and my stomach fluttered with excitement. I was about to make her mad now. "And how are you planning to sell when you're in a stalemate with your siblings?"

Fear flashed in her eyes before she snapped at me, "First, I always get my way. Second, what does that matter to your murder investigation?"

"Your father died right after alleging he signed this Yummy Foods contract," I pointed out. "It could be relevant to my case."

"How is my father's death relevant to your case? He died of an allergy. Natural causes. Luis died a month earlier."

"I'm only collecting data."

"Well, here's some data for you. There's no alleging about it. My dad signed that contract, and someone stole it."

"Who?"

Annie violently swished her hair. "Emma probably burned it on her grill for the symbolism, because Chuck wouldn't have had the nerve unless Marigold gave him the order."

I nodded at her suggestion and checked my notebook for the next question. "What was your relationship with your dad like?"

"He was a grouchy grump. Rarely saw him, especially when he took over the drive-in, or should I say, saved the drive-in. You know, no one would have been able to run it after Uncle Billy died, so it's good my dad stepped up."

"Yeah, I couldn't agree with you more," I lied. "So Uncle Charlie was a neglectful parent?"

"Of course, but you know, I'm grateful. He taught us success. Too bad you didn't learn that yourself. Maybe then you wouldn't be a sad PI who has to sniffle behind her sunglasses. And to think I used to be jealous of you—"

A baby's cry erupted from a wall speaker, cutting Annie off. It was good, too, because my pulse was racing. Groaning, Annie muted the speaker with her phone.

"You have a baby?" I said, surprised she hadn't mentioned it at the party.

"Yeah, guess I wasn't the only one keeping secrets." She lowered her voice to a whisper, "Not to sound heartless, but Zahira was an accident. I only kept her so my marriage wouldn't fall apart." She said this like she was gloating.

"Do you need to check on her?"

"No, my husband's upstairs. Do you have any more questions for me that concern the death of this nobody I never knew and don't care about?"

"So you never saw Luis even once?"

"Nope, but I hardly go to the Uncle Charlie's in Leawood." Annie stood up. "Okay, time for you to go. I need to call the funeral director back. He wants to know about the flower arrangements and what clothes to bury Dad in."

"All right." I got up and the blood rushed to my head. For once, I was eager to get back into the heat. "Thanks for your time."

"Teddy didn't give me much of a choice, did he?"

As Annie escorted me back to the foyer, I looked up at her surveillance camera and remembered her offer yesterday. "Weren't you going to send me the surveillance footage from Uncle Charlie's?"

"Right, I'll do that now." She grabbed her phone and hit a few buttons. Seconds later, my phone buzzed with a new message. "Who are you talking to next?"

"Your sister."

"Good, send her my best." She went over to a table, opened a drawer, and withdrew a Gucci shoe box. "Also, this is for you." She handed it to me. "Merry Christmas."

"It's not a bomb, is it?"

"Not a real one," Annie laughed. "But with how emotionally fragile and strung out you are, I recommend finding that out in private." She opened the front door. "Also understand this was my first and last interview, and after my father's funeral, I'll never see you again."

"What a shame," I said with a smile. "I was really looking forward to getting lunch and pedicures together in New York while hearing all about your exciting life."

Annie's eyes widened. "Get out."

With the shoe box under my arm, I shuffled outside, and the front door slammed behind me. It was when I got back to the car, though, that Annie finally succeeded in provoking my rage. Soon as I lifted the shoe box lid, I threw up right into the box of ashes.

Chapter Nineteen

T HE HIGHWAY WAS A HAZE of cooked prairie grass. My head felt like there was an angry pianist inside, banging on the keys. More tears wanted to come, but I yanked my brow ring and swallowed two more pills instead. *Don't you cry.* Annie had already wrung a drop out of me and made me regurgitate last night's ribs. "*Pathetic,*" like she'd said.

Beside me was the shoe box of the twenty-something empty envelopes, the same ones I'd addressed to her years ago, now lying in a deathbed of vomit, ashes, and chunks of paper with handwritten words, my words, the burnt ends of my heart. These were my unanswered letters telling her how miserable I was and how much I missed her. She'd burned them all. I never hated her so much. The Uncle Charlie's billboard smiled down at me from the highway. This time, I took the exit ramp for Leawood. I wanted another look at the crime scene. Though the smell of barbecue made me queasy as usual, I pulled into the drive-in, parked in the front, and flashed my headlights for service. The same lanky and fidgety curb server who hassled me on Sunday galloped out to the car to take my order of an UltraCharBurger and a large chocolate milkshake. Then he sprinted back for the Hub.

As I waited for the burger I knew I'd hardly touch, if at all, the pills continued dissolving my emotions over the burnt letters and my interaction with Annie. Meaning I was more or less becoming comfortably numb again.

I glanced around at the other meat-eaters in their cars. To my right, a large man in a station wagon was devouring an UltraCharBurger. To my left, an elderly lady in a minivan was tearing into ribs like she hadn't eaten in a month. This was why everyone loved the drive-in—even if you were having the worst day of your life, you could nurse your misery in the comfort of your own car with a pile of junk food for company. Whoever said the American Dream was dead had never been to Uncle Charlie's.

I opened the surveillance footage that Annie had sent and entered Memorial Day into the search field. There was no sound, but the video stream of the kitchen was in color.

At 5 p.m., Luis materialized for his evening shift, wearing the standard uniform of a black cap, black pants, and a black Uncle Charlie's polo. As there were no pictures of Luis online, not even for his obituary, I hadn't seen him in the flesh until now.

It wasn't that I got chills seeing a dead man cooking, but it was eerie to observe him go about a normal workday when he only had a few hours of breath left. I also wasn't expecting him to be short and bony after Walt had made him out to be a physical menace. The way Luis bounced around the kitchen suggested he wasn't nervous, not like he was being threatened by a drug lord. In fact, he couldn't stop grinning to himself.

I counted nine other employees in the kitchen, cooking or running orders. No one seemed to have tension with Luis. No secret glares or whispering. No one taking frequent trips to the bathroom. When Walt popped into the kitchen to check over everyone's shoulder like a teacher during an exam, I increased the video speed, watching Luis rapidly spritz brisket, stir sauce, and trim fat.

An hour before close, six employees were gone. An hour later, the restaurant closed at 11 p.m., and the other employees cleared out. This was when Walt, his hands shaking, approached Luis, probably to tell him he was going home early. With how much Walt was shaking, he really did look sick. Maybe he had the flu like he'd claimed. Or maybe he was sick with nerves because he knew what was in store for Luis.

The curb server knocked on my window, jolting me back into the reality of the food I was about to force down my throat.

"Tori?" He held up a greasy white bag like it was a dead goose. I rolled down the window and grabbed the burger and shake. "Want a tray?"

"No, thanks," I said. "There paper towels in the bag?"

"You bet. Want a bib?"

I shook my head. Though I had no appetite, I could always have some sugar to go with my oxies. I slurped the shake, gulp after gulp, until it was gone. Then I grabbed the two-pound burger, took out the cross-shaped toothpick, and ripped back the foil to a holy burnt end poking its head out at me, delicately draped in melted provolone and sauce.

Now I gagged. *Just try it.* With my teeth, I grabbed the meat, chewed a morsel, and swallowed. I didn't think I'd get sick from one bite, but I didn't want another. I wrapped the burger back up in the foil and shoved the rest of it into the glove box to get it out of my sight.

I returned to the surveillance footage to find out what happened after Walt abandoned Luis. The next forty minutes showed Luis texting and cleaning counters. Then he turned toward the back door like there was a knock he was expecting. He smiled, and put the cleaner back in the cabinet. After that, darkness. This was when the video feed got cut. It was 11:47 p.m. This had to be when the murderer showed up.

I didn't understand how the cops could dismiss Luis's death as an accident after seeing this footage. He wasn't up to anything unusual. Maybe they'd argued that the video was shut off because he was about to shoot heroin and didn't want the act caught on tape. But even if that was true, he couldn't have switched off a video feed while putting away a bottle of cleaner. Not to mention, only my family had the authority to shut the surveillance system down. Most likely, the cops had gotten lazy, because without direct video footage or track marks, there was no clear evidence of murder. It was easy enough to call Luis a junkie and write off his death as another overdose.

But far as I was concerned, this footage was evidence that Luis had been killed by someone who he expected would give him pleasure. Maybe he thought he was getting more money than what was already stashed in his car. Maybe he was excited for a woman who wasn't his wife. Or maybe he was waiting for a drug shipment before getting taken out by the supplier. Whatever the reason, one thing was certain—someone in my family had human blood on their hands.

Looking up from my phone, I saw the man of the hour, Walt, scurry out of the Hub to light a cigarette by the dumpsters. I grabbed my binoculars. No twitching hands this time. I started the car and drove over to him.

"Good afternoon, Walt," I said, as I got out of the car to toss the shoe box of vomit into the dumpster behind him. "Remember me? Tori Swenson? Can I ask you some more questions about Luis Mendoza?"

Walt's mouth opened in fear, before his cigarette dropped to the ground. "Sorry, gotta run back in," he gasped. "Lunchtime's real busy."

"I'm sure it is," I replied. Though I was talking to myself since he was already halfway back to the drive-in, his hands shaking more than tree branches in a twister.

Chapter Twenty

I WAS BLOATED OFF MY one bite of burger and the large chocolate shake, but at least I had something in my stomach. Stopping for barbecue had also been informative, as I knew without a doubt that Walt was hiding something. I'd chat with the liar later. For now, I had to get to my next interview with Emma.

On the surface, it was my youngest cousin who'd changed the most since we were kids. Not only had she ditched her makeup and dresses for T-shirts and jeans, but she'd stopped being Annie's biggest fangirl. It seemed inevitable, though, since Annie was always bullying her and never letting her hang out with us. Emma had turned bitter about it. As to her role at Uncle Charlie's, she was the pitmaster, the grand overseer of the barbecue pit.

The Plaza wasn't popular on weekday afternoons, so I found a parking spot right outside Emma's luxury apartment, The Bellhop. I leaned back to admire the historic building, its bricks red like barbecue sauce, and counted up its ten floors. On the rooftop was a pool, known for its wild parties so packed with bodies you couldn't move an inch without spilling your cocktail. Not exactly my scene.

I hit the buzzer. "Yes?" my cousin's voice purred from the intercom.

"It's Tori," I said.

"Great. Come on up to P1."

The penthouse, of course. The elevator took me to the top and opened to a sunny corridor with a mosaic floor. I walked toward a wall mirror, where my sleep-deprived eyes stared back at me, then stopped at a cactus sitting atop a cabinet and reached out to touch a needle. There was no pain because of the oxies, but the prick drew a dot of blood. The plant was real.

"Teeny Tori," Emma called out from her open door, where she was wearing her usual jeans and black T-shirt outfit. Meanwhile, a black Pomeranian rushed out to bark at me.

"So you say," I said, not thrilled by this nickname. As I entered Emma's apartment, the chirping fluffball tried jumping up on me. "Who's this little acrobat?" I tapped the dog's head to push him down.

"That's Hickory, sweet as his name. Did you know Pomeranians are circus dogs?"

"I could see him doing well there." I followed Emma and her clown dog into a bright living room, decorated with hickory wood furniture, oriental rugs, and at least fifty plants. "Aunt Kat would love your conservatory," I said, admiring the wiry tendrils of a fern wrapped around Emma's golden grill trophies.

Emma laughed. "Now don't get too suspicious, but I do call my apartment 'my little home of horrors.'"

"Yeah, that's not suspicious at all. Where are you stacking bodies?"

"The freezer. Want to see?"

"Not right now, but thanks." I approached the bay window with its enviable, panoramic shot of Brush Creek where the cascading brick apartment buildings, hotels, and gondolas made you feel like you were in a fairy tale. "That's quite a view," I said.

Emma rubbed Hickory's eager, panting head. "Yes, but my siblings don't think I have a life, because I'm single and live in an apartment. Truth is, they're the ones without lives in their huge boring houses isolated from civilization. In the Plaza, I'm part of the human comedy. I wouldn't have it any other way."

I scanned Emma's large country kitchen, with its red pots and pans hanging from the ceiling. She was well-stocked, but something was missing.

"How do you live without a barbecue cooker?" I asked.

"I don't. There's one in our building's courtyard. Bought it myself so I'd have the exact one I wanted, not some cheap knockoff. I'll invite you to my next barbecue party, but I have to warn you: they can get pretty rowdy."

"You don't have to convince me to come. I'd eat your barbecue any time."

"If you're hungry now, I have some brisket in the fridge I could heat up," she offered.

I patted my stomach. "No thanks, just tried the UltraCharBurger."

"Lots of meat for Teeny Tori."

Emma led me into a sunlit alcove overlooking the impeccable Brush Creek view, and we sat down at a wicker table. When Hickory jumped on her lap to pant at me like I was the one being interviewed, I got out my notebook and turned on my phone's recorder.

"All right, the first question's standard," I began. "Do you remember where you were the night of Memorial Day, the night Luis Mendoza died?"

"Yeah, I was at Uncle Charlie's at the West Bottoms location, because we'd been closed all day for the Memorial Day party. There was no one but me to prepare for the next workday, so I pulled an all-nighter."

"What were you preparing?"

"Barbecuing, mostly," she said. "It takes a long time to do a brisket, at least eight hours, but I was doing multiple briskets, pork butts, and chicken thighs."

"So you never slept?"

"I have a blow-up mattress in my office for naps."

"Can I verify your alibi with the surveillance footage?"

"Sure. There's a camera in the kitchen."

I pulled up the surveillance for the West Bottoms location and entered the time and date in the search field. True to her claim, Emma was in Uncle Charlie's cooking like a madwoman, but a half hour before midnight, she disappeared into her office. She didn't come out until a quarter past midnight.

"You were missing for forty-five minutes," I said, without mentioning her absence happened to overlap with Luis's time of death.

"Must have been napping," she said, stroking Hickory's panting head. "Go ahead and check other nights. Forty-five minutes is my standard nap time. I always set a timer."

"Why don't you have a camera in the office?"

Emma raised a brow. "Dad wanted the offices private for his business meetings. Is that a problem?"

"Not necessarily."

"Do you think I actually killed someone?" she snapped at me.

"Did you?"

"Excuse me?"

"Listen, I'm a detective. I'm just asking standard questions."

"What about standard logistics?" Now Emma was shouting. "That Leawood drive takes at least twenty minutes each way, right? To manage such a stunt, I'd have to literally jump out of my office window and speed both ways without traffic lights or getting pulled over."

"That's true." I nodded so she wouldn't kick me out of her penthouse, but I was also considering her suggestion, which though difficult, was still possible. "Did you know Luis?"

Emma shook her head. "No, I work in the West Bottoms. He worked in Leawood. Maybe I saw him when I was there for meat checks, but I wouldn't have known him by name. I don't know any employees by name. Honestly, I'm more interested in meat than people."

"Are you the only one of your siblings who regularly goes to the drive-ins?"

"No, we all have our reasons. Chuck does the finance and stops by to ask questions about expenses. Teddy orders meat and deals with the suppliers and ranchers. Annie runs the marketing and advertising side of things. But you've got the surveillance footage. See for yourself who's been coming and going."

I moved on with my next question. "How well do you know Walt?"

"I know him okay," she said. "He's been at Leawood since it opened five years ago. There was a scandal last year when an employee accused him of sexual harassment. It couldn't be proved, but I think he's still depressed about it."

"Do you think he could be involved in selling drugs at Uncle Charlie's?"

"What? No, of course not."

"What about anyone else there?"

"No way," Emma sneered like I'd called her burnt ends dry. "I mean, I wouldn't be surprised if some curb servers smoke pot, but I've never caught anyone doing or selling drugs. Dad always had a Machiavellian policy that anyone caught doing anything illegal should be fired on the spot."

"And what do you think happened to the Yummy Foods contract?"

Emma rolled her eyes. "Ugh, that stupid thing. Personally, I don't think Dad signed it. He valued quality and took pride in getting the best meat from the best ranches. He hated factory-farming, not for ethical reasons, but because the meat's inferior. He never cut corners. That's why I refuse to believe he'd have thrown away his legacy over money he didn't need."

"Right, his legacy," I muttered under my breath. "And what do you think of Annie's claim that the contract was stolen?"

"Obviously, she thinks I stole it, but that's a lie." As Emma let out a hard sigh, Hickory jumped off her lap and started barking at me even louder than before. Emma raised her voice over the noise, "But there's nothing to steal because as I said, Dad never signed."

I also raised my voice over the barking, "What about Yummy Foods' offer to buy Uncle Charlie's from you all?"

"What about it? It takes a majority vote to pass, and there's not going to be a majority."

"So you don't think Chuck could change his mind?"

The color in Emma's face drained.

"No way. I spoke to him this morning. He maintained his commitment to vetoing the offer."

Hickory was still barking at me like I was an intruder, and I gestured at him. "Do you think you could make him stop?"

"Hicky-Poo, can we please quiet it down?" she cooed. But instead of shutting up, the little yapper only yapped louder. "Sorry," she said with a shrug, "sometimes he doesn't listen to me."

"Maybe he needs a sedative." I turned back to my notebook to remember what I was talking about before my head started hurting from the noise. "What about Teddy? Why do you think he wants to sell?"

"A drunk, failure, and drifter, nostalgic for his frat days," Emma said. "Everyone knows he's a philanderer. I think he even got an Uncle Charlie's Angel pregnant. Plus, he's got unresolved daddy issues and wants to remove any reminder of Dad from his life."

"Daddy issues?"

"Oh yeah, Dad might have been more emotionally abusive to Chuck, but he put the most pressure on Teddy to succeed. He expected Teddy would run Uncle Charlie's, but whenever Dad felt Teddy wasn't up to snuff, which was often enough, he'd express his disappointment to everyone."

"Sounds like he enjoyed humiliating him," I said. "What about Annie? Why does she want to sell?"

"Because she's a cold bitch," Emma stated this like a well-known fact. "She's a performer and will do whatever it takes to get ahead in her career and make more money. Her values are for show, her family is for show, her face is for show. She's an empty, sad shell of a person. Surely, you can see that. You were close with her once."

"That was a while ago."

"You missed her, though, didn't you?" Emma smiled as she drummed her fingers on the table, adding to the cacophony of Hickory's persistent barking. "I mean, that was why you sent her all those letters, right?"

I cleared my throat, but before I could open my mouth to speak over all the noise, Hickory began making the worst high-pitched yelps I'd ever heard a dog make.

"Hickory," Emma shouted as the little dog flew to the front door. "Hick-or-y."

"Is someone here?" I asked.

"No, he's probably barking at a ghost. I've got to buzz visitors in, but let me check." Emma got up and went to the door.

The next moment, she shrieked. I dug out my stun gun from my bag and sprinted. At the door, Emma was wincing over an open box. Inside was the severed head of a piglet, surrounded by its other bloody organs and half-wrapped in butcher paper like a bouquet of flowers. With its eyes closed and mouth open, the pig looked asleep.

I sucked the air through my clenched teeth and rushed into the hallway—no one was there.

"Oh my God, oh my God," Emma panted and paced while Hickory mirrored her hysteria by barking harder and dancing on his hind legs. "Should I call the police?"

I closed the box. "Doesn't matter now," I said, as I didn't want to get the cops involved in my case. "Whoever it was is gone." I inspected the soggy box that was missing an address. "Do you usually get packages delivered to your door?"

"No," Emma shouted over Hickory. "They're dropped off in the foyer. That must be why Hickory was barking earlier. He was trying to tell us someone was out in the hall."

"Does your building have video surveillance?"

"We should," Emma huffed with irritation. "But the camera at the front door went missing last night. I filed a complaint with management, and you can bet I'll be complaining to them about this right away."

"How convenient," I said. "Any idea who might have dropped this off?"

"Of course not." Emma scooped up Hickory, and he finally shut up to lick her face. "I mean, Annie and Teddy want me to sign that contract, but would they really do something messy like this? Neither of them likes getting their hands dirty."

"Did you tell anyone I'd be here at this time?"

"I only told Chuck when I spoke to him this morning, but I can't imagine he'd do something like this either. He's so timid about everything."

"Right," I said, realizing that hardly eliminated any suspects, since I'd told Annie I was going to Emma's next, and she could have just as easily told Teddy. I picked up the box. "Mind if I take this with me?"

"Please. I want that thing far away from me." Emma cradled Hickory, peppering his head with kisses. "Do you think whoever did it might come back?"

"Sure, it's possible. Got any weapons?"

"Only knives. Should I get a gun?"

"Not if you don't know how to use it. Fortunately, you've got a strong police presence in the Plaza and an effective alarm system." I gestured to Hickory, panting in Emma's arms.

"That's right," Emma's voice softened into baby speak as she talked to her dog. "You wouldn't let anyone hurt your mama, would you Hicky-Poo?"

Outside Emma's building was a stub where a camera should have been. When I got back to the car, I squatted to examine its underbelly. No tracker. The box went into the trunk. I didn't need it stinking up the car and making me angrier.

This threat wasn't meant for Emma—it was meant for me. Someone was trying to scare me off my case. Though it didn't seem possible for Gabe to know I was here, or that he'd have been so enraged over the milkshake incident that he'd slaughter a piglet, I dialed him to be sure.

"Good afternoon, Tori—to what do I owe this pleasure?" Gabe's voice was constrained. "Looking to meet up for an ice cream social? How about I'll buy this time, and you can be the sticky one?"

"This is serious—"

"And dumping a milkshake in my car isn't? Do you know how long it took me to clean that up? Some of those stains will never come out."

I tried to stay calm, but him yelling at me wasn't making that easy. "In case you forgot, I got angry with you for screwing with my case."

"Oh, sounds like someone's still angry."

"Listen, I'm not calling to chitchat. I need to know whether this feud between us has got out of hand."

"What are you talking about?"

I sucked in a deep breath, then said, "Are you responsible for the piglet head that was delivered to my cousin's doorstep five minutes ago?"

"Are you serious?" Gabe gasped. "Tori, it sounds like you have some poor judgment right now. You know, that's what happens when you mix work and fam—"

I hung up. Covering one nostril, I tried Annie's yoga breathing technique, and it did seem to lower my heart rate until my phone dinged. A text from Gabe, sharing his GPS coordinates. He was at Rocky's in Westport, far enough to give him an alibi. I couldn't say I was relieved. I didn't think he'd done it anyway. He was an asshole, not a maniac.

Chapter Twenty-One

S A KID, CHUCK WAS a ghost. He hardly came to our parties and playdates, and if he did show up, he only talked to his stuffed animals. I knew my uncle had treated him poorly, but growing up I'd never witnessed their interactions because Chuck was pretty much inside all the time.

Now I was thinking my uncle had been especially cruel to my cousin behind closed doors. Like Emma had said, Uncle Charlie was more emotionally abusive to Chuck. That also explained why my cousin was so anxious and sensitive, especially when in the presence of my uncle at the Fourth of July party.

And after seeing how upset Chuck was at the will reading yesterday, I anticipated that my questions would be hard on him. I wasn't too pleased he thought so, as well, because he'd requested Marigold sit beside him for "emotional support." I'd done my research on her, all right, and found that she was no sweet flower. A few months ago, she'd been arrested for vandalizing butcher shops with gasoline.

I turned into historical Hyde Park with its modest 19th-century mansions, and it wasn't hard spotting Chuck's place. I pulled up at the brightly colored Mickey Mouse mailbox and parked outside the gray house. When I walked up the red and yellow front steps, I stopped short of his porch.

Holy Mickey. Maybe this was what Annie had meant when she'd said that every day was a Mickey Mouse day for Chuck. Before my eyes was a Mickey couch, a Mickey clock, a Mickey wreath, and a Mickey doormat. Secured to the house was a bronze plaque from the KC Historical Society proclaiming that *Walt Disney Lived Here.* I rang the Mickey doorbell and "When You Wish Upon a Star" chimed inside.

Marigold whisked the door open wearing a shiny, pink polka-dot dress, black bow, black heels, and furry mouse ears. Her whiskered nose was as black as her tail. In her gloved hands, she was mixing up one of Chuck's ice cream mouse-tails. The vanilla ice cream was faintly yellow.

"Hi Tori," she said, like it was normal she was dressed as Minnie Mouse.

"Nice costume," I said.

"Don't say that around Chuck," she warned in a whisper. "His grief's so bad over his father's death he needs me to be Minnie twenty-four seven."

I wasn't sure what she meant by this, but I thought it better not to ask. Marigold showed me to a living room, or "The Clubhouse" as she called it, with pink couches, children's books, and display cases holding more Disney memorabilia than a vintage museum. There was so much to marvel at—a rotary phone, wristwatches, Pez dispensers, guitars, an Elmer Fudd rifle, lunchboxes, a piggy bank—but we continued the amusement park ride into a Goofy-themed yellow kitchen where everything from the table to the napkin holders bore Goofy's grin. On the kitchen counter was a plastic pill crusher containing a bright yellow powdery substance, the same hue as Chuck's mouse-tails. Marigold had to be putting this stuff in his drinks.

"What's that?" I asked, pointing to the container of powder.

"Oh," said Marigold, raising her drawn-on eyebrows in surprise. "Just a special healing powder." I moved toward it, but I couldn't smell anything since it was contained. "This way."

Marigold pushed open a screen door. I followed her into a weedy, overgrown backyard toward a patio set up like Geppetto's workshop. At a clunky wooden table, Pinocchio smiled down at me from his highchair.

"Have a seat," Marigold ordered. "I'll get Chuck." She went back inside.

I sat beside Pinocchio and took in my surroundings. There was a princess-themed kiddy pool, a Donald Duck swing, and a red treehouse with cartoon characters waving from its windows, but with the uncut grass and pool sludge, I felt more like I was at Wasteland than Disneyland.

Just then, Chuck stumbled through the door, eyes puffy and red and wearing a black T-shirt, bright red shorts, red suspenders, white gloves, and mouse ears. In his hand was his yellow-tinted mouse-tail concoction with Oreo ears on a whipped cream cloud. He dragged his feet to the table, stinking of booze and body odor. Marigold rushed to sit beside him, squeezing his arm with her white-gloved hand. As Chuck's eyes welled up with fresh tears, he sipped his frosted drink from a plastic Mickey Mouse straw.

"Again, I'm sorry for your loss," I said.

"Thank you," he murmured, and wiped his wet eyes on his gloved hand. "It's been so hard . . . I'm sorry if I cry during our interview."

"That's fine, I get it."

"I'm sorry—" He stopped to sniffle. "I know your dad died too."

"It's okay." I looked into Chuck's moist, hazy eyes to see if he was only pretending to win me over with his sympathies, but he seemed sincere.

"Why am I so upset, though?" Chuck choked with more emotion. "My father treated the pigs at the slaughterhouse better than me. Why is it so hard to get over a monster?"

"It's okay, honey," Marigold said before whispering something into Chuck's ear that made him twitch.

"I'll make this interview as brief as I can." I turned on my phone's recorder and pulled out my notebook. "Where were you on the night of Memorial Day, the day Luis was found dead at Uncle Charlie's in Leawood?"

Soon as Chuck's trembling lips parted, his face scrunched up, and he flung himself on the table to sob.

"We were here," Marigold answered, rubbing his back. "After his dad's Memorial Day party, we came home and had a quiet night in, watching a movie."

"*The Lion King*," Chuck wailed.

"Yes, that was it."

I nodded, noting the movie's symbolism. "Do you have a surveillance camera to verify you were here?"

"There's a system." Marigold pointed to a camera over the patio. "But it only stores data for the past thirty days."

"That's too bad," I said. "Chuck, didn't you say you'd get me a copy of the restaurant's finances?"

"Yes, it's on my desk in the Mickey folder," he muffled into his sleeve.

"I'll get it. Have more of your drink, Chuck." Marigold sprung up from her chair, clicking her heels into the house to fetch the folder.

Seeing that this was possibly my only chance to question my cousin without his answers being monitored, I decided to try a new approach. "Hey Mickey," I began in a soft voice, "how's Minnie treating you?"

"Minnie?" he said into his arm, but his voice wasn't Chuck's. This was the same strange voice I'd heard Chuck make when he rushed out of the drive-in to watch Uncle Charlie die. This voice was high-pitched, soft, and upbeat like a cartoon character. Then his head sprung up like a cat's, his tears gone, his smile wide.

I swallowed. *Holy Mickey.* Now I understood why every day was a Mickey Mouse day for Chuck—he *was* Mickey Mouse. The only other guy I'd met with multiple personalities was in rehab, and he'd said that he didn't always remember what his other personalities said or did. Whether or not Chuck was aware of himself as Mickey, he was definitely not pretending. I didn't know for sure, but my hunch was Marigold was giving him that special healing powder to alter his personality and control him.

"Why, Minnie's my nurse," Chuck exclaimed in that high voice. "She takes great care of me." He let out a shrill cartoon laugh that made me sit back in my chair.

Though I found this Mickey persona creepy, I didn't know what else to do but smile back at my cousin like I would a child. "I'm glad she's treating you well," I forced myself to say, though I really wanted to confront

Marigold for what she was doing to my cousin. "Does she want you to sell Uncle Charlie's?"

"Oh no." He shook his head. "Minnie doesn't want another horrible meat chain. She says they're the devil's work, and that we must do all we can to protect the animals and environment."

"What do you think she'd do if you sold Uncle Charlie's to Yummy Foods?"

"Me? Oh, I'd never do that." Chuck was still smiling, but his eyes stared out of their sockets without emotion.

"Right, let me rephrase that," I said. "What would she do if Chuck sold?"

"That wouldn't be good for him," he giggled. "She'd be very angry and punish him."

"What would she do?"

"I don't know." Chuck snapped his suspenders. "Set the kitchen on fire again?"

"Right," I said, reflecting on her recent arrest. *Guess Marigold likes burning shit.*

"But Chuck won't change his mind," my cousin continued as Mickey. "Whenever he's weak and tempted to be a bad boy, Minnie shakes her finger at him and gives him more medicine. Then he's good as a golden raisin."

Just as I'd thought. "So she's drugging you to turn you into Mickey?" I pointed at his mouse-tail.

"Drugs are so much fun. It makes boring Chuck go away so Mickey Mouse can come out and play."

"What's she giving you?" I asked. "What's the yellow powder?" But before he could answer my question, Marigold opened the screen door, and my neck flushed in heat. I needed to snap him out of being Mickey, though I wasn't sure how.

"Chuck," I said in a demanding tone under my breath. "Chuck, Marigold's coming back."

Maybe it was being called by his name, or maybe it was the threat of Marigold's return, but Chuck slumped back into his limp arms like a dropped puppet. Apparently, he could move from Chuck to Mickey, probably by being addressed as such, and I was certain that the drugs he was on were playing a role in his hypnosis.

"Here you go." Marigold handed me a Mickey Mouse folder and returned to her spot beside Chuck to rub his back and play ventriloquist. "Are you okay, sweetie?" she murmured into his ear. "Here Chuck, drink more."

"I'm better now that you're back," he whimpered in his sad Chuck voice.

As he reached for his tainted drink, I feigned a fake violent sneeze and elbowed his mouse-tail off the table, breaking the glass and splattering ice cream on the patio. "Excuse me," I said, sniffling. "Sorry about the mess."

Marigold groaned with annoyance. "It's okay," she said, squeezing Chuck's shoulder. "We'll just have to make you another one, Chuckie."

I flipped open the Mickey Mouse folder. Inside were calculations on how much my cousins had withdrawn from the company account each month. In May, the month Luis died, the numbers showed that everyone but Chuck had taken out thousands more than in previous months. Emma had taken an extra twelve thousand, Annie ten, and Teddy a whopping one hundred and sixteen thousand. In June, Teddy even withdrew another one hundred and two thousand. *Nothing suspicious here.*

I closed the folder and glanced across the table at Chuck, now humming a lullaby. "Chuck," I said, "is it unusual your siblings withdrew so much money recently, or is there a reason for that?"

"No," he sniveled. "It's odd. But when I showed that report to Father, he didn't care. He told me I was—" Chuck's face stiffened before he cried, "A bad accountant."

Watching him break down in tears like this made me feel terrible, especially after knowing he was being drugged by his girlfriend. Maybe my cousin was a killer, or maybe it was Mickey, but I couldn't help myself. I got up, and, to Marigold's horror, gave Chuck a firm hug. For a moment, he hung in my arms, crying. Then I released him and returned to my seat.

He sniffled. "Thanks, Tori."

"You still okay to answer some more questions?" I asked.

"Yes, sorry."

"No problem. Did Uncle Charlie often dismiss large sums of money being deducted from the company account?"

"That's what was strange." Chuck blew his runny nose on his gloves. "He was always afraid people were stealing from him. His own house has more cameras than windows, and he got very angry when money disappeared from the register at the Leawood location."

"He thought Luis was the thief, right?" I said, recalling the ten thousand dollars hidden in the Mendoza car.

"Yeah, that's what he claimed, but he never had any proof. Nothing was ever caught on tape. Then I showed him proof his own kids were taking thousands from the company account, and what did he do? He got angry and called me terrible names."

"Is it possible he asked them to do something and didn't tell you about it?"

"Of course. It was no secret my father hated me. I wouldn't be surprised if he had a plan with them and kept me out of it."

"Why do you think he treated you differently from your siblings?"

"Look at me," he said. "I'm scrawny and sick. That's what he'd say before locking me in my tower when I was little. He never hit me, but he wanted me out of his sight because he was ashamed of me. I never cried about it, though, just played with my stuffed animals."

My mouth sharpened into corners of rage. So that was why Chuck had only talked to his stuffed animals as a kid. My uncle was verbally abusing and physically neglecting his son. I was so livid with my uncle that I'd have killed him myself if he wasn't already dead.

"Was Mickey in the tower with you?" I asked.

Chuck nodded. "Yes, he was my best friend. I was locked up there with him every day for years, like Sleeping Beauty, but awake." Tears ran down his cheeks, and he wiped them again with his glove, sniffling. "Sorry for all the crying, but since Dad died, all the tears I kept inside are coming out whenever I think of him. I couldn't cry before this, you know."

"It's okay to cry, sweetie." Marigold stroked his arm. "Remember you're my little mouse, and I'll always love you."

Since I was upsetting Chuck by talking about his father, I returned to the jaw-dropping financial statements. "Do you know why your siblings withdrew so much money?"

"I don't know for sure, and I never asked them about it," he said. "But I think it has to do with the Yummy Foods deal, since it was finally in the works at the time."

My eyebrow ticked up. "What do you mean 'finally'? Didn't Yummy Foods make an offer this month? These withdrawals are from May, over a month ago."

"The offer came at the end of June, but the discussion was on the table for well over a year because Yummy Foods wasn't sure which KC barbecue joint they wanted to buy. This past May, though, an executive from Yummy Foods visited a few places, and Uncle Charlie's won the bid."

This executive had to be the same person Annie was wining and dining into the early morning hours, on the night Luis died. Another possible suspect. "Do you know the name of this executive?" I asked.

"I don't remember," Chuck said. "He had a foreign last name."

"Okay, I'll try to find out." I looked at my notebook for my next question. "Speaking of Yummy Foods, why don't you want to sell?"

Chuck turned to Marigold for permission to speak. She nodded her consent, and he answered like he was a monotone recording, "It's not morally right. It would be a franchise that sells cheap, unethically produced meat. In fact, now that my father's gone, I'm thinking about shutting down Uncle Charlie's."

I sat still, stunned by this news. Chuck was now trying to do what I'd always wanted to do and shut down Uncle Charlie's. Except that this wasn't his idea. It belonged to Marigold, who was gazing into his eyes and smiling with approval.

"You have a good soul and care about the welfare of the animals, air, and planet," she said, and planted a kiss on his black nose.

"But I wouldn't have become a better man without you," he replied.

I cleared my throat to remind them I was still there. "What about your siblings?" I said. "Why do they want to sell or not sell?"

"Teddy and Annie want money," Chuck said. "And Emma's passionate about barbecue."

"Can I give my opinion?" Marigold interrupted, and, not waiting for my response, began, "Teddy's a self-entitled jerk, Annie's a greedy capitalist, and Emma's morals are as deep as that pool of slime." Marigold pointed to the kiddy pool of green sludge. "Just think of all the meat she's cooked. She feeds people the suffering of animals for a living. People like her don't deserve to breathe."

Chuck winced. "Don't talk like that about my family. They have their faults, but—"

"Why not?" Marigold smacked the table. "Don't defend them. When have they ever treated you with respect? And here you are, upset about your father when he was the worst of them all. You should be celebrating that he's dead."

First came the shakes, then Chuck dropped his head into his arms to howl out a hurricane of snot, drool, and tears.

"We must stop," Marigold declared, rising to her feet. "Chuck's too upset to answer any more questions."

"Maybe you should give him more medicine?" I raised an eyebrow at Marigold as I slid the Mickey Mouse folder into my bag.

Through clenched teeth, she hissed at Chuck before narrowing her eyes on me so tight I couldn't see them. "Allow me to show you the way out."

I followed her lead back into the house. When I looked at the kitchen counter, the pill crusher with the yellow powder was gone.

Chapter Twenty-Two

MY INTERVIEWS WERE OVER, BUT I didn't know which of my cousins, if any, had killed Luis. After all, it was possible that Uncle Charlie had killed him, not my cousins. I headed over to my jazz haven, the Green Lady Lounge, to decompress. A couple of regulars were smoking outside, and I gave them a nod.

"How's it going, Tori?" said Jerome.

"Trying not to die," I said.

Jerome laughed. I reached for the door, only to have it thrown back in my face. "Sorry baby," slurred a drunk man stumbling out.

Eric, the head waiter, jumped out after him. "Take a walk, buddy," he shouted. "Come back when you're not tanked."

I looked at the man swaying down the pavement. For his own sake, it was good he was too drunk to recognize me. Like I'd thought, Zak was lying about being sober. Guess he'd forgotten I was a jazz freak, and that KC was a village.

Eric held the door open for me. "Thanks," I said, and entered the dark room, where each tiny table was illuminated by a single candle's flame.

I stowed myself in the corner, my favorite seat in the house since I could take it all in without feeling like someone was going to sneak up on me. Per the Green Lady's code, all the musicians and waiters were dressed in formal attire. When Eric came around in his white gloves, he set a chilled glass of San Pellegrino on the coaster in front of me. He squinted at me over the candle's flame.

"Haven't seen you here for a few days," he said. "You doing okay?"

"Yeah," I said, and dropped the lemon wedge in the glass. "Was moving into my aunt's."

Eric left, and I threw back the double dose I'd earned. I'd lost count on how many pills I'd had today, but I figured I could take another when I got home and still be around my self-prescribed limits. In any case, I was nowhere near what I used to take. I'd even say I was doing a pretty good job limiting myself as much as I was.

The stage lights then fell on JJ's Big Band, the regular Wednesday night group. I'd played with them a few times before, and watching them tune up made me nostalgic for the stage. Too bad I couldn't play for a proper audience, though, when I was on oxies. If I played now, I'd only embarrass myself, since the drug slowed down my sense of rhythm.

The band kicked off with a swing number, something I hadn't heard before. I liked it enough and tapped my foot to the drumbeat while thinking about Annie and my burnt-up letters. To think she'd saved them all this time. Maybe they'd symbolized some victory over me, but I was still planning on beating her with my case. Once I found Luis's killer, there'd be no New York, New York, for her.

Eric was ready with another San Pellegrino soon as I emptied my first glass. I dropped the lemon in the second, swirled it around, and took a power gulp. The pills were kicking in hard as my body and mind dissolved into the music. Being this high wasn't the best state for thinking seriously about my investigation, but then again, it helped me momentarily escape myself. My chest expanding with euphoria, I let myself fall back in my chair and melt into the music.

Chapter Twenty-Three

HOURS LATER, WHEN I WAS sober enough to drive, I crawled back to Aunt Kat's where the neighborhood kids were setting off firecrackers for the fourth night in a row. This time, the noise didn't bother me—I was too out of it to care.

I opened the trunk, and the gust of death blew back in my face. Gagging on the odor, I grabbed the bloody box with the piglet head. For now I'd have to store it in the basement freezer so it wouldn't stink up the house. With the box under my arm, I swayed up the driveway, and had to do a double-take at what was on the doorstep—an unmarked box, like the one I was holding. I spun around. Another firecracker went off. Other than the kids, I didn't see anyone in a tree, on a roof, or on a balcony pointing a rifle between my eyes. I set the piglet head on the porch and walked across the street.

"Hey," I shouted at the kids. "You see anyone come here tonight?"

Their faces were fearful, like I was accusing them, and they shook their heads. I returned to the porch to grab a broom and knock the mystery box onto the lawn. Since it didn't explode, I pulled the flaps back when the familiar sour stench stung the back of my throat. I bit my hand so I wouldn't scream. Unlike the first piglet head, this one had a note card jammed into its limp mouth, and I yanked out the blood-stained paper. In glittery sticker letters it read, *Stop or your aunt's next.*

This sent me beelining into the house where the TV was blasting. "Aunt Kat!" I screamed. I rushed into the kitchen and bumped into her at the counter, sending her knife out of her hand and onto the floor.

"Tori," she exclaimed. "Why are you sneaking up on me like that? I could have stabbed us in the feet." She bent over to retrieve the knife.

"Sorry," I said. "I was worried."

"Why? What's got you so wound up?"

I went to the fridge, cracked open a fresh Topo Chico on my thumb, and got to chugging away my temper. After finishing the bottle, I let out an unapologetic burp and swiped a slice of pork butt off the cutting board. "You see anyone come to the house?" I said, and stuffed the meat into my mouth. As I reached for another slice, Aunt Kat slapped my hand away.

"Slow down," she said.

I swallowed the meat. "Sorry, it's been a long day, and I'm really stressed out. So can you please answer my question. Did you see anybody come here?"

"No, but I've either been crying in bed or cooking to distract myself. Why? Was someone here?"

"There was a package on the porch with a bloody piglet's head and a note card." I held up the card.

"Holy shit." Swearing was something Aunt Kat never did.

"Yeah, and this is the second piglet head of the day. One came to Emma's door during our interview." I opened the fridge for another Topo Chico.

"Tori, you know I'm not worried about myself. But for your sake, stop this investigation."

I paced around the kitchen, feeling rage in my veins. I had to get it out. As I let out a piercing scream, I cracked my bottle against the wall, spraying glass and water everywhere.

"Dear God." Aunt Kat blinked at me fearfully.

"Sorry, I'm angry."

"I can see that. Just sit down for a second and breathe."

Kicking aside a piece of glass, I grabbed another Topo Chico, snapped it open with my thumb and took a seat at the kitchen table. My hand trembled as I took a pull of water. My aunt watched me in silence, like she didn't know whether to let me be or have me hauled off to the psych ward. When my phone rang, I pulled it out to check. An unknown number. I answered it.

"Hello?" I said.

"Uhh, is this Tori?" a man's voice drawled.

"Yeah, who's this?"

"It's Victor. You called yesterday about Luis?"

Victor Green, Luis's former co-worker. I took another gulp of water. "Sure did," I said with forced enthusiasm. "Thanks for calling me back. Do you have any info on Luis you want to share?"

"Yeah, his death was no accident. I only worked with the guy for a few months, but I know a druggie when I see one, and he wasn't the type to shoot heroin. He wouldn't even drink more than three beers at the bar. All he talked about was pooling together enough money to support his family. Someone murdered him and made it look like an accident. No question in my mind about that."

"Who do you think killed him?" I asked.

"Wish I could tell you, but I've got no idea. He was well-liked. Never saw no fights or nothing."

"Do you think Luis was aware of something illegal going on at Uncle Charlie's?"

"Maybe, but I never saw anything out of the ordinary except for Walt, the manager. He was acting real strange too. Even fired me over some bogus claim on the day Luis got whacked."

"What did he fire you for?" I said, remembering that Walt had allegedly fired Victor for not showing up to work.

"Some bullshit reason about the health code," Victor said. "But if you ask me, Walt didn't want me at Uncle Charlie's for a reason. When he came by my place to drop off my things, he was mumbling, had red eyes, and stunk of body odor and booze. Seemed to me like he was struggling over something big."

"He said he had the flu."

"The flu? Nah, like I said, I know a druggie when I see one. Trust me, Walt was loaded."

Soon as I'd got off the phone with Victor, I pulled up the surveillance footage from Uncle Charlie's in Leawood. Walt claimed he'd seen Luis with a suspicious box the night before Memorial Day, but as I sped through the footage, I saw no box and no Luis. He wasn't even working. Conveniently, the footage for that night had also been deleted after close.

I shot out of my chair and turned to the clock. It was 10:28 p.m., thirty-two minutes until Uncle Charlie's closed.

"What's going on now?" Aunt Kat said.

"I'm going to Uncle Charlie's in Leawood."

"What? Why?"

"The manager is hiding something about my case. I'm going to confront him about it."

"You're doing what?" She stared at me.

"I'm going to make him confess what he knows."

"But what about this threat on our doorstep? There's some nutjob out there decapitating piglets. What else are they gonna do if you don't stop?"

"Exactly why I've got to go," I said. "They can threaten me all day long, but they went too far threatening you." I opened the fridge and grabbed three more Topo Chicos for the road.

"It's not me I'm worried about," Aunt Kat said.

"And it's not me I'm worried about." I picked up her bag and handed it to her. "So get yourself together fast, because I'm dropping you off at a hotel on the way to Uncle Charlie's."

"A hotel?" she recoiled. "I don't think so."

"You've got a bad back, your hearing sucks, and you're high all day. If someone comes here while I'm gone, you're dead."

"Absolutely not. I'm not getting chased out of my home."

"Fine," I said. "Then you're coming with me."

Chapter Twenty-Four

AUNT KAT GOT IN THE car. "You should report those piglet heads to the police and let them take it from here."

I shook my head. "Not an option."

"Why not?"

"The cops already dismissed Luis's death as an accident. You think they'll do anything about these piglet heads either?"

Aunt Kat stewed in silence the rest of the ride, which was good since I didn't feel like talking. Plus, I needed to focus on the road so I didn't get us into an accident. When we safely arrived at Uncle Charlie's, I parked across the street in the shadows of the trees.

"I don't like this place," Aunt Kat said, pulling out her silver cigarette case. "It's clinical, like a hospital. Doesn't have the same grungy charm as the gas station."

"Can't argue with you there." I raised my binoculars and scanned the parking lot. Walt's gray Honda was in the back. As a jeep of inebriated teens sped off—the last car of customers—a curb server switched off the *Open* sign.

"They're closed now," I announced. "But I got to wait for all the employees to clear out before going inside."

"How do you know this manager won't leave with the employees?" Aunt Kat asked a reasonable question.

I also had a reasonable answer. "Because he said there are two closers on weekends and holidays. Since it's a weekday, he should be the only one there tonight."

Aunt Kat lit her joint and took a drag like she was in a rush to get somewhere. "And what if he has a weapon?" Her smoke unraveled out the window.

"Doubt that," I said. "This guy's way too nervous to be pulling any stunts. I also checked today's surveillance of Uncle Charlie's before we left. He's been in there all day. Even if he had the nerve to drop off those piglet heads, there's no way he did it." I adjusted my binoculars on the drive-in, watching employees scatter to their cars like fruit flies on a wine glass. Meanwhile, Walt closed the office blinds. Only his car was in the lot now.

"He's alone." I grabbed my bag. "And he's about to have a panic attack when he sees me again. Can't say I won't enjoy watching him sweat out his lies."

Aunt Kat sighed. "As long as he doesn't do something crazy once he realizes he's been cornered."

"Don't worry. Remember, I have this if I need it." I pulled out my stun gun from my backpack. "He tries anything, he'll be on the ground for at least fifteen minutes and—"

I stopped talking as a pair of headlights barreled down the road for us.

"Get down," I whispered, pushing my aunt by the shoulders so we were out of sight by the time the truck passed. I heard tires squeal on a hard turn. Then I lifted my head and peeked through the window. A red pickup truck had pulled into Uncle Charlie's.

"Jeez, now what?" Aunt Kat whispered from the ground.

"Someone's at the drive-in. Stay down." I focused my binoculars on the truck, now at the loading dock. The driver opened the door. When I saw who it was, my jaw tensed up.

Aunt Kat poked me in the leg. "What's going on?"

"Looks like they're getting a shipment," I said, as my eyes focused on Squishy. When Walt hurried out to greet him, I could tell they weren't strangers. Squishy opened the truck, grabbed a box, and hauled it into Uncle Charlie's. Then he returned to his vehicle and grabbed another box.

Aunt Kat lit her joint again. "Drugs?"

"Don't know." My phone's camera was a poor substitute for the digital one Squishy yanked off my neck, but I could still zoom in on his license plate and snap a picture.

One after another, I watched Squishy run in with boxes until he'd emptied himself of eight and was back in the truck, slamming the door, his headlights on. He was coming toward us again. I ducked down beside Aunt Kat and we heard him whir by.

"Okay," I said, getting back up. "I'm going in."

Aunt Kat got back in her seat. "But what if that man in the truck comes back?"

"Here." I ripped out a piece of paper from my notebook, jotted down Darnell's number, and handed it to Aunt Kat. "If I'm not back in thirty, call Darnell."

"Please be careful, Tori."

I got out of the car and dashed across the street to creep behind the drive-in. Easy enough at night with no one around, but a camera was perched over the back door. There was no getting around that. I only hoped Walt wasn't watching.

With my elbow, I knocked on the door, and in the deepest voice I could muster, shouted, "Hey Walt! Got another box for you."

Seconds later, the lock twisted and the door opened. "Oh," Walt squealed when he saw me. Without his sunglasses, his eyes were bloodshot and framed with dark panda circles. "Sorry," he said, his voice trembling as much as his hands. "I wasn't expecting you. Is there something you need? It's Tori, right?"

"Yes, actually," I said. "I need to talk to you." To Walt's horror, I pushed the door back and let myself in.

"Sure." He stumbled back. "What about?"

"How about why you lied to me?"

There was no argument from Walt. He threw a pan on the floor and fled down the hall. He was fast when panicked, but I managed to reach the office door before he could close it on me. When I stepped inside, Walt cowered behind a desk covered in white powder. At the sight of the stuff I hated most in the world, I took out my hoodie from my backpack and threw it over the heroin. I didn't need to see that shit.

"Why are you shooting up in here?" I shouted at him.

"I . . ." Walt peeked his eyes over the desk.

"Don't lie to me. I know it's not flour you're weighing."

Walt's fearful pout relaxed into a resigned grin as if relieved to be caught. Then he got up and plunked down in his desk chair. "I was about to," he said.

"I thought that might be why you were wearing sunglasses indoors. You better start talking before I call the cops." I switched on my phone's recorder.

"Doesn't matter now." Walt gave a shrug. "You've already seen what you've seen. I'm toast."

"If you got nothing to lose, you might as well come clean and tell me what you know." I turned on my phone's recorder and looked Walt square in the eye. "Did you kill Luis?"

"Kill Luis?" He pulled a face. "Do I look like a killer to you?"

"Anyone could be a killer."

"Well, I'm not a killer, and I don't know who is. But if you want to know the truth, I was being blackmailed."

"Okay," I said, feeling like I was getting somewhere. I'd seen enough junkies lie to know when they were telling the truth, and Walt wasn't lying. "Who was blackmailing you?"

"Never found that out, but the day before Luis died, my locker stash was missing, and there was a note card in its place," Walt began. "Said if I didn't fire Victor and leave work early the next day, I'd be reported to the cops for drugs. I was scared I'd lose my job and go to jail, so I followed the instructions. The next morning, I found Luis dead in the cooker. I felt so guilty, too, because whoever killed Luis used my supply to do it. After that, I couldn't do nothing but shoot up at home for weeks."

I thought of the note card in the second piglet's mouth. "Was this note card handwritten?"

"No," Walt said. "The whole thing was spelled out in glittery stickers."

"I see." This meant Walt's blackmailer was the same person who'd delivered those piglet heads. I continued with my questions. "And only Uncle Charlie or one of my cousins could have opened your locker, right? Or does someone else have keys?"

Walt's head moved like a dashboard bobblehead. "Yeah, there's no other way," he sighed. "Sorry, but someone in your family's involved in a murder."

"It would seem so. Did you check the surveillance footage for the day you got the blackmail note?"

"Yeah, but it was deleted. No question Luis was set up."

"Then you never found drugs in his locker?"

"No, I only made that up because I didn't want you catching me for drugs."

"Okay, so you were the one stealing from the register?"

"Yeah," Walt sighed again. "I got Charlie thinking it was Luis after the poor guy died. I had to stop stealing after that. Wasn't sure what I'd do once my stash ran out. I can hardly afford it, managing a drive-in, but since I'm going to jail now, I guess it won't be a problem anymore."

"It's a good thing you got caught so you can straighten yourself out." This sounded hypocritical coming out of my mouth, considering how many pills I'd taken the last few days, but Walt didn't need to know that. "There are plenty of places to help you get clean."

"Hey, like Mark Twain said, quitting's the easy part," he laughed. "I've done it a thousand times before."

"You can commit to quitting again. Believe me, I stopped."

"You?" Walt rolled his red eyes over my body. "I don't see any track marks on you."

"Not heroin, opioids. See my scar?" I tugged at my brow ring. "Got it in an opioid-related car accident and had this thing put in because the hair won't grow back."

"Good for you, but I've already been in and out of rehab. As you can see, it hasn't worked out too well. Started shooting up again when that lady charged me with sexual harassment. It was a complete lie, I swear, but it gave me a hard time. The only way to escape my misery was through my old faithful girl."

"I know it's easy to slip up, but it's never too late to quit for good." I said this like I was reassuring him, but I was really reassuring myself.

"No, no," Walt murmured. "Everyone relapses in the end. Just takes one time. Of course you lie to yourself. You say nobody will know. Just one time. But then you're back to being a junkie, begging for a baggie. Unless you're one of those superhuman exceptions, I guarantee the same thing will happen to you. I'd venture to guess it already has."

A lump rose in the back of my throat.

I didn't know if he actually saw through me or not, but I didn't want to talk about drugs anymore. "Do you know why someone wanted Luis dead?"

Walt shook his head. "No clue. He must have been involved in something, though, because everyone liked him."

"What about my cousins? You ever see any of them with Luis?"

"I don't know. Whenever they're here, they're in and out. Except Teddy sometimes comes into this office to snort coke." Walt tapped the heroin-covered desk. "Right here."

"Sounds like Teddy. What about that huge man who was here a minute ago?"

"Harrison? Oh, he's a meat supplier. Sometimes we get night deliveries."

"What's in the boxes?"

"Meat," Walt said like I'd asked a stupid question. "Go ahead and check the freezer for yourself, if you don't believe me."

"Great idea, but you're showing me."

I followed Walt down the hall to the kitchen where my nose caught the scent of burnt ends, glistening on a tray under electric light.

"Over here!" Walt called out as he opened the freezer door.

I stepped inside, goosebumps erupting all over my body. I couldn't say the cold felt bad, though, especially when I had the oxy sweats and it was one hundred degrees outside. "This it?" I pointed to a stack of blue boxes.

"Yeah, have a look inside if you'd like." Walt stepped out of the cooler. "I'll be out here. It's too cold for me."

I snatched the box cutter from the freezer wall and slashed open a box. Inside were huge logs of vacuum-sealed brisket. I opened another box. More brisket. But just because there was meat in these boxes didn't mean there wasn't something else smuggled in the meat or in other boxes. I opened a third box, then a fourth, before I realized Walt wasn't standing outside the cooler anymore.

"Walt?" I shouted as I ran back to the office, but the door was already closed and locked. *You idiot.* "Walt," I shouted and banged on the door. "Let me in or I'm breaking this thing down."

I pressed my ear to the door and heard nothing. I wasn't going to try to break down a steel door, so I ran back into the kitchen, grabbed a skillet, and went outside to find Walt's office.

I stopped at a lit room with the blinds drawn and cranked my arm back to swing the skillet at the window. There was a knife crack in my ears and glass shattered everywhere. I cleared the window of the shards the best I could, then threw myself through the blinds. My legs got scratched and were bleeding, but the oxies muted the pain.

"Damn you, Walt," I groaned from the floor.

As I pushed myself up, I saw my hoodie on the floor and looked up at the desk. Walt was slumped forward, foam pooling from his bluish lips. When I saw the used syringe beside him, a memory flashed, clear as when it first happened—my dad, dead in his den, with a note saying, "Sorry." Now I couldn't move. I was sinking into the floor. I needed to escape. I reached for my bag and swallowed more pills.

I didn't know how long I'd been out when I felt a hand on my shoulder. "Tori," Darnell's voice floated into my ear.

I kept my eyes closed. My eyelids were too heavy. I was ready to sleep forever. "He's dead," I moaned. "It's my fault."

"Hush, hush," Darnell said, pulling me up and slinging me over his shoulder. "You're all right." He rubbed my back. "You did nothing wrong. Let's get you home."

Chapter Twenty-Five

ANNIE HANDED ME A LETTER. Uncle Charlie coughed up blood. Teddy kissed a nurse. Walt squeezed his fingers. Mickey Mouse laughed. A black Pomeranian barked. Dad was dead on his desk. White powder. Burnt ends.

I opened my eyes. Outside an ice cream truck was playing "Yankee Doodle Dandy," a hammer to my skull. I clamped my hands over my ears. When the truck had passed, I yanked the blinds shut with a clack. Another stab in my ears.

"Ugh," I groaned, while Rebus yawned and stretched at my feet. I was a prisoner of my body until I could get more pills.

"You're up," Darnell said from across the room. He was sitting at my desk. "How are you feeling?"

"Got a migraine." The words came out of me garbled. It even hurt hearing myself speak.

"Not surprised. You had one hell of a night."

I rubbed my legs together, the friction stinging. *That's right.* I'd climbed through the window at Uncle Charlie's and cut myself.

"Why are you here?" I asked him.

"Couldn't leave you alone," Darnell said. "Thought you might hurt yourself thinking you were to blame."

"Blame for what?" Then the memory flashed at me. After I'd climbed through the window and cut myself, I'd found Walt. "Oh my God," I shrieked. "I killed Walt."

Darnell got up and came over to me at my bedside. "No, you didn't. He overdosed by himself."

"No." I shook my head despite my head throbbing. "I was stupid. I let him out of my sight. I shouldn't have—"

"Stop. You know you're not to blame for what a person does to himself. Not to mention there are more important things to focus on." From his pocket, Darnell pulled out my orange pill bottle. A silent shriek escaped me now. My throat was closing up. *He's got your pills.* Darnell shook the bottle as if to torture me. "How long has this been going on?"

"I . . ." I fought to clear my throat. "A day."

He raised his eyebrows in doubt. "Oh yeah?"

"Okay, since Saturday," I confessed. "That's why I got kicked out of Victory House."

Darnell rubbed the bridge of his nose, trying to keep himself together. "What triggered your relapse this time?"

"You know that stakeout at Rocky's? My cousin Annie filed that case with my agency, and it triggered me bad. I'm sorry, I know I'm a failure and a huge disappointment."

"Okay," he said in a calm voice. "I'm not going to get mad or criticize you. We just need to get you back in rehab right away."

That word was another hammer stroke to my head, and I cringed into my pillow. "Does Aunt Kat know?"

"Not yet. I didn't want to worry that poor woman any more than she already was last night. She was high and hysterical and said something about a piglet head on your doorstep. I figured you could pick a better time to tell her about your situation."

"Good," I said, relieved. "Yeah, she doesn't need to know about this now." I tried sitting up, but my head throbbed, and I slid back down to the pillow. "Dammit," I moaned, rubbing my temples. *You need a pill.*

"You're all right," Darnell said, squeezing my shoulder. "Just get some rest. No more working your case."

"No, I can't rest. I found out Walt was being blackmailed by Luis's killer. That's the same person who dropped off that piglet head here." As I looked at my orange bottle still in Darnell's hands, I trembled, my breath coming out in short wisps like hiccups. "Plus . . . you know there's no negotiating with a crazy person. How can I be sure they won't hurt Aunt Kat if I stop my case? I mean, I didn't listen to their warning last night."

"I understand what you're saying," Darnell said in a more serious voice. "I can stay over the next few nights and give you some police protection."

"That won't matter. You'll leave at some point. The killer won't."

"Listen, beyond the fact you're incapacitated and would have overdosed, possibly to death, if I hadn't given you Narcan last night, you wouldn't be able to work this case even if you could move."

I ignored what he said about the Narcan. "Why can't I work?"

"Because after what happened last night, your cousin must have pulled some political connections fast because you got a restraining order against you now. You get near an Uncle Charlie's even for some brisket, you'll get yourself arrested."

My breath caught in my throat. "Which cousin?" I asked, though I already knew who it was.

"Annie, is it?"

The migraine sledgehammer stuck again. I squeezed my eyes hard. Annie had blocked me from the drive-in, but she wasn't stopping me from working. I just needed my pills to function.

"I'm not quitting," I declared.

"Oh yeah?" Darnell said, looming overhead so that I could see myself reflected in the whites of his angry eyes. "And how the hell are you doing anything when you can't get out of bed?"

"Please," I said in a pathetic tone, "give me back my pills." I held out my shaking hand.

Darnell stepped back and jammed the bottle into his pocket. "No."

"Please," I moaned, tears rising to my eyes. "I need them to keep working. I swear I'll stop using after this case, I swear."

"Tori, you're trying to negotiate, but it won't work on me. I'm not handing them back to you."

"If you don't, I swear I'll kill myself soon as you leave," I said angrily as I wiped my tears. "Because if I go back to rehab, there will be no one here to protect Aunt Kat. At least if I'm dead, the killer won't hurt her."

Darnell's eyes searched mine to see if I was lying. I wasn't. I was ready to dive out the window before going to rehab. Darnell's nostrils ballooned with fury when he saw I was serious. Then he stuck his hand in his pocket and threw the orange pill bottle at me.

"Fine," he said, "go ahead and kill yourself your way." He grabbed his gun off the desk and buckled it into his holster. "But don't expect me to come running next time you're in trouble." As he stormed out of my room and down the stairs, I knew I'd gone too far. This time he wasn't bluffing.

My hands were still shaking, but I was able to pop off the bottle's cap and throw down three pills at once. Then I lay there, waiting for the pain and guilt over Walt and Darnell to evaporate. *But you did what you had to do.* I couldn't stop this case.

Now it wasn't about getting revenge on Uncle Charlie or Annie—I had to protect Aunt Kat.

Some minutes later, my aches were mostly gone. With a lot of straining, I got my heavy body out of bed and into my desk chair. It didn't matter my mind was fogged up. The killer could come any moment. I got out my phone, found the picture of Squishy's license plate that I'd taken last night, and called up the DMV. After accepting my PI credentials, the clerk told me that the car belonged to Harrison Alan Morris.

I ran a background search on the man and, sure enough, there was a criminal resumé requiring several pages of scrolling. Harrison, or who I'd been calling "Squishy," was thirty-seven, and had been in and out of jail for selling drugs, possession, and assault. He lived in Westport across Southwest Trafficway, practically making him Aunt Kat's neighbor. Though I didn't want to call Gabe and hear him gloat, I needed to know what he knew about Squishy. His phone, however, went straight to voicemail. Maybe he'd blocked me.

"Hey, please give me a call back," I said in my message. "Looks like our cases might overlap. I want to swap notes."

Though Annie had blocked me from going to Uncle Charlie's, she'd forgotten to stop giving me access to the surveillance system. I opened the footage for the Leawood location and dialed the clock back to a week before Luis died. There had to be a clue in there leading up to his death.

I fast-forwarded through the minutes, narrowing my eyes on sprinting curb servers and cooks while Walt thumped around and Luis stirred sauce. When I got to Saturday afternoon, two days before Memorial Day, I jolted in my chair.

Here was a clue—my cousin and Luis, together. I played the video at normal speed and watched as Teddy, who'd claimed to have never met Luis, took Luis into the office. Three minutes later, Luis strutted out with the same grin he'd been wearing when his killer arrived.

There was a knock at the door. "Tori?" Aunt Kat's voice called out.

I inhaled sharply, my chest thumping with anxiety. *Just keep it together.* I slammed my laptop shut.

The door opened to my weary-faced aunt carrying a frosted Topo Chico and a blueberry chocolate chip pancake big as a vinyl record, complete with a syrup smile, butter dollop eyes, and melted chocolate chip pupils. Next to the pancake were crispy bacon strips.

Aunt Kat set the water and plate on my desk. "Darnell said you were up." She gave me a soft smile. "Thought you'd want some breakfast."

"Thanks," I said, though I wasn't hungry one bit. Plus, I knew if I took one bite of that bacon, it would come right back up. "Why are you so good to me?"

"Don't be ridiculous. How are you feeling?"

"Woke up with a killer headache." I sipped the chilled water. "But I took some meds and feel better now."

"Glad to hear that." Aunt Kat brought out a piece of paper from her robe pocket. "But after what happened yesterday, I was thinking you might want to talk to a doctor. I found a few—"

"Why would I need a doctor?" I cut her off.

"I mean a therapist. You know, someone you could talk to about what happened last night."

"I'm fine," I said. "At least, fine enough for causing someone's suicide."

"Tori, I won't listen to that nonsense." Her red eyes were beading up with tears. "I was so sick with worry last night I don't think I slept more than twenty minutes."

"Sorry, but I'm still more worried about you staying in this house alone."

Aunt Kat swallowed. "That doesn't matter now that you're off the case."

"Who said that?"

"How can you keep it? You couldn't even walk last night after finding that man dead."

I told her what I'd told Darnell. "I'm not stopping."

Aunt Kat crossed her arms. She hardly ever got mad with me, but this was looking like one of those exceptional moments. "Well, I'm not leaving my home to sit in that hot car again, especially in the daytime, or I swear I'll die sooner of a heat stroke than by some piggy killer."

I took an aggressive gulp of water. I had to convince her to ride with me, or I wouldn't be able to leave the house and continue my investigation. "But it's not safe here," I said. "Either you stay somewhere else like a hotel, or you join me on my excursions."

"Tori, I said—"

"Let me put it another way. There's a killer out there looking to kill again, specifically us, and if you're in here by yourself, I guarantee you're good as dead if they come. So if you care about me, which I know you do, you'll realize that if you die, I'll die, because I might as well be dead with your death on my conscience."

Aunt Kat let out a sigh of defeat and headed downstairs to get ready for our trip to the hardware store. I was relieved, at least temporarily, but

I'd feel better once I'd set up security equipment in the house. A gun might have also been a good idea, if I wasn't loaded on oxies.

I tossed my pancake and bacon out the window to the birds so Aunt Kat's feelings wouldn't be hurt that I hadn't eaten her breakfast, then got myself dressed.

As I was burying my pill bottle in my bag under the stun gun and handcuffs, my phone rang. I reached for it, expecting Gabe, but it was someone calling from Uncle Charlie's mansion.

I answered it. "Hello?"

"Hey there Tori," said a friendly southern voice. "It's Jean."

Jean, my uncle's pseudo-widow who was now acting like she hadn't accused me of poisoning him with an allergy. "Hi Jean," I responded in a professional tone. "What can I do for you?"

"Oh my God, I heard what happened at Uncle Charlie's last night and that you were there. How awful."

"Right." I let the pause stretch to show her I wasn't reciprocating her buddy-buddy spirit.

"I mean, wow," she went on. "Two bodies in one week. Do you think Walt's death was related to that worker's death?"

"Sorry, I can't discuss my case with you. Is there a reason you're calling?"

"Yes, hon," Jean said softly as if fearing someone was listening. "I've had a change of heart about talking to you, but I'd rather do it in person. Could you come to the house right away? I know what killed Charlie."

Chapter Twenty-Six

J EAN BOWSER, ALSO KNOWN AS Genie Bow-Bow on TV, had a short-lived career as a food model and actress posing with baked goods for *Forks N' Spoons*, slapping a VeggieChop for an infomercial, and playing her claim-to-fame role as an Uncle Charlie's Angel who squirts barbecue sauce on my uncle's face. Though her sudden eagerness to talk to me had set my skepticism meter to high, I was always interested in hearing from another suspect.

"They've already put this fortress up for sale?" Aunt Kat said, fanning herself with her straw hat.

The red sale sign in the front yard reflected the sun into my tired eyes. "Yeah, and they haven't even put Uncle Charlie in the ground yet. Someone must want their money fast."

Before I could ring the buzzer to be let in, the gate opened. Jean was watching for me.

I pulled into the driveway toward the front of the mansion where she stood at the front door, her red hair draped over her sleeveless black dress while her bloated, tear-stained face twisted into itself.

"That's Charlie's girl?" Aunt Kat whispered in surprise. "She looks a little goth for his taste."

"To be fair, she is in mourning and now lives alone in a mansion," I said.

Jean floated over to greet us. "Thanks for coming so fast," she sang in a morose twang. She pointed at Aunt Kat. "Who are you?"

My aunt smiled. "I'm Katherine, Charlie's sister."

"I've heard of you," Jean said. "I'm sorry you guys had a falling out way back when."

"I'm not," Aunt Kat said. "It was his fault."

"She's tagging along with me," I said. "But the AC's broken in the car. Mind if she waits inside while we talk?"

"Not at all." Sniffling into a tissue, Jean led us inside through a gold and marble gallery of animal paintings.

"Holy cow," Aunt Kat exclaimed, stumbling back.

I grabbed her arm, thinking she might be too emotionally fragile to handle Uncle Charlie's house. "You gonna be all right in here?" I asked.

"Tori, these are my paintings."

"Really?"

I turned to look at the smiling donkey beside me, its right-hand corner signed *K. Swenson*. A painting of a dancing barn owl had also been signed by Aunt Kat. As we walked down the hall, I scanned the other thirty or so animal paintings.

Every single one was Aunt Kat's.

"That's strange," I said. "Why does he have so many of your paintings?"

"This is so Charlie," Aunt Kat grunted, shaking her head at a painting of a calf drinking milk from a milk bottle. "He probably got off commissioning me to do these strange paintings under his pseudonym. That's why I haven't heard from Mr. Chester Butterfield about his bagpipe-playing cow painting. It was going to Charlie, and Charlie's too dead to pay for it now."

"Please," Jean said solemnly, pressing a hand to her breasts. "I know Charlie was no angel, but let's not speak ill of the departed."

Leaving Aunt Kat to admire her own work, Jean and I continued through the mansion into a cow-themed atrium. Everything here was black and white, from the dining table with its crystal udders, to the spotted lampposts, to the cow paintings and figurines, cow busts and skulls, and the hanging sculptures of cows jumping over full yellow moons. A camera peered out from a corner.

Like Annie had claimed, Uncle Charlie had been paranoid, but the question was whether he had a reason to be afraid. It wasn't paranoia if someone was actually after you.

"This way," Jean said. She directed me through a pair of sliding barn doors into a pink pig-themed room with more cameras, dancing pig wallpaper, porcelain pig lamps with pigskin lampshades, pig-faced chairs, pig curtains with curly pig tails for tassels, a pig fountain that released bubbles out of its snout, and a massive pig bust over the fireplace with a golden plaque that read *Chester*.

"Is this where Uncle Charlie came when he was feeling disgruntled?" I said.

"He loved farm animals," Jean replied in a quivering voice, ignoring my joke. She dabbed at her eyes with a tissue. "This is the pig room, his sanctuary. Pigs were his favorite farm animal." From under her collar, she pulled out a golden pig necklace. "I'm wearing this in honor of him. Please have a seat." She gestured to an upholstered mustard chair with hoof-shaped armrests. When I sat down, the chair oinked. Jean smiled, tearing up again. "Charlie just loved that chair. It was his special throne and gave him joy whenever a guest used it."

"Good. Here's hoping he's squealing with joy now."

"I think he would be. You're here to figure out what happened to him, aren't you? You want to get him justice, right?"

Two questions. Two answers.

"Yes," I said, though I didn't care too much about getting him justice. "I'm anxious to hear your theory of how Uncle Charlie died. Is it okay if I record you?"

"Of course, but it's not a theory, it's a fact. I know how he died." Her face was as stern as Chester's snout.

I got out my notebook and phone. "You mean," I began, hitting the record button, "you know what he was allergic to?"

"Absolutely. After we found out that he died of an allergy, I thought about the onset of his symptoms. And wouldn't you know? They began on Memorial Day, the same day that young man died at the drive-in. That didn't seem like a coincidence, which is why I had to call you over."

As I sat up straight at this news, the chair oinked. "What happened to Uncle Charlie on Memorial Day?" I asked her next.

"We had a barbecue party at Uncle Charlie's in the West Bottoms," she said. "He was feeling horrible when we got home, so we went to bed early. Didn't even have sex, and Charlie always wanted sex."

"Good to know. Do you have any proof you were home?"

Jean blinked, offended by my question. "You think I'm lying?"

"Hey, I'm an investigator," I reminded her. "I asked my cousins the same thing. It's standard PI procedure."

"Well, I bet none of them have an alibi, but go ahead and check the surveillance. Charlie was so afraid of thieves and killers that he installed fifty-six cameras in here." She pointed to one hovering over us. "Now that his kids can access the stream, they're probably watching me night and day to make sure I don't steal anything. That's why they're so anxious to sell this house. They want to chase me out and throw me on the street."

She got out her phone and opened the home surveillance app. After pressing a few buttons, she presented me with a video feed on an iron door.

"Is that the safe?"

"No, this was our bedroom. See the time and date?" She tapped a black fingernail on the screen where it read 11:08 p.m. on Memorial Day. "That's when we went to bed." She hit play on the video. There wasn't any sound, but I watched as Jean supported my uncle under her arm and led him inside the room.

"Do you have a camera in the bedroom?"

"No, that was the one place in the house where he wanted privacy. He didn't want our lovemaking on tape for some creep to find."

"Can you please fast forward?"

"Sure, hon." Jean increased the speed, and I watched the iron door stay shut until the next morning when my uncle tottered out in flying pig pajamas. There it was.

An ironclad alibi.

Neither Uncle Charlie nor Jean could have killed Luis.

"So what was Uncle Charlie sick with?" I asked.

"This will sound wild," Jean said, stroking her frizzy red hair.

"I'm not really shocked by much these days."

"The day after the party, I found a tick on his foot."

"A tick?" My eyebrows lifted in confusion. "Like the insect?"

"Yes, exactly."

"Is there something special about a tick in Missouri?"

"It wasn't any tick I'd seen before. This one had a white dot on its back." On her phone, Jean showed me a photo of a white-starred pumpkin seed. "It's called the lone star tick," she continued. "Ever heard of it?"

I shook my head. "Can't say entomology's my forte."

"After you brought up that worker's death at the drive-in, and I realized that it had happened on the same day I saw that tick on Charlie, I thought maybe there was something more to it. So I did some research, and now I don't think for a second that Charlie's death was natural."

"Why?"

"Turns out if the lone star tick bites you, its saliva triggers an immune system response that gives people a red meat allergy called 'alpha-gal syndrome.' It's rare this allergy turns fatal, but a few people have died from an allergic reaction. It also takes at least a month for the effects of the bite to be at their strongest, which would have been around the Fourth of July for Charlie. So the meat he was eating at the party was literally killing him."

I tried to keep a straight face, but this theory was insane.

"So you're saying Uncle Charlie died from a tick bite and eating too much meat?"

"Yes, that's what I'm saying."

"All right, you'll need a toxicologist to run the test—"

"The test is done. After my research yesterday, I called up Charlie's lawyer and urged him to get a toxicologist to test for alpha-gal syndrome. I got a call this morning with the results. That's when I called you."

Jean pulled up the toxicology results on her phone. There, in ink, and verified by Doctor G. Quigby, Uncle Charlie's allergy test read positive for alpha-gal syndrome. I reread the document, looking for some sign to indicate that it was fake, but it wasn't.

Now I was in genuine shock. "So Uncle Charlie was taken out by a bug."

Jean leaned forward, her perfumed cleavage in my nose. "Yes, and I want you to find out who's responsible."

I leaned back. "You mean, you want me to get a warrant for the tick?"

"No, I want you to find out who planted the tick on his foot," she exclaimed. "The intentionality of the act would be considered an 'unnatural death' in the eyes of the law."

The pig fountain bubbled while I imagined someone dropping a tick on my uncle's foot. The idea was so silly I couldn't suppress a laugh from squeaking out. "Sorry," I said, glancing back at Jean who wasn't amused. "This is so bizarre."

"I know, but that's really what killed Charlie."

"Okay, okay." I sucked in a long breath as I prepared myself to run with this idea. "Supposing someone did plant a tick on his foot, you still can't prove they did it with an intention to kill. If fatality with this meat allergy is as rare as you say, it's more likely an accident he died."

Jean shook her head. "The lawyer said that if planting the tick was intentional, getting its venom into Charlie would be considered intentional too. Thereby ruling his death a manslaughter by poisoning."

I thought back to the Fourth of July party when Uncle Charlie's eyeballs were blown out with rage while screaming at his kids. "Do my cousins know about this toxicology report?"

Jean shook her head again. "I asked the lawyer not to share the results with them, at least not until after the funeral. Thought it might help you find whoever did it, if they don't know you're on to them. You know, there really is that Slayer Rule in the will stating his children won't inherit a cent if any one of them is responsible for his death. The lawyer understood my concern."

"Yeah, and who's the beneficiary of my uncle's estate after my cousins?" I asked, knowing the answer.

Jean cleared her throat. "Me."

"Wouldn't you then be lucky to be right?" I gave her a smile. "But let me entertain your idea. Supposing this killer tick episode happened in the way you describe, the only way to prove it is with a confession."

"You're a PI, I'm sure you can get that."

"I don't know what you think us PIs do, but we aren't magicians. Smart people, or at least the sort of people that would calculate something like a tick bite, would probably keep that kind of info to themselves. Also, did you ever consider that a tick crawled up Uncle Charlie's leg on its own because he liked walking around barefoot?"

"No, someone did it on purpose," Jean insisted, brow furrowing. "These lone star ticks are only found in wooded areas. Someone had to have brought it from the woods to the city. The motive isn't hard either when any one of his kids could have wanted him dead. Teddy hated Charlie because he knew he'd never measure up to his father. Emma hated Charlie because he was going to sell the drive-in to Yummy Foods. Annie hated Charlie for making her do things she didn't want to do to secure the Yummy Foods deal. And Chuck hated Charlie because Charlie bullied him."

"What did Uncle Charlie make Annie do?"

"I don't know, I just heard her screaming at him once about how she should get more money for her extra work on securing the deal."

"Well, like you said, my uncle was no angel. I mean, did you actually like him?"

"Like?" Jean scoffed at me. "Honey, let me tell you that his kids have been horrible to me since Charlie died, calling me a 'gold-digger,' but unlike them, I loved their father. Why do you think I've been crying like a widow? I was in love with Charlie."

Jean goose-honked into her tissue.

I ignored the drama and tears, too overwrought to be believed. "Okay," I said, "did you see anyone get under the table during this Memorial Day picnic to put a tick on his foot?"

"No, but my guess is that it relates to the Yummy Foods contract. When Charlie was considering the offer, he got so fuming mad with his kids that he said they weren't cut out to inherit his legacy."

I remembered what Chuck said about an executive attending the Memorial Day party. "Uncle Charlie invited a Yummy Foods rep for a tour that weekend, right?"

"Yes, Annie took care of organizing his stay, but it was very tense with that man at the party. Everyone was arguing."

"Who was this guy anyway?"

"I'm glad you brought that up because I was meaning to give you something." From her purse, Jean pulled out a scarlet red folder for Yummy Foods. On the front was a post-it that read, *Nikolai Volkov, Marriott Hotel, Room 1816.*

"Nikolai is the Yummy Foods guy?"

"Yes, and he's back in KC. He returned last week to press Charlie to sign the contract. Said if Charlie didn't do it over the Fourth that Yummy Foods would renege on its offer and buy elsewhere. I thought you might want to talk to him."

"Thanks, I'm sure I would." I slipped the folder into my backpack. "Maybe it was even Mr. Volkov who put the tick on Uncle Charlie's foot, right?"

Jean flushed. "I suppose anyone there could have done it," she conceded, avoiding my eyes. "But I know in my heart it was one of his awful kids."

After Aunt Kat and I were out of the house and back in the heat, my aunt turned to me. "How'd it go?"

I turned around to wave at Jean, watching us from a window. "I'll tell you once we're on the road," I said. Then I dropped to my hands and knees and looked under the car.

"What are you doing?" Aunt Kat said with alarm.

"Just making sure no one's tracking us." I got up and gave her a thumbs up. "Next stop, the Marriott."

Chapter Twenty-Seven

A S I DROVE DOWNTOWN FOR the hotel, I updated Aunt Kat on my interview with Jean. "That's absurd," she said. "A tick?"

"Yeah, a tick," I repeated, still in disbelief myself as I turned into the hotel's parking ramp. "But it was on the toxicology report, and the lone star tick does give meat allergies. What's really hard to believe is that someone planted it on his foot."

"If they did, you know how you figure out who did it?"

"Find the tick and ask him?"

"You just start dropping lone star ticks in your cousins' laps and see who jumps the highest."

"That might work. Only problem is Chuck already jumps high at bugs."

I parked the car. We got out and walked down the ramp, through the hotel's revolving door. Inside the air-conditioned lobby were suitcase-pushers in sweaty suits and day-drinkers at the bar.

"Stay in the lobby," I told my aunt.

"Don't worry, I'll be cooling off over there." She pointed at the bar.

I headed to the elevator and pushed the button for the eighteenth floor. The doors opened to terrible jazz, that smooth, predictable bland garbage everyone liked playing in elevators and clothing stores. I stepped into a mirror box. I couldn't escape my face. *You look like shit.* In fact, I might scare

Nikolai Volkov away with my appearance before he even knew why I was there. The elevator tolled with a gentle bell and opened to a foyer with crimson carpet, faux candles, and a table holding a vase of red plastic carnations. I turned down the hall and counted the rooms until I hit Room 1816, the number on the post-it note.

As I raised my fist to knock, though, a woman screamed from inside the room like she was being gutted. Softly, I pressed my ear to the door. More screams, grunts, moans, and groans. Mr. Volkov must have picked himself up a KC girl on his business trip. This woman was screaming in pleasure, not pain.

I returned to sit in the elevator foyer and wait until Mr. Volkov's friend left. Closing my tired eyes, I watched pre-dream images flash: a lone star tick crawling across a cooker . . . Chester the Pig frolicking in a chocolate milkshake fountain . . . brisket baskets raining down from the sky . . . Rebus twitching his tail on the windowsill . . .

I must have fallen asleep, because the next thing I knew a woman was shouting in my ear. I opened my eyes. Annie was standing in front of me, her red cheeks glazed in sweat, her fake blonde hair twisted in tangles. When she clenched her jaw at me, I shot up out of my seat.

"What are you doing here?" she snapped.

"Working," I said.

"Even after you killed Walt? You know, I could call the cops on you right now for stalking me. That restraining order applies to me as much as Uncle Charlie's."

I advanced a step, my gaze digging into her blue eyes to show her I wasn't intimidated by threats. "I'm not here for you, I'm here for Nikolai Volkov," I said in my calm, professional voice. "Maybe you know him?"

Annie's red face turned redder. "You will not talk to him!" she screamed.

"Watch me." As I moved to pass her, she took a swing at me, palm open. I ducked, and she slapped the fake flowers to the ground. "Don't ruin your manicure," I said. She took another swing. Again, I shifted, and she banged the elevator instead.

"Shit!" she yelped, shaking out her arm and glaring at me like I was to blame for her injury.

I gestured to the surveillance camera above us. "Maybe I should get a restraining order against you? It's not too hard to prove who the aggressor is here."

"Are you going to blackmail me for my affair? You know, it's illegal to record people without their consent."

"Oh, you're having an affair?"

"Fuck you." She spat on my cheek. "You're such a loser addict, like your dad." She smacked the elevator button. "Hope the drugs kill you too."

"Thanks." I wiped off the glob of spit from my cheek. "But they haven't so far."

"And you know what?" Annie shouted louder, so I could smell the dick on her breath. "You're a sick, obsessive bitch with your pathetic letters. I have no regrets ghosting your ass." The elevator tolled, and she hopped on. "Go to hell" were her last words before the doors closed on her flaring nostrils.

Now it was quiet again. I felt invincible. *You won that round.* Even though Annie knew I was on drugs and was trying to create an adverse reaction in me with all her nasty provocations, I'd remained in control. But I couldn't blame her for losing her cool either. Not only was the clock ticking down on her Yummy Foods contract deadline, but I'd just discovered that she was cheating on her husband. Now it was time to march down the hall and meet her mystery lover.

"Nikolai Volkov?" I called out while knocking on his door.

"Who is it?" a sleepy voice said inside.

"Tori Swenson. I'm a private investigator, and Annie's cousin."

The lock unbolted, and a middle-aged, pot-bellied man opened the door wearing nothing but a fluffy white bathrobe. Nikolai squinted at me, puzzled by my presence. "Can I help you?" he asked.

"I think so," I said. "I'm investigating Luis Mendoza's death at Uncle Charlie's."

"You mean that accident with the heroin addict?"

"Yes, I'm investigating whether it really was an accident."

"Okay." His eyes examined me with skepticism. "But what does that have to do with me?"

"I was told you attended my uncle's Memorial Day party hours before Luis was found dead. May I please come in and ask you some questions?"

"I'd rather you not."

I gave him a grin. "Well, I'd rather I not mention your afternoon interlude with my cousin to my other cousins or Annie's husband, but—"

"Fine," Nikolai grunted. "Let me get dressed first."

He showed me into his suite, scented with fresh bodily fluids, and I waited in the living room while he changed. On the table were oyster shells and a pair of empty champagne flutes. Annie, the wining and dining queen.

"All right," Nikolai announced, once he'd tucked his gut into his trousers. He took a seat across from me and crossed his legs. "I've got a busy schedule today, so get to your questions."

"Do you mind if I record you?" I asked.

"Yes," he replied stiffly. "Not because I have anything to hide, but because I'm not going to be recorded without a lawyer present."

"Fine." I put my phone back in my bag, where I secretly switched on the recorder anyway. "Where were you at midnight on Memorial Day?"

"With Annie," Nikolai said. "We had dinner, drinks, and came back to my room."

"Do you have any proof of that?"

"I'm sure there's enough surveillance footage at this hotel to remove me and your cousin as suspects."

"And what exactly is your relationship with my cousin?" To this question, Nikolai stayed tight-lipped. "All right—how long have you been in town this time around?"

"Since July first."

"Then why weren't you at the Fourth of July party?"

Nikolai chuckled. "Oh, I wasn't going to another one of those awful parties after Memorial Day."

"Why? What happened then?"

"In two words, 'family drama.' Everyone was fighting over whether to sell Uncle Charlie's, which made my presence there a bit awkward. That pitmaster woman was especially something else. When she realized why I was there, she began swearing and throwing meat."

"Emma threw meat?"

"Yes, that was her name. She was doing all she could to scare me from the deal, screaming the usual townie rant that Yummy Foods sacrifices quality for money. Not a total lie, but we do rake in big profits. I think she even spoiled our lunch on purpose to scare me away."

"I'm sure that made my uncle mad."

"Oh yes. He was so livid he threatened to disown her. After that, she retreated into the drive-in. Never saw her again, and I hope I never do."

I remembered Emma at the will reading, snapping at Annie over the contract. Her boiling point must have been triggered when her meat got threatened.

"What about my other cousins? What was their behavior like at the party?"

"There was that weird fellow with the Mickey Mouse clothes that got wound up because the charming one—"

"Chuck and Teddy?"

"Yes, Teddy was drunk and insulting Chuck and his girlfriend for being vegans. Then Chuck started laughing in this creepy voice, and threatened Teddy with a steak knife."

"A steak knife?" I heard myself say with even more incredulity than after hearing about Emma throwing meat. Apparently, Nikolai had met Mickey, and apparently, Mickey could be violent.

Nikolai continued the story. "Teddy wrestled the knife away from Chuck and gave him a good punch in the nose. Can't say he didn't have it coming, but I got the impression this was their usual brotherly dynamic because no one else seemed to care except Chuck's girlfriend, who only looked embarrassed for herself. All very strange people."

"And Annie? How was she?"

Nikolai smiled tightly again. "Annie was a great host. She showed me around the city and drive-ins, explaining how everything works, making me feel right at home."

"I'm sure she does a great job." I nodded at the oyster shells. "Did she fight with anyone at the party?"

"With her sister, but as I said, Emma wasn't exactly a sweetheart. Charlie's girlfriend was also annoying everyone with her public displays of affection."

I nodded as I'd witnessed her same excessive fawning at the Fourth of July party. "How long are you in town now?"

"Longer than I'd like trying to get this new contract signed. But I'm leaving on Saturday, no matter what. Two more days of this boring town, and I'm gone."

"Then you don't care if you get Uncle Charlie's?"

"So be it." Nikolai shrugged. "In my line of work, there's always another deal."

Having obtained what I could from Nikolai, I returned to the lobby where Aunt Kat was laughing with the bartender. I wasn't ready to leave quite yet and headed over to the receptionist's desk, where a redheaded woman with a name tag for *Virginia* was too distracted by her phone to notice me.

I struck the desk bell hard.

Virginia flinched. "Oh," she squeaked, "how may I help you?"

I flashed her my badge. "I'm investigating a murder that might tie back to this hotel. Can you please get me access to the surveillance footage?"

Most service workers agreed to help me without realizing they were under no obligation to assist a PI, but Virginia shook her head with a sense of entitlement. "No," she said, "we can only do that for law enforcement." She then returned to her phone, swiveling around in her chair so I now faced a blue butterfly tattoo on her shoulder that I instantly remembered. I'd seen it from the top of Rocky's just a few days ago. Now Squishy stealing my camera and messing up my workers' comp case had become my good fortune, because I had leverage over this girl.

"Ginny Wolf?" I said.

She spun back around, glancing at me with stunned eyes. "Do I know you?"

"No, but I know you enough, and if you don't help me, I'll show your manager photographic evidence from the buffet line at Rocky's last Sunday, which proves that you're lying about your disability. The lump sum you received for your workers' comp claim will then be—"

"Right this way," Ginny said, grabbing her crutches.

I followed her fake limp down a hallway into an empty office, where some thirty active camera feeds ran on multiple screens. Ginny punched in a code at a computer. "You can search the database here. I hope you find what you need."

Ginny left, and I entered Memorial Day into the system and selected the main entrance camera. As I kept my thumb pressed on the fast-forward button, I watched guests come in and out until 12:27 a.m. That was when I played the video at normal speed because Nikolai and Annie were coming through the revolving door, swaying in each other's arms. The camera in the eighteenth-floor elevator foyer also showed them stumbling down the hall, with Annie pulling Nikolai by the hand.

I continued speeding through the footage until 3:03 a.m., when Annie left and got into a cab. Her alibi, which I now realized she hadn't initially revealed because she was having an affair, still wasn't an alibi. She and Nikolai had arrived at the hotel a half hour after Luis was already dead. Plenty of time to kill him and come back to the hotel to celebrate with oysters and sex.

My phone buzzed in my pocket. I had a look, hoping it was Gabe, but it was my now ex-boss.

"Hey Kev," I said.

"Tori?" Kevin's voice was extra shaky.

"You calling to yell at me for still working my case? You know I've gone rogue, and there's nothing you can do about it."

"No, that's not it."

"Then what?"

"Do you know where Gabe is?"

"Gabe? No, why should I?"

"I can't get ahold of him. I've called his family and neighbors. No one's heard from him since yesterday afternoon. His phone goes straight to voice-mail."

"Did you check Rocky's parking lot?"

"Sorry, but it's against our policy for me to discuss his case with you when you no longer work for us."

"Then sorry, but I can't help you."

I hung up, and my stomach rumbled with anxiety. So that was why Gabe hadn't called me back. Something must have happened to him.

Chapter Twenty-Eight

"**A**NY MURDERERS FOLLOWING US YET?" Aunt Kat giggled drunkenly, as I performed the customary inspection of the car's underbelly.

I got in the driver's seat beside my whiskey-scented aunt. "Don't see a tracker."

"Are we done running around town then? Because I could really use a nap."

I started up the car. "Almost, but first we need to stop at the hardware store and check out Rocky's in Westport."

"Rocky's?" Aunt Kat made a face. "Why? For your new meat addiction?" She opened her silver case and pushed a fresh joint between her lips.

I made my way down the hotel's exit ramp. "My colleague's gone missing and was last seen at Rocky's. I'm thinking his case could overlap with mine."

"Wouldn't that be your lucky day with all the problems you've already got." Aunt Kat lit her joint and took a drag. "A dead Luis. A dead Charlie. Piglet heads. A missing colleague."

"You forgot the humidity, heat, and a drunk aunt."

Aunt Kat laughed, "I'm not that drunk."

"Sure, and I'm not that hot."

As I rolled the windows down, letting street dirt bristle across my face, Aunt Kat broke out into a cough.

"Tori!" she screamed, pointing.

In a burst of adrenaline, I braked. Our bodies hurled forward in our seatbelts as a kid on a scooter passed in front of us.

"God," I said. "Where'd he come from?"

"These kids on those scooters." Aunt Kat sucked hard on her joint. "So dangerous."

I watched the boy speed off, oblivious to death, his Mickey Mouse shirt billowing behind him, and thought about Chuck wielding a knife at the Memorial Day party. Maybe Mickey had killed Luis. But it wasn't only Chuck who looked suspicious.

All my cousins did. Emma was ready to slaughter anyone to protect her barbecue. Teddy said he didn't know Luis, but there he was on tape, taking the man into the office days before his death. As for Annie, she was banging the Yummy Foods guy to get her way. Maybe she'd murder to get her way too.

"I need to question my cousins again," I announced as I took a left on 11th Street.

"Why?" Aunt Kat said.

"Because they're full of bull."

"Of course they are. They're Charlie's kids."

"And one could be a murderer," I added.

"But do you really think they'll want to talk to you again? Didn't you get the boot from all your interviews yesterday?"

"I'm not giving them a choice this time," I said, as something caught my eye in the rearview mirror.

A black Mercedes turned on 11th Street. This wouldn't have been so unusual if its windows weren't tinted, its license plate wasn't a temporary paper tag from the dealership, and its driver's only distinguishing feature wasn't a pair of lips bubbling out of a ski mask.

"Great," I muttered to myself, though I didn't especially feel afraid.

"What now?" Aunt Kat said.

"Don't turn around, but I think we're being followed."

"Followed? I thought you said there wasn't a tracker on the car."

"Doesn't mean you still can't get followed. Let me see what happens if I do this—" I swung a hard right on Broadway and accelerated through a red light.

"Tori," Aunt Kat yelped. "Jeez, I may be a little lit, but I'm not looking for a joyride."

I looked up at the mirror. Not only did the Mercedes turn on Broadway, but it followed my lead and skated through the intersection of honking cars.

"Yep, we're being followed."

Aunt Kat stiffened in her seat. "By who?"

"A pro. No marked plates. No marked anything. It's a black Mercedes."

"You think that Yummy Foods guy at the hotel told someone you were there?"

"Maybe, but Jean and Annie knew I was there too."

"What a messed-up world we live in," Aunt Kat sighed, blowing a flat flute note into her Topo Chico bottle. "To think your own family could be trying to kill you."

"It's not that crazy. Uncle Charlie appears to have already had a hand in dad's death, right? Plus, a quarter of homicides are done by family members, and when you think about it, Uncle Charlie's kids could easily afford a professional hitman to kill, dismember, and dispose of us."

"Don't talk like that."

"I'm just being realistic." I checked the mirror again. The Mercedes wasn't far behind. "We need to lose them. Hold onto your joint."

"Wha—" Aunt Kat began, before I swerved into the oncoming lane. "Watch out!" she screamed, pointing at the truck coming our way. I hit the gas to pass the car in front of us while the truck honked. My aunt was still screaming as I swerved back into the right lane.

"See? All fine."

Aunt Kat was so hysterical she was panting.

"You trying to sober me up or send me to sleep forever?"

"Sorry, but I needed to put a car between us and our stalker."

"Why don't you call your police friend?"

My stomach twisted, recalling Darnell's angry eyes this morning. It felt like it had happened years ago. That was how far away he seemed, now that he knew I was using again.

"No," I said. "He won't help because I didn't give up my case."

"That's ridiculous. Give me your phone." Aunt Kat took my phone and dialed him. When he didn't pick up, she left a voicemail. "Hi Darnell, this is Kat, Tori's aunt. Just wanted to tell you that we're downtown being chased by an unmarked black Mercedes. If you could please help us before Tori puts us in a ditch, I'd really appreciate it."

We passed the sign for I-35. The entrance ramp was in another block. Either I kept going straight through stoplight traffic until the Mercedes caught up to us, or I took the four-lane highway in rush hour traffic while trying to lose our tail.

"You better roll your window up," I instructed my aunt as I rolled up mine.

"You better not kill us."

"I'll try my best." I hit the accelerator for the on-ramp, my ponytail bobbing in the wind. In the mirror, the Mercedes flew down the ramp after us. "It's coming fast."

"Of course it is. You know this old thing can't overpower a Mercedes." Aunt Kat pointed at the semi barreling down the right lane, the lane we needed. "It's not moving over . . ."

"It's okay." I laid on my horn and rocketed out in front of the semi driver, who honked back at me.

"My God," Aunt Kat sighed and rolled up her window. When the wind's hiss was replaced by the highway's hum, she went on, "I swear, if we make it out alive after this outrageous case of yours, I'm going to a spa. My back's killing me worse than ever."

"Sorry, but we don't want to be trapped behind that semi." In the mirror, I watched the Mercedes jump out from behind the semi and switch lanes. I nodded toward my bag. "Can you grab my stun gun?"

"Really? Can you use that thing on a car?"

"Just get it out. It's all we've got."

"Whatever you say. You're the expert." She reached into my bag and dropped the weapon in my lap.

As I-35 turned into Southwest Trafficway, the speed limit cut in half. The traffic slowed down, thickening like barbecue sauce until we were at an abrupt standstill. I checked the mirror again. The Mercedes was three cars behind us, also stuck in traffic. Then it switched into the left lane for the shoulder.

That wasn't good, not when I was locked in the left lane. I couldn't pull into the shoulder, either, when there was a construction truck parked in it up ahead. Not knowing what else to do, I held onto my stun gun and rolled down my window.

Aunt Kat spun around to look out the back window. "Tori, it's coming up the shoulder."

"I know, but I can't move with a car in front of me."

I looked to my right at the semi, then to my left where the construction truck was still parked up ahead. Directly behind me, a guy in a hatchback was texting someone, looking distracted. Meanwhile, the Mercedes saddled up beside me. The tinted passenger window rolled down, revealing a gloved hand, and Aunt Kat covered her eyes. Up ahead, the cars shifted forward.

I again looked at the texting guy behind me, then hit the accelerator to jump ahead several feet. Sure enough, the Mercedes followed beside me, but the distracted hatchback driver hadn't moved yet. I switched gears and hit the accelerator to reverse the car. The hard brakes sent me and Aunt Kat forward again in our seatbelts, but now I was only a foot shy of the hatchback's bumper.

Before the Mercedes could also reverse to cut me off, I flashed my emergency blinkers and pulled a sharp U-turn into the shoulder. As I flew over concrete ripples against the flow of traffic, I watched the Mercedes shrink to a tiny dot in the mirror.

Aunt Kat grabbed a fresh bottle of Topo Chico from the cooler to roll its icy coolness over her face. "I fear my car won't survive this."

"It's still hanging in there, just like us."

I kept my eyes on the rearview mirror. A cop turned on its lights and sirens, but it was too buried in traffic to get me. At least the attention from law enforcement got the Mercedes off the shoulder and back into the traffic jam. When I pulled off the highway at the Kaufman Center exit ramp, I started chugging sparkling water.

"Is this whole chase thing over yet?" Aunt Kat asked.

"For now."

"You think someone wanted to kill us?"

"That, or make us afraid."

"And you're the one who said I'd be risking my life staying at home."

"Hey, I don't regret you coming with me. For all we know, that Mercedes could be headed to the house to burn it down."

Chapter Twenty-Nine

"RED LIGHT TORI" COULD HAVE been my nickname as I sailed through intersections, hoping a cop would follow me. Unfortunately, they only wanted you when you didn't want them.

As we neared Aunt Kat's street, I parked in a nearby cul-de-sac and jumped out with my binoculars and stun gun, then I dashed through yards, checking over my shoulder. If someone was hunting me with a real gun, I'd be screwed. For my stun gun to work, I had to be within fifteen feet of the target. When I reached Clark Avenue, I crouched behind a neighbor's car and raised my binoculars to look at Aunt Kat's house.

No Mercedes on the street. I checked the trees, balconies, and windows. No one there either.

"Coast is clear," I announced to Aunt Kat when I got back to the car.

"Thank heavens," she said, rubbing her shoulders.

"But we still need to go to the hardware store so we can be prepared if someone comes."

Aunt Kat didn't protest and fell asleep in her seat. Meanwhile, I ran into the store to charge her credit card with the most sophisticated alarm system and porch camera they had, the kind that registered broken glass and alerted your phone if it got triggered. Since I was also near Rocky's in Westport, I headed over there next to see if I could find Gabe.

Like usual, I circled around the diner to cautiously peer around the corner. Squishy's truck wasn't there, but Gabe's car was in the lot. It was even parked where I'd last seen him. I pulled out my stun gun and approached the empty vehicle, bending down to check under the car. No tracker.

I then tucked my stun gun into my shorts to cup my hands over Gabe's window. Inside were papers, binoculars, a half-eaten rib sandwich, and crusty stains of vanilla milkshake on the upholstery. No sign of a struggle, but the half-eaten sandwich was strange. Something made Gabe set his lunch down.

I returned to the loading dock where Squishy parked his truck. No blood, but there were glittering bits on the ground, like a tiny mirror had been run over. Maybe Gabe was with Squishy. Maybe Squishy had crushed his skull.

I didn't know what to do about Gabe's disappearance, so I drove me and Aunt Kat back home. After repeating my new routine of surveilling the house from a distance, I pulled her car into the garage and closed the door.

"I'm gonna set up the security system," I told her.

"Okay." Aunt Kat sighed with exhaustion as she plopped down on the couch. "Whatever you need to do."

It didn't take me long to hook up the security equipment, and it eased my mind knowing it was up and running. A warning shot was better than nothing at all. At least my poor aunt, worn down from booze and drama, had no trouble falling asleep. *You're horrible for doing this to her.* If only I hadn't taken oxies in the first place and gotten myself kicked out of Victory House. If only I hadn't been so hotheaded, pretending to be Mrs. Mendoza and giving myself this case or inviting myself to my uncle's barbecue party. If only I hadn't been so motivated to get even with my deceitful family members instead of thinking about the one member of my family I actually cared about. But there was no going back. I had to catch the killer before the killer caught us.

I continued securing the house, tying up trip wires at the front and back door entrances and the stairwell leading up to my bedroom. An intruder wouldn't notice them in the dark. Even if they were armed, I'd have enough time after they tripped to bolt out of bed and shoot my stun gun at them over the stair rail. That was my plan for tonight anyway.

Though I didn't owe Kevin anything, I called him up. Gabe was still on my mind, filling me with worry. Maybe Kevin could do something for him.

"Tori?" Kevin answered, surprised.

"Yeah," I said. "I checked out Rocky's and Gabe's car is there. I think you should know that Harrison Alan Morris, the meat delivery guy at Rocky's, might know what happened to him."

"What makes you say that?"

"Gabe was watching him, and Harrison's one bad dude with a hell of a temper."

"I'm not sure what to do with that info, but thanks for letting me know."

I hung up. Kevin really couldn't do much. It wasn't like he could send cops over to Squishy's without evidence. Maybe I'd try to find Gabe tomorrow, but for now, I had no energy and needed to escape for the rest of the night.

One more pill went down the hatch, and I dragged my feet over to the treehouse with Bird. Neighbors were drinking on their balconies, and I waved my noodle arm at them. Then I climbed up the treehouse ladder, slowly, one rung after the other, being sure not to fall, until I was peeping over the landing into the treehouse. At first, I didn't think much about why my music stand was tilted over and lying on the ground. Maybe it was the wind. But then I registered the tripod standing in its place.

Holy shit.

My feet fumbled on the rungs and I slipped, one rung after the other, down to the grass. That wasn't a tripod for a telescope or for shooting pictures.

That was a gun stand, facing my bedroom window.

Chapter Thirty

I SLEPT ON THE FLOOR all night, or tried to anyway, but it wasn't easy powering down your consciousness when a gun stand was pointed at you. Now that it was morning, I looked out the window at the treehouse and street. No Mercedes, strangers, or suspicious packages. Just another cheerful day of sunshine with a heatstroke warning.

"The treehouse?" Aunt Kat said, slapping her forehead.

"Yeah, so get in the car," I ordered as I held the door open for her. "We'll have to booby-trap it later, since someone's going up there ready to shoot me."

"Maybe you should plant a bomb there instead?" Aunt Kat sighed as she got into the passenger seat.

"Yeah, and watch a bird burst into feathers."

I closed my aunt's door and bent down to inspect the bottom of the car, where she couldn't see me swallow my third pill of the day. Then I got into the driver's seat and gave her a reassuring smile. "No tracker," I said.

"Like that matters after getting chased yesterday. So where are you dragging me off to now?"

"Today we're visiting your lovely nieces and nephews. Our first stop is Uncle Charlie's in the West Bottoms."

Her hands started trembling at this news. "I see," she said quietly.

"Sorry, I know it's a heavy place. You can stay in the car with your feet in the cooler if you'd rather not go inside."

"That's what I'll do unless you want to see me cry my eyes out. But don't they have a restraining order against you from going there?"

"Yeah, from Annie. But I'm on my way to talk to Emma before Uncle Charlie's opens, and as far as I'm aware, Emma has no reason to call the cops on me yet."

As I drove through inner-city traffic, constantly checking my mirrors to ensure no one was following us again, I pulled out my phone and replayed my first round of interviews on the speaker function. Not only could I get Aunt Kat's fresh take, but I wanted to remind myself of what I'd already learned. When Walt's nervous voice came out of the speaker, though, not even the oxies inside me could blunt my guilt. Aunt Kat listened to my first interview with him at the Hub.

"Do you really believe a word of what this Walt fellow was saying when he was cranked out on heroin?" she said. "Maybe he killed Luis, then killed himself because he was afraid you'd find out the truth."

I got defensive on Walt's behalf. "No way he killed Luis," I said. "Maybe he lied like addicts do, but he was being blackmailed by Luis's killer. His note had the same glittery sticker letters as that threat we got in the piglet's mouth. Walt was another one of the killer's victims."

We crossed the bridge into the West Bottoms, weaving through the antique warehouses until we arrived at the unassuming gas station, where only five days earlier my uncle had collapsed and died under me. Now the drive-in looked like one of those deserted gas stations in black-and-white photos. Only Emma's car was in the parking lot, which was good. We'd be alone. I stopped playing my interviews, now on Teddy, and slid my phone into my bag so the microphone was facing up and the recorder already on. It was against the law not to ask for permission to record, but right now I didn't care about the rules.

"Please don't be long." Aunt Kat leaned her seat back as far as it would go, so she couldn't see the drive-in. "This car's in the sun."

"Don't worry, I'm sure Emma will kick me out soon enough once I get aggressive with her. Then we'll stop in some air-conditioned place to cool off."

Aunt Kat flicked an eyebrow at me. "What do you mean you're getting aggressive with her?"

"After those piglet heads, Walt's death, the car chase, and the gun pointed at my bedroom window, you could say I'm in combat mode."

I got out of the car before she could argue with me, then started my trek for Uncle Charlie's across the parking lot. When I saw a guy asleep at the gas pumps, I recognized him as the same addict with the long, tangled hair who'd interrupted the party for me.

"Hey," I said, waking him up.

"Yeah?" he mumbled, looking up but too inebriated to remember me. I dug into my bag for ten twenties, the last of my cash that I'd reserved for him.

I handed him the wad. "For your service last week."

"Okay," he said, taking the cash and going back to sleep.

I continued my journey toward the drive-in, feeling charged up for my first impromptu interview of the day, because no matter how I did it, I was extracting new info from my cousins. When I reached the drive-in's glass door, I knocked with my knuckle.

Emma's head popped up from behind the kitchen counter, her apron stiffened with blood. She tried to smile but was clearly displeased to see me. When she opened the door, a gust of cooking meat steamed my face.

"What are you doing here?" she said, her accusatory tone not attempting to disguise itself. "I won't call the cops, but it's not a good idea for you to be here."

"Yeah, I know," I said. "But could I talk to you for a quick moment?"

"Why?" She frowned. "Did you find out who sent me that piglet head?"

"Not yet. Just had some follow-up questions if you don't mind." I offered her a smile.

"I guess," she said, annoyed. "But you'll have to watch me prep for lunch. The other workers are coming in soon."

"Fine by me. You said you'd give me the special tour, right? I'd love to see a great pitmaster at work."

I followed her into the beloved kitchen of my childhood, my once-favorite place in the world. On the walls were the same antique barbecue memorabilia and license plates from tourists on their barbecue pilgrimages. I looked at the cookers and tears glazed over my eyes. Maybe three pills weren't enough to handle this kitchen, but I couldn't take any more quite yet.

"I've been working since dawn." Emma lifted a cooker lid to reveal a toddler-sized brisket wrapped in greasy foil. Then she removed the foil and spritzed the brisket with apple cider vinegar. "Any guesses on who dropped off that disgusting package on my doorstep?"

"I have a lead," I said.

Emma gave a firm nod. "Good. Not that I'm grossed out by animal heads, but I've been so jostled by the appearance of one at my door that I could barely sleep the past two nights. I'm even keeping my knives out, thinking I might have to gut my first human. At least Hickory's there to bark, but I'll be going to bed on edge until you catch that psycho."

"I'll catch them soon enough." I switched the subject to something more comfortable for her. "So how do you do a brisket?" I asked like I didn't know.

Emma closed the cover on the cooking brisket, removed a grill brush, and led me to an empty cooker. "We start by cleaning."

"You clean before a cook?"

"Always before. I've already preheated this cooker fifteen minutes." Emma scrubbed the grill grate with her brush. "Massive rookie error to clean after a cook. It's much easier to wait so it's not gooey and gunky."

After scraping off char, Emma rolled out a bucket-shaped vacuum to suck up debris.

"That's a lot of gunk," I observed.

"You bet." Emma grabbed a bottle and slathered oil on the grate. "Next, we oil the grill and put in the water pan. The most important thing to smoking meat is the moisture." She placed a tin water pan under the grate before sliding pieces of wood into the tiny box jutting from the cooker's side. "Hickory logs for the fire."

"Like your dog."

"That's right. Other parts of the country use oak, mesquite, or apple wood, but it's the hickory flavor that makes Kansas City the best barbecue in the world. Plus, we cook our briskets super low and super slow." From the fridge, she picked up a brisket half her size before slamming it down on a cutting board.

"Beautiful marbling," I said.

"Yes, yes," she cooed softly, as she stroked the fat in the affectionate way a mother stroked a baby's cheek. "This was already trimmed and salted two hours ago, but it still needs to get rubbed down with seasoning. I use mustard first so it'll stick." She squirted mustard onto the brisket, smearing it all over with her tiny hands. "Then I add the seasoning I already mixed here." She held up a bottle and applied a generous coating.

"What's in it?"

Emma listed the ingredients. "Ancho chili powder, cayenne, garlic powder, onion powder, dry mustard, pepper, and dark brown molasses sugar."

That was my dad's recipe she was massaging into the meat. "Then it's ready for the grill?" I said.

"Yeah, fat side up, and place the fattiest part closest to the fire." Emma transferred the brisket to the empty cooker and shut the door. "I leave it unwrapped for the first four hours, or until the bark is soft and pliable, at which point I wrap it in foil to keep the moisture in until it hits 250F. It's important to maintain the fire and check on the meat once an hour. That way you can remove any dry spots by spritzing them with apple cider vinegar."

I nodded. "How long does it take to cook a brisket?"

"Depends on the size of the meat," Emma laughed. "Anywhere from eight to thirteen hours. By the girth and length on this one, it'll be cooking 'til sundown." She pointed to a simmering pot of reddish-brown sauce on the stove. "This sauce then gets drizzled on the finished brisket. Lots of molasses, brown sugar, tomatoes, ketchup, and spices." She gave the pot a quick stir. "Do you have questions for me about your case, or did you just want the tour?"

"Sure, I've got questions," I said, ready to fire her up. "I spoke with Nikolai Volkov yesterday."

Her mouth puckered up like she'd taken a bite of spoiled beef. "Why?" she barked. "What's that jerk still doing here?"

"I can't discuss the details—"

"He wants his contract, doesn't he?" Emma slammed her fist hard on a ladle, causing it to fly. She reached down to pick it up, clutching hard on its handle. "Well, guess what?" She pointed the ladle at me like it was a sword. "He's not getting Uncle Charlie's." Seeing the ladle in her hand directed at me in so threatening a manner, she dropped it on the counter. Then she picked up a lid and slammed it on top of the sauce pot with a cymbal clang. "Majority rules, and there's no majority."

This had to be the explosive side of Emma that Nikolai was talking about. She was so mad her face even looked different. Now it was scrunched up and red, like an infection.

I kept my voice calm. "He claimed he doesn't care if he gets the deal, that there are other deals."

"He was blowing smoke up your ass." Emma took the cheesy corn bake out of the oven and fanned the heat off with her oven mitt. "He wants the deal. Yummy Foods has wanted a barbecue chain since last year, and he knows how much money he could make with Uncle Charlie's if it goes nationwide. If he said he doesn't care, it was to make you think he wasn't a threat, because the truth is he wouldn't be camping out here unless he cared. Honestly, I wouldn't be surprised if he and Annie were breaking laws to sell Uncle Charlie's. You should be looking into that."

"He also mentioned how you treated him at the Memorial Day party," I added.

"Good for him." Emma dragged a knife through the corn bake to cut it into squares. "I don't care what that slimeball says. He was getting his ass kissed and licked by Dad, Annie, and Teddy while trying to steal my heritage. How do you think I felt?"

My eyes widened at her lack of self-awareness. It wasn't her heritage. It was mine. "Angry enough to steal a contract?" I said, my tone still professionally neutral. "Because Uncle Charlie signed, and you didn't want Yummy Foods to have the business?"

Emma advanced toward me with her knife, looking like she could cut me as easily as her corn bake. "What the fuck, Tori. You're out of line." She clapped the weapon on the counter. "Is that why you came here? To accuse me of theft?" She stirred the beans again, violently this time. "Listen, I don't have time—"

"Why did you withdraw an additional twelve thousand dollars in May from the company account?"

"Oh God." Emma banged her fist on a cooker. "Knock, knock," she said in a mocking voice. "You know, these things ain't cheap."

"You bought equipment with it? Do you have receipts?"

"I gave them to Dad since he'd asked me to replace the cookers. Sometimes he went around Chuck to get the job done faster. Now if you don't mind, I need you to get the hell out of my kitchen so I can focus on the cook."

"I understand, but could I see your office before I go?"

"No. Get out, or I'm calling the cops on you for breaking your restraining order."

"Right." I turned and sprinted down the hall.

"Bitch," Emma shouted after me.

I threw the office door open. A twin air mattress was pushed in the corner. I went over to the window and lifted it up.

"Don't open that," Emma yelled behind me. "You'll let the bugs in."

"I'm only seeing how easy it would be to get in and out." I removed the screen and poked my head outside. Below was a small jump into a flower bed that had been recently planted. "Is there a reason your flowers are so fresh?"

"How about we value what our restaurant looks like?"

"You mean, these flowers aren't here because you trampled them when you jumped out of the window on your way to kill Luis?"

"Yeah, you got me," she laughed. "I leapt out of a window into a flower bed, sped off to Kansas, killed a guy I never knew, and sped right back here with enough time to spritz the dry spots on my brisket. I never thought I'd agree with my sister, but I can see now why she hates your guts. You're a mosquito."

"And you're a fake," I said, finally calling her out. "Cooking my dad's recipes in his kitchen and pretending they're yours."

Emma bared her teeth at me. "Instead of wasting time accusing me of nonsense, maybe you should be out there trying to find the sicko who sent me that bloody piglet head. Because so far that's the only tangible piece of evidence I've seen from your pointless case."

"No, there's also this." I held up the threatening note with the glittery sticker letters that I'd found stuffed in the piglet's mouth.

"All right," Emma snorted. "We're done here. I've got workers and customers coming soon."

"What about your barbecue contests?"

Emma flashed me a cold, reptilian glare. "What about them?"

"Ever cheat? I'm only asking because I read that you were once sued for cheating."

"No, that woman was jealous. She ended up dropping the charges too. And how dare you insult my reputation. You've tasted my meat. You know I don't need to cheat." Emma waved at the wall of plaques and framed articles from newspapers celebrating Uncle Charlie's. One article even featured the world-famous chef, Tony Dean, who'd visited the historic gas station and declared it among the top ten places to eat in the world.

Above the accolades were photos of the drive-in over the years, including a black-and-white picture like the one Aunt Kat had wanted me to give Uncle Charlie—a memento from the good old days. On the opposite wall were several more of Aunt Kat's surrealist animal paintings.

I pointed to a painting of a rooster flying an airplane. "Do you know why Uncle Charlie was collecting Aunt Kat's work?"

"How should I know?" Emma pointed to the hall. "Now please fuck off so I can spray my meat and stir my beans."

I wasn't getting anything else from Emma except more vitriol, so I returned to the kitchen. As I looked at the burnt ends glistening in a pan, I felt curious to try another bite. Plus, I figured I should get some protein in me to go with the oxies.

I pointed at the pan. "Mind if I grab some breakfast to go, or should I wait for the lunch crowd?" In silence, Emma snatched a Styrofoam box, scooped out a lump of warm burnt ends, and poured a generous heap of sauce on top. "Now get out," she ordered, handing me the box. "And if I see you here again, I'm calling the cops."

Back in the car, Aunt Kat was lying under her sunhat. "Hungry for breakfast?" I held up the Styrofoam box.

She lifted her hat from her face. "From that place?" she scoffed. "I'd rather starve. How'd it go?"

"Couldn't have been better. Emma's quiet on the outside, lethal on the inside. I could see her slitting throats."

"Sounds like her father."

I wasn't hungry, but I took a bite of a burnt end, this time without gagging. Maybe it was getting easier to eat meat the more I confronted it. In fact, I had to confess I was even enjoying the taste. Emma could very well be a killer, but she could cook a mean brisket. As I swallowed the meat down, Aunt Kat brought her seat upright and gazed at the drive-in.

"Everything okay?" I said.

Tears clouded her eyes. "Yeah, it's good to make peace with this place," she said, wiping a tear away. "But let's get out of here."

Chapter Thirty-One

WE STOPPED AT A GAS station for AC, got back on the road, and made our way for Teddy's. Soon as we pulled up to the gate of Camelot Castle, Aunt Kat covered her mouth. "Is that supposed to be a house or an amusement park?"

I reached out my window to ring the buzzer. "I'd call it a resort prison."

"Hello?" Susanne's thin voice squeaked through the intercom.

"Hi, this is Tori," I said in a pleasant tone. "I'm here for Teddy. Is he home?"

"Did you make an appointment? He's at the country club."

"No appointment. Do you know when he'll be back?"

"You must schedule an appointment with Teddy. Can I give him a message for you?"

I was about to tell her to calm down when a red Porsche pulled up beside me. "Tori?" Teddy said, looking sober for the first time, his hair messy from driving with the top down. "Bring a friend for the big castle tour?" He winked at Aunt Kat.

She winked back at him. "I'm your aunt. Don't you remember me?"

"Not with purple hair," Teddy laughed. "Cool though. Everyone should have a wacky aunt with purple hair."

I pointed to the empty golf bag in his passenger seat. "Golfing?"

"Yeah, but we called the game early."

"Where are your clubs?"

"Oh." He blushed. "They roll out of the bag when I drive so fast." He bent down and picked one up to show me. "Anyway, what are you doing here?"

"If you could spare a few minutes, I'd love to ask you some follow-up questions for my case."

"Yeah?" His voice vibrated with nerves. "You close to figuring it out?"

"I think so."

"Sure you don't want the house tour first?"

"I'd love to, but how about next time? I've got lots of work."

"All work and no play makes Tori a bore." Teddy pulled a dramatic pout. "But fine, we can chat so long as you don't tell Susanne what we're talking about. Deal?"

I gave him a reassuring smile. "Fine by me."

"All right. Let me get changed out of these sweaty clothes and grab a couple of brewskis. I'll meet you at the fire pit."

With his clubs in one hand and golf bag in the other, Teddy dashed through the medieval doors, and Aunt Kat and I got out of the car into the cloudless, sunny day. While Aunt Kat marveled at the monstrosity of Teddy's fortress, taking in all its towers and turrets, I seized the opportunity to open a Topo Chico and swig back another pill without her seeing. After all, my tolerance was going up. I needed more to be where I needed to be.

Aunt Kat rolled her eyes. "You really believe his golf clubs just rolled on the floor of his car?"

"Nope," I said, drinking more sparkling water. "He's hiding something. Maybe he got back from a rendezvous and was hiding sex toys in his golf bag."

"He's having an affair?"

"You really surprised?"

I led Aunt Kat around the castle until we reached the arcade, where she took a seat at the patio table to wait in the shade. Then I walked across the lawn toward the lake and got out my phone to check the security camera's live streams from Aunt Kat's porch. The question wasn't whether someone was coming to the house, but when. If only Darnell had returned Aunt Kat's call yesterday, he could have stood guard. But he didn't want anything to do with me and my relapse, and I couldn't blame him for that.

I opened the video feeds where one camera faced the front door, while the other showed the street of neighborhood kids setting off firecrackers. I put the phone away and grabbed a seat at the fire pit to guzzle more sparkling water and take in the beauty. Lake Weatherby was cleaner than the Missouri River, but I still wouldn't go swimming in it. Not when it was hot as bathtub water.

"Teddy said you were out here," a meek voice said behind me. I turned to find Susanne in a sleeveless summer dress with a tray of iced tea, sugar cubes, and cookies. "I thought you could use some refreshments, especially in this heat." She had as much life in her as a Hallmark card as she set the tray on the table.

"Thanks," I said, though I didn't want any of her cookies. Even if I was hungry, I didn't trust her enough to eat her food.

"What do you need to talk to Teddy about?" she asked.

"Uncle Charlie's funeral tomorrow."

"I see." Her voice softened, though there was still suspicion in it. "Yes," she went on, "Charlie's death has been hard on Teddy. He's been grieving by golfing and boating every day."

"Was Teddy close to Uncle Charlie?"

"Close?" she repeated with confusion in her face. "I suppose he admired him for his achievements, but I wouldn't say they were close. No one could be with how paranoid and terrible Charlie was."

"That's what I keep hearing—"

"Tori," Teddy shouted, while trotting across the lawn with a bottle of beer in each hand. When he reached us, I could see by the wrinkles in his face that he was worried I was talking to his wife without him. "Thanks, Suzie." He pecked a kiss on her cheek. "I'll talk to Tori alone now."

"About funeral matters?" She lifted an eyebrow.

"Exactly."

Susanne still looked dissatisfied by our meeting, but headed back for the house. Meanwhile, Teddy dug through the cookie jar and sugar cubes before pressing his ear to the pitcher of tea, lifting the tray, and taking a cookie.

"What are you doing?" I said.

"Making sure everything's good. Want a cookie?" He pushed the jar of chocolate chip cookies toward me, but I especially didn't want one after he'd fingered them all. Teddy took a bite and chased it down with some beer. "Thanks for the white lie about the funeral." He let out a burp. "She doesn't need to hear any of this murder talk. Would upset her unnecessarily."

"It's confidential anyway," I reminded him, and put my phone on the table to record our conversation.

"Are you here because of what happened to Walt? What a tragedy. I know he was awkward, but overall a decent guy. Or was there something else you wanted to discuss?"

My memory of Walt dead on his desk floated back to me. Again, I saw the purple face, the foam-filled mouth, the rolled-back eyes.

"Tori?" Teddy said, pulling me back into the present.

I blinked, then looked back at my cousin. "Yes. What happened to Walt was horrible, but that's not why I'm here. I want to know more about your role as the food supplier at Uncle Charlie's. Do you know many KC meat suppliers?"

"Of course." Teddy took a pull of beer.

"Then maybe you can help me. The night Walt died, I was surveilling Uncle Charlie's and saw a night delivery. Walt said this was normal, is that right?"

"Yeah, we occasionally have night deliveries."

"Would you know the name of a particular meat supplier? He's a giant with an ugly blond haircut."

Teddy reacted to this description of Squishy by knocking his bottle on the table and spilling its contents. "Dammit," he muttered and grabbed a napkin to wipe up the mess. "And yes . . . that's Harrison. He only delivers at night."

I pointed to the bottle shaking in his hand. "You afraid of him or something?"

"Oh. No, no, no. I'm upset I spilled my beer."

"You ever argue with Harrison?"

"Argue? I mean, we don't always see things eye to eye. He's not happy delivering at night, but what can I do about it? It's the only time he's free and we're not busy."

"Would you be surprised if he was a murderer?"

"A murderer," Teddy laughed uncomfortably. "Wait, do you think he killed Luis?"

"I don't know. I just want to know your thoughts. He does go to Uncle Charlie's at night, which is when Luis was working alone. But another question. What do you think of Chuck's accounting skills?"

Teddy laughed again, comfortably this time. "Is Chuck good at anything besides drawing cartoons? Even that's debatable."

"You're saying he's not good with numbers though he's the company accountant?"

"Yeah, Dad gave Chuck that job because he gave us all jobs, but there's been more than one occasion when Chuck royally screwed up. Dad was so angry about it at the barbecue party on Memorial Day that he said he'd kick him out of the business."

"What did Chuck miscalculate?"

"No idea," Teddy sighed. "All I can remember is how amusing it was watching Dad scream and Chuck squirm."

"Chuck gave me this." I pulled out the financial records from Chuck's Mickey Mouse folder. Now it was time to watch Teddy squirm. "It says here that you took out one hundred and sixteen thousand dollars in May. Is that accurate?"

Teddy shot up from his chair. "No," he shouted, "that weasel must be up to something."

I remained calm. "So you're saying these records aren't right?"

"Of course not. Either he's making me look bad on purpose, or he really is that incompetent. You know, I wouldn't be surprised if he stole that money and blamed me for it."

I nodded. Though it was possible Chuck had falsified the records, I was at least certain that either he or Teddy was lying. As Teddy sat back down and chugged his beer like a hungry infant, I proceeded to my next question. "You've mentioned that you didn't get along with your father, but did you fear him enough to do what he asked?"

"What? No. What kind of question is that? My father never owned me. Do you see where I live?" He pointed at his castle. "I have more than double his assets."

"What I meant was, how much did you seek his approval? Did you want to be the next face of Uncle Charlie's, but he wouldn't let you?"

Teddy now pointed at the front gate. "Okay, I think it's time for you to leave."

"I don't think so," I said, pointing at his chair for him to sit down. "Unless you want me to play our last interview for your wife. I can skip to the part about the Crown Room with her cousin."

Panic lit up in Teddy's eyes. "You wouldn't."

"Try me."

"But that's a breach of your confidentiality rules. You can't do that."

"I can if I'm conducting a murder investigation, and someone wants me dead. Can't say I care too much about the rules right now, so can you please sit down and answer my question?"

"This is so fucked." Teddy sat back down and twisted the cap off another bottle of beer. "But to answer your question, yes, I often did what my father asked of me because he was my boss."

"Did he ever ask you to commit a crime? Like do something about Luis?"

"What? Of course not."

"You might have an alibi for when Luis died," I began, "but you're also on tape at Uncle Charlie's speaking to Luis a few days before his death. You claimed you didn't even know who he was, so what were you doing in the office with him? Or were you too drunk to remember?"

Teddy's face reddened while he squeezed his beer bottle. "Excuse me?" he squealed.

I opened the surveillance footage from Uncle Charlie's. Teddy covered his mouth when he saw himself on the screen.

"See," I continued, tapping on the screen at the image of himself, "you went into the office with Luis for three minutes. When he came out, he was happy. Why is that? Or were you having an affair with him too?"

"Hell no." Teddy's exclamation came out as a burp. "It was illegal what we were doing, that's why I kept quiet."

"Were you doing coke?"

"How'd you know?"

I gave a closed smile. I didn't mention Walt had told me Teddy was snorting in the office. "So you gave Luis drugs?"

"Sure, we did a line or two together. No big deal. But that's why he was glowing when he left. Now you know the truth."

"I don't know if I do. His widow said he never did drugs."

"And wives always know what their husbands are up to, right?" Teddy smirked.

"I thought you said your wife knows you're having affairs."

"Yeah, but we don't talk about it. If you brought it up, she'd deny it before trying to cut your tongue out. It isn't proper etiquette to speak of these things in our society. I expect Luis's wife behaved similarly, whether in denial or not, to preserve the integrity of his character and reputation."

"And you don't think it's strange Luis died a few days after you gave him coke?"

"How's that strange?" Teddy brushed a hand through his hair. "Makes total sense to me. He switched from coke to heroin and overdosed. Probably didn't know what the hell he was doing, or maybe it was cut with something fatal. That happens all the time with opioids, especially fentanyl."

I held up the threatening note with the sparkly letters. "What about this? Do you recognize it?"

Teddy took the note from me before dropping it like it was two hundred degrees. "Of course not."

"Listen." I leaned toward him. "I know you didn't kill Luis since you were busy banging your wife's cousin in your wife's castle, but maybe you played a role in his death in another way. Maybe by accident. Is there something you're not telling me?"

"No, no." Distressed, Teddy grabbed another chocolate chip cookie and shoved the entire thing into his mouth. "I admit I gave him coke," he garbled through the cookie. "But like I already told you, I had nothing to do with his death. I swear."

A figure in the distance made me swivel around in my chair. It was Susanne, charging across the lawn for us. Now she was full of energy, and as she got closer, I could see it was an energy driven by fury.

Teddy jerked in his chair. "Hey Suz—"

She hit him on the back of the head and grabbed the sugar jar. "Tori needs to leave right now." From the jar, she pulled out a white cube and twisted it open. Inside the Styrofoam that looked like any other sugar cube was a tiny microphone. She shot me a glare. "You lied to me. You said you were here to discuss Charlie's funeral."

"Tori's a private investigator," Teddy said. "But don't worry, our conversation's confidential."

"I don't care. Your meeting's over." Susanne pulled a gun from her dress pocket, and I stood up.

"Suz." Teddy reached for her arm. "Please, we don't want a scandal. Give me the gun."

"Shut up, or I'll point it at you."

I didn't need to get shot to know when it was time to leave. "Don't worry, I'll go," I said and started power walking for the car.

Aunt Kat was fanning her face in the arcade, and I gestured at her to join me.

Soon as Aunt Kat hustled beside me, she nodded back at Susanne holding the gun. "What's going on? Is that woman going to shoot us?"

"Nothing's going on," I said. "Everything's great. We're just leaving."

In silence, Susanne followed us all the way to the car. "Don't come back here again," she said, as if this wasn't obvious.

"Have a fantastic day," I told her and turned on the car.

Once I'd driven outside the castle gates and was safely beyond the aim of Susanne's gun, Aunt Kat turned to me. "Jesus, what happened there?"

"I guess Teddy's wife wasn't too happy hearing about his infidelities."

"That's why she pulled a gun on you?" Aunt Kat shook her head. "Seriously, is there anyone in this family who isn't insane?"

"You and me."

But I wasn't so sure of that as I drove toward Overland Park for Annie's, my foot trembling on the pedal, my hands choking the steering wheel. With all the drugs in me mixing with fury toward my cousin, I was feeling a little insane myself. This encounter would also be different from running into Annie at the hotel by accident. Now I was expecting to see her. I didn't even care that Aunt Kat watched me knock back two more pills. She'd think they were anti-narcotics anyway. *You'll be fine. You'll be fine.*

Except I was lying to myself.

Chapter Thirty-Two

TRUTH WAS, I KEPT REPLAYING what Annie had said at the hotel: *You're such a loser addict like your dad.*

Insulting my dad like that made me want to wring her neck. Flying down the open highway, I let myself fantasize about knocking on her taupe door. She opened it, screamed at me, threatened to call the cops. I didn't say a word. I threw myself on her, pinned her to the ground, held her by the neck. She grabbed my arms. Her legs flailed beneath me. She wheezed, her blue eyes pleading with me not to kill her, but I squeezed harder, my thumbs pushing into her esophagus to cut off her breath, my nails digging deep into her throat until her painted face shriveled to a prune.

Aunt Kat's scream ripped me back into the present. I yanked the wheel before we hit the traffic barrier. Our bodies rocked a hard right. Back in the lane, like I didn't almost kill us. My trembling foot relaxed on the pedal, and I reached for the Topo Chico between my legs.

"Sorry," I muttered, before taking a long pull of water.

"My God am I glad I didn't doze off," Aunt Kat said. "Why are you driving like that?"

"Sorry, I'm tired. I'm not sleeping great these days."

"Then you shouldn't be driving. You're already lucky to have survived one bad accident."

I disagreed with my aunt on that point. I wasn't lucky to have survived that crash, not when I was trying to die as the fuck-up I was. I turned into Whispering Winds, Annie's boring cream and taupe neighborhood, and my arms shook even more on the wheel.

"What's going on?" Aunt Kat said. "You're all flushed. Your hands are shaking."

"I'm fine," I said, parking at Annie's.

I climbed out of the car to the scent of pesticides in the humid air. As I moved up the driveway, my neck felt extra tight. To kill or not to kill Annie, that was the question. Maybe the sweetness of revenge was worth a lifetime sentence.

When I reached the floral welcome mat, I thumped both of my fists on the taupe door. This is why I preferred knocking to ringing the bell. You controlled the rhythm and volume of your presence, letting the person inside know you weren't messing around. Her high heels came stabbing across the floor toward me, and I formed two fists. For all I knew, she could try throwing another punch at me. When her shoes stopped clicking, the peephole clouded.

"I'm calling the cops," Annie's voice rang out.

"If you don't talk to me, I'm telling your husband about Nik—"

The door flew open to Annie in a hot pink yoga outfit. She was scowling. "You're such a fucking nuisance."

"Sorry about that."

"Yeah, whatever. Meet me at the Smoothie King in the Plaza in thirty."

Back in the car, Aunt Kat blinked at my news. "You blackmailed her? That's against the law."

"So is killing people," I said, my clammy hands gripping the wheel. Now the euphoric combination of pills and power was giving me a great high. "I had to," I added, "or she wouldn't have agreed to talk to me."

"I hope pissing off your cousins is helping you solve this case."

"I think so. The more pissed they get, the closer I am. Angry criminals are more likely to screw up too."

"And angry criminals are also more likely to attack those who threaten them." Aunt Kat tied her purple hair back into a ponytail. "How's the house anyway? Are you checking the video feeds?"

"Only every twenty minutes. Nothing happening so far."

"That's a relief. You ever talk to your cop friend about our highway chase?"

My hold on the wheel loosened at the mention of Darnell, but in my present state, I was fairly immune to sadness. "No, I told you he's done with me."

"I can't believe that. He's your best friend."

"Annie was once my best friend too. Every relationship has an expiration date."

We rode the next twenty minutes in silence, the hot air blowing at us through the open windows. The wind made it too loud to talk anyway, but I was all right with that when all I could do was smile to myself about how frightened and furious Annie must have been, knowing she was about to lose her big city dreams because of me. I pulled into the parking ramp across from Smoothie King, and Aunt Kat got out of the car too.

"I'm going to grab lunch at Chickee's," she said, pointing across the street at a restaurant with giant window pictures of fried chicken thighs smothered in ranch sauce.

"Fine. I'll meet you back here. Shouldn't take too long."

As I had a head start on Annie, I got to the patio first and ordered a giant iced tea. I was already halfway done slurping when I saw her charging toward me.

She sat down at the table and pointed at my phone. "Turn that fucking thing off," she ordered.

"All right." I switched off the recorder.

"You know it'll ruin my marriage if Rick finds out about Kolya. Are you really so jealous of me that you want to destroy my life?"

"That's funny," I said, my voice calmer than ever. "It doesn't seem like you had a problem watching mine get destroyed after my dad died."

Annie let out an irritated grunt. "How much do you want?"

"I don't want money. I want to solve my case."

"Bullshit. You're crying over your restraining order and your stupid letters I burned. By the way, I don't regret that either."

"It's interesting you held onto them for so long."

"Want to know why? In case I needed to blackmail you. Sorry, not sorry."

I changed the subject. "A car chased me yesterday after I left the hotel. You have something to do with that?"

Annie rolled her eyes. "Oh, please."

"You tried attacking me in the hotel," I reminded her. "You spat on my face. Is it that crazy to think you sent someone after me?"

"Is it that crazy to think I'd hate you for trying to bring my drive-in down while spying on me? But to answer your question, no, I didn't waste my money sending a hitman after you."

I looked at her face, and the hate in it made my heart fist. I wanted to lunge at her. If she wasn't here to watch, I'd swallow more pills.

"Hello?" Annie tapped on her gold watch, and I flinched. "Mind getting to your questions? I have an appointment soon with the funeral director to drop off Dad's tux and makeup."

"Right." I gulped down the rest of my iced tea. "Why are you sleeping with Nikolai?" My question came out like an accusation. "I met him yesterday. He's not an attractive man."

"No, but he's got a surprising amount of spunk." She smirked. "I'm doing all I can to sell Uncle Charlie's to Yummy Foods. When Kolya visited over Memorial Day weekend, he took a liking to me, and Dad suggested I do what I needed to land the contract."

"So Uncle Charlie asked you to have an affair to secure the deal?"

Annie's mouth puckered into a frown. "He never explicitly asked that, but I knew what he meant. There was too much money on the line."

"And what else would you do for this deal? Commit murder?"

"Funny," Annie laughed.

"Are you laughing because you and Kolya did commit murder?"

"Please, I didn't kill Luis. My alibi for that night is working my ass off in a hotel suite. And you know what? It worked because Kolya offered us a contract the next day."

Although Annie was proud to have been a successful prostitute for her father, I didn't tell her I couldn't account for her whereabouts during Luis's death. The hotel footage showed the drunk pair stumbling into the hotel half an hour later.

Annie added, "What would have been my motive for killing a cook anyway?"

"Maybe he knew about your affair?" I offered. "That's a common motive for murder." Annie scowled at my explanation. "Another question," I said, getting out Chuck's Mickey Mouse folder to pull out the financial records. I pointed to the number beside her name. "It says here you withdrew ten thousand in May."

"Yeah, to entertain Kolya. I put him up in that presidential suite for a week while serving him gourmet sausages and eggs in bed. You think that was cheap?"

"Do you have receipts for these transactions?"

"You kidding? You think I'd keep evidence of my affair lying around? I'm not like my drunk stupid brother."

I nodded, agreeing with her on that point. "Is this the first time you've slept with a client?"

Annie gave a tight smile. "Marketing's about selling yourself, and what can I say? I'm good at it. There's nothing wrong with that in the business world. The way I see it, sex is like a handshake."

I didn't ask how many people she'd shaken metaphorical hands with. "Does your husband know?"

"No way. He's too obsessed with his spiritual healing practice and thinks I have postpartum depression after the baby. Anyway, that's my excuse for coming home at odd hours. I tell him I'm sweaty from yoga. He's always very understanding."

"And did you resent your father for making you have affairs?"

"How absurd," she said, flicking her hair back. "My father never made me do anything." Her eyebrows squeezed together, probably because she didn't want to admit he had controlled her. "The next thing you'll say is I gave him the allergy."

"You certainly had a motive—" I stopped myself mid-sentence at a black car coming down the street. The windows were tinted and the license plate was missing. It was the same Mercedes from yesterday. Like Chuck seeing a bug, I jumped up from my chair.

"Interview over?" Annie spun around to see what I was looking at.

"That's the car that followed me yesterday." I pointed. "We need to hide right now."

I bolted for the door and went inside the restaurant. But Annie stayed put. Inside Smoothie King, I watched her on the other side of the glass, feeling like I'd either abandoned her to her death, or that I'd only imagined she was there. It was like she was in a glass box beyond me. I motioned for her to come inside, but she only waved at the Mercedes.

When it passed by, I ran back outside and told her, "Okay, we need to move."

"Why?" Annie smiled.

"Are you having me followed?"

"My God, you're as paranoid as my dad." She rolled her eyes. "Just do some more oxies and calm your shit."

I cleared my throat uncomfortably. "I don't do that stuff anymore. It was that one day, that was all."

"Right, whatever you say," Annie laughed. "I recall one of your tear-stained letters saying that it was 'the perfect day.' Remember? We snuck into Uncle Billy's dresser, found his pills, and filled the kiddy pool with barbecue sauce."

The image of the sauce-filled pool flashed at me, but I blinked it away. "I'm not paranoid," I declared. "That car followed me from the hotel. Don't you think it's suspicious you're with me now when it turns up again?"

"I don't care what you think." Annie picked up her bag and stood up. "Now if you'll excuse me, I need to drop off my father's tux at the funeral home." As she hustled across the street for the parking garage, I kept up beside her. She couldn't leave. I needed to keep asking her questions.

"Did you tell anyone I was at the hotel?" I said, checking over my shoulder for the Mercedes.

"Yes," she said. "I told my siblings that you had stalked me there where I was having a business meeting and to watch their backs for you." So all my cousins knew I was there. Any one of them could have had me chased.

"And now?" I said as we entered the parking garage. "Did you tell anyone we were meeting at Smoothie King?"

"No one. On Betty Beef's honor." Annie did our secret blood sister cow horn sign above her head. "I only told my husband I was meeting you for lunch, but I didn't say where I was going."

I continued following Annie to her burnt orange SUV. In my panicked state, I didn't know what else to ask, but I felt like she was getting away with all the answers I still needed. When she unlocked her vehicle with a double beep, she snatched off her sunglasses and looked me straight in the eye.

"Listen," she said, softening her tone, "I know things are shit between us, and that's a real shame it worked out that way, but I need to know something. Are you going to tell Rick about my sexual indiscretions?"

"I don't know," I said. "Depends how I'm feeling."

"You'd better not," she warned. "You already saw how I can throw a punch when I'm threatened. Just imagine if I had time to plot something out."

"Oh yeah? Like a murder?" I opened my bag and pulled out a threat of my own—the threatening note with the sparkly sticker letters. "Maybe you did this?"

Annie's eyes widened. Then she swiped the note out of my hand, oddly excited, like she'd found something she thought was lost. "Where did you get this?"

"From the killer. Reminded me of the marketing materials on your dining room table."

"Yeah right, I made this. I've got way more taste than to have this font. Helvetica, it looks like. How do I know this thing's real anyway?" She threw the note back at me. "I know you PIs lie to get what you want. Dad was probably onto something when he said you'd invited yourself to our party."

"Maybe he was—"

I stopped myself. The shark fin of the Mercedes had resurfaced across the street. I squatted behind the concrete barrier, pulling Annie by the wrist so she was down with me.

"What are you doing?" She shook her arm. "Let me go."

"You're staying here until that car passes." I held onto her while she continued trying to shake herself free, clawing me with sharp nails I couldn't feel. It almost felt fun, like we were kids again.

"Jesus, let me go." She grabbed my bag with her free hand, and I released my grip. The last thing I needed was her finding my pills and chucking them into a street gutter.

With a huff, Annie stood up and got into her car. I peeked over the concrete wall. The Mercedes was gone.

"Nice chatting with you!" Annie called from her open window as she started her car. "And see you at the funeral tomorrow. That is, if you make it there alive." She flashed me a fake smile. "Oh, and one more question for you, Miss Detective. Why is Virginia Wolf still employed at the Marriott?"

My mouth dropped open. "You knew that I was the PI put on your case?"

"Some PI you are. Once you showed us your PI card for Bullseye Services, I knew you were the one who had my case."

"How?"

"Because you'd mentioned at dad's party that you'd been to Rocky's the day before. And I looked up Ginny Wolf's social media page. She'd also been at Rocky's that day. Hardly a coincidence."

"So why did you file that claim?" I said. "Who's this Ginny to you?"

"She works at the front desk at the Marriott, and I saw her run out of Kolya's room with the diamond necklace he gave me. She even swiped his

Rocky's gift cards on top of it, the cheap bitch. But I couldn't report her for theft because the surveillance tape had been conveniently erased." Annie took a deep breath. "Anyway, I saw her stumbling that afternoon in crutches, so I knew she was lying about her injury and looked for a PI to catch her breaking her workers' comp. Too bad you didn't catch her."

"I had evidence of her lying, but my camera was stolen."

"What a shame. You know, maybe it's a good thing I cost you your PI job. I don't think you're suited for investigative work."

I lunged at her window. "You're the one who got me fired?"

"Sorry," she said with a bright smile. "But now you'll have way more time to do drugs. I'll send you a postcard from New York to make you feel better."

With a giggle, Annie flipped her hair, the equivalent of her middle finger. Then she zipped out of the garage, gone. As her car sped off and the quiet returned, I pulled on my hair and screamed so hard it felt like there was a knife in my throat. Then I opened my bag and swallowed more pills.

A few minutes later, I was woozier than ever. When I headed back to the car, Aunt Kat was leaning against the trunk with a chicken sandwich in her mouth. *The Mercedes.*

"Get away from the car!" I shouted at my aunt.

My energy was low, but I started running toward her. Aunt Kat was confused, but she moved back. As for me, I didn't care whether I got blown up. I got out my phone's flashlight, dropped to my hands and knees, and rolled under the car. No bomb, but a red light was blinking.

The Mercedes had been following me.

Chapter Thirty-Three

I YANKED OFF THE TRACKER, the same model as the one I'd found on Luis's car, and stuck it on another car's bumper. Then I got me and Aunt Kat out of the garage.

"Who do you think did it?" Aunt Kat mumbled through a bite of chicken sandwich, as I turned on a side street in the direction of Chuck's house. "You've been inspecting the car every time."

"Not every time." I checked my rearview mirror. "I didn't look when we left Teddy's since Susanne was chasing us out with a gun."

I splashed water on my face to keep my eyes open. *You were stupid taking more.*

Still not enough to overdose, but too many. I was losing steam.

"It was probably his crazy wife," Aunt Kat suggested.

"Maybe, but it could have been Teddy while I was waiting for him. He's the one who took Luis into the office to apparently snort coke. I don't know if that's true, but what happened in that office could explain why there was a tracker on Luis's car."

She frowned. "But how did that Mercedes know we were at the hotel yesterday? There wasn't a tracker on the car. You checked."

"I did. But Annie told her siblings I was there, so any one of them could have called that Mercedes driver to follow us."

Aunt Kat swallowed her last bite of sandwich and squished the paper bag into a ball.

"Well, we know one thing. Whoever's driving that Mercedes isn't too smart using the same car today as yesterday."

"More reason Teddy's involved."

We arrived at the Mickey Mouse House to find a giant moving truck in the driveway. No longer dressed up in her polka-dots and mouse ears, Marigold stood on the porch giving orders to movers. I got out of the car and walked toward her.

In the heat, and with all the drugs coursing through me, the air felt like wet sand.

"The princess floor lamp," Marigold said to a mover. "Be careful with that one." When she saw me, her face shriveled into coldness. "What are you doing here?"

"I need to talk to Chuck."

"He's not here."

I stepped aside so a mover could move by with a display case. "Where are you guys moving?"

"I'm the only one moving. We broke up last night, but that's all you need to know."

"Know where I can find him?"

"He left his phone here when he ran off this morning, but he's probably at Loose Park meditating in the rose garden. He's been going there every day since his dad died to get away from everything." She rubbed her forehead, as if to ward off a headache.

"Okay, I'll check it out," I said. "Where are you headed now?"

"None of your business."

That was the answer I expected. I got back in the car and gulped down half a bottle of sparkling water, but no matter how much I drank, my throat was still dry.

"My goodness, you're pale as a parsnip," Aunt Kat exclaimed. "What happened?"

"Just a hiccup is all." I hoped my aunt didn't attribute my weakened physical state to drugs, but she wasn't asking, so I figured I was still in the clear. "Chuck's likely at Loose Park."

My mind was fogging and my breathing slowing down, and I drove even slower so we wouldn't get into an accident. At every stoplight, I drank more water. All the while, Aunt Kat was worrying about me, but I couldn't listen to her. *Focus on the road.* When I got to the hill and rolled up for Loose Park, I was just relieved we'd made it there in one piece.

"Seriously, Tori," Aunt Kat said. "You should let me drive next time."

"I'm fine." I gestured to the park's main pavilion, where a group of drunk teenagers were having a party. "Looks like the kids are enjoying being out of school." It reminded me of when I was last here, celebrating the success of Swensons Barbecue. The memory only added to my nausea. I handed Aunt Kat my stun gun. "Here."

As she took it, she looked at me in bewilderment. "Why are you giving me this?"

"In case you need to use it, all you got to do is switch it on and pull the trigger. Just be sure you're within fifteen feet of your target."

Before she could say more, I got out of the car and started toward the rose garden. The people passing me were fuzzy figures, indistinct witnesses to my staggering feet who were likely disturbed by me, but I kept moving. I had to talk to Chuck.

When I turned into the circular garden, the roses were in bloom, and a stone fountain gurgled at its center. On a bench in the shade sat Chuck in black shorts and a black T-shirt. His eyes were closed, his head poorly shaved. There were at least a dozen razor cuts on his scalp. I started recording on my phone. More than any other interview, I needed this one on tape, because with all the pills I was on, I might not remember it.

"Chuck?" I poked his arm. He recoiled, opened his eyes, and looked at me with a tearful gaze. "Sorry to hear about your breakup."

"You went to the house?" His voice was quiet. "I told her she could take whatever she wanted."

I sat down beside him on the bench. "Why?"

"They're material attachments that remind me of her, but it doesn't matter now since I'm moving to Myanmar this weekend."

"Myanmar?" My head jolted at this news, which was almost as ludicrous as hearing that a tick had killed Uncle Charlie. "Why are you moving there?"

"To meditate."

"About what?"

"Everything. Marigold never loved me. My father never loved me. No one ever loved me." The tears rolled out, and he didn't bother to dab them.

"Sorry you feel that way." I offered him a tissue. "But I was hoping to ask you some more questions about my case."

"Sure." Chuck took the tissue and honked into it.

I pulled out his financial records. "Your siblings claim you've made miscalculations in your work. Is that true?"

Chuck swallowed and nodded bashfully. "Yes, I've made errors, but when it's your job to be perfect, you fail sometimes. Haven't you ever made mistakes in your work?"

The question felt too painfully relevant, so I ignored it. "I've heard from your siblings that there was a scandal with your accounts at the Memorial Day party. You know what that's all about?"

More tears came. "Yes," he sniffled. "I miscalculated how much we were spending on meat, at least, according to my father. But I don't think I was wrong."

"What did you find out?"

"That we were spending twice as much on meat. Father got so angry with me when I showed him that he threatened to fire me at the party. He was so scary."

"Do you think Uncle Charlie was hiding something?"

Chuck nodded again. "I checked my numbers three times. Same results."

"So why would Uncle Charlie spend twice as much on meat?"

"I don't know. No one ever told me anything."

I looked back at the financial records. "Teddy told me the large sum of money he took out from the company account was your mistake. Is that possible?"

Chuck turned to look right at me, his eyes serious. "No, he's lying. He was the one buying all that extra meat."

I shook my head. Unless Chuck was lying, which I didn't think he was, I still didn't know why Uncle Charlie would buy extra meat and how that would play into Luis's death. It was also especially hard thinking through my jelly mind, but I went on with my questions. "What about Emma?" I asked. "She claimed she bought cookers and gave those receipts to Uncle Charlie."

"Maybe, but I never saw her receipts. Like I told you already, my family often keeps me out of the loop—" He jumped off the bench as a buzzing bee landed on a nearby rose.

I pulled myself up to approach my frightened cousin, now clinging and heaving to the fountain rim like he might get sick in it. "How do you expect to survive the wilderness when you run away from bees?" I said. "You'll be surrounded by all kinds of jungle bugs in Myanmar."

"That's just it." Chuck splashed dirty fountain water on his face. "I need to flush out my demons, attachments, and fears to find the true path to enlightenment. Nature is the ultimate test. I need to reconcile myself to her by loving her, not fearing her."

"Don't you think you might just be running away from the things that you need to face here?" As I said this, I felt like I was talking to myself.

"Maybe, but I need a new start," Chuck said. "A new place with no pain."

"Except that place doesn't exist. The kind of pain you've got is going with you wherever you go." Chuck looked at the ground and stayed silent. "Anyway," I went on, "how does Mickey feel about this plan?"

"Mickey?" Chuck's blue eyes grew pale with confusion. "What do you mean?"

"Didn't you know Marigold was drugging you to bring out your Mickey Mouse personality?"

"She was?" he said, sounding genuinely surprised and confused.

"Yeah, it seemed like you were under hypnosis when I saw it happen, like you could switch in and out of it."

Chuck let out a sudden gasp of understanding. "So that's why I have some memory gaps. Marigold told me bad things that I'd done, and I couldn't remember them. Sometimes I felt like I was waking up somewhere strange and couldn't remember how I'd got there."

"What did she say you did?" I asked.

Now Chuck dropped his head. "I don't want to talk about it."

"Like hurting people?"

Chuck teared up and started panting. "I'm sorry, but I really don't want to talk about it. Not now, please."

"It's okay," I said, trying to calm him down. "It's not your fault if it was Mickey and you were being drugged."

"What was she giving me?"

"Did you see any yellow powder around? I think that's the drug she was using on you."

He nodded. "Yes, I saw her putting that powder in my drinks, but I thought it was part of the recipe. And it tasted so good and made me feel so nice. I didn't want to ask and upset her either when I was just so happy to have a girlfriend."

"Chuck, you know you deserve someone who isn't going to drug you, right?"

"I don't deserve anything," he said, rubbing his nicked-up bald head. "Everything must go that was weighing me down. In fact, before you touched my arm, I had decided to renounce my inheritance."

I scanned Chuck's distressed face. His emotions seemed authentic, but I had to wonder, on some level, whether he was only becoming a monk and running out of the country because he felt guilty or fearful of getting caught for murder.

And now he'd even told me he knew of things he'd done. If only I could push through his fragility and get a confession.

I held up the same threatening note with the sparkly sticker letters I'd shown all my cousins. "Does this mean anything to you?"

"I don't think so. Like everything else, I know nothing." Already, Chuck sounded like a monk.

"Do you know if Mickey made it?"

"I don't know."

"What about Marigold? Did she make this card with the sparkly stickers?"

"Not that I know of," Chuck said, his breathing getting shorter again with anxiety.

"Okay, it's okay," I said, squeezing his shoulder. "Can you tell me if you remember her asking you to do anything for her at all?"

"Yeah, all the time," he said. "She wanted me to vote to sell the drive-in, push for vegan items on the menu, or buy her vacations, jewelry, clothes, and furniture."

"And you always did what she asked?"

"I usually obeyed. But last night was different. That was the first time I refused her."

"What happened?"

"I didn't drink my mouse-tail, that was the first thing. I told her it was upsetting my stomach. Then I said I didn't want to close Uncle Charlie's anymore, that I was going to sign the Yummy Foods contract and sell it instead."

"Why would you do that?"

"I told her I wanted to distance myself from the drive-in and forgive my father. Marigold got so mad she screamed and ripped up all the drawings I'd made for her. Then she said it was over."

"Why did you change your mind about signing the contract?"

"Annie convinced me."

"Annie?" My fingers twitched.

That must have been why she was so confident that she was still going to New York when she flew out of the parking garage.

"Yes, she's coming over tonight with the contract for me to sign."

My eyes blew open, and I lunged toward Chuck. "What time?" I said.

"I don't know. She said she'd text first."

"Did she threaten you if you didn't sign?"

"Threaten me?" He shook his head, his panicked breathing coming out like hiccups. "No, she only thought it would be a good idea for my self-growth and self-care to release my attachments to the barbecue business and my father's abuse. I think she's right, don't you?"

I didn't want to upset Chuck any more than I already had. I feared he might have a panic attack if I kept asking him questions or saying what I thought, so I pushed my tongue into my bottom lip. Annie might have been manipulating her naïve brother, but I was still in her way. Soon as the sun went down, I'd be running a stakeout at the Mickey Mouse House. Maybe then, I could also get Chuck to confess what Mickey had done.

Chapter Thirty-Four

WHEN I GOT BACK TO the car, Aunt Kat's eyes lit up. "Jesus, Tori," she exclaimed. "You can barely stand. What's going on?"

I struggled to pop the cap off a new Topo Chico with my thumb ring, my hands vibrating so much I splashed water on my thighs and the car seat. "Nothing," I muttered. "Just mad I don't have answers."

"I think I should drive us home."

I ignored my aunt's suggestion and started the car. "No need. We got another place to go first."

"Where?"

"Chuck's."

"But we were just at Chuck's."

As my aunt continued talking, my pocket buzzed. I took my phone out to check and swallowed despite my cotton-dry mouth. The security system. Both video feeds had been cut on the surveillance app.

I replayed the footage. Two minutes earlier, the Mercedes had pulled up to the house, rolled down the driver's window, pushed a gun through the gap, and shot the camera dead without a pop. A silencer—and a perfect shot.

"No," I said under my breath.

"What?" Aunt Kat shouted. "What now?"

I didn't want to worry her, so I kept my mouth shut. I still had time before Annie went to Chuck's tonight. Now I wanted to confront who'd been following me. I put the car into drive and pulled out onto the road.

"Watch out!" Aunt Kat shrieked before I clipped a stop sign. "My God, you're on drugs again, aren't you?"

I was still rolling down the street in a squiggly line. "I'm fine," I whispered, "I'm—"

"Stop the car," Aunt Kat ordered with tears in her eyes. I stopped in the middle of the street. "Get out. I'm driving." I slunk out and switched seats with her.

"Sorry," I slurred. "I think I'm having a heatstroke out here."

"No, I think it's more than that." My aunt started driving while the tears came out hard. "I had my suspicions, but I wanted to be wrong." She wiped her eyes. "Pains me to say it, but we're sending you back to rehab. I thought you were better. What happened?"

There was no point lying when she already knew the truth. "It's this case. I only started taking pills last week for the stress."

"Opioids?" she choked on the word.

I didn't have to give her an answer. She knew. So I slumped back in my seat, sipping on my water while she drove us home without realizing someone was waiting for us there. It was a good thing, too, that I hadn't warned her about it, or she'd have gone straight to the police station.

I pulled out the stun gun in the passenger side door. Fortunately, it had a wide berth since I'd be an especially bad shot. *Just got to stun them before they shoot you.* When we turned on Aunt Kat's street, I squinted through my hazy vision at the neighborhood. I didn't see a Mercedes on the street, but that didn't mean much. A pro would hide the car after taking out the cameras.

Soon as Aunt Kat pulled into the driveway, I grabbed her by the wrist. "Don't get out. Someone's in the house." With my stun gun, I pointed at the blown-out cameras on the porch and the half-open front door.

Aunt Kat clapped a hand over her mouth. "Oh God, we need to go."

"No, no, stay here." I opened my door.

Aunt Kat jerked me back in the car. "Don't be dumb."

The front door of the house kicked open next, and I didn't need fully functioning eyesight to know who the enormous person was standing there.

"Squishy," I said.

Aunt Kat blinked at me. "Who?"

Seeing how messed up I was, I didn't feel threatened by him. I raised the stun gun and pulled the trigger. When nothing happened, I groaned. "He's too far away."

"And you're not getting any closer. We're leaving right now." Aunt Kat restarted the car, but before we could pull out of the driveway, Squishy raised his gun and shot at the tires. My aunt and I ducked down. "Please don't shoot us!" Aunt Kat shouted at him.

"Where's the folder?" he demanded.

"The folder?" Aunt Kat looked at me, confused. "I don't know what you're talking about." She turned to me, her face desperate. "Tori?"

He had to be talking about the Mickey Mouse folder. "Don't got a folder," I said, like this was a normal question in a normal situation.

"Yeah, you do," Squishy said, advancing toward the car. "And if you don't give it to me now, I'll shoot more than your tires."

Another gunshot fired, and the windshield shattered all over me. Beyond the broken glass, terror blanched Squishy's face. Then he sprinted down the driveway and disappeared.

Aunt Kat hurried to sweep the glass off my lap. "You hurt?" she said.

"No." I raised myself to look around.

Aunt Kat raised herself up too. "Why'd he run off like that?"

"Because he wasn't the one who shot out the windshield."

"What? Then who was it?"

As I turned toward the treehouse, another pop whizzed in my ear. The next thing I heard was the horn blaring. Aunt Kat was lying face-down on it, blood everywhere. I gagged pulling her back. She was bleeding—a lot.

"Aunt Kat?"

She moaned in a deep unrecognizable tone. It was the sound of agony. I looked back at the treehouse. A figure in black jumped from the ladder and ran through the backyard. I was too weak to chase them, and anyway, I needed an ambulance—if only my hands weren't shaking so much.

I activated the voice command on my phone and shouted for 911. Soon an operator was reassuring me that help was on the way. At least we were near Saint Luke's, but this wasn't a consolation. Aunt Kat was still bleeding. She could be dying.

I grabbed her hand and squeezed. "Hold on," I told her. "Help's coming."

"Tori," she murmured. "Please don't hurt yourself, okay?"

Tears beaded up in my eyes. Here she was suffering, maybe even dying, all because of me, and still worrying about my well-being. "I won't."

"You promise?"

I struggled to nod as I heard the sirens coming. "Yeah, I promise."

The medics got Aunt Kat on a gurney, but they couldn't tell me anything except to call the hospital later. Leaving fast as they'd come, I watched the blue and red strobe lights flash down the road before I threw up on myself. Then I stumbled for the porch, where the front door was shot through. I pushed it back and stepped into a living room that looked like a cyclone had visited, with every drawer pulled out, every piece of furniture overturned, mail and magazines everywhere. Even Aunt Kat's cow painting was on the floor, slashed. At least Rebus was all right, meowing from under the plum couch, but I didn't wait to keep my promise. I stumbled to the bathroom, emptied the rest of my pills into the toilet, and flushed.

After that, I couldn't move or think. The world was heavy and spinning. The only thing I could do was lie on the bathroom floor and unravel toilet paper. I kept pulling, looking for an end, but only more tissue came. At some point, though, I gave up because my eyes closed themselves for sleep or for death. Whichever came first, I didn't care.

Chapter Thirty-Five

OPENED MY EYES TO dusk. A boxer was stuck in my head, trying to punch his way out. I reached over the toilet and hit the lever to flush. The whooshing water masked my inner noise, but I still winced hearing it. Sound, light, touch. Everything hurt.

It had been hours since I'd had a pill. I looked around the bathroom floor. My pill bottle was lying there. I crawled over to it, picked it up—my stomach dropped. It was empty.

Now I vaguely remembered what had happened, and my stomach dropped again. Because I'd gone overboard with the oxies and thought I was invincible against Squishy, Aunt Kat had got shot. Then I'd flushed the pills down the toilet like an idiot.

Rule number one of quitting oxies: never quit cold turkey. That was signing up for hell. Already, the withdrawal symptoms had started—the runny nose, the sweats, the muscle aches, the rising anxiety. The symptoms would only get worse. I figured I had twenty-four hours at best before they were so bad I wouldn't be able to move at all. I swallowed some aspirin for my aches, though it wouldn't help much. And nothing could help my guilt over Aunt Kat. I didn't even know if she was still alive. *If only you weren't such a selfish addict.* But that's what I was.

I picked up the phone and called the hospital.

"I'm calling to find out about Katherine Swenson," I said to the nurse. "I'm her niece."

The nurse paused to review her records. "Yes, she was brought in for surgery a few hours ago. They removed a bullet, but her condition is still unstable. Call back tomorrow."

I hung up and wanted to die. I scrolled down to Darnell's number, my finger hovering over the button, but I couldn't press it. Not only had he ignored Aunt Kat's call yesterday, but he was serious about cutting me off. Plus, it wasn't like he could help me arrest Aunt Kat's shooter when I didn't know who it was either. The only thing I knew for sure was that it wasn't Squishy.

I went to the living room and slammed an open table drawer, which I immediately regretted because it was another stab in my ears. I grabbed my head, trying to think through the pounding headache. Squishy was looking for something, but I couldn't remember much except Aunt Kat getting shot by that person in the treehouse.

I opened my phone to see if I'd recorded anything from the shooting, but the last thing I had was my interview with Chuck, something I also barely remembered.

I played it to fill in my memory gap. When I got to the part where Chuck was talking about signing the contract, I hissed. *That's right.* Annie was manipulating Chuck.

I looked at the clock. It was 8:12 p.m. Maybe she hadn't gone over to his place yet. If I went there now, I might still be able to stop her. But soon as I reached for my bag, I saw my aunt's slashed cow painting on the floor, and the cow's brown expressive eyes gazed back at me to slash my heart. *You can't go to Chuck's.* Because much as I wanted to punish Annie, Aunt Kat was more important. I needed to find who'd shot her before the withdrawal effects rendered me completely useless.

The only place I could think to go was Squishy's. Maybe he hadn't shot my aunt, but he knew something about my case I didn't. After changing my clothes so I wouldn't stink of blood and vomit, I checked my bag. My cuffs and stun gun were still there. Then I headed out the blasted front door. I'd have to walk to Squishy's since the car tires were shot out, though I also wasn't exactly in any condition to drive.

As I hobbled down the street toward Southwest Trafficway, Darnell's angelic words flitted in my ear to warn me again: *He could crush your skull.*

Chapter Thirty-Six

MY CLOTHES WERE SOAKING IN sweat and my body aching inside-out by the time I'd arrived at Squishy's gray bungalow. I stopped at the mailbox and groaned. Already my head was throbbing harder. Music was blasting inside. Still, I moved toward the shabby house, slithering through the shadows of the trees alongside Squishy's driveway. The nearer I got, the clearer its disrepair. Paint cracking, wood splitting, windows broken. Even the slats of the attic vent dangled out like someone had kicked them from the inside.

I pulled out my stun gun and approached the dark porch where the music, which I could now discern was country, rattled the rusty gutter. There was a small window on the front door, but it was too high for me to look into the house. I held out my stun gun, ready to pull the trigger, and raised my other hand to knock.

But a car was coming, and it was slowing down. When the headlights stopped outside Squishy's, I lowered my hand and squinted through the darkness. It was a taxi, and a figure was stepping out with a large, cylindrical object. I didn't wait to be discovered. I scurried around the side of the house to hide by the garbage cans.

Squishy's guest knocked with little gusto, but they didn't need to bang on the door to be heard. A small dog with a yappy bark alerted Squishy to his visitor. The dog, yet another obstacle in my way. At least it didn't sound big and threatening. The door opened, letting out more music.

"You're late," I could hear Squishy say over the music and barking dog. There was a silent pause between the two people. "Well," Squishy went on, "what are you waiting for? Come on in."

Footsteps followed. The door slammed shut.

The appearance of a mystery guest meant my plan had changed. Instead of confronting Squishy, I needed to eavesdrop on his conversation. Outside the house, though, I couldn't hear a thing. Not with the windows boarded up and the music playing. I returned to the front of the house, careful not to step on a twig and alert the dog to my presence.

Softly, I pressed my ear to the door, cringed at the sound, and pulled back. Again, nothing but music. If I was going to hear any conversation, I'd have to get inside. I stepped back to examine the roof with its broken shingles flaking off. If I could somehow climb up there, I could pull out one of those dangling slats from the attic vent and sneak inside. The question, though, was whether I was capable of climbing anything with the withdrawals already turning my arms and legs to putty. I was pretty sure I wouldn't make it.

There was a stand-alone garage on the far side of the property, and I headed over to see if Squishy had a ladder. The door was locked, but I cupped my hands over the window. Inside was the Mercedes, lots of tools, and sure enough, a ladder.

I grabbed a rake and propped the window open wide enough to climb through. Again, a benefit to being small.

When I was in, I grabbed the ladder, unlocked the door, and dragged my prop across the lawn until it was leaning on the side of Squishy's house. I climbed up all the rungs, somehow managing not to fall, and stepped onto the vibrating roof that made my stomach turn. The shingles were crumbly too, but at least the slope wasn't that steep.

I moved onward and upward, trying not to slip, until I reached the attic vent with its slats that looked like a child's mouth, with the teeth hanging loosely. One needed to pop out for me to fit through the hole, so I took ahold of the bottom plank and pulled—it wasn't coming out easy. I pulled harder and this time it came out, but I stumbled back with it, sliding down the roof as the shingles ripped over my cut-up legs. My pain was at a level ten out of ten, but my fear of falling off the roof was greater, and I grabbed onto the plumbing vent sticking out and held on.

I'd saved myself from breaking my neck, but my phone slid out of my pocket and clanged in the gutter. Of course, the dog started barking next. *Shit.* I swallowed, trying to keep still, my heart beating hard against the pulsating house. Then I heard the door open.

For a moment, I just heard loud music. Squishy was investigating his property, but I hoped he wouldn't come around to the side of his house. If he did, he'd see the ladder, and then I'd be in serious trouble. "I can't believe it," I heard Squishy say. "Damn squirrels."

The door slammed after that, leaving me to rest on the roof with relief. I lay there, taking hot, heavy breaths, my drenched body hurting everywhere. It was no wonder, either, with how scraped up I was, but I peeled myself back up, leaving my phone to lie wherever it was. It would be too risky looking for it anyway without a flashlight.

I made my way back up to the attic vent, poked my head through the hole I'd made, and shut my eyes. *Jesus.* My throat burned, and I gripped on the vent's side so I wouldn't fall again. When I opened my eyes again, I saw what I thought I saw—Gabe, on the ground, wrapped like a moth in a spider's lair. As I'd suspected, Squishy had done something to him. A faint light came in from under the attic door, enough that I could see Gabe's swollen and bruised eyes looking up at me.

"Tori?" he muffled through the bloody cloth in his mouth.

"Thank God you're alive," I said, trying not to get sick at the foul sauna I was crawling into. I bent down to untie his gag. Soon as it was off, his hungry mouth snapped at the air.

"Tori," Gabe coughed, "I'm so glad—" But he couldn't finish because he started sobbing.

I never thought I'd feel sorry for Gabe, but I certainly did in this moment. This was one broken man. I had to give him a hug.

"You're okay now," I tried reassuring him while holding him and rubbing his back.

"I'm so glad to see you," he cried into my shoulder.

"Me too. But right now we need to act smart. Can you tell me what happened to you?"

Gabe pulled back from me, his mouth twitching. Then he nodded, took a quick breath, and began in a raspy tone, "I've been investigating why Rocky's hasn't been receiving their meat shipments. Harrison's the main meat supplier, so he's been under suspicion for theft. Yesterday, he caught me snooping around in his truck. That's when he took my phone. I managed to throw my sunglasses to leave a clue, but after that, he locked me inside the truck. Then he drove me here and beat—"

Gabe stopped. I wanted to hear more of his story, but I could see he was too traumatized to go on. "It's all right," I said, rubbing his shoulders.

"Is help coming?"

"Just me I'm afraid. I can't call anyone either. Lost my phone on the roof."

Gabe's eyes widened. "You need to go get help."

"No way. I'm not leaving you here."

"But it's not safe. If he catches you, he'll hurt you much worse than me."

I allowed myself to glance over Gabe's body. Not only was he covered in cuts, bruises, blood, and his own bodily waste, but his beautiful face looked like roast beef that had been sitting under a heat lamp all day.

"I'm not leaving you here," I repeated. "Plus, I'm armed." I showed him my stun gun tucked into my shorts. From the blank look on his face, I could tell he wasn't confident in me. Still, he didn't argue while I untied his feet. When I got to his hands, I saw they were cuffed. "Where's the key?"

"Harrison's got it."

"Okay, stay put while I go get it," I said like it was no big deal.

"He's got a chihuahua, you know."

"Yeah, I heard it." I gave him my best attempt at a smile, but he was somewhere else. "You know," I added before I realized what I was saying, "the reason I broke things off with you back in the day had nothing to do with you. I even kind of liked you."

Gabe looked at me intensely. "Why are you bringing that up now?"

"Guess I don't care about hiding the truth when we might die." I gave a shrug. "See, I'd relapsed my third time then and was too ashamed to tell you about it."

"Relapsed on what?"

"Oxies. And you know what's funny? I relapsed for the fourth time this week and then quit again tonight. Couldn't have picked better timing, right?"

"Wait," Gabe said and looked at me with concern. "So you're going through withdrawals right now?"

"Yep, full force. They're only getting worse from here on out, too, so I'd better find Squishy before I can't move."

"You really shouldn't confront him, Tori."

"Don't worry. When this is all over, we'll get together for milkshakes and have a good laugh."

Gabe looked scared for me as I opened the attic door. The music was louder than ever, with the subwoofer downstairs making my temples throb to their own drumbeat. Holding the stun gun in front of me, I wobbled down the hall toward a staircase, where I could smell the acrid scent of coke and was close enough to hear voices.

"I'm thinking of selling again," Squishy announced. "Lots of dough in the white stuff."

"Yeah, this is some high-quality shit," his guest said and snorted a line. "Where did you get it?"

I drew in a quick breath. I knew that voice. It had been nervous today when I'd threatened it with exposure, but now the voice sounded different. Now it sounded invincible.

Chapter Thirty-Seven

M Y GASP MUST HAVE GIVEN me away, because paws began clipping the hardwood stairs, slowly coming up.

I stepped back with my stun gun. A chihuahua wrapped its head around the corner and bared its underbite at me. I didn't want to stun such a small dog, but when it jumped toward me and bit my leg, I had no choice but to pull the trigger. There was a shrill whimper, and the dog slumped back to disappear down the stairwell, its paralyzed body rippling over the steps.

"Holy shit, your dog!" Teddy shrieked.

Squishy screamed like a father finding his kid wedged under a car, but before he could reach his dog at the bottom of the stairs, I stumbled down first, my stun gun still drawn. I stepped over the injured animal into a living room where the music was at peak volume. My head was really going to pop. At the sight of me, Squishy clenched his jaw, but he didn't attack. Not when my weapon was aimed at him. Instead, he turned to his dog whelping in pain.

Teddy was sitting on the couch wiping his nose as if I hadn't heard or seen anything unusual. "Tori?" he shouted over the music, his eyes bloodshot. I yanked out the stereo plug and for a moment the silence was so disorienting it hurt. "What are you doing here?" Teddy said.

My head spun as I took in the room, my cousin, Squishy, the yelping dog, the coke pile on the table, Teddy's golf bag on the couch. "That was my question for you."

Teddy stood up. "Harrison's a meat supplier, I told you that. And you know I like drugs. No secret there. We were only having some fun. Want to join us?"

"Fuck that," Squishy said, as he stopped petting his dog to turn his murderous gaze on me. "She hurt my dog."

"Not as bad as you hurt my colleague," I said, still aiming my stun gun at Squishy.

"So?" Squishy raised himself so he was towering over me by two feet, making me feel like I was at a disadvantage, even though I had a weapon. "That pretty boy deserved it for being in my business."

"Come on, guys," Teddy interjected. "We don't want a scandal."

"Sorry, but she's dying tonight," Squishy announced. "Then I'm feeding her to Bubbles. If you didn't want your cousin getting hurt, you shouldn't have asked me to chase her."

I raised my stun gun at Squishy's face. "So," I said, nodding at my cousin, "you were the one who put that tracker on my car yesterday, weren't you?"

"What?" Teddy said. "I don't know what Harrison's talking about. I didn't ask him to chase you."

Squishy redirected his anger from me to Teddy. "You calling me a liar?"

"No, I—"

"Don't tell me you didn't want that fucking folder."

"What folder?" I said, playing dumb as I had Chuck's Mickey Mouse folder in my bag.

"You have it, Tori," Teddy said. "I've got access to Dad's home surveillance system, and I saw Jean give it to you."

"Jean?" Now I thought back to when she gave me that Yummy Foods folder. It had a note with Nikolai's location on it. Maybe Teddy was looking for Nikolai, and Annie was keeping him a secret for some reason, but I wasn't about to check my bag now.

"Yeah, it has something in there I need," Teddy continued. "That's why when Annie called yesterday and said you were at the Marriott, I told Harrison to find you and get it. That was all, I swear. I never told him to hurt you."

"Well, I've got no idea what you're talking about," I said. "Don't got a folder."

"Yes, you do. Look in your bag." Teddy advanced toward me, and I shifted my aim on him.

"Stay back or I'll shoot."

He put his hands up. "Please, just give it to me. I'll give you ten grand for your trouble."

"I told you I don't have it. I threw that thing away thinking it was trash."

"Where did you throw it away?" Teddy advanced toward me, forgetting my warning and the weapon in my hand. I pulled the trigger, holding it a few seconds longer than with the dog to be sure I'd got him good. No noise went off, but you knew you'd hit your target when you heard a scream.

Sure enough, Teddy let out a high-pitched squeal and fell to the ground to twitch. His muscle spasms would incapacitate him for at least fifteen minutes, if not longer. I repositioned my aim back at Squishy who stared at me like he didn't care I could sting him next.

"Why are you stealing meat from Rocky's?" I asked him.

"That's the question that put your friend in my attic, the same place you're going."

Something hard then hit me on the forehead—keys, now at my feet. My focus was blurred, but I could see Squishy move toward me as another shape emerged at the top of the stairs. It was Gabe, and as Squishy turned around to face him, Gabe threw his chained arms over Squishy's tree trunk neck. At once, they both fell back on the steps, with Gabe trying to strangle Squishy while Squishy slammed Gabe into the stairs.

This time, I didn't fumble. I raised the stun gun at Squishy and fired. Squishy sucked on his teeth and threw his head back.

Dropping the weapon, I rushed over to Gabe and lifted the chain over Squishy's head. Though Squishy was 250 pounds of muscle, I pulled his feet down the stairs to free Gabe beneath him. Gabe was wheezing, but still breathing while I got out my cuffs. I threw a metal claw on one of Squishy's meaty wrists, but as I went for the other, he grabbed my wrist hard with his free hand. I swallowed. The stun gun hadn't worked right.

I tried to pull back, but Squishy took me by the throat and squeezed hard. I dug my nails into his hand, but he pushed me against the staircase railing so that the iron dug into my spine. Rage burned in his protruding eyes. I spat on his face and he flinched, lessening his grip for a moment. I slapped at his face with both my hands, digging my thumb ring into his cheek and carving it until blood came. He yelped and squeezed my neck harder. I couldn't breathe. My chest was tightening. As my vision started going splotchy, a light glinted at me—the open bracelet. I reached to take ahold of it and snapped it on the stair rail. The click made Squishy stop strangling me to turn around.

"Shit," he said, and released his grasp on me to yank the chain.

I slid down the stairs and hit the ground. As I tried to breathe, Squishy attempted to rip the rail out of the wall, his grunts overtaken by metal clapping metal. I crawled to the stun gun on the floor, picked it up, and pointed it at Squishy. This time, I fired a few feet away and held the trigger until Squishy let out a horrendous scream and fell to the floor. Now he really was down. Beside me my moaning cousin was still lying on the floor. I took his phone from his pocket to call 911.

A woman answered, "What's your emergency?"

I choked getting the words out. "I need— the police— I've restrained two men— and I need an ambulance for a man who's been badly beaten." I gave her the address.

"What about you? Are you in need of help?"

"No, I'll live."

I lay on the ground to cough and rub my bruised neck. It was from this vantage point that I saw what was in Teddy's golf bag. Money, clean wads of it. That was why his bag didn't have clubs in it yesterday. He wasn't golfing, he was getting money for Squishy. I also remembered what Chuck had said about Teddy withdrawing more money from the company account to pay for double the meat.

I slid over to my groaning cousin. "Hey," I said, "were you paying Harrison to steal meat from Rocky's so you could sell it at Uncle Charlie's?"

Teddy wrestled to open his mouth. "You're not getting a word out of me," he moaned.

"Is that why you put the tracker on Luis's car? So you'd know where to kill him before he could tell anyone about your meat conspiracy?"

"I don't know what you're talking about."

"Listen, I'll shoot you again if you don't tell me the truth."

"I killed no one," Teddy shouted. "I told you I'm not a murderer."

"Then why did you go into the office with Luis? I know you weren't doing drugs. He didn't do drugs."

"He was blackmailing me, all right? Luis overheard me bribing Harrison to steal meat from Rocky's."

So that was the motive. Luis was blackmailing Teddy because Harrison was stealing meat from Rocky's. My head hurt to think, but this explained why Rocky's only had chicken wings and the Holiday Rib Sandwich Special the other night.

"Why were you stealing meat from Rocky's?" I pressed my cousin. "Were you running low or what?"

"Of course not. But Yummy Foods was considering a sale between us and Rocky's, and Dad thought they'd definitely pick us if Rocky's looked incompetent running out of their own supply while we added an extra meaty burger to our menu."

"The UltraCharBurger," I said, remembering my unfinished lunch still in the glove compartment of Aunt Kat's car.

"Yeah."

"Did your dad also tell you to kill Luis for blackmailing you?"

"No, I keep telling you I didn't kill anyone or have anyone killed," Teddy said, getting angry. "Dad didn't even know about Luis blackmailing me. I didn't tell him because he'd have blamed me for it. Anyway, that's the reason you saw Luis smiling on the camera after leaving the office. I'd just given him blackmail money."

"How much?"

"Ten thousand."

The exact amount I'd found in Luis's car. Teddy's story added up to the right numbers. "Still sounds like a motive to kill," I said.

"Maybe, but I didn't do it, and you know it. You saw my sex tape. It proves I wasn't at Uncle Charlie's when Luis died."

"And maybe you made that tape to have an alibi because you hired Harrison over there to kill him for you."

Teddy shook his head. "No, absolutely not."

"Then why were you tracking Luis?"

"Why not? He was blackmailing me."

There was a pounding at the door. "Police."

My heart swelled. It was Darnell.

"Don't shoot!" I called out. "The suspects aren't armed."

Darnell kicked the door open, his gun drawn, with two cops behind him. He looked at me with raised brows. "Tori?" he said. "What are you doing here?"

"Yeah, I know. I'm still alive." I tried to laugh but it came out as a cough.

"Shit, you look horrible."

"Yeah, and I feel even worse than I look."

"Here." He offered me his hand and pulled me up off the floor. For a moment, we stared at each other, not sure what to do.

"I'm sorry," I said, breaking the silence.

"Me too, Tor." Darnell grabbed me for a hug. This was the best feeling I'd had all week. "I shouldn't have abandoned you like that, but I was pissed. I didn't have the energy to deal with another one of your relapses."

"I get it," I sighed. "It's not easy being my friend."

"But friends shouldn't leave friends." He rubbed my back. "I hope you can forgive me."

"There's nothing to forgive."

Darnell stepped back to point at Squishy. "Isn't that the guy who stole your camera at Rocky's? Is that why you're here?"

"No, that's nothing compared to what else this guy's done. He was stealing meat from Rocky's and selling it to Uncle Charlie's. The money's in that golf bag." I nodded at it. "Also, Harrison nearly killed my colleague." I nodded toward Gabe, still lying on the stairs.

After Darnell and the other cops did a quick sweep of the house to be sure no one else was being kidnapped and assaulted, Squishy and Teddy were placed into separate cop cars and taken to jail. A detective would come tomorrow with a search warrant and do a finer sweep of the house.

Meanwhile, an ambulance arrived to take Gabe to the hospital. He couldn't talk on the gurney, but I gave him a hand squeeze, and he gave me a half-smile. He was going to be okay. As for Bubbles, Darnell called animal control to take her somewhere safe.

After Darnell had retrieved my camera from Squishy's bedroom and fished my phone out of the gutter, he lit a cigarette on the porch. Though the smoke irritated my throat, especially with my withdrawals, I didn't care too much when I was just happy to have my best friend back.

"I swear you'll give me a heart attack one day," he said as smoke swirled over his head. "But tell me, what's happened in your case since I last saw you?"

"Aunt Kat got shot today," I said, shivering at those words.

"Oh my God. Is she all right?"

My body felt so nauseous thinking about it again that I had to lean against the side of the house so I wouldn't collapse. "I don't know," I said. "But I got so upset about it that I flushed my pills down the toilet a few hours ago. Going through withdrawals now."

"Jesus. No wonder you look so terrible."

"Thanks."

"Dang it, Tor. I'm pulling for your aunt, of course, but I've got to say I'm relieved you quit again. Now that you got some closure on this Mendoza case, I hope you can really focus again on your self-recovery."

"Yeah, I want that, but—"

"What?"

I hated to think it much less say it to Darnell. "I'm not sure this case is over," I confessed.

"What do you mean?" He squinted at me. "You don't think Teddy and his friend were the ones involved in Luis's death?"

"I don't know. Teddy said he didn't hire Squishy to kill Luis. He could be lying, of course, but if that's true, that means the real murderer is still out there. I still don't have any evidence of murder."

"Well, let's hope you got the right guys." Darnell put his butt out on Squishy's front door. "In the meantime, I'm taking you to the hospital."

"No, no," I winced. "I'll be all right. Trust me, I've suffered worse withdrawals. I didn't swallow enough pills this past week for them to kill me."

Darnell lifted a brow but gave a nod. "Okay, but I'm sleeping over tonight. Then we're getting you back in rehab tomorrow."

"I'll go back," I reassured him, but I didn't tell him rehab wasn't happening tomorrow. Not only was Uncle Charlie's funeral in the afternoon, but I couldn't check myself into a clinic until I was certain I'd found the killer. After all, my gut was telling me I hadn't.

And my gut never lied.

Chapter Thirty-Eight

THE DARK PURPLE DOOR HUNG from its hinge, barely open in the night breeze. Darnell pushed it back, to disaster. Again, I was confronted with my aunt's broken things and how I was the one to blame for it all. Warm tears stung my eyes. *Let her be okay.*

"What a mess," Darnell said. "What was this Squishy looking for anyway?"

"Don't know," I said, though that was a lie. Now I knew what Squishy wanted, or rather, what Teddy wanted, but I didn't want to get out the Yummy Foods folder until I was alone. Maybe there was something in it I didn't want Darnell to see. "Could you help me up the stairs?" I asked. "My legs might as well be liquid."

"Yeah, let's get you to bed." Darnell threw me over his shoulder, carried me up the stairs, and got me under the covers. Then he brought me a cold Topo Chico and some aspirin.

"Thanks." I swallowed a few pills and felt ready to pass out. I wondered if I'd be able to sleep, though. Exhausted as I was, insomnia was another classic withdrawal symptom.

"All right, you're safe here," Darnell said. "Need anything else?"

"Yeah, can you feed Rebus?" I pointed at his empty bowl. "He's probably starving."

Darnell opened a can of wet food and scooped the contents into the bowl, but when Rebus didn't come running, my stomach pinched with a mother's fear. I sat up in bed, looking around the room for him.

"Rebus," I called out, but there was still no sign of him. "Rebus!"

"Maybe I scared him off?" Darnell said.

"No, he knows you. And he loves food." I didn't care that I was weak. I rolled out of bed and dropped down to my hands and knees to look under the bed, but Rebus wasn't there. As I got up and stumbled for the doorway, Darnell blocked my path.

"Stay put," he ordered.

"But Rebus is missing. He's not here. I need to find him. I need to—"

"You need to rest, Tori. Don't worry, I'll go look for him."

While Darnell made me go back to bed to sit there and worry, he searched the house. When he returned, his unhappy expression told me what I didn't want to hear. Again, I got myself out of bed only for him to block my path. "Please," I begged, trying to push past him. "We have to find him. We have to."

Darnell wouldn't let me go. "Listen, he must have gone outside while the front door was open," he said. "I don't want to lie to you. He could be anywhere."

"No." I shook my head. "He's a cat. He's got a homing instinct. You know, cats go back to where they used to live. That's why you're not sup-posed to let them outside right after you move."

"You mean, he went back to Victory House?"

"Yeah, so long as he didn't get hit by a—" I stopped myself from saying more for fear it would come true. More tears came. Rebus was my baby boy, and the kitten Aunt Kat got me when Dad died. And with her already in the hospital, I was sure to lose what sanity I had left if something had happened to Reebs.

"Okay," Darnell said. "I'll go look for him at Victory House, but you have to stay here. You're in no condition to do anything. You need rest." He led me back to bed and handed me my Topo Chico.

I had no choice but to agree to this arrangement. With Darnell gone, I tried distracting myself by reaching for my backpack and pulling out the folder Jean gave me, with the post-it detailing Nikolai's whereabouts still tacked on the front. This time, I opened the flap. Something was tucked into the pocket—a sheet of paper.

I took it out, and my burning eyes widened. No wonder Teddy wanted this bad enough to have me chased. He wasn't looking for Nikolai. He was looking for Uncle Charlie's contract with Yummy Foods, signed and notarized on July 1. My heart beat in my head seeing my uncle's signature, dated only three days before the party. Why hadn't he given this to Nikolai if he'd already signed? Maybe he'd signed thinking he was dying from the allergy that actually was killing him, but kept the contract because he wasn't sure he wanted to sell the drive-in. That was what he'd told me in the parking lot, that he didn't know what to do.

Now I also had to question Jean's motives in giving me this, and whether she knew the contents of the folder. That was something I'd confront her about at the funeral tomorrow. I filed the contract back in my bag. If I wasn't so worried over my missing cat, I could almost laugh that I had this document since it didn't matter anymore. Even if I did destroy it, Annie had already won in getting Chuck to sign the new contract last night. Uncle Charlie's was going nationwide.

I heard the front door open, and my heart flipped in my chest. Darnell's footsteps were coming up the stairs, but I didn't hear any meows. Now I was entering panic mode, my breaths growing shorter and shorter.

"Tori!" Darnell called out at me from the doorway. "It's okay, he's fine."

I stopped panting. "He is?" I said in disbelief.

"Yeah, he was at Victory House like you said. Was entertaining everyone too. He's under the couch downstairs because he clawed himself out of my arms as soon as I opened the door. I fixed the hinge so he won't get outside again." Darnell held up his arms to show me the bloody cat scratches, turning my panicked breathing into laughter. I jumped out of bed and handed him a box of tissues for his arm.

"I'll go get him," I said. "He'll come to me."

"Hold up, there." Darnell wiped his bloody arm with the tissue. "Just let me carry you so you don't fall down the stairs and break your neck."

Darnell lifted me up again and took me downstairs to set me on the couch. Then I got down to the floor and pushed aside the broken bong to see the best sight on earth—my little boy, glaring at me with his mismatched eyes.

"Come here, Reebs," I sang out to him. But he was too mad to move. I didn't care if he was yowling, I pulled him out and cradled him. He was filthy and full of bugs from his evening adventure, but I didn't care about that either as I peppered his angry face with kisses.

Chapter Thirty-Nine

THE NEXT MORNING, I WOKE up in wet sheets. Though the sleep had been somewhat restorative, the withdrawals had only gotten worse. More body aches, a sharper headache, and wet, clammy skin. I reached for the aspirin and swallowed several pills, though I knew they'd do little to help.

Darnell was already awake. "Morning," he said in the doorway. "Heard you sleeping."

"Yeah, guess I got some, but I still feel like death," my voice crackled out of me like I'd been chain-smoking last night. "Here's hoping the hospital news doesn't kill me."

"She's gonna be okay," Darnell hurried to reassure me. "I called a few hours ago. They removed the bullet from her shoulder. She's stable now."

For a moment, the rush of endorphins at hearing my aunt was going to live masked my pain.

I couldn't even open my mouth to speak.

"But she needs to rest in the hospital a few days," Darnell continued. "If you want to see her, we can stop by this morning on the way to rehab."

I cleared my sore throat at his suggestion. "Sorry," I said. "I can't go to rehab today."

Darnell narrowed his eyes on me. "Why not?"

"Uncle Charlie's funeral. Then there's a barbecue party in the West Bottoms for the family."

Darnell rubbed the spot between his eyes. "Why would you want to go to his funeral after everything that's happened and how shitty you feel?"

"I know it's nuts, but I want to see my family one more time before I move on from them for good."

"Well, that sounds stupid to me, but I guess I won't stop you. I'd go with you too if I wasn't on duty all day. I want to try questioning that Squishy guy if he'll talk. You know your cousin lawyered up right away after we charged him with conspiring to steal from Rocky's, as well as the kidnapping and assault of your colleague. Guess he didn't realize he could be charged with crimes he didn't commit if they related to a conspiracy he was involved in."

"Not surprised there."

"Anyway, I'll come back this afternoon and take you to the church if that's what you still want to do. Until then, try to rest up and reconsider what you're doing."

Darnell left me alone in the house, and I started recharging my stun gun in case I needed it again. My phone had lost power overnight as well, and when I plugged it in, it lit up. A new text from Jean was waiting for me. I stared at the words, trying to process them in my slow brain.

Tori, she wrote, *don't know if you've heard, but Yummy Foods pulled out of their new contract deal to buy Uncle Charlie's after Teddy's arrest last night.*

It was as I'd expected. Yummy Foods had backed out because there was a scandal at the drive-in. Consequently, Uncle Charlie's wasn't going nationwide and Annie wasn't getting her way, which in theory meant I was getting mine.

But I didn't feel particularly like a winner. Maybe that had more to do with the severity of my withdrawal symptoms. I pulled out the signed contract to have another look. *You could still change the outcome.* Because even if Yummy Foods had reneged on their offer to my cousins, this original contract had already been signed by both parties and notarized by Uncle Charlie himself, making it absolutely valid. I could turn it over to

Nikolai, and Uncle Charlie's would belong to the conglomerate whether they wanted it or not.

Rebus jumped up on the bed to knead my queasy stomach. "Not now, Reebs," I moaned as I pulled him up to rock him in my arms, nuzzling his fluffy cheek with my nose. Sick as I was, I was still so relieved that Rebus and Aunt Kat were all right. And I reminded myself that soon enough, I'd be back in rehab for round four and that maybe I'd be all right too. There was always hope in that, however small, that I'd stop the drugs for good. If Darnell could do it, so could I.

I scratched Rebus behind his ears, and as he meowed with pleasure, the fur at his rear started moving. "You pick up a bug last night or what, Reebs?"

I sifted through his black hair. At the base of his tail was a critter from his nightly excursion, and when I plucked it off, I wondered whether I was hallucinating—but no, in my hand was an eight-legged pumpkin seed. A standard Missouri tick. Maybe I was losing my mind from the withdrawals, but I got an idea.

"It's like you knew just what I needed," I told Rebus, petting him for a job well done.

With the tick crawling in my closed fist, I went down the hall to Aunt Kat's studio. Though my hand was shaking, I grabbed a tiny paintbrush and dropped a dot of white paint on the bug's back. Now it wasn't just any standard Missouri tick. It was a lone star tick.

Chapter Forty

N O KILLER VISITED WHILE DARNELL was away, but by the time he'd returned to take me to the church, I was doing worse than ever. Now I'd officially gone eighteen hours without an oxy.

"And you still want to go to this funeral?" Darnell said in his judgmental tone as he zipped up my black dress since I couldn't do it myself. "You're looking real corpselike, Tor."

"Then I'll fit right in," I said. "Anyway, I've probably got a few hours in me before I collapse."

Darnell shook his head. "I really don't understand you sometimes."

"It's about closure, you know?" This was partially true, but I didn't tell him the whole truth, that I was still in case mode despite having half a functioning body and brain. There was no point worrying him since I was going through with my plan anyway.

Darnell helped me out of the house and into his cop car. "Got some news to tell you," he announced, once we were buckled inside.

"About what Squishy said?" I asked.

"Yeah, this is confidential, but I'm making an exception telling you since it's your case and family."

"I understand."

Darnell lit a cigarette and sucked so hard the tip crackled.

The smoke made me feel even more nauseated, and I redirected the AC vent to blow it away from me. As Darnell exhaled a jet stream through his nostrils, he began, "Harrison's trying to make a deal to get off easier, saying that he's got proof Teddy asked him to kill Luis. Harrison says he refused and seems to think Teddy had someone else do the job."

"Do you believe him?"

"I don't know." Darnell took another drag. "He's a professional slime-ball, so I don't trust a word out of his mouth. But maybe he's telling the truth."

I thought about Teddy hiring someone else to kill Luis. He certainly had a motive since he was getting blackmailed, but I still wasn't convinced. Unless Teddy was a master at pretending to be a dimwit, he'd have already given himself away if he'd ordered a hit on Luis. And I didn't think Teddy was pretending.

"I also got some news at the station about your other cousin, Annie," Darnell said.

I jolted forward hearing her name. "What do you mean?"

"Her husband filed a missing person report today. Said it's been twenty-four hours since she left home to meet you for lunch. Said she never came back. No one's seen her car either. Do you know anything about that?"

"No."

Darnell looked at me with suspicion. "Anything strange happen between you and her yesterday?"

I thought through my muddy memory. "I interviewed her around lunchtime. She was going to meet the funeral director after lunch to drop off Uncle Charlie's burial clothes. Did you check that out?"

"Yeah, but her husband said she never showed for that appointment. Apparently, Jean went to see the funeral director instead."

"Jean?" Now I really was confused. Then I thought back to how giddy Annie was speeding out of the parking garage, which wasn't how someone would act on their way to see a funeral director. Only getting what she wanted could make her that happy. "Annie must have changed her plan," I said.

"She was also supposed to get Chuck's signature last night on the new Yummy Foods contract. Did you check in with him?"

Darnell gave a nod. "I tried calling him, but he didn't pick up his phone."

"That's not a surprise considering he surrendered his worldly possessions overnight."

"Why would he do that?"

"He wants to reset himself and be a monk in Myanmar. Don't ask me to explain these things."

"Man, you've got some weird relatives."

"Tell me about it."

"Anyway, Annie's husband seems to think something serious happened for her not to be home getting ready for her father's funeral."

My chest contracted at the word "serious." Now I wasn't sure whether to be concerned for her or suspicious of her. Maybe both.

"That's true," I agreed. "Annie would want to spend time putting on her face."

"So you have no idea where she could be?"

I tried thinking. Was Annie hiding because I'd caught Teddy and she'd been involved in his meat conspiracy? Even if that was true, it still didn't explain why she was suddenly so overjoyed in the parking garage before I caught Teddy. And it had nothing to do with her arrangement with Chuck to sign the contract either, not when she'd have already thought she had her deal in the bag. Her enthusiasm had switched on as soon as I'd showed her that threatening note card.

I looked at the clock. The funeral started in half an hour.

I pointed to the exit sign for the Kaufman Center. "Mind if we take a quick detour to the Marriott?"

Darnell flicked his cigarette in his ashtray. "Why, what's there?"

"Just got a hunch."

Chapter Forty-One

DARNELL SMOKED ANOTHER CIGARETTE IN the car while I went into the hotel. Ginny Wolf was at the front desk, but in my present zombie state, she didn't recognize me.

"Excuse me?" she called out. "Can I help you?"

I didn't reply as I charged for the elevators, especially since she was flagging down a security officer to possibly stop me. I pushed the button to go up, and got on before anyone gave me trouble.

Then I made my way up to the eighteenth floor to knock again at Nikolai's door.

"Mr. Volkov?" I said. "It's Tori Swenson. Please open the door. This is an emergency."

Nikolai opened the door, wearing a suit and stinking of some nausea-inducing citrus and tobacco cologne. Behind him was an expensive suitcase, packed and ready to go.

"Ms. Swenson," he said, forcing a smile. "What good timing you have. Are you here to bid me a Kansas City farewell? I'm on my way to the airport."

"Have you seen Annie?" I said. "She's gone missing."

"Has she?" Nikolai's forced smile turned genuine. "Oh, good."

"How's that good?"

"Because she was supposed to come here last night to celebrate the contract she was bringing me, but she never showed. I thought she was standing me up, and it hurt my feelings."

"But if you didn't see her—" I stopped myself, unsure of where I was headed.

Nikolai shrugged. "Maybe she's hiding because she was working with her sleazy brother? She could also be upset and embarrassed by this whole affair, no pun intended. You must know by now that Yummy Foods withdrew its offer to buy Uncle Charlie's. We're buying Rocky's instead, which is better for us since we'll get more revenue from the sympathy of the Rocky's patrons after your family got caught stealing their meat. Yes, I imagine Annie's hiding out in a Missouri cave with several bottles of wine. Now if you don't mind, I must catch a flight to a real city." Nikolai grabbed his suitcase handle.

I remembered the signed contract in my bag. "Wait," I said. "What about the original contract with Uncle Charlie? What would you do if that came to light?"

Nikolai laughed. "That would be most unfortunate for Uncle Charlie's, because in that case we'd be forced to take ownership. Which would mean liquidating its assets since we can't do anything with that place now that it's tied up in this dreadful meat scandal. But as the situation stands, your uncle didn't sign that contract, or at least if he had, it's lost to the wind."

"Right. Lost to the wind."

"Now I really must get to my taxi," Nikolai said with more urgency. "A shame it didn't work out with the barbecue drive-in, but as I said before, there's no end of sellers out there. At least it was fun while it lasted with your cousin. Do send her my regards." Nikolai moved past me to roll his luggage down the hall.

I dug out the contract from my bag to look at my uncle's swollen signature, but I didn't call after Nikolai. It wasn't Uncle Charlie who should decide, but me. And there was still time to liquidate it if that's what I wanted, but for now I needed to get to the funeral. Maybe someone there would know what happened to Annie.

To avoid the security officer who might be looking for me, I exited the hotel through the parking garage. But I hadn't even taken one step out the door when my stomach flipped at what was there, in the corner of the lot—Annie's orange SUV.

Chapter Forty-Two

"FIND WHAT YOU WERE LOOKING for?" Darnell said when I got back to the car.

My skin was crawling like there were lone star ticks all over me. "I didn't find Annie," I said. "But her car is parked in the hotel parking garage."

"What the hell?" Darnell's eyes widened. "How'd you know she'd be here?"

"I didn't know for sure, but she was sleeping with the Yummy Foods exec in this hotel. He told me he never saw her last night either. Apparently, she was supposed to bring him the signed contract and never showed up for their rendezvous."

"Another planned meeting missed."

"Yeah, but her car's at the hotel." I reached for the Topo Chico in the cup holder and opened it with my shaking thumb ring. "Maybe Nikolai was lying and knows exactly where she is. Otherwise, I don't know why she'd be here."

"Okay, I'll come back here and ask to check the hotel surveillance after I drop you off at the funeral."

We arrived at the church right on time, and I watched from my window as Emma strutted inside. With how grungy she always looked in her cooking attire, it was strange seeing her in a formal dress and ballet flats. She almost looked like the little princess she was as a kid.

"Thanks for the ride," I said to Darnell. "Let me know what you find out at the hotel."

"I will," he said. "Please be careful, Tor."

"I'll do my best."

"And call if you need anything. I'll pick you up from the drive-in when you're done with your barbecue party."

I made my way inside a mostly empty church. All the guests from the Fourth of July party must have had better things to do with their Saturday afternoon. Half of Uncle Charlie's children were also missing, and while Annie's absence was the most puzzling because no one seemed to know where she was, it was Teddy's and Susanne's absences that attracted the most gossip. Both had been arrested. Apparently, Susanne was in police custody after trying to shoot her cousin, Penelope Hall, for sleeping with Teddy. No wonder Teddy didn't want his wife finding out about his affair.

As for my dead uncle, he was lying in an open coffin at the altar. I waited in the short line to examine his lifeless face, which had been powdered with so much blush that he looked like he was having another allergic reaction. As I leaned over to inspect his hands, folded over his abdomen, someone squeezed my shoulders from behind. Though I was running low on fuel, I still spun around with my fists out.

"Oh," Jean exclaimed fearfully from behind a black veil. "Sorry hon, I shouldn't have snuck up on you like that."

"Yeah, you could say I'm a bit on edge," I said.

"You poor thing, you look like you've been through a war. I was beyond myself with grief hearing about your aunt getting shot." Jean moved closer. "Can we talk outside in private?"

"I was meaning to ask you the same thing."

I followed her into the parking lot, where the hot wind blew dandelion fluff from the cemetery. Jean lifted her veil, revealing frizzy red hair and a face free of makeup, and said, "It's about Annie."

"Yeah? You know where she is?"

"I know she's gone missing," Jean began, "but I want you to know I know nothing more than that although I saw her yesterday. Honestly, when she came over to drop off Charlie's clothes and asked me to go to the funeral director instead of her, I thought it bizarre."

"Did she say where she was going?"

Jean shook her head. "Only mentioned she was in a hurry to meet someone."

"A man?"

"I have no idea," Jean blurted out defensively. "Me and Annie weren't exactly best friends."

"How was she acting?"

"That's the strangest part. She was as excited as a kid on Christmas morning. I just hope she didn't get into an accident on the way to whoever she was meeting."

I knew an accident wasn't possible since I'd seen her car at the Marriott, but the idea of Annie getting into one made me choke on the humid air. Mad as I was at her for everything she'd said and done to me, I didn't want anything bad to have actually happened to her.

"Oh hon, I'm sorry." Jean extended a hand toward me.

I stepped back. "Don't touch me."

"All right, all right. I was only trying to offer my sympathies, but I'm sure Annie's fine. She's probably too ashamed to show her face after losing that Yummy Foods deal."

"I'm not sure of anything," I said stiffly.

"On a different note," Jean said, her sad face transforming into an enthusiastic grin, "did you ever find out who gave Charlie that alpha-gal meat allergy?"

I stared Jean down at this question, as I didn't like how she was dismissing my cousin's disappearance so she could inquire about the status of her pending inheritance. "Guess you'll have to find out," I told her. "And I have a question for you too."

Jean gave me a knowing smile. "You mean about the signed contract I gave you in that Yummy Foods folder?"

"So you did give it to me on purpose."

"I figured you'd know better than me what to do with that thing being a Swenson and all. Not to mention it was your daddy's drive-in in the first place, right? I didn't want to say anything to you about it at the house because of all those cameras and your cousins watching. What did you end up doing with it anyway?"

I didn't know what game Jean was playing, but I had nothing more to say to her. My withdrawals were also reaching new depths as my nausea churned in my stomach with a warning, and though I raced back into the church to find a bathroom, I didn't make it there in time.

Chapter Forty-Three

THE GRAVEDIGGER CLEANED UP MY vomit while I waited outside the church, because I couldn't listen to the priest praise my uncle without getting sick again. When the church bells started ringing and the people poured out, I saw Chuck dabbing his eyes with a wad of tissues.

"Hey Chuck," I called out to him. "Can I catch a ride with you to the West Bottoms?"

I certainly wouldn't be partaking in the barbecue, cake, and booze, but I needed to get to the family party to get my answers.

"Sure," Chuck said.

I got into his Mickey Mouse Mobile, a red and yellow sedan with big black mouse ears on the hood. Inside was a Disney clock where Mickey's whiskers told the time. Soon as Chuck pulled out of the parking lot, I rolled down my window to get sick on the road. "Sorry," I said, wiping my mouth. "I think I got some vomit on your car door."

"I don't care. I won't have a car anymore after today anyway. Got a flight booked this evening for Myanmar. But maybe I should drive you home instead of the party so you can rest? You look very sick, Tori."

"No need," I said, though it had been twenty-one hours into my withdrawals, and I wasn't sure how much longer I had until I couldn't function at all.

The drive continued to be rough, but at least I didn't get sick again. When we got to the drive-in, Jean and Emma were already sitting at the picnic table, gorging on meat, corn, and potato salad.

I sat down beside Emma, my bag on the other side of me so no one would notice I was switching my phone on to secretly record the conversation.

"Guess it's wise you're not eating anything when you're sick," Jean said to me as she salted her baked beans. "Know what you got?"

"No," I said.

"I hope you're not contagious," Emma sneered as she rubbed a scratch on her arm like I could contaminate it with my disease. "You look absolutely disgusting."

"Thanks," I said. "I think I'm not feeling well because of Annie. Aren't you guys worried about her?"

"Oh God, why do you even care about that bitch after she banned you from coming here?" Emma stabbed a burnt end with her fork. "Good thing she's not here or you wouldn't be."

My phone dinged in my bag, and I pulled it out. A text from Darnell. *You won't believe this,* he wrote. *Don't know if this was Annie, but the surveillance footage shows that whoever was driving her car showed up around 10 p.m. last night wearing gloves and a bedsheet. We're considering the vehicle abandoned now so we can impound it and do an inventory of what's inside.*

These words stabbed my stomach, and I clutched at my abdomen like I might get sick again. I didn't think it was Annie in that bedsheet.

"You okay, hon?" Jean asked. "You need the bathroom?"

"I don't know," I said, my body feeling extra hot. "I'm worried about Annie." I looked at their faces and saw only blank stares.

"If you want my opinion," Jean sighed, "I'm not worried about her at all. I mean, I knew she was selfish, but what I don't understand is how she could have missed her own father's funeral."

"She's probably mad Yummy Foods yanked their offer off the table," Emma said.

"Or maybe she's upset about Teddy?" Chuck offered softly, stirring the mouse-tail he'd made for himself, which I noticed had a yellowish tint. "They've always been pretty close."

"Or maybe she was involved in his meat conspiracy and is avoiding arrest?" Jean suggested. "That wouldn't surprise me a bit. What do you think, Miss PI?"

Everyone looked at me. "I think she's—" I couldn't even say the word without gagging.

"Gross," Emma said, leaning away from me. "Don't throw up here while I'm eating."

Chuck passed me some paper towels, but I waved my hand at him to stay away. I swallowed my urge to get sick.

"Dead," I said. "I think she's dead."

Jean clapped a hand on her chest. "Good God, really?"

"Tori, how could you say something like that?" Emma said with over-wrought emotion, as if she cared about her sister.

"Annie's dead?" Chuck stuttered. "What do you mean?"

"Why else would she be missing?" I said.

"There are many reasons." Jean grabbed her beer. "Do you have any evidence for this horrible claim? Those are some pretty big words you're putting out."

"No evidence," I lied. "Just got a gut feeling."

"You don't go on gut feelings in your line of work, do you?" Emma asked.

"Sometimes I do. Maybe that's why I'm sick all of a sudden."

"She never came over last night," Chuck revealed, then took a gulp of his drink.

"Really?" I said.

"Yeah," Chuck said, eyeing the greasy meat chunks on Emma's plate. "Em, mind if I have a burnt end?"

"I thought you were a vegan," she said. "Not to mention I heard you telling people at the church you want to be a monk."

"I want to eat meat this one last time in honor of Dad," said Chuck.

Groaning, Emma pushed the plate across the table to Chuck. He picked up a burnt end with his grubby fingers and shoved it into his mouth. As he chewed, he closed his eyes.

"Amazing," he murmured. "I'm so glad I had a chance to appreciate Dad before going to Myanmar." He licked his sticky fingers.

"Myanmar?" Emma cocked her head at him.

"I'm moving there this weekend. You can buy a visa at the airport."

"What?" Emma gasped. "You can't move across the world. You have to help me run Uncle Charlie's."

"I don't care what you do with it, Em. I don't want anything to do with this place anymore. Everything in my life was ruined because of Dad. In fact, I signed away my share of the inheritance this morning. Thought it would be better to be free of it all. You, Teddy, and Annie will have to run it without me."

"Why on earth would you do that?" Emma squeezed her eyebrows together. "I guess that means Uncle Charlie's will be run by me and Annie, so long as she's alive." Emma gave me a smile. "I'm sure that'll be a fun partnership."

Ignoring Emma's mocking tone, I decided to try answering my other question. I reached into my bag for the orange pill bottle and tapped the tick with the white dot of paint on its back onto the table. It just sat there, as if on trial. Meanwhile, I turned to observe everyone's reactions.

"What are you doing?" Emma shouted at me. "What is that gross thing?"

Jean looked at me with curiosity. Chuck started crying into his hands.

"That's what killed Uncle Charlie," I announced.

"Are you crazy?" Emma said.

"Nope, isn't that right, Chuck?" I looked at him while he wailed into his hands.

Chuck stopped crying, the tears hanging off his lashes like morning dew on grass blades. "How did you know?" he said softly.

"Because you broke down in tears, and you said you only started crying again because of your dad's death. You didn't cry at the stink bug at the Fourth of July party, but I think you're crying now because this tick reminds you of how you planted it on your father's foot at the Memorial Day party. Marigold told you that you did that, right? Is that the bad thing you didn't want to tell me about yesterday?"

When Chuck didn't say anything, Emma slapped a hand over her open mouth. "Oh my God," she said. "Chuck, is that true?"

Chuck wiped his eyes with a paper towel. "It's for the best I confess, if I'm going to live an honest monk's life," he began. "I can't carry the guilt anymore." He took another big gulp of mouse-tail.

Jean slapped her phone on the table to record this conversation for her own benefit, and shouted into her microphone, "Chuck, you killed Charlie?"

"No, it's not like that," he said, the tears still coming. "Marigold told me I put the tick on his foot to give him a meat allergy, but I couldn't remember doing it. She said I must have blocked it out because it was too painful a memory, but after learning from Tori that I was getting drugged by Marigold into becoming Mickey Mouse, I now know it was Mickey who did it."

Emma stared at her brother in disbelief. "Mickey Mouse?"

"Marigold was drugging him," I repeated. "Not sure with what, but it could change his personality and make him forget what he did. Right, Chuck?"

Chuck nodded through his tears. "Yeah, I think he's been out a few times around you all, and that explains why I can't remember some things. Like when he apparently threatened Teddy at the Memorial Day Party with a knife. I guess Mickey isn't the nicest mouse."

"So why did you just willingly drug yourself right now?" I nodded at his drink.

"Yeah, that might have been a mistake, but after you told me about the yellow powder Marigold was drugging me with, I found some in the kitchen cupboard and thought it would help me deal with my grief." Chuck took another sip. "You know, like putting on a band-aid." He pointed to the cut on my arm that I'd got last week when Squishy pushed me in the Rocky's parking lot. Though I'd gotten more marks on my body last night at Squishy's house, that cut was almost healed.

"Okay, I'm still having trouble understanding all this," Emma said to Chuck. "You're telling me you turn into Mickey Mouse and do crazy shit? You know what? Never mind, don't explain that part, just tell me why you or Mickey wanted to give Dad a meat allergy."

Chuck sniffled, "Because Marigold said we were teaching him a lesson for not putting vegan items on the menu. She said Dad was trying to spread the evil meat problem in this country by selling out to Yummy Foods and that we were doing good by stopping him."

"Why would you agree to hurt Dad?" Emma said.

"I told you I didn't have a choice. Marigold was giving me those mouse-tails and then hypnotizing me to make me turn into Mickey. It was Mickey who hurt Dad through me. And after Marigold told me what happened with the tick, I didn't know what to think because I couldn't remember doing it. But Marigold said I'd done it, so I knew it was true, and she said to never tell anyone or we'd both get in trouble and she'd have to leave me. I was really upset hearing about what I did, but she reassured me that the chances of death by allergic reaction were practically nonexistent."

"Yeah, but that's how he died, isn't it?" Jean shouted at Chuck, and threw a burnt end at his bald head. "Sweet Jesus, you should be in jail for manslaughter."

Chuck turned to Emma with tearful, imploring eyes. "That's why I refused my inheritance. How could I take Dad's money after what I'd done?"

"That's really messed up, Chuck," Emma said.

"I should go home and pack for my trip now." He drank down the rest of his mouse-tail, wiped his mouth free of ice cream, and stood up. "I'm sorry, Em. Tell Annie and Teddy I'm sorry too."

"You're not going anywhere but prison, Mickey," Jean said.

At Jean's threat, Chuck's features contorted, his sadness turning into amusement. By addressing him as Mickey, Jean must have triggered him into an episode.

"Sorry, time to go," he said in his shrill cartoon voice. Then he picked up a knife and held it across the table at Jean who retracted in her chair. "Unless you want to try to stop me?"

No one said or did anything as Chuck, or rather Mickey, marched toward the parking lot.

Chapter Forty-Four

"HOLY SHIT," EMMA MUTTERED, BEFORE casting an accusatory glare at me. "How'd you know about this tick anyway?"

I pointed at Jean. "Ask her."

Emma redirected her glare to my uncle's former girlfriend. "Is that why Marigold moved into Dad's house yesterday? Was she working with you?"

"How do you know Marigold's there?" Jean grinned. "Or have you been watching me on the cameras?"

"I think the better question is why she's there with you when she was just dating my brother."

"I'll tell you," Jean said, "but first you both need to put your phones on the table."

"Whatever." Emma placed her phone down.

As I got mine out, Emma and Jean saw that I'd been recording the conversation. "Turn off your recorder, Tori," Jean ordered. I did as she asked. "All right," Jean went on, "I'll tell you the truth, only because I have a proposition for Emma that she won't be able to refuse."

"Excuse me?" Emma squinted at Jean.

"You see, I didn't want to sell Uncle Charlie's when my motives were pure in stopping the spread of meat consumption in the world. Me and Marigold, we're in HETA together." She pulled out the golden pig necklace from under her dress collar. "And we infiltrated your twisted, spoiled family so we could destroy your meat empire."

Emma gnashed her teeth. There was a carving knife in front of my cousin, and I moved it away from her reach, fearful she might pick it up and try to gut Jean.

"Of course, it was a long-term plan," Jean continued. "When we'd first heard about Yummy Foods' interest in Uncle Charlie's last year, we decided to win the affections of your brother and father, which was easy enough, and then collect as much info as we could about your business while gaining Charlie's and Chuck's trust. It wasn't until Yummy Foods wanted to move forward two months ago and buy, however, that we knew we had to act fast to stop the drive-in from becoming a chain. As you just discovered, Marigold was able to easily seduce Chuck into becoming Mickey by adding PCP to his ice cream drinks, and oh boy, did she have him on a string with her cute little costume too." Jean batted her eyelashes like she was Minnie Mouse.

"So that's what the yellow powder was," I said. "PCP can certainly make people hallucinate."

"Maybe Marigold was operating Chuck like a cartoon robot, but you couldn't convince my father what to do," Emma said. "And he was the only one who had the power to sell."

"You know, you shouldn't be so unhappy with me, hon," Jean said. "I was on your side at the time. But you're right, Charlie didn't care a damn what I said. Not even sex was a bargaining chip, and not to brag, but I'm pretty good in that department. He really was undecided about what to do. That was when I had the brilliant idea to make him allergic to his own product. Some of our activists had done it with success, but I had hopes that if I fed him enough meat after he'd been bitten, maybe he'd die."

Emma jumped up, grabbed the platter of burnt ends, and showered Jean with the meat. "Murderer!" she screamed.

Jean laughed as she picked a burnt end out of her cleavage. "No, no," she said. "You heard your brother confess. He's the one who did it."

"No, he didn't. He was drugged by Marigold. You both should be in jail."

"Go ahead and prove it, dear. But so you know, the Slayer Rule will go into effect for you and all your siblings. You won't receive a penny of your inheritance."

As Emma raised a fist to strike Jean, I grabbed her with my putty arm. "Stay out of this," Emma barked at me.

"That's impossible." I turned my attention back to Jean. "You gave me that contract. Why did you do that if you didn't want to sell Uncle Charlie's?"

"What contract?" Emma said with fearful eyes.

"The original one your father signed for Yummy Foods." Jean smiled.

"No, no, no." Emma beat her fists on the table. "He never signed."

"Not true," Jean said. "Anyway, call me a greedy hypocrite, but once I'd heard at the will reading that I was next in succession after you kids, I realized I'd inherit everything if that tick bite was linked to Chuck with that unnatural death clause." Jean turned to shake her head at me. "But you were supposed to give that contract to Nikolai, so he'd buy Uncle Charlie's and make me even richer than I'm about to be."

The contract was still in my bag. "Sorry," I said. "I destroyed it."

"That's fine," Jean said. "It's not like Yummy Foods would want it now after Teddy's big scandal anyway." She turned back to Emma with a smile. "Which is why I'll make a deal with you, sweetie—"

"Eat shit." Emma spat on the table.

"Just hear me out, before you start unloading profanity on your future benefactress. I won't destroy your precious drive-in, and I'll even let you run it, but only on the condition that you put vegan items on the menu so I can keep HETA and Marigold pleased enough while we turn your dad's mansion into our new KC headquarters. What do you say?"

Emma spat again, this time hitting Jean's cheek. "You're fucking dead meat."

Jean wiped the globule off. "Okay, I'll give you a few days to cool down and think about it." She stood up. "I'll be speaking to Charlie's lawyer now. Thanks for your help, Tori. Couldn't have done it without you."

Emma got up from the table and shouted at Jean, "You're not going anywhere, bitch."

"Oh no?" Jean opened her purse and drew out a gun. "Sit back down, sugar. Unless you want to be shot with your father's pistol."

Emma huffed and sat back down.

"Why didn't you pull that out earlier when Chuck threatened you with that knife?" I asked Jean.

"I didn't care if he left," she said. "I'll turn my recording over to the police right now, to make sure he gets arrested before he tries flying off to Asia."

Jean left me and Emma to sit at the table in tense silence. That Mickey Mouse had taken out my uncle with a tick was something, and that Jean and Marigold, so concerned with animal welfare but not so much that of humans, was another thing. All I could think about was Annie. I didn't think I was wrong when I'd said she was dead. Now I wondered whether Jean killed Annie yesterday. Maybe Annie had stumbled on Jean and Marigold's plan.

I glanced across the table at Emma, who stared glassy-eyed at the drive-in. I couldn't blame her for being angry. After all, she'd just found out her dad's death was carried out by her own brother, all her siblings were gone, her family's pseudo-empire had been humiliated by Teddy's scandal, her inheritance had been stripped, and she was now under Jean's thumb.

"Can I help clean up?" I offered, though I could barely move.

Emma didn't respond, so I gathered the plates and utensils and took them into the kitchen. When I opened the dishwasher, there was a water pan, meat cleaver, and skillet, all clean. I removed the items, setting the cleaver on the counter while searching for the cooker with its missing water pan.

Of the ten cookers, the one in the corner with its lid thrown back was missing its pan. As Dad had taught me, I filled the pan with water at the right level and slid it back into its proper place. But before I could close the lid, I noticed the grill grate was shiny. Emma's words from her kitchen tour returned to make my spine tingle: *Massive rookie error to clean after a cook. It's much easier to wait so it's not gooey and gunky.*

Beside the cooker was a bucket-shaped vacuum. I rolled it toward me, hands shaking as I popped the lid off. Inside was char, ash, and a piece of metal that glittered in the light. I dug it out. The *om* sign. A needle stabbed me right in the heart. It was Annie's silver toe ring.

Chapter Forty-Five

A SCREAM RIPPED OUT OF MY throat as I dropped the ring. My ash-coated fingers moved to cover my eyes from the truth, the horrible truth that my blood sister had been killed by her real sister.

"Looks like Teeny Tori found some treasure," Emma declared from the doorway.

I lowered my quivering fingers so I could see her. Her eyes were smiling at the ring on the floor. Now my anger was surfacing. I grabbed a spoon on the counter and threw it at Emma.

When it brushed by her ear, she giggled. "Nice try, but I wouldn't cry over her if I were you. I mean, did she mind screwing you over and stealing your inheritance? That must have hurt as bad as when Uncle Billy died."

"You killed your own sister."

"Yeah, but it wasn't my first kill. Actually, my first time was your dad in a way. I was the one who set up the boiling sauce to fall off the cooker and onto his hands. I was only eleven, but I was a smart kid back then."

My breath whipped into the back of my throat. I couldn't breathe. I was panting for air. The room didn't have enough oxygen. I gripped the cooker beside me to keep myself from falling.

"Dad asked me to do it after Annie refused," Emma continued. "At least she obeyed him once Uncle Billy died, or she'd have been thrown into the gutter along with you. And you know, it was great once you were gone. I was so tired of you and Annie always having fun, never letting me join."

I wanted to strike her, but I couldn't even stand without holding onto the cooker. I thought of my stun gun and phone, both in my backpack. My backpack was at the picnic table. I couldn't defend myself. I couldn't call Darnell for help.

"You're a demon," I wheezed.

"That's judgmental of you." Emma shook her head at me. "Aren't you supposed to practice objectivity as an investigator? For all you know, maybe I killed my sister in self-defense. That's what I'll say when they find you dead."

"Fuck you."

Emma laughed. "You know, it's too bad you're not a challenge. It's going to be super easy killing you, unlike my sister. See this scratch on my arm?" She pointed at the spot. "That bitch put up a real fight."

My hands were still shaking, but I managed to grab the clean skillet on the counter.

"Nice symbolism," Emma said. "I banged Annie in the face with that thing, but I'm afraid you're not using it on me."

She held up my stun gun and pointed it at me. *Fuck.* She'd gone through my backpack. I wobbled back, trying to put distance between us, but it didn't matter. She fired an electric volt that knocked me and the skillet to the floor. When I hit the tiles, I felt like butter seething on a hot pan. Every muscle fiber in my body twisted in a different direction. A charley horse for the whole body.

I moaned as Emma approached, stooping down beside me. "Don't worry," she whispered. "I promise it won't hurt too bad."

She stood back up, and I watched her ballet flats skip away from me toward the office. The skillet was on the floor, a few feet away, but I couldn't reach it.

The only thing I could do was wait to regain my mobility. By then, it would be too late even if I had any strength left. *You're gonna die.*

I knew Emma had gone to fetch some instrument of death. When she returned, I saw what it was—the thing I feared most in the world—the drug that had killed my dad. Emma wrapped a tube around my arm and looked for a vein.

"You know brown sugar is my favorite ingredient," she said eagerly. "You can thank me in heaven. Because unlike Annie, your death will be sweet."

Emma stuck me with the needle of heroin and hit the plunger. I gasped as an intense warmth rushed through me, instantly evaporating my muscle aches. A switch had been flipped. For while I'd remain incapacitated by muscle spasms, Emma had just cured me of my withdrawal symptoms by giving me an opiate. Everything was golden. I was flying higher than ever.

"You know what they'll say when they find you dead in here?" Emma's voice was distant, like it was trapped in a snow globe. In fact, the whole kitchen now floated in a snow globe. Or maybe it was me in the snow globe. "That poor Victoria Swenson almost died in a car crash two years ago." Emma picked up the meat cleaver. "She was in rehab a few times and was an outstanding little investigator in our community. But in the end, she relapsed like her daddy. Then she went so crazy she even killed her poor cousin and tried killing the other."

Emma sharpened the blade against a steel rod, but the grating noises didn't hurt my head. I was drifting in a state of euphoric bliss and about to die. I felt so at peace as I considered Emma's words. Aunt Kat and Darnell already knew I'd relapsed and would believe her story.

They'd think I'd died a murderous junkie. Aunt Kat would think I'd broken my promise not to hurt myself. They'd be devastated. And they'd never get over it.

For so long, I thought leaving this world would unburden those who cared about me. If I was dead, they'd be free. But now that heroin had been forced on me, I could see I'd been wrong. I didn't feel free when Dad died. The end of my suffering would only be the beginning of theirs. Of course, I wasn't in a great position to fight Emma, but I had one advantage. She didn't know I had a high opioid tolerance from my pill-popping this past week, and she'd given me strength in removing the withdrawal symptoms.

Still, I couldn't do anything so long as I twitched on the floor. I'd regain more mobility over time, but until then I needed to keep Emma talking.

"All ready for Teeny Tori," Emma announced as she raised the cleaver over my head.

"Wait," I moaned.

"What?" Emma gave an exasperated sigh and lowered her arm. "You got some special last words?"

"Luis. Why?"

"My God, you still want to solve your case even when you're on the chopping block. Well, I suppose someone should appreciate my genius, right?" Emma stepped back to lean against the cooker while I slid an inch toward the skillet. "So as you already know, Luis was blackmailing my bone-headed brother for his stupid bribery scheme at Rocky's, but what you don't know is that Luis got greedy trying to blackmail me too. Obviously, I had to protect our reputation."

"Reputation?" I rasped, the four syllables slow and heavy in my mouth.

"People come from all over the world for our burnt end burger. I wasn't about to let it out that we were using subpar meat from Rocky's."

"But it's out now."

"No thanks to you." Emma shook her head at me. "It'll be rough recovering from that exposure, but I can play the ignorant card and say I didn't know what my dumbass brother was doing. With all my siblings out of the business, I'm also considering rebranding Uncle Charlie's to Miss Emma's. A new name, a new vision. Of course, I'll have to kill Jean if she doesn't give me the drive-in. What do you think?"

"Miss Emma—" I cut myself off and pretended to gasp hard, so she'd think I was much weaker than I was. "That's street talk for morphine."

"Really?" Emma laughed. "You know, it's too bad I have to kill you. I think we might have gotten along without Annie around."

"Yeah, too bad," I slurred, moaning as I rolled another inch toward the skillet. Emma picked up the cleaver again. "Wait. Why Annie?"

With another annoyed sigh, Emma set the blade back down on the counter. "Because that crazy bitch was trying to blackmail me. She came over here yesterday looking like she'd won a lifetime supply of free yoga lessons, saying if I didn't sign the new contract that she'd tell you and the cops all about how I'd blackmailed Walt and killed Luis. Obviously, I couldn't let either of those things happen."

"But how'd she know it was you?"

"That's the best part," Emma laughed. "In your impromptu interviews yesterday, you showed her the note card that I shoved into the piglet's mouth. Since you showed it to me first, I expected she'd come over here once she saw it. You see, she'd have recognized those stickers belonging to her, and she knew I was always taking her stuff."

My heart was beating slow like a clock wrapped in cotton. That was why Annie had sped out of the garage, overly confident, when I'd showed her the note card. She'd been excited to beat her sister. After all, she'd never needed Emma's signature for the contract when she'd already had Chuck's. She'd just wanted to put Emma in her place. That's what got her killed: being the winner. But now she was dead. I remembered I needed to keep Emma talking.

"So Annie went to see you yesterday," I said.

"Yeah." Emma smiled. "I shut down Uncle Charlie's early for a false fire. When Annie came by, no one was around to see me smack her in the face with that skillet. She fought back, of course, but she got her ass thrown on the grill like Luis. Then I drove her car over to the Marriott, since she'd texted all of us siblings that she'd run into you there two days ago while visiting that vile Yummy Foods executive."

"And you don't have remorse about what you've done?" I moved another inch on the floor toward my weapon.

"Hell no. I was being threatened, and I won't feel remorse for you, either, when I cut off your head and throw it on the barbie."

I asked my next question before Emma could follow through with that plan. "Like the piglets?" I pretended to laugh, like I was stupid so Emma wouldn't get suspicious that I was becoming too lucid in asking such relevant questions.

"A fun touch, right?" she said.

"How'd you do it? I mean, the time I was visiting you and it showed up at your door."

"I told you Hickory was a circus dog. I gave him the special hand signal, and he barked like someone was at the door. Then I went into the hall to grab the package I hid in the cabinet and act like it had just been delivered. Right after you left, I drove over to Aunt Kat's to drop off another piglet head, the one with the note card. I was even watching you from your treehouse when you came home that night. Man, did I have a good laugh at your reaction. Pretty brilliant, right?"

"You shot Aunt Kat too," I added.

"Yeah, but I meant to hit you. Didn't know she was in the driver's seat." Emma shrugged. "There was also Teddy's henchman doing his dirty work, confusing you with who was who, but what can I say? I guess we Swensons have a violent gene, though it seems like yours was directed toward self-harm, which reminds me that we need to get to the end of your story." As Emma raised the cleaver over my head, I rolled another inch and grabbed the skillet handle. It was heavy, but I swung, striking Emma's arm and sending the cleaver across the kitchen.

"Dammit!" she screamed. "You clipped my thumb." She gave me a kick in the side that I couldn't feel. "That was dumb, Tori. Now I'm really going to make you suffer." Emma marched off to retrieve her blade.

I had to get up now or I was dead. With the skillet in one hand, I grabbed the counter with the other to pull myself up. I staggered back until I was leaning against the open cooker, where Emma had cremated Annie. Meanwhile, Emma grabbed her weapon from the floor. When she turned around and saw me standing, her eyes widened with rage.

"What are you doing?" she shouted.

"Guess I'm harder to kill than you thought," I said, tightening my grip on the skillet. "Then again, you've made mistakes before. Sometimes your burnt ends are a bit dry."

I knew that would set Emma off, and sure enough, she charged at me, the cleaver drawn in front of her. I had only one shot to get this right. I swung my arm and threw the skillet—right in her face. She cried out in pain, dropping the weapon to grab her head. I didn't wait for her to recover. I stumbled toward my cousin and pushed her into the cooker, slamming the lid down on her neck so hard it nearly closed all the way. Emma's feet twitched for a moment, then went still.

I slumped back to the floor, where Annie's toe ring sparkled at me. I picked it up, my tears plus the heroin making everything blurry. Pressing her ring to my lips, I then closed my eyes and let myself fall back on the cool tiles, as if floating in a kiddy pool of barbecue sauce.

Chapter Forty-Six

DIDN'T REMEMBER DARNELL COMING FOR me. I didn't remember getting the Narcan either.

I woke up in a hospital bed feeling buried in sand. It was black out, the moon outside my window half-full, a mandarin orange slice amid the stars.

Across the room, Darnell was watching me.

"Hey Tor," he said. "How you feeling?"

I opened my mouth, but words were heavy. "Like a sedated manatee."

"Yeah, no kidding. You're lucky to be alive."

"Am I alive?"

"You'll feel better in a few days."

"Just gotta go through more withdrawal symptoms." I smiled weakly. "Then back to rehab for round number four, the final round."

He got up and came over to my bed to squeeze my hand. "If you want me there, I'm there."

"Thanks, I might take you up on that."

Darnell uncapped a cold Topo Chico and handed me the bottle. "I'm not sure if this is funny, but did you know that your latest relapse is what saved your life?"

"Oh yeah?" I took a sip of delicious sparkling water.

"The doctor said that the dose of heroin Emma gave you would have killed you, if you hadn't already reintroduced opiates into your system last week and built up a tolerance."

"That is pretty funny." As I took another sip of water, a memory flashed at me of Emma with her cleaver. "I killed her, didn't I? And she killed Annie."

"Yeah, what a shitshow." Darnell shook his head. "But you're okay now, and you won't get charged with anything since it was clearly self-defense."

"Well, that's a relief."

"And you know who wants to see you besides your buddy Gabe down the hall?"

I sat up higher in bed. "Is Aunt Kat still here?"

"Yeah, how about I take you to her."

Darnell helped me into a wheelchair and gave me my bag. As he wheeled me down the fluorescent-lit hall, I peeked inside to be sure—the folder was still there. Though Emma had taken my stun gun, she hadn't found the contract. Darnell turned me into a room where Aunt Kat was lying in a bed on the phone. I couldn't be happier to see her. When she saw me, her face also broke into a smile.

"Sorry, I need to go," she said into the receiver. "My niece is here." She hung up. "Tori." She reached out her hands, and Darnell pushed me up to her bedside so we could side hug. "I'm so relieved you're okay."

"I guess I wanted to keep you company in here," I said. "How's the shoulder?"

"Can't feel a darn thing with all the painkillers they've got me on." Aunt Kat tugged on her arm tube. "But don't get me started on all this absurdity that it's illegal to give me my own marijuana—that I've legally grown with a medical prescription—but completely legal to dose me up on a dangerous narcotic. I can't complain too much, though, since I had a bullet in me. How are you doing?"

"Besides feeling like my head's a water balloon," I said, "I finished my case without dying. Looking forward to going back to rehab as soon as I get out of this place."

"That's a good plan," Aunt Kat said, tears beading in her eyes. "You can stay at mine for as long as you need, okay?"

I just nodded, not wanting to say anything sentimental for fear I'd cry and exhaust myself more.

"Who were you talking to?"

Aunt Kat's sadness shifted into a sudden grin. "You won't believe it."

"A mechanic to fix your car?"

"Oh gosh, I think at this point it's time to get a new one," she laughed. "But no, it was Charlie's lawyer."

"His lawyer? Why?"

"Tori, I'm still in shock. He told me the horrible news about Charlie's kids, that they're either dead or in jail, which means Charlie's fortune is mine."

"What?" My head jerked back. "How's it yours? What about Jean? Wasn't she next in line to inherit his fortune after the kids?"

"Yeah, but Chuck's former girlfriend shot her dead this evening."

"Marigold?"

"That's her name." Aunt Kat nodded. "She moved into Charlie's mansion yesterday, and when she found out Jean was keeping Uncle Charlie's open, she went ballistic, calling Jean a hypocrite and shooting her with Chuck's Elmer Fudd rifle. It was all caught on the surveillance footage. As for Teddy and Chuck, they can't inherit a cent, since Jean had already sent the lawyer a recording of Chuck confessing to planting that lone star tick on Charlie, thereby enacting that Slayer Rule and nullifying the children's claim to his estate. Chuck was later arrested at the airport with a ticket to Myanmar in his hand, and has been charged with manslaughter. He's down at the jail with his brother now."

"Guess he'll just have to meditate in a cage," I observed.

"So after your cousins and Jean," Aunt Kat went on, "I was next in Charlie's will."

"He was collecting your animal paintings in his house and office. Maybe he kept a soft spot for you."

"Maybe, or maybe he didn't have anyone else in mind. In any case, most of his money will be used to pay off this antitrust conspiracy lawsuit with Rocky's. Then I'm signing the drive-ins over to you."

"Me?" I blinked. "You don't have to—"

"Of course I do. It was Billy's baby. It should have been yours all along. Whether to keep the drive-ins, sell, or shut them down, that should be your call."

I squeezed the bag on my lap where the Yummy Foods contract was still hiding.

"All right, I'll have to think about it."

"If my vote matters," Darnell interjected, "I hope you don't shut it down. I don't know what I'd do if I couldn't get my brisket fix after a long hot day of arresting drunks and delinquents. Not to mention KC sure wouldn't be the same without that gas station drive-in."

"That's true," Aunt Kat said.

A nurse entered the room. "You guys need to go," she said to me and Darnell. "I got to check on Miss Katherine's vitals now."

"All right." I gave my aunt another hug. "See you tomorrow."

Darnell wheeled me back into the hall. "Man," he sighed, "this day keeps getting weirder and weirder. You go from almost getting killed to owning Uncle Charlie's."

"Yeah, and I'm way too drugged up to appreciate any of it."

"You think you'll keep it? I know that place is loaded for you."

"It is. But it was my dad's before my uncle stole it. If I keep the drive-in, though, I'm going to have to really work on getting over my meat aversion. Also, I'm definitely changing the name back to Swensons Barbecue."

"Yeah, I like the sound of that. Swensons Barbecue."

My heart tingled, hearing the words. That was my dad's place, not Uncle Charlie's. I pointed to the elevator across the hall. "Could we step out for some fresh air? I think it would help clear my head."

"Sure, I could always use another cig." Darnell steered me toward the elevator. "I've pretty much become a chain-smoker after this week."

We rode the elevator down, and Darnell pushed me through the sliding glass doors and into the cool darkness. For once, a pleasant midsummer's night. Darnell lit up and took a drag of his cigarette, releasing a thin stream of smoke. Then I opened my bag and removed Uncle Charlie's contract.

"Mind if I see your lighter?" I said, opening my palm.

Darnell blew smoke through his nostrils. "Don't tell me you want to start smoking now."

"No, just need the lighter."

He gave me one of his skeptical looks. "You're not gonna do something crazy like set yourself on fire, are you?"

"Not without gasoline."

Darnell dropped the lighter in my hand. "What's that?" He nodded at the paper on my lap.

"It's me, deciding to run the drive-in." I flicked the lighter's wheel, and as the flame licked the paper, it crackled, curled, and charred, its burnt ends whirling into the wind and up to the stars.

— THE END —

Acknowledgments

I HAVE TO START BY THANKING my father, who had the patience to read who knows how many drafts and always offered his honest feedback. I also want to thank my mother for her earnest advice, and my Uncle Steve and Lewe Sessions for letting me interview them. Thanks to my exceptional friends for their critical eyes—Quinn Phillips, Justin Hanuska, and Beth Johnson. Finally, I want to express gratitude to my editor, Kayla Webb, for her expert guidance and enthusiasm.

About the Author

BURNT ENDS (CAMCAT BOOKS | 2024) was inspired by Laura's uncle, who ran a successful burger drive-in chain in Ohio, as well as her experience living in Kansas City, Missouri. She has bachelor's degrees in Russian and English literature from the University of Wisconsin-Madison, and a master's degree in Russian literature from Northwestern University. She lives in Washington, D.C., with her two cats, Sasha and Ginny Wolf.

If you enjoyed
Laura Wetsel's *Burnt Ends,*
please consider leaving a review
to help out our authors.

And check out another CamCat book:
Jennifer Sadera's
I Know She Was There.

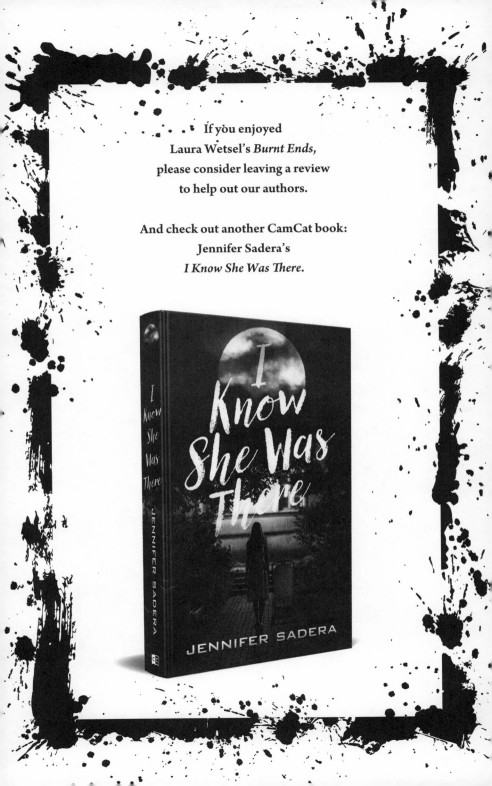

CHAPTER ONE

J ANE BROCKTON was going to get caught.

My heart raced when Jane emerged from the side door of her home; what she and I were *both* doing was risky, but it was too late for regrets. I wondered if she thought so, too. Probably. Her behavior was becoming alarmingly brazen. I pulled Emmy's stroller closer and pushed aside boxwood branches, widening the portal I peered through. Although Jane's across-the-street neighbors' hedge was directly in front of her farmhouse-style McMansion, it was too dark this late at night for me to be seen.

Go back inside if you know what's good for you. I pressed my fingers to my lips as the man emerged from the house next to hers. Even if I'd yelled a warning, Jane Brockton wouldn't heed it. Who the hell was I? Certainly not someone her neighbors on Woodmint Lane knew. If Jane observed my late-night excursions through the streets of her stylish suburban New York neighborhood, her first instinct wouldn't be to worry about *her* behavior.

I was prepared. If confronted by any resident of the exclusive enclave, I'd explain I walked the streets late at night to lull my colicky baby to sleep.

I couldn't admit my ulterior motive—worming my way back onto Primrose Way and into my former best friend's good graces. And there was no need to share how lately the lives of this neighborhood's inhabitants lured me like a potent drug—or how Jane Brockton was fast becoming the kingpin of my needy addiction. Jane stood out, even in this community of excess: gourmet dinner deliveries, drive-up dog grooming, same-day laundry service, and weekly Botox parties.

Her meetings with the mystery man were far from innocent. The first tryst I'd witnessed was late last Friday night—exactly a week ago. I'd strolled around the corner of Woodmint Lane just as the pair had emerged from their side-by-side houses and taken to the dark street like prowlers casing the block. I followed their skulking forms up Woodmint, being careful to stay a few dozen yards behind, until all I could discern was their silhouettes, too close to each other for friendly companionship.

They'd eventually crossed Primrose Way and veered into the woods where the bike trails and picnic areas offered secluded spaces. When they didn't emerge from the wooded area, I backed Emmy's stroller silently and reversed my route, heading away, my pulse still throbbing, echoing in my temples.

It was impossible to deny what was going on as I watched similar scenes unfold three nights this week: Jane slipping soundlessly from her mudroom door like a specter, the flash of the screen door in the faint moonlight an apparent signal.

Tonight, as they hooked hands in the driveway between the houses, I slicked my tongue over my dry lips. She risked losing everything. I knew how that felt. Tim had left me before I'd even changed out his worn bachelor pad sofa for the sectional I'd been eyeing at Ethan Allen. I watched them cross through the shadows, barely able to see them step inside the shed at the far end of Jane's yard.

And all under the nose of her poor devoted husband, Rod. He couldn't be as gullible as he appeared, could he?

A voice called out, shattering the stillness of the night. I flinched, convinced I'd been discovered. I looked around the immediate shadows, placing a hand over my chest to still my galloping heart.

"Jane?" It was Rod's voice. I recognized the timbre by now.

Settle down, Caroline.

My eyes darted to the custom home's open front door. Rod had noticed his wife's abandonment earlier than usual. Warm interior light spilled across the porch floorboards and outlined Rod's robed form in the door frame.

"Are you out here? Jane?"

The worry in his voice made me hate Jane Brockton. I flirted with the idea of stepping away from the hedge and announcing I'd witnessed her heading to the shed with the neighbor. Of course, that would be ridiculous. I was a stranger. My name, Caroline Case, would mean nothing to him.

Rod closed the door and my gaze traveled to the glowing upstairs window on the far left of his house. The light had blinked off half an hour ago, like a giant eyelid closing over the dormered master bedroom casement. I knew exactly where their bedroom was because I'd studied the Deer Crossing home models on the builder's website. I knew the layout of all three house styles so well I could escort potential buyers through them. I'd briefly considered it. Becoming a real-estate agent would give me access inside, where I could discover what life behind the movie-set facades was really like. Pristine marble floors, granite countertops, and crystal vases on every conceivable surface? Or gravy-laden dishes in sinks and mud-caked shoes arrayed haphazardly just inside the eye-catching front doors?

I suspected the latter was true for almost every house except for my former best friend Muzzy Owen's place on Primrose Way. Muzzy could put Martha Stewart to shame.

I wedged myself and Emmy's stroller further into the hedge. Becoming a real-estate agent wouldn't connect me as intimately to Jane and Rod Brockton (information gleaned by rifling through the contents of their mailbox) as I was at this moment. Trepidation—and yes, anticipation—laced my bloodstream and turned my breathing shallow as I waited for Rod to come outside and start his nightly search for his wife. Some may consider my interest, my excitement, twisted but I didn't plan to *use* my stealthily gathered information against anyone. It was enough to reassure myself that nobody's life was perfect, no matter how it appeared to an outsider. A faint click echoed through the still night. I squinted through the hedge leaves, my eyes laser pointers on the side door Jane had emerged from only moments before. Rod appeared.

As he stepped into the dusky side yard, I thought about the people unknown to me until a week ago: the latest neighborhood couple to pique my interest. Even though they were *technically* still strangers, I'd had an entire week to learn about the Brocktons. A few passes in my car last Saturday morning revealed a tracksuit-clad GenX-er, her wavy hair the reddish-brown color of autumn oak leaves, and a gray-haired, bespectacled Boomer in crisp dark jeans and golf shirt standing on the sage-and-cream farmhouse's front porch. Steaming mugs in hand, their calls drifted through my open car window, cautioning their little golden designer dog when it strayed too close to the street, their voices overly indulgent, as if correcting a beloved but errant child. The very picture of domestic bliss.

I studied the Colonial to the Brockton's right. On the front porch steps, two tremendous Boston ferns in oversized urns stretched outward like dozens of welcoming arms. The only testament to human activity. Someone obviously cared for the vigorous plants, but a midnight peek inside that house's mailbox revealed only empty space. It made me uncomfortable not knowing who Jane's mystery man was.

And did Rod usually wake when his wife slipped between the silk sheets (they had to be silk) after her extracurriculars? He obviously questioned her increasingly regular late-night abandonment. He wouldn't be roaming the dark in his nightwear if he hadn't noticed.

Perhaps Jane said she couldn't sleep. She needed to move—walk the neighborhood—to tire herself. Hearing that, he'd frown, warning her not to wander around in the middle of the night. Rod was the type—I was sure just by the way he coddled his dog—to worry about his lovely wife walking the dark streets, even the magical byways of Deer Crossing. Hence, the need for new places to rendezvous each night. But the shed on their very own property! Even though tonight's tryst was later than usual, it was dangerously daring to stay on site. Maybe Jane wanted to get caught.

A scratching sound echoed through the quiet night. I looked at the side door Rod had just emerged from, saw his silhouette turn back and open it. The little dog circled him, barking sharply. The urgent yipping cut clearly through the still air, skittering my pulse. I quickly glanced at Emmy soundly sleeping in her stroller. If the dog didn't stop barking, I'd have to get away— fast. Emmy could wake and start her colicky wailing, which would rouse the Brockton's neighbors whose hedge I'd appropriated. One flick of their front porch light would reveal me in all my lurking glory.

As if to answer my concerns, the dog ceased barking and scampered toward the shed. I rubbed at the sudden chill sliding across my upper arms. That little canine nose was sniffing out Jane's trail.

Rod stepped tentatively forward. It was too dark to see what he was wearing beneath the robe, but I pictured him in L.L. Bean slippers with those heavy rubberized soles and cotton print pajamas, like Daddy used to wear. Daddy's had line drawings of old-fashioned cars dotted across the white cotton background. Model T's and Roadsters. I felt angry with Jane all over again. *How dare she . . .*

"Sorry, darling," Jane called, striding from the shadows, stopping a few feet in front of him. "I was potting those plants earlier and thought I left my cell phone in the shed." Her voice was soft, relaxed. She was a pro.

"I saw it on the bookshelf in the study earlier this evening," Rod said, bending to calm the little dog who was bouncing between them like a child with untreated ADHD.

"Oh geez, I'm losing it," she said, laughing.

Not yet, you're not, I thought. Not yet.

CHAPTER TWO

SATURDAY, AUGUST 12

THE BABY'S cry jarred me out of sleep.

I fought with the down comforter, kicking free and swinging my heels over the edge of the bed before I realized there was no longer any sound coming from the adjacent room or the baby monitor. Was that good or bad? Was Emmy lying face-down on the crib mattress, a victim of SIDS? Were the cries she'd managed to wake me with the last she'd ever make? I raced across the room, falling into the bedroom door, my left wrist taking the brunt of my weight. I clumsily straightened and yanked the door open with my right hand and ran from the room like a fugitive, breath coming in halting gasps.

She lay in the crib on her back. The gently slumbering infant of diaper commercials: wispy nutmeg curls; cheeks glowing through the night-light gloom like shiny copper pennies. Her chubby limbs and tiny Buddha belly enveloped in warm flannel footed pajamas with no blanket. No toys or stuffed animals crowded into the enclosure; the firm, Greenguard Gold-and CertiPUR certified mattress hemmed by the Babyletto Premium crib's perfectly proportioned slats, too close together to trap a small child's head. I'd done my research.

I took a deep breath, arms and legs shaking as the adrenaline coursing through my bloodstream dissipated. Normalcy returning in syncopated tremors. It was going to be a challenge, this day. Like all the others before it. Massaging my left wrist, I felt a sting in my smallest fingertip. Looking at the hand cradled in my other palm, I noticed the gleam of blood seeping into the ridge around my nail bed, the nail tip partially severed. Served me right. I couldn't remember the last time I'd filed and clipped my nails, much less gotten a proper manicure.

Truth was I couldn't recall exactly what I'd been doing during the months since Tim left, except worrying he'd take Emmy away. Now I had to endure another day. Close to fourteen hours until twilight would usher in soothing darkness. That's when I'd gently lift Emmy from her crib or ease her out of the ever-present infant carrier strapped to my chest. I'd transfer her to the state-of-the-art BabyZen Buggy, complete with bassinet top. Tim had scoffed when I bought it because it had cost half a week's salary, but it was well worth the money, encasing my precious girl in cozy warmth as the soundless wheels rolled smoothly over the paved streets.

I'd always found it soothing to explore the area. Tim and I used to take post-dinner summertime strolls when we first moved into the neighborhood, years ago. Back when we enjoyed doing things together.

He'd quickly tired of those walks. Despite how I'd forced the issue when I became pregnant—recalling my mother's adamant advice against letting the baby, once born, come between us—Tim stopped accompanying me. I kept at it, wandering familiar streets, and discovering new routes. Keeping myself fit even before I had Emmy, yet something new sprouted in my mind. Realizations and suspicions growing like the child in my womb: Why was I spending so much time alone? Where was Tim most evenings when I returned from my strolls to our stark, empty house?

Emmy was born in January, a dangerous time to take a newborn outside in upstate New York, but it was an unseasonably warm winter and by late March I was once again crisscrossing the streets of our development, this time with Emmy for company.

Our walks quickly became a nightly ritual, each foray into the dusky suburban streets calming us more than the previous stroll. Before long, I was walking for hours each evening, widening our horizons, and building my stamina. I'd occasionally head out during daylight hours, even though there wasn't much outdoor activity during cold winter afternoons. I preferred the anonymity of my night-time strolls.

That was when things started to fall apart at home—or maybe it was a continuation of the downward spiral that had begun with Emmy's refusal to nurse, my baby blues, and Tim's inability to keep us or himself happy. I thought about his after-hour stints at the firm. He'd claimed to be overwhelmed by a new project, but he'd never had to work through the dinner hour in the early years of our marriage.

The night I found a matchbook from a local bar in Tim's jacket pocket, I shoved Emmy in the stroller and beelined it through the front door, anger sparking my movements, spurring me through the dark streets and farther from home. That was the evening I discovered Deer Crossing, just a mile from my house. It changed everything, sparking an odyssey into a realm previously unknown to me. I'd dutifully returned from the exclusive enclave that night and all the others that followed, but I never really made it back to the place Tim and I had been before.

It was to be expected, of course. How could I settle for the dreary happenings around my house when others were living such charmed lives? These people were like my own neighbors, but younger, fitter. Happier. Especially the couple I'd been stalking lately: Barbie-and-Ken look-alikes I'd named Matt and Melanie at 21 Pine Hill Road. Just like the couples I'd noticed through their unguarded windows that very first night who'd laughed together and cuddled on sofas in front of large-screen televisions and flickering fireplaces, the positioning of Matt and Melanie's trim, athletic bodies struck me upon first glimpse, weeks ago: The way their entwined forms rocked in rhythm to the strains of a song I couldn't hear, their beauty highlighted by the warm wash of incandescent light overhead. Framed by the living room window, their faces were a blur, but I was transfixed by how her long dark hair spilled against his cheek and mingled with his blond waves. A pang sliced at my throat, making swallowing painful. The pair was maybe a few years older than Tim and me; I couldn't recall the last time Tim and I danced together. Perhaps our wedding reception? Why didn't we focus on each other the way the dreamy couple in front of my greedy eyes did? I squeezed my lids shut, trying to recall my husband's touch on my skin, but I couldn't arouse the sensation.

I felt nothing.

I spied on them all.

Every neighbor too careless or too foolish to keep their shades drawn. Hundreds of houses on display, their interiors glowing with life and bleeding it out into the night. A hemorrhage of strangers gathered around dinner tables; texting on phones while gearing up Netflix; doing yoga. The activities were as varied as the people performing them. And that's what it seemed like, a show, with the homes' inhabitants cast as theatrical versions of themselves.

I needed this—the feeling of being a part of something without the responsibility of involvement. Oddly, I felt a connection to these blurry-faced strangers I hadn't been able to maintain with Tim since before Emmy was born. He blamed me for the divide. I knew he did. His seemingly innocent remarks rankled. Like his comment after my mom's fatal accident when I'd been three months pregnant: *Maybe you'd feel less devastated if you and your mother had gotten along better.*

I stared blankly at him. "My mom was my best friend," I'd said, amazed that her death seemed to be tearing us apart rather than bonding us in grief—especially since he hadn't been overly fond of her.

And then there was his advice after the postpartum depression that had set in a week after I'd given birth: *If you force yourself to get out of bed and tend to Emmy, the mother-daughter bonding will help you overcome your depression.*

I snorted just thinking of his self-righteous remarks. What the hell did *he* know, anyway? After Doctor Ellison explained that stress, hormonal changes, and sleep deprivation combined to create a textbook case of the baby blues, Tim grudgingly attended to Emmy amid my crying jags and unending desire for sleep.

He was always willing to do pharmacy runs. I suspected he just wanted to get out of the house, away from Emmy's endless crying and my incessant requests for help. Hours after departing for the drugstore he'd reappear with excuses of long lines, drug shortages, pharmacist consultations. Anything to make the extended absences seem believable.

I couldn't pronounce the name of the script Dr. Ellison had prescribed for postpartum depression, but I'd eagerly anticipate the Xanax the doctor told me to take only in emergencies. The medication calmed me far better than my husband did. Tim, watching me pop the pills like a halitosis sufferer scarfing down breath mints, scoffed at what he called my *weakness*.

"You can't be hoovering those pills while you're taking care of Emmy," he'd complain.

"That's why you're here," I'd point out. "Until I can get myself back on track."

He'd roll his eyes and sigh. Often, he'd storm out of the house, slamming the door behind him, not returning until my frantic texts begged him to soothe our wailing child.

The postpartum meds hadn't worked, and I wasn't able to sleep without Xanax. Claiming to worry about the potential for drug dependence, Tim began monitoring and restricting my intake, leading to endless nights without more than an hour or two of rest, giving my waking hours a surreal, nightmarish quality. Every sound became oddly amplified, as though my ears had reverberating speakers tucked inside; morning light scorched my retinas, sending shards of throbbing brightness straight into my brain, settling into a baseline headache that no amount of ibuprofen could touch. That was the *weakness* Tim so readily diagnosed. I suppressed my resentment, convincing myself he was only looking out for my health.

Exercise helped. In the soothing dark and silence of my nightly strolls, I could function normally. My stiff legs relaxed into an easy, elongated ramble, and my lungs unclenched, turning my shallow breaths into deep, full inhalations. The later my strolls stretched into the night, the more I felt like myself.

That's when I realized how much I needed the residents of Deer Crossing. Muzzy Owen and her tribe were the first to catch my eye, and her reciprocal attention bolstered my confidence. I didn't live in the development, but I had every right to stroll the storied streets. Lately, I'd even taken to waving at Matt as I passed him. He'd wave back if he wasn't preoccupied by a strenuous yard task, like raking out the flowerbeds or mowing the lawn.

This August evening the temperature hovered around seventy degrees in low humidity. Emmy cooed like a chickadee content in its nest as I increased my speed up an incline, my arms laboring under the increased weight of the carriage. Gritting my teeth against the pain slicing through my left wrist—a reminder of my morning's sleep-deprived plunge into my bedroom door—I focused on the exertion. It felt cleansing, just like Dr. Ellison said it would. Now that Tim no longer lived with me, I could walk the streets any time of the day or night. I didn't have to get back from my evening strolls before he did. Didn't have to figure out where he'd been while I was walking off my resentment.

Even so, Emmy needed a mother *and* a father, no matter our difficulties. I texted Tim every day about important child-related topics. Asking his opinion about starting Emmy on rice gruel, sharing a milestone she reached, or a worry over a minor health issue. Even though he seldom answered me, I was determined to keep him involved in our child's life, and eventually get him back home. I knew only too well how impossible it was to endure a childhood without a dad.

I scooted across the three-lane thoroughfare separating Highland Knolls, my neighborhood of modest ranches and bilevels, to Deer Crossing. Consisting of a few hundred dwellings, the upscale development had two parallel main roads leading off Route 55 and into the neighborhood: Pine Hill Road on the west side, and Woodmint Lane on the east. Connecting them at the northernmost end of each road was Primrose Way which stretched from the bike trails at Woodmint to the pond on Lakeside, just beyond Primrose and north of Pine Hill. Each of these roads had multiple connecting paths and cul-de-sacs with winding streets and expertly land-scaped lots. As I started up Woodmint, I wondered if the neighbors banded together to create a cohesive planting plan. Even in the muted glow of the HPS streetlights, the perennials peeking around stately birches shut out the memory of the ragged, yellowing hostas lining my house's walkway. To-night, I meandered, noting how the light layered over the smooth expanse of lawn extending from house to house like an unending carpet. I could dis-cern no weeds in the seamless stretches of grass.

This should have been my life, my neighborhood. As a mechanical en-gineer, Tim made a decent buck, and my home-based medical-billing job helped cover the extras. My virtual position meant no childcare expenses, which was fortunate. With my parents gone and Tim's entire family across the country in Seattle, my salary would have been swallowed up in daycare costs had I been forced to commute to an office each day.

Still, I'd wanted the big, impressive house, and we could have swung it. Our other expenses were minimal. We preferred our television to mov-ie theaters; takeout to dining out; comfortable clothes to designer labels. And we'd been saving for the future. I'd talked about a big family, like the four-sibling clan Tim had been raised in, not the sad little twosome that had comprised most of my childhood. But my husband decided for us both that prudence was called for. We'd start in a house we could afford rather than live in a "monstrosity" we'd struggle to make payments on.

I'd reluctantly agreed to our simple two-bedroom ranch on Tim's as-surance that as our salaries and family grew, we'd expand to a bigger place. Seemed like a good plan, until my mother died, and my world began to un-ravel. Now the modest house felt like a condemnation. I needed a home like the one we'd envisioned ourselves eventually living in, a validation of sorts. No chance I'd ever have it unless I could get Tim back.

At the end of Woodmint, I'd eventually turn left onto Primrose Way, and pass Muzzy's house at the other end of that street, near Pine Hill. With any luck she'd be outside, maybe sitting on her front porch. It was early enough—much earlier than most of my treks into the neighborhood. I walked faster, my gaze lasered once again on the Brockton's sage farmhouse as I neared it.

One low light was on in the living room. I glanced at the completely dark Colonial next door, which I recalled was the tawny tone of a caramel chewy in daylight.

"Good evening," came a female voice from somewhere in the shadows. Jane Brockton.

I jumped, heart slamming into breastbone. A dark figure stood like a sentinel at the end of the driveway, next to the mailbox. "Oh, uh, hello."

"I didn't mean to frighten you," she said, stepping forward. Her tone suggested otherwise.

"No, that's okay, I'm just . . ." I trailed off, my pounding heart making breathing and speaking at the same time impossible.

"You spend an awful lot of time on this street, don't you?"

She'd noticed my snooping. My mind clicked into survival mode, sending desperate messages to my mouth. "Well, you know how it is with colicky babies." I looked down at the carriage and back at her advancing form. "Whatever it takes to get them to sleep."

"No, I don't know. I don't have children." Jane's tone sounded oddly challenging. "What's the baby's name?"

"Emmy," I said, my quivering voice hinting at my reluctance to tell her anything about myself.

She stopped a few feet in front of me and raised her hand which held an iPhone. She turned on the built-in flashlight, creating a harsh halo of light around her stunning figure. I'd clearly not been able to properly appreciate her attractiveness from a distance. "May I take a peek?"

Seriously? She wants to shine a high-intensity beam into my infant's face? Good thing she doesn't have children. I raised the bassinet hood, an urgency to get away from her overwhelming me. "I just got her to sleep; she's hyper-sensitive to light."

"Oh," she sounded disappointed. Perhaps she wanted a child and Rod was unwilling or unable to provide any for her? He was, after all, a good bit older than she was. She stepped back, giving me the impression of a balloon deflating slightly. "You'll have to stroll by in the daytime when the baby's awake." She accented the word *daytime*.

"I'll do that," I promised, pressing on the carriage handle.

"I'm Jane, by the way."

"Alice," I lied. "Nice to meet you," I called over my shoulder as I stepped forward.

"You look like that woman who used to go to Muzzy Owen's house." Her voice had a hard edge that sent a shiver down my spine. "But her name wasn't Alice."

I froze. "You know Muzzy?" I tried to suppress the surprise in my voice.

"I know everyone in this neighborhood. But I don't know you."

"Well, I don't actually live here."

"I know that. I can follow people, too. Your name is Caroline, so why would you tell me it's Alice?"

My throat went dry. I turned toward her, my legs shaking. "Look, I don't want any trouble."

"Then don't lie to me."

"I don't even know you," I said and held my hand up. "I never tell strangers my name."

"You're the stranger here, and I'd prefer you keep it that way. Stick to your own neighborhood. Keep your stroller, your car, and yourself off these streets. You don't belong here."

Her petty threat burst my fear like a soap bubble. Who the hell was *she* to tell me where I could stroll my child? I lowered my chin until my gaze was level with hers. "I can walk wherever I please. If you have a problem with that, too bad."

"You need to mind your own business. Keep your nose out of—"

"Out of what?" I sighed, impatience warring with the good manners my mother instilled in me. "Your *business* looks like a lot more fun than mine."

Jane's mouth dropped and I could see her face redden in the ambient light from her cell phone, now glowing beside her thigh where she'd dropped her hand. Before she could sputter out a reply, I turned on my heel and headed down the street, vigorously pushing the stroller ahead of me.

Was that a good idea? asked a voice. The voice that sounded like my mother's.

"Probably not," I muttered. But it felt fantastic to tell her off.

I couldn't properly catch my breath until I was in front of Muzzy's dark house. So, Jane had followed me home one evening? So much for my stealth. Gazing at the shadowy box that was Muzzy's house, I wondered if my former BF had filled Jane in on my story.

Sadness encircled me like a heavy woolen cape, weighing me down, and notching my body temperature up a good ten degrees. I didn't care. Even if my one-time friend had gossiped all over the neighborhood about me, I deserved it. And it would be a small price to pay to get Muzzy Owen back in my life. My gaze lingering on the dark house, I walked on. Ignoring the trickle of the fountain in the loathsome pond to my right, I turned left onto Pine Hill Road and approached Matt and Melanie's house on the corner. A porch light flicked on, illuminating the "21" over the front door which was open to reveal the profiles of two people.

Melanie, her long tresses recently chopped to her shoulders, thrust her arms around the shoulders of a tall, dark-haired man and pressed herself intimately against him.

"I don't care," she declared. "Let him find out about us. Let them *all* find out!"

MORE MYSTERIOUS READS FROM CAMCAT BOOKS

CamCat
Books

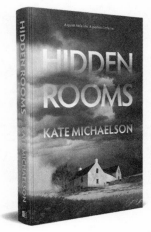

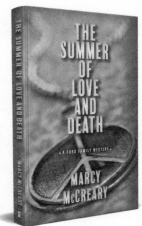

Available now, wherever books are sold.

CamCat
Books

VISIT US ONLINE FOR MORE BOOKS TO LIVE IN:
CAMCATBOOKS.COM

SIGN UP FOR CAMCAT'S FICTION NEWSLETTER FOR
COVER REVEALS, EBOOK DEALS, AND MORE EXCLUSIVE CONTENT.